PRAISE FOR *WALTER'S MUSE*

For those who believe in second chances in love and life and who aspire to aging graciously and with a zest for life, *Walter's Muse* provides a warm and engaging blueprint. Okimoto's loveably quirky characters become a reader's friends and family. I hated to finish the last page.

– **Connie Burns,**
SCHOOL LIBRARY JOURNAL reviewer, ret.
soon-to-be retired school librarian

Walter's Muse by Jean Okimoto is an exhilarating portrait of a woman in her prime, post-divorce, post-retirement, and ready to start life anew. One wonderful summer on Vashon Island changes Maggie Lewis' life in ways she never could have anticipated–and revives in all of us a lust for life, with its splendid twists and turns, gifts of love and friendship, and promises of more surprises to come.

– **Nina Sankovitch,**
HUFFINGTON POST, author of
Tolstoy and the Purple Chair

In *Walter's Muse* Jean Davies Okimoto captures what life is like on an island in the middle of Puget Sound. In an engrossing story full of twists and turns she describes the locals, the retirees, the eccentrics, and the farmer's market crowd all of whom are suspicious of the dreaded new comer waving the banner of threatened gentrification. All in all it's a delightful story told with wit and charm.

– **Ann Combs**
EAGLE HARBOR BOOKS

A retired librarian resetting her compass immerses us in a neighborhood of warm, resourceful people who respond to personal dilemmas with unique collaborative style. Okimoto portrays lightly and humorously the regenerative power of friendship: *a joy to read!*

– **Rayna Holtz**
Librarian, KING COUNTY LIBRARY SYSTEM, ret.

Brimming with wit and wisdom, *Walter's Muse* is a delightful celebration of mature love, the exasperating bond of family, the power of community and the unbridled beauty of living on an island in Puget Sound. *Walter's Muse* is sure to enchant fans of *Major Pettigrew's Last Stand!*

– **Juli Morser**
BOOKS BY THE WAY

For those of us who are also aging children's writers, *Walter's Muse* is both frighteningly authentic, and blessedly amusing. It was a pleasure to spend time on Vashon Island with such a well-drawn cast of characters.

– **David Lubar**
author of *Attack of the Vampire Weenies:
And Other Warped and Creepy Tales*

Also by Jean Davies Okimoto

Plays:

Hum It Again, Jeremy
Uncle Hideki
Uncle Hideki and the Empty Nest

Novels:

The Love Ceiling
Walter's Muse

Nonfiction:

*Boomerang Kids: How to Live with Adult Children Who
Return Home* (coauthor)

Young Adult Novels:

My Mother Is Not Married to My Father
It's Just Too Much
Norman Schnurman, Average Person
Who Did It, Jenny Lake?
Jason's Women
Molly by Any Other Name
Take a Chance, Gramps!
Talent Night
The Eclipse of Moonbeam Dawson
To JayKae: Life Stinx
Maya and the Cotton Candy Boy

Picture Books:

Blumpoe the Grumpoe Meets Arnold the Cat
A Place for Grace
No Dear, Not Here
Dear Ichiro
The White Swan Express (coauthor)
*Winston of Churchill: One Bear's Battle Against Global
Warming*

Walter's
Muse

a novel

Jean Davies Okimoto

ENDICOTT
and HUGH
BOOKS

This is a work of fiction. All the characters and events portrayed in this novel are either fictitious or are used fictitiously.

WALTER'S MUSE

ENDICOTT & HUGH BOOKS
P.O. Box 13305, Burton, WA 98013.
www.endicottandhughbooks.com

paperback: 978-0-9837115-1-3
hardcover: 978-0-9837115-2-0
ebook: 978-0-9837115-3-7

Publisher's Cataloging-In-Publication Data
(Prepared by The Donohue Group, Inc.)

Okimoto, Jean Davies.   Walter's Muse / Jean Davies Okimoto. -- 1st ed.

   p. ; cm.

  ISBN: 978-0-9837115-2-0 (hardcover)
  ISBN: 978-0-9837115-1-3 (pbk.)

  1. Librarians--Fiction. 2. Retired women--Fiction. 3. Man-woman relationships--Fiction. 4. Sibling rivalry--Fiction. 5. Neighbors--Fiction. 6. Vashon Island (Wash.)--Fiction. 7. Love stories, American. I. Title.

PS3565.K46 W25 2012
813/.54   2011938340

Book design by Masha Shubin
Author photo by Roger Davies

LCCN 2011938340

Printed in the United States of America
10 9 8 7 6 5 4
First Edition

For Artis Palmer

ACKNOWLEDGEMENTS

It is a pleasure to thank those who either provided helpful information or a careful reading—and often both: Amanda Devine, Barry Foster, Margy Heldring, Rayna Holtz, Donna Kaplan, Dan Klein, Laurel Kuehl, Juli Morser, David Pfeiffer, and Ann Leda Shapiro.

Thank you to Jill Andrews for her haiku, which I love, and the other writers from whom I learn so much on Wednesday mornings: Jean Carpenter, Marta Cou, Kathy Olsen, Edeen Parrish, Arlene Schade, Faye Wilkinson, Ina Whitlock, Bee and Bo Bonow and our generous host at Books by the Way, Jenni Wilke.

It's been just delightful to work once more with the creative designer Masha Shubin, and Linda Franklin, who brings her skills and an eagle eye to any manuscript. Thanks to my agent, Robert Astle, for his continued enthusiasm and support, and for leading me to Ali Bosworth Mancini. Again, I'm so pleased to be the beneficiary of her editorial talent and many years of experience at Viking Penguin.

I am grateful to and for my daughters: Amy Kirkman and Katie Klein. And my husband, Joe. As always, Joe makes everything possible.

WALTER'S MUSE

CHAPTER ONE

By the third time Maggie heard the wail, she was convinced she'd really better check on Walter. At first she hadn't been too concerned; the odd noise sounded a bit like the foghorn on the Tacoma Narrows Bridge only with a higher note, like a falsetto foghorn. Maybe they'd been working on it and the horn had ended up with a higher pitch, maybe they'd installed some type of new fancy digital equipment. Or would it be analog? She got all that sort of thing mixed up and frankly didn't know the difference. Then Maggie looked out at the water and realized this didn't make sense. There wasn't any fog. Not a trace or even a misty wisp. A brisk wind rippled the surface of the cove, but the evening was perfectly clear with the sky the deepening blue of dusk and at least another hour 'til sunset. Probably a boat horn somewhere had gotten stuck was more like it, she decided. But as the wind picked up and Maggie listened more closely, the wail got louder and she knew that cry had to come from the lungs of a living creature. Part wolf howl and part Bessie Smith bone-crushing blues, it completely unnerved her. And although she couldn't pinpoint the exact location, she was pretty sure it was coming from Walter's place, which unnerved her even more.

It was around eight o'clock when Maggie first heard the strange wail. She was down at the beach, lifting her kayak to the landing of her boatshed, when she stopped to listen. The breeze had picked up, slowly gathering steam like an ancient locomotive, at first rustling the leaves of the trees edging the beach and sending ripples over the surface of the water. Within minutes, the branches were swaying as waves furiously whipped against the shore and small pieces of driftwood skittered across the sand. Everyone on the island knew the storm was coming, they just didn't expect such high winds this time of year. Summer on the island was beautiful and they all remembered again why they chose to live here. During the dreary soggy winters in this rainy northwest corner of the country it wasn't always evident. But stunning summers provided vindication. It was the delayed gratification they expected, one to which they felt entitled: warm, sparkling days; starlit nights; crisp, clean air; the splendor of the Olympic Mountains and the majesty of Mt. Rainier all against the bluest of blue skies. They did not expect storms.

As Maggie shoved the kayak in the boathouse, a gust of wind from the south blew the door open with such force she had to brace her shoulder against it to keep it steady as she tried to secure the lock. On the island some people never locked their doors, but the boathouses on the beach occasionally attracted pilferers. Fishing tackle, boat cushions, oars and paddles, life jackets, small outboard motors and sometimes kayaks had all been known to disappear. To play it safe, in the summer Maggie hung the padlock key hung around her neck so she'd remember to lock her boathouse. She thought of it as her Baker's Beach jewelry.

She snapped the lock shut and as she scurried up to the house, a shingle from someone's roof went flying by. She watched it sail overhead, hoping it wasn't from her roof. Climbing up the steps to her front porch, she thought she heard the strange sound again and again stopped for a second to listen, but all she could hear was the wind—and it was getting stronger by the minute.

At 8:30 the power went out. Maggie had just finished watching *Washington Week*, the PBS Friday night weekly roundup of the news from the other Washington, and went to get candles from the kitchen so she could at least have light for reading. She was getting them from the cupboard next to the sink when she saw a tall dark shape in a hooded parka loping toward her house. The parka was flapping every which way and there was no mistaking the tall form and the long strides. It was her neighbor, Howie Frankel.

Maggie opened the door a crack for Howie and the wind tore into the house, rattling the shades and sending papers by the phone sailing around the room, including a scrap with her sister's number. Maggie had jotted it down from a voice mail message Leslie left about being somewhere her cell phone wouldn't work. If it blew away, Maggie knew she'd call again. Leslie always surfaced when she wanted something or to make an announcement—usually about a new man. At fifty-five, Maggie's little sister continued to change men the way a lot of women change wardrobes.

Howie quickly stepped in and the door slammed shut behind him. "I'm going to start the generator in the pump house, so at least we can all have water." Howie seemed excited; Maggie thought he actually enjoyed the drama of these storms. "Everything okay, here?"

"So far, thanks. I've still got a roof, and I'm about to make a fire for a little more light. And especially to warm up."

"As soon as I get the pump going, I'll start the generator at our place. Mark wanted me to tell you we've got plenty of room in our refrigerator if you've got anything in yours you're afraid might spoil. Or just come on over if you get bored. Martha Jane's hanging out with us. She has one of those emergency radios that you crank and we're trying to get news of when they think this thing will blow over."

"Thanks. I'm fine, but if it drags on I might bring a few things over." The wind practically ripped the door off as she opened it for Howie. "Be careful."

The idea of sitting out the storm with them was appealing. Maggie loved being around Martha Jane Morrison—just her presence was inspiring, and she wasn't the only one who felt that way. There were a number of people on the island, mostly women in their sixties and seventies, who were in awe of Martha Jane. They hung on her every word, even when she nattered on and they couldn't always follow her. It was her spirit they loved. At ninety-one, Martha Jane had a curiosity and optimism about life that was more typically found in the very young, and she attracted groupies. Maggie was one of them.

The front of Martha Jane's house faced Hormann Road, a gravel road that came to a dead end at her lot, giving her a Hormann Road address. But the back of her house faced Baker's Beach and that's where she told everyone she lived. Over the years, the culture of Hormann Road had shifted; the prime waterfront had attracted wealthy retirees and summer people who tore down the ramshackle cabins they'd purchased, replacing them with upscale homes that could have come from the pages of *Sunset* magazine. There were even a couple of mini-mansions that looked as though they'd been plucked from the shores of the eastside of Lake Washington, the heart of Microsoft country. It was not Martha Jane's cup of green tea, and her house shared its aesthetic with the three houses on Baker's Beach that had retained their original, weather-beaten character. The residents were also more to her liking. As much as Maggie wanted to hang out with Martha Jane and Howie and Mark, she decided she'd better stay put and quite literally hold down the fort.

From her front window, she watched Howie lope along up the hill toward the pump house. At least six feet four, he had a heron-shaped body and with his knobby Adam's apple and macaw nose he made her think of Ichabod Crane. Howie had dark soulful eyes, sparse gray hair, which he wore in a ponytail, and a sad, sweet sense of humor. He'd been the head of the drama department at Pacific Community College and retired two years ago. Howie's specialty was theatrical direction and he always said his mission was to bring out the best in actors. But it was more than actors, Maggie thought, Howie brought out the best in everyone.

The temperature had dropped and the house was getting chilly, so she went to the back porch to get kindling and logs from the wood box. It was a challenge just to get in and out of the back door with her arms full without the door tearing off in the wind. Maggie was laying the kindling in the woodstove when she heard the howl again.

Ouw-ooooo.

It was strange: wolf-like and eerie, but so faint, Maggie wondered if the creature could be an owl. Or maybe some other bird traumatized by the wind, which now sounded like God was flapping a giant towel over the roar of a huge waterfall. The only other sound came from the pump house where Howie was trying to start the generator, which started like an outboard motor. It took Howie several tries to get the thing going and between each yank on the generator, Maggie heard the howl.

Ouw-oooo. Sputter.

Ouw-oooo. Sputter sputter.

Then the pump house generator started. It rumbled like a motorbike with a dangling muffler and she thought either the howling seemed to stop, or she just couldn't hear it over all the racket.

Maggie got the kindling lit and waited for it to catch and the flames to hold, then she carefully positioned the logs on top. Making fires was something she enjoyed very much. It made her feel quite capable in a primitive, basic kind of way—the opposite of how she felt when confronted with technology. Why did a librarian have to be a media specialist, she'd once complained to Martha Jane. "I went into this field because I loved books—not machines!"

Across the cove at Howie and Mark's, Maggie saw the lights come on as they started the generator to their house. Maggie wondered if it was time she got a generator, too. But it seemed like a hassle: having to keep fuel for it, making sure the thing had batteries. Why bother? She could always take her food to Howie and Mark's if the power outage lasted too long. And besides, there was something kind of lovely and charming about relying on candlelight. Although seeing their lights come on certainly was comforting. It was dark at Martha Jane's house and down along the cove it was dark at Joanne McKee's. Joanne was the only one at Baker's Beach who didn't live on the island year round. She usually came a couple of times a month and last weekend she'd mentioned she'd be at a conference this week. This spring she'd showed up with a retired professor, Bob Cameron. They didn't leave her house much, and Joanne had kept unusually quiet about him, which made Maggie and Martha Jane wonder if he had a wife somewhere. Joanne was a psychoanalyst, and had been working for years on the book she called her life's work, *The Hoax of Penis Envy.*

Maggie pulled her chair and a little table closer to the fire, then lit the candles, intending to read her way through the storm. Lighting three of them made for pretty good light. They were beeswax candles that Martha Jane had given her for her birthday and had a honey vanilla smell she loved. They were probably better suited to romance than providing reading light, although the former was a state of mind Maggie hadn't encountered in more decades than she cared to remember. She had to admit, however, that in spite of the fact that her neighbor Walter Hathaway was an old grump, he was a handsome and rather virile looking old grump and she'd found herself thinking about him much more this summer than was at all sensible.

Maggie pulled the candles closer and opened her book. Determined to read some classics this summer, she was making her way through Joyce's *Portrait of the Artist as a Young Man*. Stephen Dedalus had just had his first sexual experience with the prostitute in Dublin when she heard the howl again. Louder, and now unmistakably some canine creature, a wolf or a dog. And since no one, to her knowledge, had ever seen a wolf on Vashon Island outside of the wildlife refuge Wolftown—it had to be a dog and Maggie was now positive it was Walter's dog.

She didn't bother calling Walter. If he needed help and the phone lines were still working, he would have called someone, most likely Martha Jane. That is, if he were capable of phoning. Maggie grabbed her rain parka and a flashlight and blew out the candles. As she opened the heavy cedar door, the wind accosted it and slammed it back against the front of the house, like it was made of paper. It did occur to her that she was probably crazy to go out there, but that terrible howl pulled her toward it the way people are drawn to stare at a crash on the freeway.

Her front porch and the steps to the yard were completely littered with twigs and small branches. Maggie clutched the railing and pushed the small branches off to the side with her foot and as she went down the steps, she lifted the larger ones, tossing them into the yard. She was making her way along the side of the house and was a few feet from the path to Walter's cabin when she heard a loud crack. In the dark she couldn't tell where it came from and ran back and huddled under the carport shining the light every which way until she saw a huge limb. It was close to twenty feet long, covering the compost pile with half its branches as it sprawled across the shed. About ten yards east of it Maggie saw a long ragged yellow gash on one of the tall cedars that towered over the path. And then she heard the howl. This time it was louder and she grabbed her bicycle helmet from its hook on the carport wall and plopped it on her head, and headed on foot down the path to Walter's cabin, hastily fastening the helmet as she went.

Maggie hadn't ridden her bike in three years. She quit when the back tire went flat and she never got around to fixing it. It was probably time anyway. The hills had simply gotten harder and harder. It was one thing to see some smiling, silver-haired crone sailing along on a bike, the picture of health and fitness—like the women in those ads for arthritis medicine—but quite another if she was grimacing, red-faced, puffing, and drenched in sweat. The picture becomes pathetic, and wisdom—Maggie was convinced—was, in part, knowing when to hang it up.

She kept her head down, trying to hold the light steady on the path, walking as fast as she could. Running with all the branches scattered everywhere seemed rather risky. Her balance, like everything else, was not what it used to be. Ever since breaking her wrist when she fell playing tag with her granddaughter last summer, she'd been a bit gun-shy about running. Of course the bike helmet was ridiculous. She knew that. As if it was going to protect her from being bonked on the head by a two-ton fir tree. But it seemed like she should have equipment and other than the flashlight, it was the only thing she could come up with.

It was hard not to step on the branches that were strewn all over the path and Maggie just hoped that if one of the power lines had come down, she'd see it and not just step on it as if it were some innocuous little twig. She could just see the story in the *Beachcomber*, the island weekly newspaper...Maggie Lewis, 65, died tragically in the windstorm that swept the Northwest on July 17th having been electrocuted from a downed power line between the property owned by Ms. Lewis and that of noted children's author, Walter Hathaway. Ms. Lewis, recently retired from Evergreen Elementary in Seattle, where she served as the librarian for nearly four decades, was wearing a bicycle helmet.

Who would miss me? Maggie carefully stepped over a large limb that had fallen across the path. Her daughter Becky, of course, and Ashley, her granddaughter, and Martha Jane, and Howie and Mark—a handful of people she supposed. But everyone would get over it. Life would go on. We're made to re-attach after all, she thought, carefully stepping across another large branch. It's our animal nature, like members of monkey troupes.

Walter Hathaway's cabin was separated from Maggie's house by less than a half-acre of forest, and although his lot was technically part of Baker's Beach, the huge old growth cedars and dense brush blanketing the southern portion of Maggie's property kept Walter hidden from the other residents of the beach. Hidden and private, which was the way Walter liked it. Walter lived quietly at the end of the beach—with one notable exception that drove everyone at Baker's Beach nuts. Even Martha Jane. Several times a day and at least once or twice in the evening, they could hear Walter Hathaway "calling" his dog, Bill Bailey. A big, reddish-brown, shaggy bear of a dog of untraceable parentage, Walter had purchased him from a panhandler for fifteen dollars. He was the latest in a succession of Bill Baileys. All mongrels, all rescued in one form or another. All named Bill Bailey. Walter accompanied himself on a ukulele as his rich baritone voice boomed through the woods, echoing across the water belting out his up-tempo rendition of "Won't you Come Home, Bill Bailey." His neighbors had never heard him sing anything else. They assumed it was the only song in Walter's repertoire and for everyone at the beach it was one song too many.

But he wasn't totally isolated—every once in a while Maggie would see him at the post office or the grocery store and occasionally on the beach if they each happened to be walking at low tide. The conversation, if you could call it that, was always the same.

"Hello, Walter."

"Hello, Maggie."

When they meet they are awkward, tense and uncomfortable, and Maggie, who is typically friendly to animals, never even greets Walter's dog. Cut. End of scene. They move on. Walter Hathaway and Maggie had some history: a history they were both quite careful to avoid ever mentioning, especially to each other.

Walter hadn't always been a loner, but ever since he came to Vashon Island last year, with the exception of attending Martha Jane's ninety-first birthday party in March, Maggie didn't think Walter ever went anywhere except Thriftway for groceries and the Burton post office near Quartermaster Harbor. Martha Jane had also known Walter before he came to the island, probably for at least twenty years, and she was one of the few from his past life that hadn't given up on him.

The howling got louder as Maggie neared the end of the path. She ceased contemplating getting zapped off the face of the earth by a downed power line and emerged from the woods to shine the light on the source of the howl. Bill Bailey, with his head lifted toward the sky, sat howling next to a heap on the ground that looked like trash to be hauled off from a construction site: a big slab-like panel, a rusty aluminum ladder tipped on its side, and what seemed to be the top half of a broken windmill. Then Maggie saw the work boots jutting out from under the slab.

"Walter!" She rushed over and knelt down and peered under the slab. "Is that you under there?"

"You were expecting Harry Potter?"

With the noise of the generator and the noise of the wind, the only words she caught were "Harry Potter." Walter considered Harry Potter his nemesis. He blamed the Harry Potter phenomenon for ruining his career.

"Just out for a little bike ride, Maggie?"

Then Maggie noticed that his speech was slurred and her first thought was that Walter had fallen off the wagon. Ignoring his comment about her bicycle helmet, she looked at the slab and saw it was one of the solar panels from the roof of his cabin. And the broken windmill must have been the top of Walter's wind turbine. "Let me see if I can get this off."

"Good idea, because I can't seem to move my arms. I tried to kick the damn thing off but it bounced back on my head. I found that somewhat discouraging."

Bill Bailey, who had ceased howling, licked Maggie's face as she squatted like a weight lifter and grabbed the edges of the panel, then slowly stood, holding the thing over Walter.

"I don't seem to be able to move. Just push the damn thing all the way over, Maggie."

She gave it a shove and the solar panel landed next to Walter with a thud.

Then he saw the broken windmill. "That too! What a crock. It's not easy being green."

"I don't think I should try to move you—"

"You couldn't if you tried," he said, his speech slurring.

Oh my God. He didn't smell like booze. *Walter could be having a stroke...*she turned and ran to his cabin.

She'd never been inside before. There was a huge river rock fireplace in the middle of one unbroken space which had the kitchen, an eating and living area, and what looked like an office at the end of the room that faced the beach. Near the office area, floor to ceiling bookcases flanked the entrance to a short hallway that ended with two doors off the "T", and Maggie ran and opened the door on the left. Wrong. It was a bedroom. She spun around to the other door and flung it open. A towel was tossed over the shower curtain rod, the toilet seat was up and over the sink there was a mirrored medicine cabinet. Maggie pulled on it, but it was stuck. She gave it a quick pound and then yanked it open. She grabbed a bottle of aspirin and the glass next to the sink and filled it, thankful that Howie had gotten the pump house generator going and they still had water. She pulled the towel off the shower rod and charged out of the cabin, across the yard and knelt next to Walter.

"Walter, you've got to take a bunch of aspirin."

"I think I'm going to need more than aspirin, Maggie."

"Look, you might be having a stroke," she said in her best Ms. Lewis–the–Librarian voice. "Take these now. Open your mouth." Maggie lifted Walter's head and scooted behind him so he lay against her lap. She propped one knee behind his shoulders and was relieved when he obeyed, opening his mouth like a baby bird, and she dropped the aspirin in his mouth, two at a time, then lifted the glass to his lips. Walter drank and gulped down the aspirin.

"Good. Now two more."

"How many?"

"Don't argue. You're taking six and then I'm calling the medics." Maggie had no clue if this was the right amount, but she was sure you couldn't overdose on six aspirin and it seemed like a good number. Walter couldn't move either arm and as she cradled his head she felt a surge of tenderness. A big man, one of the few who had ever made her feel almost petite and quite female, Walter had a large head with rugged features. His hair was very white and thick, except at the temples and on the crown, and she imagined Richard Burton might have looked a lot like Walter had he lived to be Walter's age. He had broad shoulders and a thick build and when they gave out testosterone, Maggie was sure Walter must have been near the front of the line. He was the last person you would peg for a children's author. To look at him you'd immediately think of someone like Mailer writing about prisons, or Hemingway and war and bullfights and all that dashing about. But Walter's big hit was one of the dearest stories

Maggie had ever read, a sweet tale filled with kindness and good will.

He swallowed the last of the aspirin. Then she put the towel on the grass and laid his head back down. "I'll be right back."

Bill Bailey stayed next to Walter. He licked his face then lay down beside him as Maggie ran to Walter's cabin to phone, hoping the phone lines were still up and working. Usually when the power was out they didn't lose the phone, those lines were the sturdiest—which was a good thing because some parts of Baker's Beach were in those pockets where cell phones didn't work.

Maggie shone the light around the cabin and saw the phone on the desk in front of the window that faced the cove. Praying that there would be a dial tone, she picked up the receiver and when she got one, muttered thanks to the heavens as she quickly dialed 911. She tapped her fingers on the desk, waiting for them to answer. Maggie knew they had to be swamped with calls, but the wait was dreadful and to calm herself she looked around the cabin, trying to focus on anything other than poor Walter lying out there in all that rubble.

The bookcases were crammed with books, both hardcover and paperbacks, and she was struck by the odd mix, a hodge-podge of adult and children's titles. *The Blind Assassin* next to *If You Give a Mouse a Cookie*; *Naked Lunch* next to *Curious George*; *Slaughterhouse Five* wedged in between *Green Eggs and Ham* and *Lilly's Purple Plastic Purse*.

On the wall across from the door, she noticed the framed movie poster of the hit film based on *The Adventures of Fric the Chick*. It was hard to believe twenty years had gone by since that film first came out. Those were the glory days for Walter, at least in terms of his career. Maggie also knew for a fact it was when his personal life hit bottom.

The dispatcher came on the line...they thought they could be there in about ten minutes, and flooded with relief, she ran to tell Walter.

"They're on their way, Walter." Bill Bailey licked her face as she bent down to sit next to Walter. The ground was hard and cold and she closed the hood of her parka tight around her neck and pulled the sleeves over her hands. At the edge of the clearing, the huge limbs of the fir trees flapped in great arcs like feathered wings of some gigantic greenish-black bird.

"Did you tell them to take the right fork off Baker's Beach Road? In case the sign blew down—"

"Of course." Would a woman have reminded her of this...as if she were a ninny? Maggie doubted it. It was hard for her not to see things through a gender lens, but she reminded herself what a challenge it must be for Walter to be so helpless. And with his life literally in her hands...the guy had to be acutely uncomfortable, to say the least.

"I'm going to write them a letter. False claims." Walter turned his head toward her.

"Just be patient, Walter. They said they'd be here right away."

"Not the *medics*," he croaked, rolling his eyes.

"Shh...I don't think you should talk, save your strength."

"I'll put it all over the Internet and ruin them. Better than a law suit," he said, ignoring her, his words slurring together.

"Ruin who?" Maggie asked. She knew she shouldn't have asked him. He really needed to stay quiet, but her curiosity got the better of her.

"The damn Danes, their crappy alternative energy company. All this crap was supposed to withstand up to 150 miles per hour. This is just a little breeze and just look at it!" Walter nodded his head toward the broken wind turbine and the solar panel, which lay toppled on the ground a few feet from them and now had a crack in it.

"Maggie?" Walter's voice was almost a whisper.

"What?"

He looked up at her. His eyes were still very blue underneath his bushy white brows. "Maggie—"

"Shh—" She lay her hand over his.

"I have to say this."

"Save your strength, Walter. We can talk later."

"No," he growled through clenched teeth. His breathing quickened and his eyes were pleading. "I want you to know I'm sorry. I'm very sorry about what happened."

Maggie patted his hand. "It was a long time ago."

He closed his eyes. His breathing seemed to quiet for a minute. Then they heard a loud crack and a terrible crashing thud. A huge tree must have blown over somewhere.

"Oh no, what if it's blocking the road!" Maggie scrambled to her feet, rolling to her hands and knees, then pushing up with her arms. She could almost jump up from this peculiar stance.

Walter said something, but the wind was so loud, she couldn't hear him.

"What?" She bent over him. He mumbled again, but it was still unintelligible. Maggie leaned closer, her ear next to his lips. She felt his breath on her cheek, the short gasps of someone in acute distress.

"Don't leave," he muttered.

"You're not going to die, Walter. It's not your time." Maggie spoke with absolute certainty and with a clarity that felt almost mystical but nonetheless very factual. Whether he felt reassured or not, she had no idea. Trust, especially trusting women, did not come easily to Walter. "I'm going to call Howie and Mark, I'll be right back."

The wind continued to howl and she trotted to the cabin, leaping over the debris of broken branches best she could, praying again that the phone lines were still working. As she picked up the phone, her heart started racing. Oh great, that's all we need here, she thought. A little cardiac arrest while I'm trying to get help for Walter.

Thank God, a dial tone. "Mark, it's Maggie—" She was panting so much it was hard to talk.

"What's wrong?"

"It's Walter. He's collapsed and I've called the Medics but I'm afraid the road could be blocked. Could one of you guys bring your chain saw and check it out? I need to stay with him."

"Of course. Be right there."

The wind was still ferocious as she made her way across the yard. Bill Bailey, with his head resting on his paws, lay right next to Walter. His dark eyes were unwavering, fixed on Walter's face, and his ears were perked as if he were ready to spring into action if he only knew what he was supposed to do. Maggie patted Bill's head then sat on the other side of Walter. His eyes were closed, but his color was good and his breathing seemed less labored.

"Maggie."

"I'm here. Mark is coming to check the road."

"I hate this," he muttered.

"I know it must hurt ho-n—" She stopped herself from saying "honey" as if she were trying to comfort her daughter or granddaughter.

"Not that...I hate causing trouble."

"Yes, you were a dreadful man to have caused this storm. Now please be quiet and save your strength."

Bill Bailey heard Mark before they did. He sprang to his feet, barking furiously as Mark, carrying his chain saw and bobbing behind the beam of a flashlight, emerged from the path. Bill kept barking and Mark shouted something but they couldn't hear until he got closer.

"Quiet, Bill! It's just me," Mark commanded and the dog immediately stopped barking. Mark was someone who gave off an air of authority to people as well as animals. Before he retired, he had been a social worker attached to the Tacoma Police gang unit. Maggie also thought his take-charge presence came from his military background. His father was a Navy admiral and Mark had prepped at The Citadel, but defied his father when he didn't apply to Annapolis as he'd been programmed to do since birth. Instead he went to UC Berkeley, which provided not only a good education but a better atmosphere for a young man to come out in.

"There's a huge tree down, but it narrowly missed the road." Mark knelt next to Walter and patted Bill, who had settled down again by Walter's side. "We'll get you out of here, Walter."

Walter nodded and mumbled. Maggie knew he wished they would both just go away.

"We had Martha Jane's radio on and they're saying the wind's starting to die down, but it sure doesn't feel like it." Mark looked up at the trees swaying furiously.

"At least the road's clear. Thanks for checking it, but listen— maybe you should go back to your house." Maggie put her hand on Mark's arm, "It's wild out here with the trees blowing down. We don't both need to wait."

Mark shook his head. "A tree can crush us in the house, too."

Bill Bailey jumped up and faced the road and began barking and in a minute they saw the lights of the Medics aid car turn into the drive. It parked next to the house and two young people jumped out, a man and a woman. Maggie was reassured the minute she saw that the guy was Derek Whitlock—Walter couldn't be in better hands. Derek was something of a celebrity on the island after he'd saved Elmer Piedmont's life, a local contractor who had gone into a diabetic coma in the ferry line during morning rush hour.

Derek was in his late twenties and he looked so much like Bruce Springsteen that a lot of people called him Boss. He knelt next to Walter and asked him to describe what happened to determine his responsiveness and level of consciousness. Maggie stepped back to give Walter some privacy. Derek took Walter's vital signs and then she heard him giving Walter a mental status exam. Asking him if he knew what year it was, what month, what day, where he was, who was the President, all that sort of thing, and she just hoped Walter wouldn't get impatient and bite his head off. While Derek was making the assessment of Walter's condition, the other medic, an attractive young woman with curly brown hair and a pert little nose, brought the gurney from the back of the aid car. She looked to Maggie like she'd be more at home in a majorette outfit than her fire department uniform, but she certainly seemed to know what she was doing.

Bill Bailey leaped toward Walter as they lifted him onto the gurney. Mark went to help but the young woman waved him off.

Maggie grabbed Bill Bailey's collar and struggled to keep him from jumping on the gurney next to Walter and Bill began to howl. It was heart wrenching, a wail that reverberated pain, and Walter's eyes filled with tears at the sound of it.

"You're going to be fine," Maggie whispered to Walter.

"My dog—" he said, struggling to sit up.

"Just take it easy, sir." Derek fastened straps around Walter's body and he and the young woman pushed the gurney over the gravel. "Only medics can ride in the vehicle with him," Derek said to Maggie, "but you can follow us. The family has priority to board the ferry right behind us."

"I'm just a friend." Maggie walked beside them, hunched over, holding fast to the squirming, howling dog.

"No matter," the young woman said kindly. "You can follow us. We'll be taking him to Harborview Hospital."

"Okay, I'll just put Bill in your cabin and then follow you—"

"Maggie—" Walter tried to lift his head as they loaded him into the aid car. "Don't follow us. Just take care of Bill Bailey." Then he closed his eyes.

The dog's howl changed key and tempo, dropping a few octaves to become a whimpering cry, full of despair.

"Please, Maggie."

As the medics were closing the doors of the aid car, she assured him she'd stay with Bill Bailey. Maggie couldn't stand the thought of Walter lying alone in the hospital, but it was clear that all he wanted from her was to look after his dog.

CHAPTER TWO

Bill Bailey did not calm down. As the aid car drove away he began to howl and then whine, and the pain of it made Maggie think of Billie Holiday's "Strange Fruit"—and she wanted to weep.

Mark set his chainsaw down and massaged Bill Bailey's neck, which just made him howl all the more. His authority seemed to have worn off. "Do you think he's eaten?" Mark looked over at Walter's cabin. "I suppose he's got a good supply of dog food. Maybe it wouldn't hurt to try feeding him."

"I should've asked Walter." Maggie held tight to Bill Bailey's collar. Still howling and whining, he was trying to bolt in the direction of the road. He jumped up and down and squirmed with such force Maggie thought he'd pull her arm off. "I think he's too upset to want to eat anyway," she said, gasping for breath, as she struggled to hold onto him.

Mark picked up his chainsaw. "Once you get him in your house, I'm sure he'll be fine." Mark had to yell to be heard over both the wind and the howling dog. He stared at the wreckage of Walter's solar panel and his wind turbine. "Howie's with Martha Jane and you've got Bill Bailey," he shouted. "I suppose I'm the only one that can go to the hospital. Do you think I should?"

"Walter would be furious, you know how he is. I'll call the hospital in a few hours. Even though the Medics have priority boarding on the ferry, it's still going to take them awhile to get him to Seattle and checked in at Harborview. Look, you might as well go home and I'll just let you know what I find out."

"Why don't I give you a hand getting Bill to your house?" Mark bent down to help hold the dog.

"No, seriously, just go ahead. I'm sure the minute he gets out of Walter's yard he'll settle down."

"Well, if you're sure. I did tell Howie and Martha Jane I wouldn't be long."

"I am. He'll be fine."

After Mark left, Maggie dragged Bill Bailey, still jumping, squirming, and whining, across the clearing. When she got to the path and tried to pull him into the woods, Bill Bailey plunked his butt down and with his paws rigid in front of him, lifted his head and looked up at the trees, which were still swaying in the wind. Then he howled. It was a loud, awful wail. On either side of the path the wind was whipping the branches and then Maggie heard a loud crack. Why had she been so quick to tell Mark she could handle this herself? The poor animal was terrified and he was having none of her. What was she thinking? Well, at least he hadn't tried to bite her. She would need to be patient. Take time to comfort him. Calm him down. Leaning over, her face inches from his, she gently stroked the top of his head.

"It's okay, Bill. Walter will be back. Come with me now." Her voice was kind and soothing. Bill Bailey stopped howling, but didn't budge. Maybe she needed a little more authority in her voice. She patted his head, then said, firmly. "Come."

Bill started howling again.

"Bill," she commanded. *"You must come with me."* She tugged at his collar, which resulted in his flinging himself down on the ground where he lay on the path and whined.

"Come, Bill!" She put the flashlight down and bent over and with both hands on his collar gave it a strong tug. This time Bill Bailey sat up, but no matter how hard she yanked and the louder she yelled *"COME!"* he refused to stand. Maggie had to resort to dragging him, sitting on his butt. He continued to whine as she struggled along the path, pulling him with one hand tight on his

collar, while the other held the flashlight. It seemed like a journey of a thousand days and the whining was soon accompanied by swearing. More than once, as her arm and back ached with pain, she was tempted to let go of the damn dog and let him just stay there howling in the woods. But she didn't. Walter would only blame himself for leaving Bill Bailey in the first place. He'd see it as a failure and Walter didn't need another one of those. Besides, she'd promised.

When she finally got him inside, Maggie let go of his collar, shut the door with her backside and then slumped against it. She rubbed her hands, her arms, then her back. They were all killing her.

When the door closed, Bill Bailey stopped howling. He sat quietly in the middle of the dark room and Maggie, relieved at the quiet and rubbing her sore back, looked around for the matches to light the candles. Well, at least he's shut up, she thought, but the minute she lit the candles, Bill Bailey began to whine and started pacing back and forth in front of the door. *Oh for God's sake.* How long would he stay so agitated? The way he was pacing reminded her of a wolf. But Maggie, true to her nature, tried to look on the bright side. At least that terrible howling stopped, she told herself. And for that she was grateful.

Maggie looked at her watch. It was 11:30. The power had been off for three hours and there was no telling when it might come back on. She figured she'd better transfer the food from the refrigerator to her ice chest. As she went to the basement to get it, she wondered if Bill Bailey might follow her. But he kept whining and pacing, his eyes fixed on the front door. Clearly, they had not bonded.

Maggie emptied the ice cubes into the chest and put the frozen food on top of them, then the milk. There wasn't that much food: a bunch of Lean Cuisines and some frozen chicken breasts. Over the years, her interest in cooking had been rather erratic. There were occasions when Becky was growing up that she'd have little bursts of creativity and would read recipes, try new dishes, and she quite enjoyed it. But on a regular basis, she felt like a plow horse, plodding along with the yoke of having to get people fed, and she found it about as interesting as doing a load of wash. The microwave had been the happy hearth of the Lewis kitchen, with frozen pot pies the staple.

She looked around for something to feed Bill Bailey. There probably wasn't much that would appeal to him. She had planned to go to Thriftway but then the storm had hit. A grapefruit, some limp green beans, a bagel and some leftover pizza was about it for the refrigerator; and in the cupboard there was only cereal and canned soup. She decided to try the soup: Campbell's chicken noodle, comfort food from her not-so-comforting childhood. Her electric stove was no good with the power out, but then she doubted Bill Bailey needed his food warmed. Maggie pulled off the top of the can and dumped the soup in a small aluminum mixing bowl. She decided to add water, thinking it might be too salty for him if she didn't dilute it a little.

"Here Bill!" Maggie plopped the bowl down in front of the door.

He stopped pacing and looked at the bowl.

"Mmm—mmm good," she tried to encourage him.

Bill Bailey stared at her.

"Try it. You'll like it."

The dog looked at the bowl and then turned away.

"Fine. Don't eat it. Hurt my feelings, I don't care." She left the bowl by the door in case Bill Bailey changed his mind, and went to read her book. Stephen Dedalus, having been with the prostitute, was now struggling with his Catholic conscience. Maggie knew something about this because her mother had been raised Catholic and although she left the fold when she married her father, a Jew, her fear of displeasing God never left and was transmitted to Maggie in oddly distorted ways.

In the flickering candlelight, Maggie found herself reading the same paragraph over and between worrying about Walter and worrying about the dog, she decided to try the hospital and then just go to bed. But what to do with Bill Bailey? Still ignoring the soup, he'd been pacing the whole time in front of the door and it seemed to her that he'd probably traveled a mini Iditarod. Where did he sleep at Walter's? she wondered. Maggie couldn't remember seeing a dog bed. Maybe he slept on the couch, or curled up next to Walter.

She went to the phone, got a flashlight and looked in her Seattle directory for the number for Harborview. She was sure they wouldn't give her much information until morning, but if they at least told her what unit he was on that might be a clue. While Maggie waited for the hospital receptionist, she watched Bill Bailey pacing back and forth in front of the door, wondering how she'd ever sleep with the sound of his nails clicking over the floor all night. When the operator came on, Maggie was told that in the morning Walter would have a direct line to his room and she could call then. She was told he would be on 3East. Maggie thanked the operator. The lack of details wasn't a surprise; she hadn't expected much information. But what happened after she hung up was quite unexpected. Slowly, she put the phone back, steadied herself on the desk and turned toward the door where Bill Bailey was pacing. She looked at the dog, then went to him, knelt down and threw her arms around him and began to weep. She pressed her face against Bill's big head and tears rolled across her face onto his shaggy fur.

This display of emotion seemed to disturb him and he threw his head up and howled. "I thought we'd moved beyond that, dog." Maggie stood up and wiped her eyes on her sleeve.

She went to the kitchen and got a tissue and blew her nose. The tears had been a bit of a shock. But she chalked it up to the storm, the stress, and her struggle with the dog—to say nothing of her aching back.

Bill Bailey continued to howl and Maggie wondered again how she was going to get any sleep. It would be bad enough trying to sleep with the wind still blowing so hard and now that he was back to this wretched howling, it would be impossible. Bill Bailey was bereft. Nothing about Maggie, her house, or her offering of Campbell's soup was of solace. He needed something familiar, so finally, with a sigh of resignation, Maggie decided that if she wanted any peace at all she'd have to "call" him. She went to the living room and stared at Bill Bailey as he paced in front of the door. She held her arms loosely at her sides and took a deep breath.

"Won't you come home, Bill Bailey, won't you come home," she sang out.

Bill Bailey stopped pacing.

"She moans the whole day lo—ong."

Bill stared at her.

"I'll do the cooking darling, I'll pay the rent." She was getting into it now, Maggie stood up and grabbed one of the candles, blew it out and it became a mike. *"I knows I've done you wro—ong."*

Bill Bailey perked up his ears.

"'Member that windy eve that I drove you out," very clever, Maggie thought, a little improvisation here, changing "rainy" to "windy." *"With nothing but a fine tooth comb?"*

She was really belting it out when Bill Bailey stuck his nose in the air and began to howl. Not about to stop, Maggie kept going for the big finish. No way would she let that dog drown her out. Maggie strutted back and forth, then whirled to face him on the last line.

"I know I'se to blame; well ain't that a shame? Bill Bailey won't you please come home?"

She fell back, collapsing in the big overstuffed reading chair and Bill Bailey, still howling, flung himself against the door.

"It wasn't *that* bad, dog." Maggie put her head back on the chair and closed her eyes. The empathy she felt for Bill Bailey was waning as he continued to howl and leap against the front door. To regain some feeling for him, Maggie imagined his pre-Walter life, his life with the panhandler, no doubt a Dickensian existence, the victim of terrible cruelty and abuse. Maggie began thinking of him as Pip and felt her heart softening. She sighed a deep sigh. The only hope to shut him up might be to at least get him in a familiar place. In his own home. She'd have to take him to Walter's house and spend the night there with him, that was all there was to it.

Grabbing the flashlight from the kitchen, she went to the basement and cut a length off a clothesline for a leash. There was no way she was going to walk all the way to Walter's cabin hunched over, struggling to hold onto Bill Bailey's collar. Maggie assumed Walter had candles and matches, but just in case, after she blew out the candles she stuffed some matches and two of her candles into the deep pockets of her parka.

Bill Bailey was very strong and along with the flashlight, Maggie had to hold the rope in both hands just to hang onto him. The minute she set foot on the path, he was like a horse heading for the barn pulling her along, stumbling after him. "If I fall, dog, that's it—we're finished. You can wait in the woods for Walter by yourself, for all I care."

When they got to the end of the path next to the clearing in front of Walter's cabin, Bill Bailey leaped up with such force that Maggie dropped the flashlight. She struggled to hold him as she picked it up, then Bill galloped up to the cabin, the rope whizzing after him, burning her hands.

"Damn dog," she muttered. "Walter better appreciate this." Maggie rubbed her hands together to stop the stinging and followed Bill Bailey to the cabin. Lying in a heap a few yards from the porch were the solar panels and broken wind turbine. Poor Walter. It made her think of the wreck he'd made of his life. True, it was his own bad behavior that had driven so many people away, but Maggie still felt sorry for him.

"Come on dog. Let's go to bed."

Maggie shone the light around the cabin and didn't see any evidence of a bed for Bill Bailey, who was frantically looking in each room, hoping to find Walter. This pursuit seemed to occupy him and Maggie was thankful that at least he'd stopped that god-awful howling. In the kitchen, she found two aluminum dog dishes, one empty and the other about half filled with water. She began opening the cupboards trying to find dog food. Even though her purpose was noble, she felt a little uneasy going through Walter's cupboards. But the truth was, Maggie was a bit of a snoop. The discomfort she felt was because she had an impulse to go though all his stuff—not just the kitchen cupboards. She didn't deny this personality trait, but simply acknowledged it as not one of her more attractive qualities.

There was a bag of Paul Newman organic dog food in the lower cupboard next to the cupboard under the sink. Leave it to Walter to buy the best and with profits to a good cause to boot. On the bag there was a photo of Paul Newman, "Pa" Newman, and his daughter, Nell, each holding a yellow lab puppy. Now there was one handsome man, she thought. Still gorgeous up into his eighties. It broke her heart when she'd heard he'd died. Walter was aging almost as well as Paul Newman had, which was quite something considering Walter's many years of decadence. Maggie supposed it was probably a genetic thing. She imagined him in the hospital, lying back against the pillows with his broad shoulders and handsome face, with the female staff hovering all around, attracted by all that seductive virility.

She dumped some of the dog food into Bill Bailey's dish and called his name in a normal tone of voice. To her great relief, he came to the kitchen and immediately began eating.

Maggie decided to check her voice mail before she turned in. She went to Walter's desk and set the flashlight where it could shine on the phone and put in her number for messages. There was only one new one.

"Maggie—" Her sister still spoke with the breathy little-girl Marilyn Monroe voice she'd carefully cultivated in high school when she first wanted to be an actress. "Did you get my new number? I haven't heard from you and I have some very big news! Do call! As soon as you can! And here's the number again. 310-879-9654. Got that?" Leslie repeated it again, slowly, carefully, the way you speak to the elderly. "I can't wait to talk with you! Bye-bye!" Maggie wondered why she'd never gotten used to Leslie's signature goodbye, the second "bye" lilting upward in a cheery little trill. It always made her feel a little squirmy, the kind of squirm she felt listening to an actor who didn't have much talent, or a rather sad stand-up comic trying too hard to be funny.

Walter's computer and printer were on his desk and several sheets of paper were stacked in the tray of the printer. It looked like the power had gone out when it was in the middle of a printing job. Maggie was aroused by a burning curiosity. Authors were movie stars to a lot of librarians, and Maggie was no exception. Even though Walter had not had a success in years to rival *The Adventures of Fric the Chick*, he was still a great talent and she yearned to see what he was up to. *Can I stop myself from grabbing the pages off that printer? Of course I can*, she decided. In spite of her sorry little episode with Walter all those years ago, she reminded herself that she actually was able to control her emotions if the situation called for it. But Maggie didn't see how this situation could possibly call for it, and since she was being nice enough to care for Bill Bailey, it was only fitting that she read those pages.

The heading said "Chapter Four" and there were five complete pages with a sixth sticking halfway out of the printer. Maggie positioned the flashlight on the desk so she could read and sat in Walter's chair. The header at the top across from the page number said, "A Goose Called Hope/Hathaway" and Maggie assumed *A Goose Called Hope* was the title and the protagonist was some kind of goose. From what she could tell the story was told from the third person omniscient point of view and Chapter Four opened with a meeting of townspeople demanding that the mayor of the town do something about the geese who were pooping all over their property. From the rallying cries of "Round them up! Send them back to Canada!" Maggie assumed that Hope was a Canada goose. The page before the one stuck in the printer had the owner of a bicycle shop, a Mr. Hedgehopper, calling for the extermination of all the geese. It described the goose, Hope, sitting on the roof of the town hall, hearing the cries of "Kill! Kill!" echo up the chimney. Walter's writing was lush and lyrical and Maggie loved the few pages she read. Her only regret was that she wouldn't be able to tell Walter how excited she was about it.

Maggie put the pages back in the order she'd found them and carefully placed them on the tray of the printer. She started to pick up the flashlight from the desk and then she just couldn't help herself. There were a few papers under a paperweight, a beautiful white rock that Walter had probably picked up on the beach, and she slid the rock to the side to take a little peek. Nothing too interesting. Just the stuff of life: a few bills, a warranty for some piece of equipment, some phone numbers scribbled on a small scrap, but then on the bottom there was a letter from Walter's agent. The stationery was quite nice: a good weight, creamy ivory with "Madeline Gordon Literary Agency, Inc." embossed in navy blue lettering with a dignified font across the top. How rare to receive an actual letter these days with so much correspondence done by email. Maggie assumed Walter's agent must be even older than Walter to be sending an actual letter.

Dear Walter,

I have now had the chance to read your first three chapters of *A Goose Called Hope* and I've enjoyed it very much. Hope is an engaging character and I immediately felt for her and the goslings. However, as I mentioned when we spoke a few weeks ago, the market is dreadful for this kind of thing. Animal stories like this seem to be out of fashion and the editors are now interested in vampires, zombies, and ghosts. That said, I do think you should proceed with the story. When you finish the manuscript, send it along and even though I predict it will be a hard sell, I'll do everything I can to place it.

Best,
Madeline

Maggie put the papers back under the white rock and felt a surge of guilt. This generally followed any snooping that she did, but was usually not of the magnitude to disturb her sleep. It would predictably subside within a few hours, especially after she reminded herself that as far as vices go, this one was less than a misdemeanor type vice, it was just a little blip on her otherwise reasonably good character.

While Maggie had been snooping at Walter's desk, Bill Bailey had finished his food and was sitting on the couch, staring out the window. Maggie was sure he was hoping Walter would appear any minute. He didn't look at all relaxed, more like a sentry, but at least he was quiet.

"I'm going to bed now, Bill, good-night." Maggie patted his head but he didn't look at her, or even move.

Walter's bedroom and the bathroom were off a narrow hallway beyond the main room of the cabin. Maggie stopped to use the bathroom and did a little more investigating, this time checking out the medicine cabinet before she went to bed. There was the aspirin that she'd given him before the Medics came, some Aleve, and Lipitor—the same dosage she took. Maggie noted that there weren't any condoms or Viagra and she wondered if Walter had closed that chapter, thinking it would be quite a waste if he had.

In the bedroom there was a very comfortable looking queen-size bed with forest green sheets and a comforter that was a warm brown, like the color of pine paneling. The whole thing had an LL Bean feel to it. The bed was positioned in front of a large window that looked out toward the beach. It was so much quieter now, the storm seemed almost over, and Maggie wondered how long it would take the power company to fix the damage and get the power back on. She took off her shoes and got under the covers and was beginning to doze off when she heard Bill Bailey's nails slowly clicking across the hardwood floor. There was a dip in the mattress as he sprung on the bed and settled down with a sigh by Maggie's feet. She felt quite flattered by this breakthrough.

Bill Bailey was the first male of any sort that she'd slept with in a very long time.

CHAPTER THREE

Maggie was jolted awake by a repetitive, persistent and high-pitched beep. Disoriented and confused, she thought it was the alarm on a hospital heart monitor and she didn't know where she was or what had happened. It was a terrible feeling. Totally unnerving, and it didn't go away until her eyes focused in the dark and a big shaggy form took shape and she realized it was Bill Bailey. Grabbing the flashlight next to the bed, and still a bit foggy, she followed the sound to the main room of the cabin where Walter's printer was beeping and it dawned on her that the power had come back on. There was probably some button to push to make the printer resume printing, but Maggie didn't want to fool around with the thing. She did manage to find the printer's on/off switch and turned that off. The refrigerator was humming in the kitchen and she saw the light on the microwave blinking. Maggie checked her watch. Almost three a.m. She'd set the microwave clock in the morning, she decided with a yawn, and went back to Walter's bed.

Bill Bailey had followed her when she went to turn off the printer, and as she crawled back into bed, he stood at the foot of it and began to whine. Then he started pacing around the cabin.

"Come to bed, Bill. He's still not here!"

She said this with conviction, she thought it was quite commanding...she who must be obeyed...but it only served to make him whine with more vigor.

"You don't want to sleep with me, dog? You think I'm over the hill?" she yelled from the bedroom.

Maggie put the pillow over her head to muffle the sound of his whining and didn't remember much after that. But when she woke up in the morning, Bill Bailey was on the bed. She sat up and yawned and Bill Bailey jumped down, trotted around to her side of the bed and sat and stared at her.

"I suppose you want breakfast, dog," Maggie said, yawning. "Well, you'll just have to wait a minute."

Bill Bailey followed her to the bathroom. "Do you mind—" she said, shutting the door in his face. He immediately began to whine and it reminded her of having a two-year-old when you couldn't get a minute for yourself. Although she supposed he wasn't this needy around Walter. When she came out of the bathroom, he stopped whining and she let him outside. "Your turn, dog." She watched him pee on a salal bush, let him back in and was about to feed him when the phone rang.

She wasn't sure if she should answer it, but her prying mind had been uncorked the night before and there was no stuffing it back and keeping a lid on. Besides, if the caller didn't want to speak to her, the person could call back and she wouldn't pick up and they could leave a message.

"I'm calling for Walter Hathaway. Is he available?" A high youthful female voice. New York accent.

"I'm sorry, he's not available, but I'd be happy to take a message," Maggie replied with evasive good cheer, figuring Walter might not like her broadcasting the fact that he was in the hospital.

"Well, I'm not sure..."

"Or perhaps we could hang up and you could call back and leave the message on his voice mail," she suggested.

"No, I really should speak to him personally...do you know when he'll return?"

"It could be a few days."

"Oh...well...maybe I should—are you related to Walter?"

"I'm his friend. I'm here taking care of his dog."

"I'm not quite sure what to do, but I wouldn't want Walter to hear this anywhere else, so I'd like you to tell him..." she paused, "this is Jenny Schnieder calling and I'm afraid I have some very sad news. Walter's agent Madeline Gordon passed away last Thursday in Maine."

"Oh dear."

"It was a heart attack, quite sudden and we're all just devastated. I'm her assistant. The family asked me to call all her authors."

"I'm very sorry."

"I'd appreciate it if you could tell Mr. Hathaway for me, and of course, have him call me whenever he can."

"I'll tell him and I'm sure he would want you to extend his deepest sympathy to the family."

Maggie hung up and sat down at Walter's desk and looked out at the beach. Oh my. Poor Ms. Gordon. Poor Walter. Poor Ms. Gordon's family, and the assistant. Poor thing, having to make these calls.

Staring out at the water, Maggie shook her head; the water was calm but she could hardly recognize the beach. It was piled with enormous driftwood logs strewn every which way like a giant had dumped a box of his toothpicks on the sand. And a tall fir to the east of Walter's lot had blown over and lay covering everything for half the length of a football field. Its enormous limbs sliced across the beach and jutted far out into the water. But now there was no wind at all, just an eerie stillness broken only by the sound of a chainsaw off in the distance.

Poor Walter.

He must have been with Madeline Gordon quite a long time. Probably since the beginning, which had to be at least twenty-five years. And Madeline Gordon. What a shame, her letter had sounded so pleasant, and she must have been quite a good person to have put up with Walter all these years.

Bill Bailey came to sit next to Maggie and she stroked his head. "We never know, do we, doggie? We never know when it will be our time." Maggie sighed and continued absently stroking his head, looking out at the water and wondering how Walter was this morning. She went to the desk and reached for the phone. "Well, there's only one way to find out."

Maggie was on hold for a long time, and didn't much care for the music...some old country song "If you've got the money, honey...I've got the time..."

She heard more chain saws start up and wondered if their road was still clear. That's all we'd need, she thought—a tree, like the one that went down over the beach, blocking the whole road. She tapped her fingers on the desk, and was starting to open one of the drawers when the hospital operator answered. She said Maggie could call Walter's room directly. Maggie jotted down the number, hung up and sat there trying to decide when would be the right time to tell him about Madeline Gordon. The whole thing made her nervous. She was getting involved with Walter Hathaway far more than she ever intended when all she'd set out to do last night was just check on the old grump. But Maggie felt protective of Walter. What kind of shape was he in? How bad off? He wasn't in intensive care, so whatever had happened to him must not be critical or life-threatening. Nonetheless, Maggie hated to be the one to deliver a blow.

She looked at the number, gathered her nerve and called. The phone rang and rang and Maggie was about to hang up when it stopped and there was the sound of a lot of clunking and rustling. Finally Walter croaked, "Hello."

"Walter? It's Maggie."

"Ahhh," he sighed, "...Maggie..." His voice was raspy, but it had a bedroomy, sleepy- after-sex intimacy to it—so unlike his usual curt growl that Maggie was sure he was undoubtedly gorked out on pain medication.

"What's happened, Walter? How are you?"

"Ahh...Maggie..." his voice trailed off. It sounded like he was about to fall asleep.

"What does the doctor say?"

"They're... keeping me for... observation," he said slowly. Long pauses between his words. "It seems... I had...a little stroke. They...call it...CIA...ha-ha...a spy blowing up my brain...

no—it's...*T*...*TIA*...but it's just...a brain fart...there's nothing wrong with me...except..." his voice trailed off like he was losing steam.

"Except what?"

No answer.

"Walter? Can you hear me?" She used her Ms. Lewis–the–Librarian voice.

"Right. Yes. I'm here." He perked up like a kid caught napping when the teacher called on him.

"What else is the matter with you?"

"Just a minute, Maggie."

She waited and heard fumbling, then it sounded like he took a drink of water. Perhaps he sat up, she thought.

"I may have to have surgery for my shoulder." Walter was still speaking slowly, but he sounded more alert. "Something happened to it, but I have no memory of anything. Probably that damn solar panel did it."

There was a long pause and Maggie thought she was losing him again. "Walter? What about the surgery?"

"Oh...that. Well, they're bringing in a specialist. An orthopedic person to take a look and then he'll...or I suppose it could be a she...anyway, then they'll tell me what's next." There was another long pause.

"Maggie? Are you still there."

"Of course."

"How is Bill Bailey?"

"Frankly, he was miserable at my house. There didn't seem to be any other solution than to take him back to your cabin. He was quite upset, so I just stayed with him."

"Thank you." His voice caught in his throat.

"I can stay with him until you come home."

Walter coughed. He seemed quite undone, and Maggie just couldn't do it. She'd tell him later about Madeline Gordon. It was terribly early and he'd been through a lot and sounded exhausted. Maggie closed her eyes for a minute, promising herself that, of course, she would tell him—but just later. She'd do it when she called back this afternoon to find out about the surgery.

Maggie hung up and looked at Bill Bailey, who sat by the window staring at the road. He seemed tense and hyper alert, but at least he'd quit that terrible howling and pacing. She went to the kitchen and when he heard her dumping dog food into his bowl, he trotted right in and ate it all up. He still seemed a little tentative, but overall he appeared to be getting more comfortable with her and Maggie decided she and Bill Bailey were developing a relationship. After all, they had slept together and that had to count for something. *Not unlike me and his master all those years ago,* she thought, *but of course that had led to a disaster.* Maybe she and the dog would fare better.

After he finished eating, Maggie decided it was time to take him to her house. She got the rope and when she tied it to his collar, Bill Bailey didn't seem to mind. So far, so good.

She grabbed Bill Bailey's dog food and his dishes and they headed out the door. But when they got to the steps at the edge of the porch, it was like a switch flipped in his doggie brain because Bill Bailey lay down and wouldn't budge.

"Get up, dog."

Maggie tried her Ms. Lewis–the–Librarian voice and she might as well have been talking to a pile of rocks. Bill put his head on his paws and refused to look at her. Then she yanked on the rope.

Argggh. Bill made a terrible gagging sound.

Oh, great. Walter comes home and finds out his agent is dead and that I've strangled his dog.

Maggie let the rope dangle and tried another approach. "Come on Bill. Come with me, you'll love my house. You are a good fellow—such a handsome, good doggie," she said, each word a drop of honey. "Now come along with Maggie, sweetheart."

A big sigh this time. He actually sounded bored. Maggie opened the bag of dog food and took out a few pieces and held them in front of him. "Come on, Bill. You can have this nice treat!"

He closed his eyes. Passive aggressive, that's what he is, she thought, and she was getting pissed.

"Fine. Stay on the porch all day you cantankerous canine. I'm out of here." Maggie dropped the rope and stomped down the steps and hadn't gotten more than a few feet when she noticed a male grosbeak, bright orange and black, sitting on top of an empty bird feeder to the right of the porch. She wanted to ignore it, but just couldn't. They were such beautiful birds, flying about as if every day were Halloween, and it seemed to be sitting there chirping "Trick or Treat." Maggie went back inside and finally found a metal garbage can full of sunflower chips by the kitchen door. Bill Bailey ignored her as she walked past him, which she interpreted as an act of hostility. Maybe the grosbeak would be grateful.

After she filled the feeder, which immediately became a bird buffet for the grosbeak's entire family and a bunch of assorted finches, she tried one last time with Bill Bailey.

"I'm not kidding, dog. This is it. Come with me now, or I'm leaving with your food and water and you'll just have to come by yourself when you can't stand it anymore."

Another "forget it lady" type sigh.

"I'm not singing the song, dog. I'm going to count to ten and if you don't come with me by the time I get to ten, I'm leaving."

Maggie began counting, and got to ten and Bill Bailey didn't budge. She untied the rope from his collar, went inside and filled his water dish, plunked it down on the porch, said goodbye and left.

Walter's yard and the path between their lots were strewn with broken branches and Maggie wondered what she'd find when she got to her house. What if the roof had blown off or a tree had fallen down and crushed the whole house? She imagined herself having to live at Walter's for months while her house was repaired. Would he sleep on the couch and give me the bed? Did he snore or make obnoxious throat-clearing noises in the morning? And what about the scourge of the elderly—gas?

Maggie climbed over a large branch that lay across the path and came out of the woods to see that a patch of the carport roof was missing some shingles, but the house itself looked fine. She walked toward the carport to get a closer look at the roof and remembered that she'd left her bicycle helmet at Walter's. She certainly had no need for it. Putting it on had been ridiculous anyway and she decided she'd wait to get it when she went back to feed Bill Bailey, who, Maggie was sure, knew her whole exit with his bag of dog food had been a big bluff.

The garbage can from the back porch lay six feet from the door in the dahlias. A raccoon, or perhaps Tanner, Howie and Mark's garbage-loving black lab, must have had quite a feast because the stuff he probably found inedible—orange juice cartons, wet paper towels, deli food containers—was decorating the bushes and flower beds. Maggie thought her garden looked like a garbage truck had taken a turn too fast and rolled over, dumping a good portion of her carbon footprint in her yard.

Maggie was typically not one to avoid things. Responsibility could be my middle name, she thought. The oldest child of a depressed mother, Maggie had developed the habit quite early in life of doing the hardest or most difficult task first. But today she spent the morning practicing the fine art of procrastination. She did everything but call Walter. She showered, dressed, ate breakfast, answered emails, and messed around on the Internet where she read the *New York Times*, the *Washington Post*, and *School and Library Journal*. She even googled Walter's name—there were ninety-five thousand items—but she did not call him.

Hello Walter, I hope you're feeling better today. Well, I'm terribly sorry to be the bearer of some bad news but I received a call when I was staying at your cabin with Bill Bailey and it seems that your agent has died.

She couldn't do it. She'd wait until he was home: rested, stronger, more resilient. Instead, Maggie decided to make the other call that was on her things-I'd-rather-not-do list. Call her sister.

Leslie had had the same cell phone number for years. The fact that Maggie couldn't remember it and always had to look it up, she knew, was telling. She checked the address book on her computer and then looked out the window at the garbage in her yard. I really should pick that stuff up, she thought, realizing that particular chore had more appeal than talking to Leslie, who invariably wanted something. It was all take and no give with her, and Maggie put the computer on sleep and went out to clean up the garbage.

Howie came by with his chain saw as she was getting the last juice carton out of the rosemary bush.

"Party animals, I take it." Howie laughed and set down the saw. "This time I don't think it was Tanner—he hates the wind and was home all night under the bed."

"The raccoons, no doubt," Maggie said, with a smile. "Did you guys have any damage?"

"One of the shutters on the window nearest the beach has disappeared. I'm hoping to spot it on my way over to the Wigginses. Carl called and asked me for a hand. There's a tree down over his drive." Howie looked toward the woods. "Any word about Walter?"

"I talked with him a little while ago. They say he had a minor stroke and may have to have surgery for a broken shoulder. But he's going to be okay. I'm going to call a bit later, I'll let you know what I find out."

"Where's Bill Bailey?" Howie asked.

"I left him on Walter's front porch. He had no interest in coming over and I had no interest in spending more time at Walter's place, but I'll find out what Walter wants me to do about him when I call."

"It's good of you to help him, Maggie." Howie picked up the chain saw. "Especially after he treated all of us like phone solicitors who were annoying him when we were just trying to welcome him."

Maggie winced a little at Howie's take on Walter's interpersonal skills. True, he was a crusty old grump and appeared quite tough, but she suspected it was a veneer designed to shield a very soft underbelly. She gave Howie a cheery wave as he left for the Wigginses.

Maggie supposed she could spend the rest of the morning searching for the missing shingles from the carport, but she couldn't quite bring herself to engage in such an obvious effort to avoid calling Leslie, let alone Walter.

Leslie answered on the first ring. "Oh, Maggie," she said breathlessly, her voice oozing relief. "I saw on the news that you'd had a terrible wind storm up there and I was so worried about you. Oh, I'm so glad you've called! Are you all right?"

"I'm fine. Thank you."

"Oh, thank God," she said, dramatically in her breathy voice. Maggie could picture her with her hand over her heart, swooning. Drama came quite naturally to Leslie. Decades ago she had a minor part in *Bottoms Up*, a *Cheers* spin-off in which she played Brandi, a ditsy sexpot. Type-casting to be sure, Maggie thought. But Leslie's best, longest-running gig was in the late eighties and early nineties when she made a fortune in television commercials as the PerkySweet Prune lady.

"Well, I have some good news," she said, with a bright little chirp, "and..." she paused here as her voice lowered and became very distressed, "...some bad news."

Then she sighed deeply and waited. Maggie knew it was what they call a tease on the cable news shows where they want you to be so intrigued that you'll sit through that little green lizard thing that wants you to buy insurance until they come back and tell you the whole amazing news story.

Leslie sighed again, a little more deeply this time, which Maggie knew was her cue to ask her what had happened, but she just didn't feel like it. She hit a key on her computer to wake it up and checked her email.

"Well," Leslie said with another sigh, "I guess I'll tell you the bad news first and get it over with..."

Another pause and Maggie still didn't bite.

Then a really tragic sigh. "...Leonard and I have split up."

"I'm sorry it didn't work out," Maggie said civilly, opening an email from Avon offering a special on Anew Reversalist Illuminating Eye System for $30.00 with free shipping.

"I suppose I should have seen it coming." Leslie sighed again.

Surely you jest, you bubblehead. Leonard was her fifth husband. Maggie opened another email. This one from a local island shop, Giraffe Global Gallery & Fair Trade Store, advertising Sugar Shea

Body Scrub from Southern Sudan. They had color photos of the Sudanese women working to make the stuff in rural processing centers and a paragraph which explained that the Sudanese variety of shea nut was known by its Arabic name of lulu.

Lulu, meaning nut. *My sister's a real lulu*, Maggie thought, picturing the contrast of Leslie's latest struggle with the women in the photos.

"Would you like to hear the good news?" Leslie asked timidly.

"Sure."

"You don't sound like it, Maggie."

"Look. I'm sorry about you and Larry—"

"Leonard."

"Right. Leonard. I'm sorry it didn't work out and of course, I want good things for you." This was true. In spite of the fact Leslie had been quite an albatross after their lives fell apart when Maggie was sixteen and Leslie was six and their mother turned into a lifeless zombie, Maggie had, in fact, always wished her well.

"I'm coming to visit!" Leslie gushed.

"Visit who?"

"Visit you, on Vashon Island! A little peace and quiet is what I need right now and some family support, I mean, I really thought it was going to work out with Leonard and I've been so upset and when I told my therapist about this idea of spending time on the island with you he thought it might really do me some good…"

Even her therapist wants to get rid of her. Now it was Maggie's turn to sigh.

"Maggie?"

"Hmmm," Maggie muttered absently, still looking at the photos of the Sudanese women.

"You don't sound excited." Leslie sounded hurt.

"Just surprised, I guess, but it's fine if you want to come." It was the best Maggie could muster in the way of enthusiasm. And telling Leslie that she couldn't come, making up some excuse about why it wasn't a good time, was something Maggie just wasn't capable of even though she often entertained such thoughts. She was hard wired to respond to Leslie.

Leslie announced she was arriving Monday and magnanimously stated that Maggie wouldn't have to pick her up at the airport, that she'd be renting a car. After they hung up, Maggie went down to the beach for some fresh air. The news of her sister's upcoming visit had a suffocating effect on her, and she needed to get a grip before she could even think about calling Walter to see what the surgeon had said.

By June most of the harbor seal pups had been weaned, and as Maggie sat on a large driftwood log, she saw one stick its glistening silver head out of the water to stare at her with big liquid, dark eyes. It disappeared after a few seconds, only to pop up again a few feet to the right of her, a little farther out. They're curious creatures and it made her laugh. Near the water, her perspective would shift. Not a colossal seismic shift but just one that helped her to recognize the vastness of the universe and how her own particular dilemma, whatever it happened to be, was in comparison, quite small. The world would go on.

She ran her hand over the warm sand, scooped up a little and let it fall through her fingers. How long would Leslie stay this time? There was no way to predict; the only pattern Maggie had figured out was that she typically visited when she was between men. Not that Maggie felt superior to her in the relationship department; she could certainly admit they both had lousy track records. Maggie had one long, pathetic marriage that had limped along on life support and finally fizzled and died when Becky went off to college whereas Leslie had a string of marriages that all met the same fate: all expired. Their marital journeys had been totally different, but at fifty-five and sixty-five they'd both ended up in the same place.

CHAPTER FOUR

Maggie put off calling Walter for at least a half hour after she got back from the beach. She poured herself some iced tea, leafed through the latest issue of the *New Yorker*, mostly reading the cartoons, some of which she didn't get, and a poem that she thought was quite terrible. Then she went to her computer and answered an email from her granddaughter. Ashley was at a summer camp on the Oregon Coast and she wished they were corresponding with real letters sent with a postage stamp through the snail mail. She knew letters from camp were mostly a thing of the past, at least they were at Camp Ravenswood and she supposed it made some sense in today's world. But she used to love the letters Becky sent when she went to Hidden Valley Camp. It seemed like that was centuries ago and then Maggie realized it wasn't just a figure of speech: it *had* been in the last century when Becky was ten—Ashley's age now. How did this happen? It was a question that seemed to be on the lips of a lot of people her age and she wondered if that surprise about getting old was unique to her generation. Maggie didn't remember her own grandparents commenting so frequently on their age, wondering where the years had gone. Maybe we boomers somehow thought we'd stay young forever, just gliding through life, never grasping that we would inevitably go downhill, falling apart like poor Walter. She pictured him with his broken wing lying in the hospital and just couldn't put off calling any longer. Maggie finished the email to Ashley, hit "send" and picked up the phone.

When Walter answered, Maggie thought he sounded a bit more alert than he had when they first spoke. "Walter, it's Maggie. How are you now?"

"I've been better," he said, sounding quite cranky. "I get that painkiller every four hours and I wish they'd get here. I need the hit."

"I'm sorry."

"It's not your fault for crissake," he snapped.

"I know it's not. I just meant I'm sorry to hear you're in pain, Walter."

"Hmmph," he muttered something unintelligible, then asked, "How's Bill Bailey?"

"I'm afraid I have to tell you that he wouldn't budge when I left this morning. He's probably still on your porch."

"It's about time!" Walter shouted.

"What?"

"Not you, Maggie. The nurse is here. Just a minute, hang on."

Maggie heard a clunk that she supposed was Walter putting the phone down, then a female voice that she couldn't understand and the low murmur of conversation before Walter picked up the phone again.

"Sorry," Walter mumbled. Apologies were never his long suit. "Now where were we?"

"Bill Bailey. I left him on your porch, and I need to know if I should feed him again, and when? And how much food does he get? And I really don't think he should spend the night on your porch. I just need to know what you'd like me to do."

"Look, sorry I was a grouch. I don't like it here."

"Walter?"

"What?"

"What should I do about Bill Bailey?" she asked.

"I don't like not being able to take care of my own dog."

"They won't let him sleep at the hospital, so you'll have to tell me what you want me to do."

A long sigh of resignation, then he finally said, "He gets two scoops—heaping ones, and the scoop is in the bag. I feed him in the morning and again late afternoon, usually around five. And you don't have to sleep with him at my place, just tell him firmly to come with you."

"I tried that and it didn't work."

"Oh. Well, maybe put on his leash and then try."

"I had a rope that I tied to his collar and—"

"He hates ropes. The guy I got him from used to yank him around with a rope, no wonder he didn't go with you. I'm sure he thought you were going to take him back to the streets."

"Yes, I wanted to put a little bandana around his neck and make a sign so we'd could stand under the bridge by First Avenue." Walter didn't say anything, he just sighed. "Walter, just tell me where his leash is."

"It's on a hook by the back door. If you don't see it, my coat's probably hanging over it."

"I want to have a positive attitude about this, and assume that when he sees the leash that he'll trot along right over to my place, but just in case he still won't budge, what do you want me to do? I suppose I could get Howie…maybe Bill Bailey responds better to men…as a last resort, maybe Howie could carry him to my house," Maggie said, thinking aloud.

"Don't bring anyone else into this—it's bad enough that I have to depend on you!"

And YOU better believe I'd rather not be involved with you OR your dog! Maggie had an impulse to hang up on him, but then she imagined Walter alone in that hospital and also losing his agent—which he still didn't know about—so she cut him some slack and resisted the urge. But she couldn't think of anything to say that didn't sound sarcastic, and he didn't say anything for such a long time that she wondered if the nurse had come back in to do something and he'd put the phone down.

"Walter?"

"I'm grateful to you, Maggie," he said, quietly. His voice had softened and she wondered if the painkiller had kicked in. "If it doesn't work with the leash I don't suppose you could…" his voice trailed off.

"Could what?"

"You know…a few verses…"

"I'm not singing the song."

"Okay, fine. Just leave him at my place by himself. If you come over to feed him and let him out in the morning that should be fine. They're doing surgery on my hand and shoulder tomorrow and I'll be home the day after that, so a couple of nights by himself won't kill him."

"So it wasn't just bruised or sprained. I'm sorry."

"I'll be in a cast for about six weeks, but it could've been worse. I'm alive, which is better than the alternative."

This seemed to be the time for Maggie to tell him about his agent. She recognized that the segue was there with the reference to death. She could say, "We never know when it's our time, do we? And I'm so sorry but I have to tell you about a phone call I got when I was staying at your house…you see, I answered the phone in case it was the hospital and—"

No, not now. He was facing that surgery. She'd wait until he was through it. A person needed to be in the best possible shape to get through any kind of surgery and having a terrible blow like the awful news of his agent's death could make it much more difficult. Even minor surgery wasn't a breeze. Being put under and having someone cut you open made most people anxious and especially someone like Walter who couldn't stand not being in control. She would definitely wait. It was better this way.

"Will you need a ride home from the hospital?" she asked.

"No, you've done enough. I'll take a cab to the ferry and then have the Ride-On Vashon, that new taxi service, pick me up." His voice was soft and mellow and Maggie was quite sure the medicine had taken effect.

"What about groceries? I can pick some up for you if you'd like?"

"Ahhh, Maggie my girl…"

"I'm not your girl. I was just trying to be helpful. I'd do it for anyone."

"Of course. I know that," he said, softly. "I'll have the taxi stop at Thriftway and I'll pick up stuff at the deli. It may take me awhile to learn how to cook with my left hand. And I don't know what I'll do about writing my book...well...I guess I'll have to figure that out later."

Walter's voice was a little fuzzy and he sounded like he was getting sleepy. Maggie told him to get some rest and she hung up feeling like a coward. Cowardice frightened her, she wondered sometimes if it existed in DNA, some kind of defective little cell, a minus "C" cell for lack of courage. Whenever she felt cowardly she worried that she might have inherited the gene from her father.

Maggie got a broom and went out to the porch to clean up all the mess from the storm. First she carried the larger branches out to the yard and began a pile next to the carport—when they dried out she'd use them for kindling. She'd given up burning brush, even though outdoor burning was still allowed in some rural areas of King County, and Vashon Island certainly qualified as rural. Mostly she'd given it up to avoid Jeanette Bugsby, who lived a half mile down on Hormann Road. Jeanette was a self-appointed green policewoman and lectured anyone she found burning outdoors. She could get quite nasty about it. Of course, she was right about how the smoke polluted the air and all, Maggie knew that. But the woman was so self-righteous and rigid that Maggie had given up outdoor burning as much to avoid Jeanette Bugsby as to keep the air clean.

It was a clear day, dead calm and getting quite warm; now close to eighty and it wasn't even noon. After Maggie had made a pile of branches and swept all the twigs and smaller debris from the porch, she was sweating and sticky and quite hot and decided to take her kayak out for a paddle.

She went in to call Martha Jane before she headed down to the boathouse. Years ago Martha Jane had made Maggie promise not to go out without telling her, insisting that someone needed to know where she was. Martha Jane said it was like checking in at the ranger station when you're hiking alone in the wilderness and Maggie had always appreciated her concern. People didn't often feel protective of Maggie. She used to think it was because of her size. Tall, big-boned and wide-hipped, she thought it was because she had the physical appearance of someone who could literally be leaned on, that she projected an image of stability, like a broad-bottomed boat. But deep down, she knew it was a little more than that. Unlike her sister, she'd learned to be alone with her sorrow and to shield her vulnerability with a sturdy armor of efficiency and reliability. Maggie was capable. She was the one who could cope.

It seemed to be getting hotter by the minute. Even the phone felt sticky in her hand when she picked it up to call.

"Hi, it's me. Just wanted to let you know I'll be out in my kayak."

"Thank you for letting me know, Maggie dear." Martha Jane's voice was weak and raspy with age, and she spoke with long pauses between words. But it had retained a sweet, musical quality and Maggie never grew impatient with the pauses. "And Maggie—"

"Yes?"

"Well now—how is Walter? Have you—have you—heard anything today?"

"He's supposed to have surgery tomorrow for his shoulder, and then he'll be home the day after that."

"Oh my. It's such a shame—they let—they, you know—shove people out so soon these days..." There was a long pause and her voice trailed off.

"I know."

"And especially someone like Walter—who will look after him, dear?"

"He didn't say. I'm sure he thinks he doesn't need anyone."

"Oh, my—well, he may be forced to accept help whether he likes it or not. Now what was it we wanted to talk about, again?"

"I just wanted to let you know I was going out in my kayak."

"Right, yes, right—of course. Can you stop in for some iced tea when you're back?"

"Love to. I shouldn't be out more than an hour." Maggie wondered if Martha Jane would remember their conversation when she got back. It was hard to predict. Her memory seemed like the weather: sometimes so clear and sharp and then other days when it was muted, gray, with everything a bit cloudy. But the shifts in the patterns of Martha Jane's mind, even at their most cloudy, never troubled Maggie. When she was with her, she felt blessed with gentle warmth, as if she was in the center of a soft summer breeze. They'd first met when Maggie started working at Evergreen Elementary, where Martha Jane taught kindergarten. Their time on the staff only overlapped a few years as Martha Jane was close to retirement when Maggie started there, but it was more than enough time to develop a solid friendship. Early on, it had occurred to Maggie that checking in with Martha Jane before she went out in her kayak might not always serve its purpose. If Maggie had a mishap and didn't return as expected, it was quite possible that Martha Jane might not even remember that she had called to check in before she left. But futile or not, it had become a ritual, and one that meant a lot to her.

Maggie was not a person who was especially enamored of possessions. Stores and shopping confused her and in fact, could make her feel a little unbalanced. A little unhinged in very large stores. She avoided them as much as possible. Except for bookstores, of course. Her car, her clothes, her furniture—none of it meant much to her. But there was one possession to which she was deeply attached: her kayak. She loved her kayak. It was made by a local company, Pacific Kayak in Silverdale, Washington, and she even loved the name of the model: Gossamer. She'd chosen light carbon over fiberglass, and it weighed only forty-seven pounds. The only anxiety she'd experienced when ordering her kayak was when it came time to choose the deck color. There were twenty-two different choices and they all had lovely names. For safety, she thought it might be wise to pick one that would show up well against the water, such as Pylon Orange, Goldenrod, Bright Aztec Yellow or Lime Green. But the one she fell in love with was Spruce. A beautiful blue green and she decided if she blended too much with the water, making it a reckless choice, well, so be it. But when Maggie put in the order, she fizzled and chose Goldenrod.

Unlike a lot of what she owned, which came from thrift shops, or like her car, which had been bought used, the Gossamer had been purchased when it was brand new and she paid top dollar. In fact, the paddle she bought, a Werner Camano fiberglass and carbon blend, was also quite expensive, as were her black paddling booties and paddling gloves. All top of the line. All brand new. Except for the color, Maggie had thrown caution to the wind, splurging on her kayak the way some women splurged on spas. She was also quite sure that the abandonment with which she threw herself into buying it had more than a little to do with the major event in her life at the time: her divorce from George.

As she got close to the boathouse, Maggie could see the effects of the storm. The deck was dotted with twigs and a large fir branch was lodged in the railing. She pulled the branch out and tossed it onto the bank, and stared at all the twigs, contemplating going back up to the house for a broom. But the water beckoned. It shone cool and clear, like dark blue silk spreading out from the huge driftwood logs that had washed up on the beach, and Maggie proceeded to unlock the door of the boathouse. She picked up the kayak and headed to the water. The Gossamer was less than two feet wide across the beam and just over eighteen feet long with the rudder, and she managed it easily. Her father used to say, "Maggie, darling, you are a big, sturdy girl." At least he'd added the endearment "darling" and she supposed he meant it as a compliment, but it never felt like one. Especially after Leslie came along.

Her sister was an "oops" baby, she later figured out, and their parents, especially their father, adored Leslie. He called her "little kitten," or "lil kit" and without question, her sister possessed a sex kitten sensuality that only increased with her age in its power to attract men. Leslie was blessed with their mother's looks. Small, blonde, and soft, she was a brown-eyed Susan with huge dark eyes and golden skin like the beautiful tow-headed children in the old Coppertone ads. Maggie saw herself as more of a plow horse creature, and there was some truth to it. Large-boned with something of a peasant body, she had big features and her father's dark hair. She'd been told she looked like his mother. The only feature she had that favored her mother was her eyes. She had her mother's startlingly blue eyes.

Maggie pulled on her black paddling shoes and slipped on the life vest, a narrow inflatable device with a cord that you tugged to inflate. She'd come to especially appreciate it on a hot day as it added so little bulk, and offered a freedom of movement that she really loved. As she carried her kayak and the paddle to the edge of the beach, a large powerboat went by about twenty yards from shore, creating waves from its wake. She waited for them to subside, leaning over, steadying the kayak. Even in the summer, there were only a few places along the shores of the island where the water was considered by some hearty souls as warm enough for swimming. But Baker's Beach, unlike the long stretch of beach around the Burton peninsula, was not one of them. Even on the hottest days, the water was still icy cold and as soon as the waves stopped splashing against the sides of the kayak, Maggie waded out and climbed into the boat, getting out of the water as quickly as she could.

For a half hour, she paddled close to the shore heading north beyond Baker's Beach. When she was close to Sylvan Beach, she glided over at least a half dozen starfish, some of them over a foot long in amazing colors: light blue, orange and a stunning deep lavender, a color like a lilac in full bloom. She stopped paddling forward, turned the paddle over and slipped it back in the water lightly pulling the water forward so she could go back to get a better look. It was slack tide without much of a current and she floated above them, mesmerized, gazing down at the beautiful creatures. Farther north about twenty feet, a blue heron stood motionless on its long spindly legs, silently fishing in the shallow water. A white gull flew overhead and Maggie could hear the sound of its wings. She didn't feel like a foreign invader as she floated quietly above the starfish, near the heron, and just below the gull. There was a sense of being part of it. It was a familiar, exquisitely peaceful feeling. She often experienced it on the water when there were no other boats in sight and it could feed her soul for quite some time. But today, when she spotted a beautiful little golden starfish, thoughts of her sister began to contaminate her psyche. It was like an emotional oil spill. Maggie dubbed her sister Leslie Valdez or Leslie BP, wondering what kind of mess she'd want her to clean up this time. Maggie took one last look at the heron, then slipped her paddle into the water and headed back.

As she was putting her kayak in the boathouse, Martha Jane waved from her deck. "Yoo-hoo, Maggie dear—tea time!" Maggie shaded her eyes and looked up from the beach. Martha Jane was wearing one of her painting smocks. This one had large, multi-colored stripes and the way it draped over her plump figure, Maggie observed, not unkindly, it made Martha Jane look a bit like a beach ball. Martha Jane had taken up painting a few years ago, studying with Fred Weiss, who Maggie thought was probably close to ninety himself. He had an informal art school on Margot Road, on a hill above Fisher Pond just south of Cove Road, and Martha Jane went to paint at Fred's studio almost every day. There were many things Maggie admired about her friend, but probably one of the qualities she appreciated most was the way Martha Jane stayed engaged in life. It was the passion she had. Martha Jane often seasoned her conversation with little philo-sophical snippets, which Maggie loved even though they usually came with a long preamble where Martha Jane would struggle to remember the source. She would eventually give up but then go on to quote whatever it was with great clarity. A favorite was "It is the soul that is afraid of dying that never learns to live."

As Maggie walked up the steps to the deck, Martha Jane brought out a tall pitcher of iced tea. She walked slowly, shuffling a little and moving each foot forward with care.

"Here, let me help." Maggie reached for the pitcher. It was clear cut glass and quite beautiful. The ice cubes rose to the top, floating with thin slices of lemon and sprigs of mint.

"Thank you, dear." Martha Jane slowly lowered herself into one of two white wicker chairs. "Just put it there," she said, smiling and motioning to a little teak table between the chairs. "Well, let's sit and have our tea—the mint you know is from..." she paused, her brows knit together in a little scowl, "there's something I forgot..."

"I think we'll need some gla—"

"Glasses!" Martha Jane shook her head. "That's it! I'm sorry, dear—" She started to pull herself up.

"Stay there, I'll get them." As Maggie went in the house, Martha Jane sat back in the chair and sighed, folding her hands across her stomach.

Like a lot of beach houses, Martha Jane's house had a damp seawater smell along with a hint of cedar and mildew: a summer place smell that many cottages, cabins, and camps all seemed to have. For Maggie that summer place aroma evoked a feeling of comfort as wonderful as if there had been chocolate chip cookies baking in the oven. Martha Jane's house also had the odor of oil paint in the mix. In the middle of the living room, which doubled as her studio, was a large table covered with tubes of paints, palettes, little jars and brushes. Canvases were propped against every wall and at least a half dozen leaned on the furniture. Some of the paintings seemed finished and a few looked like works in progress. And there were books. Piles and piles of books. On the floor, the windowsills, every table—except the one that held the art supplies—even the seats of most the chairs were covered with books. Only the sofa was somewhat uncluttered. Although a hardcover book lay open, face down next to a pair of reading glasses near where Maria Montessori, Martha Jane's large orange cat, lay curled in a big furry heap. Martha Jane had adopted the cat from Vashon Island Pet Protectors, the local animal shelter, and not long after she got the cat, she made a slipcover in fuzzy orange fabric. She wanted the couch to match Maria Montessori, hoping it would blend nicely with the cat hair.

Maggie returned with the glasses, poured tea for each of them and sat next to Martha Jane. "This is perfect," she said, taking a sip. "Nothing better on a hot day."

"Mint adds such a nice touch, don't you think? It's from Howie and Mark's garden."

Maggie and Martha Jane were often the beneficiaries of the bounty of Howie and Mark's garden. It was a serious garden, covering almost an acre behind their house, completely surrounded by high fencing to keep the deer away. Maggie had tried to grow deer-resistant plants with inconsistent results. But Martha Jane not only made no attempt whatsoever to garden, but would feed any deer she thought were in need of a little extra nutrition. She loved the deer so much that at one time she'd been dubbed the Deer Lady of Hormann Road. One of her first paintings was of two little fawns whose mother had been found dead on the road across from Baker's Beach. Martha Jane had taken them under her wing, feeding them little pieces of apples. She named them Jane Doe and John Deere and for many years they hung around at Martha Jane's place as if it were a wildlife refuge. And now their descendants came on a regular basis and everyone at Baker's Beach was pretty sure Martha Jane continued with her nutrition program, whether any of them needed it or not.

"This is lovely," Maggie said, looking at the pitcher. "Do you ever make solar tea?"

"Oh no. I always thought that was a little silly. I could never tell the difference from solar and any other kind of tea and the one time I tried it, putting the pitcher in the sun the way Sondra Wiggins said to do it, a lot of bugs flew in."

"I think you're supposed to cover it."

"Maybe that was the problem." Martha Jane looked over toward Maggie's house. "What a storm that was—looks like you didn't have too much damage."

"Except for a big fir tree that fell across my shed, I was lucky. Your place looks fine, too."

"It is, and Howie and Mark have already cleared most of the debris. But poor Walter."

Maggie nodded. "I've been taking care of Bill Bailey while Walter is in the hospital...or at least trying to—"

"It's very good of you. I'm sure you know, for many years now Walter hasn't been the easiest person to help. Of course in the beginning, it was different. I was on one of those committees for the International Reading Association. IRA, not the gun people you know," she paused and took a little sip of her tea. "I've been working on talking faster, so I don't forget what I started to say. Like about the gun people. I cannot for the life of me understand why they allow hunting on this island. It's an outrage."

"I agree."

"Was that what we were talking about, dear?"

"About Walter?"

"Oh yes, well I don't mind taking a little credit for bringing his wonderful book to the attention of a lot of reading specialists and I believe he was—and for that matter—still is appreciative. But his work is wonderful and if it hadn't been me, it would have been someone else."

"I'm glad he appreciates you."

"Well, perhaps so, but he can be difficult, but you know that, don't you? I'm sure you must—well, you did know him before he moved to the beach—I think, as I remember..."

Maggie knew Martha Jane sensed there'd been something between her and Walter and supposed she was curious. It was only natural that she would be, although it wasn't in her nature to pry.

"I did know him. After you retired from Evergreen, I invited him to do an author visit one year when the American Library Association mid-winter meeting was in Seattle."

"Oh, really?" She looked at Maggie and smiled. "And how did it go?"

"Not well."

Understatement of the year, Maggie thought, and then decided to leave it at that. "But I really would like your advice about something—"

"Good. I like to give advice."

"Well, I need it, because while I was at Walter's place feeding Bill Bailey there was a phone call from the assistant to Walter's agent with the awful news that his agent had died."

"Oh dear."

"Yes, and it was quite sudden and the assistant didn't want to just leave a voice mail message and she asked me to tell him."

"Oh dear—oh my..." Martha Jane put her hand on Maggie's arm. "How difficult."

"Yes, so difficult that I haven't been able to get the nerve to tell him. Every time I've tried, I just chicken out. I mean, there he is in the hospital and it will just be inflicting a blow and he's facing surgery. I just don't know what to do."

Martha Jane patted Maggie's arm. "You have to tell him. First thing, soon as he gets home. There's no good time, but the longer you avoid telling him the worse it will be for both of you. You have to get it over with."

Maggie stared out at the water for a few minutes. Finally she said, "I know you're right. But I'd certainly like to avoid it. Today, when I was out in my kayak, I just wanted to keep going. Just paddle off into the sunset. And besides all this with Walter—Leslie's coming. She's always so draining and I just don't feel up to it, although as you know, I never feel up to it with her."

"I don't suppose you could suggest that it's not the best time for you—"

"Leslie has a very well developed sense of entitlement, it never occurs to her to ask if it's a good time for me."

"Then could you limit the visit in some way?" Martha Jane asked.

"Things with me and Leslie always feel complicated. But I've told you about all that. About our mother."

"I'm not going to pretend I remember, Maggie dear. I'm sure you've told me. But I'm not good at faking it. I know many people who are, but it just doesn't work for me. I'd rather ask and I just assume that if it's important the person will want to tell me again. I hope you don't find that annoying."

"Oh no. Because I know you're interested."

"I am, now what was it I didn't remember?"

"About our mother. I was ten when Leslie was born and our mother went into a severe postpartum depression. I'd talk to her and try to engage her, but there was nobody home inside this very sad, almost lifeless person. She spent most of the day in bed, our father was always traveling and except when I was at school, I had to take care of Leslie."

"That's a lot of responsibility for a ten-year-old." Martha Jane shook her head. "Too much."

"Actually, I think I clung to her as much as she did to me. I'm sure I gave that little baby the mothering I wished I'd had for myself. And to this day, I think I still yearn for some kind of closeness with Leslie, but instead I always end up feeling ripped off." Maggie drank the last of the tea and chewed on a piece of ice. "But at least she never stays that long." She gave Martha Jane a sad smile. "I can always count on that."

CHAPTER FIVE

Maggie was relieved Bill Bailey was still on Walter's porch. He'd moved under the swing so he could be in the shade and when he saw her, he scooted out and trotted down the steps, wagging his tail and panting. He seemed so pleased that Maggie hoped it meant he'd had a change of heart and that he'd go to her house and stay there until Walter got home. She really hadn't liked leaving him by himself on Walter's sunny porch that morning. The poor thing looked so hot with all that fur, and at least her house stayed cool.

"Hi Bill." Maggie patted his head, "let's see how you're fixed for water." She'd put the water bowl by the door in the shade when she left in the morning, but now the sun was beating down and it was empty. She took it inside to fill and Bill Bailey followed, still wagging his tail and panting. Walter's house was stuffy, Maggie hadn't noticed it last night, but there wasn't anything covering the windows. She supposed he didn't feel the need, the cabin was so secluded, but it seemed to her some nice shades or curtains would have looked attractive and certainly would help keep it cooler on these hot days. At Home Depot she'd gotten some wonderful shades for her house, ones that actually worked without the cord getting all messed up. And they'd had all kinds of colors. She remembered a very pretty woodlandy green and thought it would look quite nice in Walter's cabin.

Maggie filled the water bowl and gave it to Bill Bailey, who drank greedily like it was an oasis in the Sahara. He slopped so much water on the floor, it looked like a pipe had burst or the roof was leaking. She spotted a roll of paper towel hanging under a cupboard, but as was her habit at home she looked for a rag, always trying to conserve on paper products. She opened the cupboard under the sink and knelt down, peering in only to find a jumble of scrub brushes, half-empty plastic soap bottles, rusty SOS pads, bug spray, mousetraps, loose charcoal briquettes and crumbly sponges. The only rag was oily and black from what she assumed was the charcoal.

Not as spry as she once was, Maggie had to grab the counter to pull herself up and almost slipped on the wet floor. Frustrated, she yanked on the paper towel, which sent the roll flying, bouncing down on the counter and then to the floor, unrolling the paper towel like a scroll as it went. "Damn," Maggie grumbled as she rolled it up and fastened it back on the holder. Then, knees creaking and holding a big wad of paper towel, she got back down on the floor. It was a cheesy brand of paper towel and she had to pull herself up to get more. This time she was careful, and gingerly, not yanking, she pulled off another half dozen sheets. How that dog had gotten so much water on the floor was beyond her, but as she mopped it up, Maggie had what she believed to be an out-of-body experience, because she suddenly saw herself from a completely different perspective. It was as if she were looking down from somewhere else and could hardly believe what she saw.

I am down on the floor on my hands and knees in Walter Hathaway's cabin, cleaning up after his dog.

To Maggie this was none other than a Gloria Steinem moment; it was almost an epiphany and she decided that the only way to regain some measure of parity having found herself in this humiliating situation would be for her to become quite forthright and proactive, and therefore, she concluded, she would be quite justified to snoop around a little more. After all, she did need to look around for the leash. Perhaps it was in a desk drawer.

Bill Bailey had stopped panting and he followed her into the main room of the cabin and jumped up on Walter's couch. Taking up almost two-thirds of it, his big bulk disappeared into the dark brown couch. Maggie shook her head—it certainly was a good thing the color of the fabric matched Bill Bailey because it was covered in dog hair, making the whole couch look like it was wearing a brown mohair sweater.

From the couch Bill Bailey watched Maggie as she went over to Walter's desk. Having his eyes on her was not the ideal condition for snooping. She hesitated for a minute, worried that his opinion of her would drop considerably when he saw what she had in mind. But then Maggie dismissed this as some minor paranoia—the fact that she was about to behave dishonorably could not possibly register in his dog brain. It was her own guilt she'd have to contend with and she'd had decades of practice in rationalizing this particular shortcoming.

What she really wanted was to see what was on Walter's computer, that's where people kept everything, but she was afraid she'd hit the wrong key and really screw things up and get found out. So Maggie snooped the old-fashioned way. The desk had a center drawer and four deep drawers on each side. She pulled out the center drawer first. It had the typical stuff: pens, pencils, scotch tape, mailing tape, an assortment of stamps with out-of-date postage, a pack of sticky notes, rubber bands and a bunch of loose paper clips. There were also some lottery tickets and a bunch of business cards. Sorting through the cards, Maggie didn't see any names she recognized. There were bookstore managers, librarians from different parts of the country, and people from various publishing houses. They all had something to do with books. And they were all women. This wasn't exactly a surprise as children's books was a field dominated by women, but Maggie still took note of it and wondered why Walter had kept the cards of all these people. Had there been a little fling with each of them?

"I know you think I'm behaving like a jealous wife, Bill," she said to the dog, whose presence was making her nervous, "but you've got it wrong. I'm just a very curious person."

Maggie closed the center drawer and opened the top one on the right hand side. It was filled with neatly labeled, legal-sized file folders. She was surprised that it was so tidy, surprised, she supposed, because Walter's life had been such a mess. The labels in the first section of the drawer all indicated files for business type papers: social security, bank statements, health insurance, tax returns, real estate tax, and the like. As she flipped through the files, Maggie saw that the ones in the second half of the drawer related to the business of writing. The labels read, "contracts," "reprint rights & permissions," "royalty statements," "speaking engagements," "foreign rights," and then she noticed a label on the last folder at the back of the drawer which begged to be opened, and with Miss Marple deftness, she lifted it out. The label, all in caps and typed in a font that was styled in bold, said "PERSONAL."

Just as Maggie sat down at Walter's desk to settle in for a good look, Bill Bailey leaped off the couch and went to the door and barked. She didn't know why he chose this particular time to inform her that he needed to go out to do his business, but she jumped up to oblige him. Maggie had no idea what kind of bladder or bowel control Bill Bailey possessed and she didn't want to test it. Cleaning up the water he'd slopped all over Walter's kitchen floor had been quite enough. Maggie opened the door for him and he took off down the porch steps. Did Bill Bailey want out because he didn't like her snooping in Walter's stuff? That seemed far-fetched and even more paranoid, but nevertheless, she ran back to the desk and put the file back in the drawer before she opened the door to let him back in. But Bill Bailey was nowhere to be seen.

He couldn't have gone far, after all up to now he didn't even want to leave the porch, but Maggie got panicky at the idea of losing him. What if Bill Bailey was so forlorn, he just wandered off somewhere, never to be seen again? It was bad enough that she had to tell Walter about his agent, what if she had to tell him that his dog disappeared? That she'd lost Bill Bailey? Oh, God. Maggie ran toward the yard, taking the porch steps two at a time, but her ankle wasn't cooperative and buckled as she reached the last step and she stumbled and slid on the lawn not far from the solar panel and broken wind turbine where she'd found Walter.

A few minutes later, Howie came down Baker's Beach Road and saw Maggie sitting on the grass a bit out of breath, rubbing her ankle.

"Are you okay?" He came across the yard, set down his chain saw, and bent down next to her.

"I was trying to run after Bill Bailey, but my legs had a different idea." Maggie pulled up the leg of her jeans and looked at her ankle.

"Do you think you've sprained it?"

"I don't think so, it doesn't hurt that much. It's more one of those annoying little reminders that I'm not a kid anymore." She looked around the yard at the solar panel and broken wind turbine. "This place must be jinxed."

Howie laughed and put out his hand and helped her up. Her ankle was a bit sore, but she was able to put her weight on it. She looked around the yard and all along the edge of the woods but there was no sign of Bill Bailey.

"Howie, I've got to find that dog."

"Which way did he go?"

"I don't know. He barked to go out and I opened the door for him and then I went back inside for a minute. I never dreamed he'd take off."

"Maybe he decided to go for a little walk on the beach. Let's take a look." Howie led the way around the cabin and down the narrow, grassy path to the beach. The tide was out and the beach was empty except for Jordan Wiggins, Carl and Sondra's grandson, who was squatting over a tide pool a few yards to the north of them. Jordan spent part of every summer with Carl and Sondra, and Maggie loved watching him come back each year, a little taller, a little more grown-up. He was twelve now, and it seemed to her like he'd grown a foot since last summer. There was also a new addition: braces. But even with all the wire, he had a winning smile. Jordan had dark hair and large brown eyes and got a deep tan. This summer he was so long and lanky Maggie thought he looked as if he'd been stretched over the winter like a piece of caramel taffy. Jordan was great kid and everyone at Baker's Beach was fond of him. Even Walter.

There wasn't much wind and the air was briny and hot, although it got cooler as they neared the beach. Howie and Maggie made their way over the gravelly sand, carefully avoiding the rocks frosted with barnacles that had been exposed by the retreat of the sea.

"Have you seen Bill Bailey?" Howie called, when they got within earshot of Jordan.

Jordan looked up and yelled something neither of them could hear. They got closer and Howie asked him again if he'd seen Bill.

"He was here just a minute ago," Jordan said. "I'm catching hermit crabs, and Bill Bailey seemed very interested for a while, but then he left."

Maggie pointed to the Ziploc bag that Jordan held. It was filled with seawater, sand and about three hermit crabs. "Those are pretty cool little guys, what're you going to do with them?"

"Walter and I race 'em."

"You know he's in the hospital, right?" Maggie thought it was possible Jordan hadn't heard about Walter, although the news on Vashon Island, like most small communities, traveled quickly and people seemed to know everything about everyone's business.

Jordan nodded. "I'm saving them for when he gets out."

"I see." She tried to sound casual, but it was actually a bit of a surprise. Ever since Walter had been on the island he'd seemed like such a crank, and so solitary, it was hard to imagine him doing something playful like this with Jordan.

"May the best crab win," Howie said. He walked across the beach to the edge of the water, and shaded his eyes and looked up and down as far as he could see. "No sign of him. I'm not sure where we look now."

"Maybe he went back to Walter's," Jordan suggested.

"Let's hope. Listen, if he comes back, be sure and let me know," Maggie said.

They left Jordan to his crab round-up and made their way back over the rocks to the path to Walter's and Maggie imagined some screwball Keystone Kops scenario where she and Howie and Bill Bailey chased each other round and round Walter's cabin.

As they went, they each shouted Bill's name. But unlike the sound of voices over the water, which carried great distances, the sound of voices on the beach seemed to end up muffled and

Maggie thought if Bill was nearby he either heard them with his superior dog hearing and was ignoring them, or their voices were whispers even this dog couldn't hear.

As they got to the cabin and walked to the yard, Howie grinned. "Do you think I should call him using Walter's method?"

"Absolutely!"

He walked to the center of the yard. "A little duet, Maggie?"

"I think it's better if it's only a male voice. Bill may be a bit of purist and it's closer to the manner in which he's become accustomed to being summoned."

"Good point." Howie cleared his throat, and began. *"Won't you come home, Bill Bailey, won't you come home?"* Howie was a natural mimic and his voice sounded so much like Walter's it was as if he'd channeled him. He really got into it, strutting around the yard with his arms spread wide, belting it out at the top of his lungs. *"She moans the whole day lo—ong. I'll do the cooking darling, I'll pay the rent..."* Just as he got to the next line, *"I knows I've done you wro—ong,"* Bill Bailey tore out of the woods near the road, bounding across the yard. But when he saw Howie and Maggie, he screeched to a halt like a cartoon dog, then lay down with his head on his paws as if he'd been hit and flattened with a wave of grief.

"I'll get his leash." Maggie ran in the cabin, taking the steps more carefully this time, while Howie crouched next to Bill and grabbed his collar.

She didn't see the leash at first, but finally found it hanging on a peg by the back door under Walter's red and black checked lumber jacket. She thought Walter looked like one of those silver-haired guys on a *Field & Stream* cover in that jacket. Very rugged and handsome. Although she doubted he'd look so fit when he came home from the hospital, and wondered if he'd let any of them help him. Maybe he'd warm up to Howie if she told him how Howie had sung the song.

She came back with the leash and knelt next to Bill Bailey. "After he left the beach, I guess he went through the woods to the road—he was probably hanging out there, waiting for Walter."

Maggie snapped the leash on his collar. "I'm going to try to get him to come to my house. I don't think he should be alone."

She stood and tugged on the leash, but Bill didn't budge. "Come on, Bill," Maggie said, firmly and tugged again. This time Bill gagged a little when the leash yanked his collar, which made her feel terrible.

Howie reached for the leash, tugged on it and got the same reaction; this time the gagging was even more pathetic. "I don't think we can get him to your house, Maggie. And I'm afraid if I tried to pick him up, besides wrecking my back—he might take a chunk out of my arm. I'll go up on the porch and call him Walter's way and at least maybe we can get him back in the cabin."

Maggie sighed and knelt down and patted Bill's head. She was getting annoyed with this dog, but she also felt sorry for him. Maggie knew what it felt like to be abandoned by someone you counted on to care for you. She looked up at Howie. "I think you're right. I'll just leave him in the cabin and come back to feed him at the end of the day."

Howie went in the cabin where Bill couldn't see him and began his best Walter Hathaway imitation, belting out another chorus of "Won't You Come Home, Bill Bailey?"

Bill perked up his ears, stood up and trotted into the cabin. Howie and Maggie high-fived and Maggie thanked him for all his help. "You sounded so much like Walter, if Martha Jane and Mark heard you, they'd think he'd come home from the hospital."

"Let me know if you need anything else."

"Will do, and thanks again, Howie."

After he left, Maggie went around opening all the windows. The day had gotten even hotter, and Bill Bailey was panting harder. She couldn't blame him for wanting to be down by the water and then in the woods.

She filled his water bowl to the top and told Bill Bailey that she'd be back later to feed him. The kitchen was the coolest part of the cabin and Bill lay on the floor near the back door under the pegs that held Walter's coats. She slipped out the front door, thinking about how she'd looked for the leash in Walter's desk, wondering what she might have found in the file marked "PERSONAL."

As she closed the door behind her, Maggie decided that after all the trouble she'd gone to when Bill Bailey went missing, to say nothing of the worry, she'd certainly be entitled to have a little look-see, just a little peek when she came back to give Bill Bailey his dinner.

CHAPTER SIX

"Maggie..." It was her sister's breathy, little-girl Marilyn Monroe voice, the first of two messages that were waiting for Maggie when she got back to her house. "...My plane gets in around three and I'm not going to worry about the ferry schedule, I'll just take my chances and get there when I get there. Oh, and Mag-gie..." Leslie lowered her voice, teasingly drawing out Maggie's name, "...I have a sur-prise for you. And don't you dare call to get it out of me because I'll never tell until I get there! Bye-bye."

Maggie rolled her eyes. A new man. What else? The minimum duration of her sister's dry spells, her manless intervals, usually lasted a few weeks. But now it seemed, it was days. This must be some kind of record. Maybe desperation had set in. When Maggie thought of Leslie showing up with a new balding, pot-bellied, powerboat-driving, red-faced, boozy millionaire, it was more than annoying. In the past few years, as Leslie entered her fifties with the bloom most definitely off the rose, these seemed to be the types that were available to her. Maggie couldn't think of a single one that didn't fit that description. And there were other predictable factors as well. They all had a history of multiple marriages, and they all moaned about capital gains taxes. Maggie thought it was bad enough to have to put up with Leslie—but to have the latest boyfriend invading her peaceful sanctuary? Simply an outrage.

She went to the phone and paused, taking a moment to rehearse, searching for the right words. She wanted to be sure her response would be conveyed with a clarity that would be understood, but with grace. But Maggie was short on grace and all that came to mind was "*Don't bring the bozo.*" It was satisfying imagining shouting that into the phone. It would be quite cathartic, but she immediately knew what Leslie would say and she began to hear the whole conversation in her head before she'd even lifted the phone.

LESLIE: You've ruined the surprise, Maggie.

MAGGIE: I don't like surprises.

LESLIE: You don't care about my happiness.

MAGGIE: Your happiness? What about me? Have you ever given one second of thought to what I might want, or need, or think, or feel? It's always been a one-way street with you, Leslie—and I'm sick of it.

Then Maggie imagines she hears Leslie's voice break as her sister begins to cry...soft little hiccupping sobs and then Maggie sees their street, Lee Road near the University, and it's early spring with the days finally getting longer and the cherry trees beginning to blossom. A few spindly daffodils bloom in the weedy bed next to the front porch and the grass is bright green from the rain. Their mother is asleep and Maggie is in the kitchen, cooking dinner. She opens a can of Hormel Mary Kitchen Roast Beef Hash and dumps it in the cast iron skillet. On her wrist, dangling from a gold charm bracelet, is her scholarship medal: a gold and black tiger, the Jefferson High mascot, holding a book. It's the academic equivalent of the medals the athletes earn, which are only worn by girls when given to them by their boyfriends. The gold and black tigers hold the icons of the athletes' sports and are proudly displayed on a little gold chain around their girlfriends' necks. It's a symbol of their value, signifying that they have risen to the pinnacle of success that a girl can attain at Jefferson High School: they have won an athlete. Maggie wears her medal on a bracelet to avoid any embarrassing confusion. While the hash cooks, she opens a can of Del Monte Canned Fruit Cocktail to complete the meal. Outside on the front porch, Leslie sits on the bottom step in her yellow rain slicker. She is six years old and, holding a stick, she draws lines in the wet dirt of the flowerbed, writing her name, or words she is learning in first grade. Words like "dog" and "mop" and "top" and then "dad," the word she writes most often. And although she's been told, she still sits on the porch every night waiting for him to come home.

Maggie deleted Leslie's message and looked out at the water. The tide was higher now, covering the rocks, leaving the beach an unbroken arc of sand curving around the cove. The breeze had picked up but now was only a gentle summer wind, and the leaves of the old vine maple fluttered like brilliant green fans against the blue of the sea. If only she were someone like Thich Nhat Hanh, who could feel this beauty and be mindful, staying in the present, instead of feeling totally pissed off about Leslie descending on her with some bozo. Looking at the beach, Maggie took a very deep breath and exhaled slowly, trying to stay focused, absorbing only the wonder and beauty of the world in front of her...breathing in...breathing out...breathing....brea...oh screw it, she said and turned back to the phone to pick up the other message.

It was from Walter. He sounded flat and matter-of-fact, but spoke precisely and without the mellow affectionate tone of his lovely painkiller voice. "Maggie, the surgery is scheduled for eight tomorrow morning. In case anything happens, there are two wills, both a regular will and a living will in my desk. Thank you for taking care of Bill Bailey."

She saved the message. She wasn't sure why, maybe so she could still hear his voice if something happened to him. Maggie didn't think Walter was being dramatic. She was sure that any time a person was going to be put under anesthesia, especially to hand control to another human being who had sharp instruments with which to cut open one's body, there was the fear of not making it. Undoubtedly a common fear, the way many people about to take a trip wonder if the plane they've just boarded will ever land safely—at least she always did.

Maggie was suddenly starving and scarfed down a bagel, spread thick with cream cheese, and three leftover pieces of cold pizza. She did this when she was tense. Food pulled her to it with the strength of an industrial magnet and only occasionally could she muster the will power to resist the wild call of the carbs. And this was not one of those times. But the satisfaction of the food was fleeting, as it unhappily often was for her, and after she stuffed her face, fatigue swept over Maggie as if an energy-saving switch had kicked in and she now operated on half power. She went to her bedroom and curled up on top of the comforter like an old, tired cat.

She fell into a deep, weary sleep and dreamed. It was a recurring dream, one she'd had off and on over the years as long as she could remember. The scene is a toy store, the Disneyland of toy stores, a technicolored child's paradise and she is riding a pearly white horse on a merry-go-round. Her beautiful mother grabs her hand and yanks her off the horse. They begin to run. Maggie is in front with her mother stumbling behind, she is running as fast as she can toward a two-car garage, terrified that she'll be late and won't make it in time. And then Maggie always wakes up.

The feeling of being late for something urgent was profound— and seemed to belong to the present, not the dream. Maggie looked at the clock. She couldn't believe it was almost eight, and she had the nagging feeling there was something she was supposed to have done, although she was having trouble remembering what it was. This happened a lot. She recognized it as a sign of an aging brain, and she was not accepting it gracefully. As she sat up, it came to her. Walter's dog. She needed to feed Bill Bailey.

On the way over to Walter's cabin, Maggie thought about the message he'd left and realized that she indeed now had a legitimate excuse for looking into his file. Looking. Not snooping. It would be important for her to locate his will in case something happened to him. It was only natural that she would want to be prepared. The situation called for it.

Bill began barking as Maggie climbed the porch steps and when she opened the door, he was there to greet her. His tail was a brown hairy pendulum, wagging back and forth with vigor, and he licked her hand with a big, sloppy dog kiss. He must be famished, she thought. Too bad he'd been so obstinate about not coming to her house—he might not have had to wait so long for his dinner. Maggie patted his head, thinking he must have been lonely all afternoon.

Maggie knew something about being lonely and she identified with Bill Bailey. But he only had Walter in his life, whereas she had always found comfort in her friends, in her work, in nature—especially the sea—her books, and most of all, her daughter and then, of course, Ashley. But she'd been having memories lately of the September when Becky left home for college. Even though Lewis and Clark wasn't all that far, the nest left empty by the exit of her only child had been devastating. She didn't know what she would have done that year without her work. This September would be the first time Maggie wouldn't return to Evergreen Elementary in forty years and she wondered how she'd fare. At least Bill didn't have those issues, she thought as she leaned down to pat him. "Ready for dinner, Bill?"

He planted another big dog smooch right on her chin. "Oh yuk." She wiped her chin with the back of her hand. This was a little more affection than Maggie cared for and she made a quick exit to the kitchen, where she got the dog food from the cupboard. She thought it seemed odd to remember exactly where Walter kept it, as if she'd been taking of care of Bill for months instead of just a little over twenty-four hours. Especially in the light of her unreliable memory and the frequency with which she'd find herself going into one room or another at home, only to find she hadn't the foggiest notion of what she'd intended to do.

Bill licked her hand again when she put his food down next to his water bowl and when he began to eat, she washed her hands, then went to Walter's desk. She pulled out the file marked "PERSONAL." Going right to it, as easily as she'd remembered which cupboard had the dog food.

Placing the file on the desk, Maggie sat down and carefully opened it. She wanted to be very sure not to change the order, so after she looked at each document, with great care, she slowly turned it over, leaving it face down on the other half of the file folder. His passport was on the top. He looked quite handsome and was smiling in the photo. She was certain it had been issued before they required unsmiling photos, which made people look so bleak and dismal, like in mug shots. Leafing through it, Maggie saw that he hadn't been anywhere since a trip to Bologna four years ago, and the trip before that was to Frankfurt. She was pretty sure those had been for the Bologna Children's Book Fair and the Frankfurt International Book Fair. Other than that, Walter didn't seem to have been much of a traveler.

Right behind his passport was the Living Will, although it wasn't called that, it said "Health Care Directive" and it said, "I, Walter S. Hathaway, having the capacity to make health care decisions, willfully and voluntarily make known my desire that my dying shall not be artificially prolonged under circumstances set forth below," and then it went on in great detail for three pages. Well, now she knew where it was. She turned it over and went on to the next document: Walter's Decree of Divorce, setting forth his terms and conditions of divorce from Lorna L. Hathaway.

Bill Bailey had finished eating and came in and jumped up on the couch. He let out what seemed to Maggie to be a contented sigh, clearly unconcerned that she was sitting at Walter's desk scoping out Walter's most private stuff.

As far as divorces go, it seemed pretty straightforward. California had community property and they'd split everything down the middle. There were no children, no gory custody battles and he'd even been able to keep all future income from *The Adventures of Fric the Chick,* which made sense considering what Maggie knew of the situation.

The next one was the will itself, which she found more interesting. There was a list of specific assets. It seemed that in addition to the cabin, Walter owned a small apartment building near Green Lake in Seattle and the Trust Department of US Bank had been named executor. Guess he didn't blow all his money, she thought, as she turned the page and read a separate document listing his royalties and residuals, and naming his agent, Madeline Gordon, as his literary executor.

The section after that listed the beneficiaries. Walter was leaving everything he had to be equally divided among the Seattle Humane Society, Vashon Island Pet Protectors, the Authors Guild, UNICEF, and Veterans for Peace. Not a single person was named, just these organizations. Maybe there weren't any nieces and nephews anywhere, or if there were maybe they were deadbeats or neo-Nazis. Who knew? Certainly, they were worthy organizations, but it spoke to a lack of human connection and for a man who created something that had so profoundly connected him to children, to her it seemed so very sad.

But then Maggie saw a bunch of letters that turned her sad picture of Walter on its head. They were written on various kinds of paper: yellow lined legal paper, plain white copy paper, and scattered between them was an assortment of note cards with varying designs. They were all in the same handwriting, none had dates and they were all signed "With love, Charlotte." Leafing through them quickly, she saw they were all from this Charlotte person and she intended to study them all, except that in the middle of them, Maggie saw a familiar letterhead and the sight of it was shocking. Centered at the top of the page, in neat block letters was the name and address of Evergreen Elementary. The letter was from her!

Dear Mr. Hathaway:

We were delighted to learn that you've agreed to be the keynote speaker at the mid-winter meeting of the American Library Association to be held in Seattle this coming year. I was on the ALA program committee this year, but am writing now in my capacity as the librarian of Evergreen Elementary School. It is my hope that while you are in the area, you might be available to visit Evergreen Elementary to speak with our students. We are a small school in West Seattle serving a low income population; and although more than half our students are part of the free lunch program, we do have funds available from a literacy grant and would be able to offer a stipend.

Your wonderful books are favorites, not only of our students, but of mine as well. It would be a great honor to

have you visit Evergreen Elementary and I look forward to
hearing from you.

Respectfully yours,

Margaret Lewis

Margaret Lewis,
Librarian

Maggie had not saved the reply she received from Walter
Hathaway. Most librarians would keep a letter signed by a
Newbery Medalist, but she remembered quite clearly what had
happened to it: torn to bits and burned in her woodstove. But
why had he kept her letter? As a reminder to keep him on the
wagon? She couldn't make sense of it, and turned her attention
back to the letters from this Charlotte person. As she began to
read the first one, Bill started barking. Maggie heard footsteps on
the porch, and as Bill jumped down from the couch and went to
the door, Maggie quickly put the folder back in the drawer.

Bill wagged his tail as she opened the door. It was Jordan
Wiggins. He bent down to pat Bill, who immediately licked
his face, affection that Jordan seemed to expect and enjoy. He
scratched Bill's ears for a minute, before he asked about Walter.

"I just wanted to make sure you found Bill Bailey and if you
heard when Mr. Hathaway was coming home?"

"The day after tomorrow." Maggie smiled at Jordan, resisting
the temptation to give him some kind of explanation about what
she was doing there.

"Great. I'll see him then."

"He might not be up to seeing visitors right away, Jordan."
Maggie had no idea if she was trying to protect Jordan from a
predictably very grumpy Walter—or Walter, who would be just
home from the hospital, needing rest.

"He'll tell me to go away if he doesn't want company," Jordan
said, confidently.

Maggie thought about asking Jordan to help her get Bill Bailey
to go to her house. Obviously they had a nice relationship and he

might have better luck than she and Howie had, but she didn't have the energy for what could be another failure with this dog. And he had done pretty well alone in Walter's house today and she thought he could probably stay by himself that night. It did occur to Maggie to stay a little while longer herself; she was certainly curious about those letters from Charlotte-With-Love. They'd probably been written before emails became such a common form of communication and for all she knew, Walter and Charlotte could currently be exchanging love emails. But Maggie didn't have the nerve to look on his computer. After all, she had her limits. Besides, it was starting to bother her that Jordan had seen her at Walter's and she decided she'd better get home where she belonged.

Maggie turned in early. It had been a long day. As soon as her head hit the pillow, she was just drifting off to sleep when she heard a terrible sound. A terrible sound she had heard before, and immediately recognized. The deep, mournful wail of Bill Bailey. Night had fallen, and even though he'd been alone during the day, she supposed he didn't like being alone in the dark cabin. It was that grief-stricken cry of abandonment and she got up, dressed, grabbed a flashlight and headed back to Walter's place. It wasn't just to comfort Bill Bailey. Getting him to shut up would be the only way *she* was going to get any sleep. When she entered Walter's yard, Bill Bailey's wail stopped, paused for a couple of beats and became an aria of barking.

"Oh, just deal with it, dog," she said, stepping up on the porch. Maggie opened the door and he greeted her with even more affection than he had when she'd come over to feed him. She snapped on the light, and leaned over to pet him, getting another one of those slobbery dog kisses on her hand. Yuk. She wiped her hand on her jeans, then looked over at the desk. For coming over here again, having to leave the comfort of my own bed, I certainly should be rewarded with a bit of a look-see into that file of Walter's, she thought. But with the light on, and no shades or anything covering the windows, if anyone came by she realized she might as well be sitting in Macy's window. Maggie considered turning off the light and using her flashlight to snoop into the file, but that had a cat burglar quality that she found unappealing. So Maggie went again to Walter's bed, seduced by the dog's pain just as she had been by Walter's all those years ago.

They had exchanged letters and a few phone calls, arranging for his school visit following his appearance at the mid-winter ALA meeting. She loved his voice, it was deep and mellow and to her great surprise, he never seemed to be in a hurry to get off the phone. She nervously made a few inane jokes, she couldn't remember what they were, but she remembered that he laughed. It had been years since she'd looked forward to anything as much as that conference.

After Walter's keynote speech, a handful of people had gone over to the bar in the Sheraton Hotel across from the convention center: Walter, his editor at Scholastic, their marketing director, and Maggie. Rayna Starr, who was president of ALA, didn't join them; she said she was still on East Coast time and was going to bed. After one round of drinks, the Scholastic people said goodnight, leaving Maggie alone with Walter. Like more than a few of her colleagues, Maggie was a bit of an author groupie, and to find herself alone with one of the most popular children's writers of all time made her feel like she'd just won the lottery. She sipped her wine, her head spinning with all the usual questions: where did he get the idea for *The Adventures of Fric the Chick*? Had he grown up around animals? When did he know he wanted to be a writer? How had he gotten his start in publishing? What was his process like, did he write every day, or in spurts? Did he have to do a lot of research for the character of Sally Ann, the twelve-year-old girl in the story? Was she based on someone he knew? And what was it like to see it made into a film? The questions danced and twirled in her head, but she couldn't get them out. It had been so much easier to talk with him when they'd had those few phone conversations, but sitting across from him, she found herself stuck behind a heavy curtain of shyness. All she could muster was a mumbled thanks for his agreeing to visit Evergreen Elementary when the conference was over.

"I'm happy to do it." Walter took a long sip of his drink.

"We have that literacy grant, you didn't have to waive your fee. But we're grateful."

"It's the kind of school that can use a break. I like kids... always thought I'd have some. What about you?"

Her wine was taking effect; he seemed genuinely interested and she began to relax. "I love working with kids." Maggie smiled. "And when I see them discover books, well, you know—it's like I've done something worthwhile. And I can't think of a day that kids don't make me laugh, at least at some point. She smiled again and took another sip of wine. "What are you working on now? Is there a new book coming out soon?"

Walter signaled for their server, caught his eye and pointed to his empty glass. "Want another?"

"No I'm fine, thanks."

He was drinking scotch rocks and he emptied his glass, then chewed on an ice cube. He seemed tense, and Maggie thought better of asking him again about what he was writing. Maybe he found the question intrusive. She knew there were writers who thought if they talked about the story it would diffuse it and they'd lose the drive to write it.

When the server came, Walter exchanged his empty glass for the fresh drink. He took a long gulp, set the glass down and looked at her. Even in the dim light his eyes were astoundingly blue.

"To answer your question, I haven't been able to do a damn thing since Lorna left me."

"Your wife?"

"My ex-wife. A dumb cliché, predictable in every way. I'd written the screenplay and we'd gone to LA for the filming of *Fric* and three weeks into the shoot Lorna ran off with the film's producer." Walter laughed, but his eyes were sad.

"I'm sorry."

Walter shook his head. "No matter...what about you?" He glanced at her left hand.

"I have a daughter in college—my marriage ended as soon as she finished high school, but it'd been pretty dead for a long time."

"You seem to be doing very well." He took another long sip. "Is your daughter doing okay?"

"She is."

"I always wanted kids, I'm sure that's why I created Sally Ann, the daughter I'd wished I'd had."

"I loved that character. She was funny and dear and feisty."

Walter's eyes brimmed with tears, he pinched the bridge of his nose. He was on his third drink and she supposed that had loosened him up. "I'm sorry…shit, I don't know why I'm telling you all this."

She didn't know what came over her, but she reached for his hand and Walter held on as if she'd thrown him a life ring. "Lorna and I had decided to start a family, the book was a big hit, the money was coming in. Everything was coming up roses, or so I thought. Then she met Alan Wolfe. Of course, I wanted to kill him. I wanted to kill them both."

"Naturally," Maggie said, nodding her head. "But I'm very glad you didn't. You need to write more wonderful books and your fans wouldn't like it if you went to jail."

Walter put his other hand over hers. "You're very attractive, Maggie. You're what I would call a handsome woman."

She laughed. "It's the kind of compliment I think they give a woman who's big."

"Well, it does imply stature, a kind of substantial beauty, I'd say." He smiled, but there was such a deep sadness to Walter, he seemed almost lost. He leaned across the table and whispered, "Would you like some mixed nuts?"

"Mixed nuts?"

He leaned closer. "Or potato chips?"

"Not really, I—"

He leaned even closer and put his lips near her ear. "Or some trail mix?'

"Trail mix?" She laughed, uncomfortably, "Walter, I don't quite get it, why would I want trail mix?"

"It's the stuff in the mini bar. We could have a picnic in my room." Walter smiled, then whispered seductively, "There's chocolate, too."

Maggie could feel her face flush and she quickly glanced around the lounge. She didn't recognize anyone she knew, which was a relief. She didn't know what she was worried about, they were both single consenting adults—although she didn't want to be the subject of a lot of gossip. But truth be told, even if Maggie had seen the entire executive committee of the American Library Association in that bar, she doubted it would have been a deterrent. She wanted Walter Hathaway. It's hard to say how much had to do with the intense physical attraction she felt, how much she loved what he wrote and the kind of soul she assumed he had to write such wonderful stuff, or how hurt he seemed—which made her feel needed. And then there was her ego. She was flattered that he wanted her.

"Oh, well, if there's chocolate, then I think I'd like to go to this picnic."

And they did have a picnic in his room. Maggie had had enough to drink so she went with the Diet Coke, but Walter had more scotch. They got all the goodies out of the mini bar and spread them out in the middle of the bed, where they both flopped and began devouring them. They began rating each item as if they were giving restaurant reviews. First they sampled the trail mix.

Walter chewed slowly, twisting his mouth around as if he were tasting wine. "Dry. Too fruity. Overly salted."

She put a handful in her mouth chewed slowly. "Two stars."

Walter shook his head. "I disagree. One at best."

They continued rating the mixed nuts, then the potato chips, which were the kind that came in a little can.

Maggie took several out of the can, and slowly chewed them. "It doesn't compare to Lay's Classic," she pronounced. "But they're not terrible. Maybe three stars."

Walter ate a few chips and agreed with her rating. Then he picked up the chocolate, Fran's Blend Dark Chocolate Bar. He kissed it gently, then carefully unwrapped it, ever so slowly slipping off the paper, then inching off the gold foil. He offered her a little bite, then kissed her lightly on her lips before he took a bite. They kissed between each bite, each kiss lasting longer than the previous kiss, and after they had devoured the chocolate, they devoured each other. Walter was passionate, eager to please and exceptionally tender. She wanted to spend the entire conference in this room with this man. Maggie felt rebellious and a little wild, like the teenager she'd wished she'd been.

"You're incredible," she said softly, her cheek against his chest.

"Sex can be easy," he whispered, "it's love that's difficult."

She caressed the side of his face and it was wet with tears.

The day of Walter's visit to Evergreen, Maggie was as excited as a fifteen-year-old on a first date. She brought a huge bouquet of flowers to school and put them in the refrigerator in the teacher's lounge. They weren't just grocery store flowers. She'd sprung for a fifty-dollar bouquet from the florist at the Four Seasons Hotel, the closest thing they had in Seattle to a florist to the stars. It had ferns and woodland wildflowers and miniature ceramic forest creatures peeking from the ferns. It was beautifully tied in to *The Adventures of Fric the Chick* and Maggie hoped Walter would be touched.

Typically, the principal and janitor were the first ones to arrive at Evergreen in the morning, but the principal, Elaine Martinez, had a principals' meeting at district headquarters, so she wasn't there when Maggie got to school that morning. Elaine wasn't expected back until close to noon, and was really disappointed that she'd miss Walter's presentation. She was a big fan.

As soon as Maggie arrived at school, she found Eddie Bergstrom, the janitor, and got him to set up the podium on the stage. It had a built-in mike that you had to plug into an outlet on the floor of the stage, which then got covered by the podium. It used to be that a librarian just had to know about books, but with all the new technology they'd become "media specialists" as well, and at Maggie's school that meant she had to know about all the video projectors, PowerPoint presentations, and all the equipment for assemblies. It didn't come naturally to her and she had to force herself to learn it. That morning, she became somewhat obsessive about the mike, turning it on, flicking it with her fingers, announcing "testing...testing..." and repeatedly adjusting the volume. She finally drove Eddie crazy, who had agreed to stand in the back of the auditorium to let her know if the volume was okay. After the tenth time she announced "testing," Eddie threw his hands up in the air and yelled, "*Enough!*"

The fifth graders had made a huge banner "WELCOME WALTER HATHAWAY" that they'd decorated with cutouts of chickens and it hung across the entrance to the auditorium across from the main office. Maggie was tempted to ask Eddie for a ladder because she thought it was beginning to droop, but thought better of it. Maggie knew the school janitor is not someone you ever want to annoy.

She went to the library and straightened all the chairs, then rearranged the copies of Walter's books, which she'd placed in the center of each of the eight tables where the kids sat. She could hear them out in the hall arriving and going to their classrooms, and then the bell rang. The assembly was going to start right after the teachers took attendance and the kids filed into the auditorium.

The big clock on the wall at the end of the library said nine-fifteen and Maggie left for the foyer near the main door to wait for Walter. January in the northwest is often dreary, and the day of Walter's visit was no different. The sky looked like it was made of bunches of gray lint from a clothes dryer and as she huddled by the front door, it began to rain. Seattle rush hour traffic had become a nightmare. But once Walter got through downtown and came across the West Seattle bridge, he'd be through the worst of the morning congestion and would be going against the traffic. Maggie didn't think it would be a problem.

The rain came down harder and she waited and waited, but there was no sign of Walter. When they'd made arrangements for his visit to Evergreen, Maggie had offered to have him picked up. She knew it would have been easy to find a parent volunteer who'd be willing to do it, but he'd refused. Maggie looked at her watch. It seemed like she'd been waiting an hour, but it was only ten minutes after he was supposed to arrive. She decided to wait another five minutes and then call his hotel.

"Maggie," Barb Robbins, the PE teacher, came up to her. "Where is he? The kids are getting really antsy."

"There's probably some traffic hang-up. Maybe get them singing?"

"I don't sing and it's not Helen's day." Barb said, scowling.

"Oh, right." Evergreen shared Helen Klemke, their music teacher, with three other schools and Maggie never could remember which day Helen came to Evergreen. It was too bad Elaine had that meeting; she'd been a camp director years ago and knew all kinds of rounds and sing-a-longs, plus the kids here always paid attention to the principal. "Ask Margaret, her fourth grade is always singing, even when it's not Helen's day."

"Good idea."

Barb went back to the auditorium and in a few minutes Maggie heard everyone singing, "Take Me Out to the Ballgame." After going through it once, it sounded like they were dividing the kids into groups and singing rounds. Maggie thought it sounded like an old seventy-eight record of chipmunks played backward, a garbled mess and she was worrying how long they could keep it up and the teachers could stand it, when she saw a cab turn into the parking lot and drive up in the front of the school.

Maggie held the door open. "Glad you made it!" she called to Walter who seemed to be having a lot of trouble getting out of the cab.

"Ahhh, Mag-gie," he slurred.

Maggie watched in shock as Walter stumbled up the steps into the school.

"Just need to stop in the men's room," he muttered and then staggered to the door across from the office next to the auditorium. He opened it, toppled in and she heard the unmistakable sound of a stream followed by a big thud and a crash. Walter Hathaway had peed in the janitor's broom closet and passed out.

CHAPTER SEVEN

Maggie sometimes thought that in another life she might have been a dog. She was a creature of routine; she liked to eat at the same time, take walks at the same time, and go to bed at the same time. This preference for habit suited her quite well for the structure of the school day and the school calendar, and she'd created a life on the island that had its own kind of predictability. Deviation in her routine had always thrown her a bit, and she had to admit it had gotten worse as she'd gotten older. The arrival of her sister was a major deviation. Besides invading her territory and disrupting her routine, the presence of Leslie always caused the eruption of an emotional skirmish within her psyche, as the militias of guilt and resentment went at each other.

Leslie was due to arrive the same day Walter was getting out of the hospital, and that morning after she fed Bill Bailey, Maggie went to Thriftway to get a few groceries—but not to really stock up. Leslie was always on some kind of diet and there'd be no telling what she could or couldn't eat. The most memorable (or the one Maggie wished could be forgettable) had been the cabbage soup diet. Leslie made a huge pot of this soup and the diet allowed eating as much as one wanted, and as often, for five days. The soup consisted of a large head of cabbage, V-8 Juice, onion, celery and some hot sauce. It was guaranteed that you would lose five pounds in five days, but instead of the desired weight loss, all it gave Leslie was gas. She almost exploded. At the grocery store Maggie was going to get food *she* liked and Leslie would have to adapt. She also wanted to make a point of not having food for more than a day or two, hoping it would give more than a hint that she expected Leslie's visit to be short.

At Thriftway, Jordan Wiggins was standing in front of the magazine racks near the door as Maggie came in. He waved when he saw her, flashed his metallic grin and sauntered over, hands stuffed in his pockets.

"Hi, Jordan.

"Hi.

"Waiting for your grandmother?" Maggie asked.

"Nope. She's getting ready for the garden tour and Grandpa Carl is playing golf. I'm just hanging out until the movie starts."

The Vashon Theater got a lot of first-run movies and although Maggie didn't care for the kind of action films that kids liked, she loved the theater. Nothing seemed to have changed too much since it was built in the late 1940's and it brought back sweet memories of going to the movies with her father on rainy Saturday afternoons, when her mother was home with Leslie. The Vashon Theater also had superb popcorn. With real butter.

"I guess you're not a golfer or a gardener."

"Not really." Jordan grinned. "But Mr. Hathaway called this morning and asked if I'd be his helper. He talked to my grandparents and it's cool with them and he's going to pay me and everything."

"I think that's great—he really will need help. Did he say when he'd be home?"

"He said he wasn't sure which ferry he'd be able to get, but he thought he'd be home by early afternoon. I'm supposed to go over there around four."

Maggie looked at her empty cart. "You know he might not have anything to eat in his cabin. Maybe I should pick up a few things while I'm here. Want to help?"

Jordan checked the time on his cell phone. "I have some time before the movie starts. I'll go with you. I know he gets stuff from the deli because last week he shared a burrito with me that he got here."

Maggie started to push the cart, but Jordan grabbed it. "I'll do it." He flashed his wire smile. "I mean, if you want."

"Thanks. Maybe you can advise me about what you think he might like." Maggie wondered if Jordan must be a little lonely. He seemed happy enough, but his summer visits to the island were never long enough for him to make friends his own age.

On the way to the deli section, they passed the flowers. There were some gorgeous Gerber Daisies, a stunning coral color. They were kind of pricey, but Maggie thought a lovely little bunch to put on Walter's kitchen table would make a nice, cheerful welcome for him. She doubted anyone had sent him any flowers in the hospital and she reached for a beautiful bunch and started to put it in the cart. Then it occurred to her that maybe he *had* gotten flowers in the hospital. For instance, from that Charlotte person. She looked at the price again and quickly put them back.

Jordan pushed the cart past the flowers and then stopped by the bread. "He likes Bill's Bread."

"Okay, so do I. It's fabulous bread." Maggie put two loaves in the cart. "Anything else?"

"Just deli stuff, I think. And then he always seems to have grapes and melons."

At the deli counter, Jordan pointed to some of the salads and meat and cheese he'd seen at Walter's and Maggie was surprised he seemed so sure about it. "I guess you must spend a lot of time with him—"

Jordan nodded. "He's fun. I have lunch at his cabin a lot. And he's not my family so he doesn't buy me stuff and then want me to spy on my other grandparents."

Maggie looked in the deli case. "Okay, so we'll get the turkey, and then the potato salad and the Greek salad."

"And cheese, I'm pretty sure he usually has cheese," Jordan pointed to slices of Swiss and cheddar.

"Okay, that too." After the order was filled, they went toward the back of the store to get fruit. On the way, as Maggie picked up a rotisserie chicken for herself, Jordan mentioned that Walter ate those, so she got a second one.

She walked abreast of Jordan as he pushed the cart toward the islands piled high with fruit and vegetables. "What did you mean when you said Mr. Hathaway doesn't buy you stuff like all your grandparents?" Maggie leaned down and lowered her voice, "—if you don't mind my asking."

"I have a ton of grandparents and step-grandparents. See both my mom and my dad have parents who got divorced, then they got married again to other people. And even Grandpa Marty got married more times than that, and most of these grandparents don't like each other. Grandma Betty used to be married to Grandpa Bob and she can't stand him or his new wife, who is Grandma Sharon. I have to be with all of them in the summer when I'm not at camp, and then they ask me what I did with the other grandmas and grandpas and they buy me stuff. It doesn't really make me feel that great to get all this stuff. Maybe that sounds weird, but it's just that I'm pretty sure it's so I'll think their stuff is the best."

"Sounds kind of confusing." Maggie went to the island where melons were piled and brought back a honeydew and two small cantaloupes. "Do you think I should get a watermelon?"

"Good idea. And I'll eat it, even if Mr. Hathaway doesn't like it." Jordan put a large watermelon in the cart. "Don't worry, it won't go to waste. I can eat a lot of this."

After they got through the checkout, Jordan pushed the cart to Maggie's car, helped her load the groceries into the trunk and then trotted off to the movie. What a neat kid. Maggie shook her head, why would Sondra Wiggins put her house on the garden tour when Jordan was visiting? And Carl—off at the golf course instead of spending time with Jordan. Some people had gold under their nose and didn't even know it.

As she pushed the cart across the parking lot back to the store, Maggie saw Martha Jane drive up in her ancient red Mercedes. It ran on recycled cooking oil and gave off a great whiff of French fries. Maggie wasn't the only one who worried about Martha Jane driving at her age, but whenever her friends brought it up, she said, "I'm a much better driver than most sixteen-year-olds and they let them on the road." It was hard to argue with her. Most of the accidents on the island seemed to involve kids. And Martha Jane would remind everyone that she never drove off-island, she never drove at night, and she was very, very careful. She also reminded them that she also needed her car for her special mission, one to which she felt she had a calling. Like quite a few islanders, Martha Jane thought it was an outrage that hunting was legal on Vashon Island and every year in the fall, she drove on all the back roads looking for hunters, hoping to harass them. She had shrunk considerably and therefore peered out just over the top of the steering wheel and relished the fact that it seemed to terrify the hunters to see someone her age behind the wheel.

"Hi there!" Martha Jane opened the door, hung onto the steering wheel and very slowly pushed herself out of her car. It amazed Maggie how she kept her spirits up when her joints must hurt all the time. Martha Jane closed the car door and then stood by the car with her head cocked as if she were trying to think of something. She glanced at a young woman going toward the store carrying cloth bags, and then smiled. "Oh, that's it, the bags. I knew I'd forgotten. I think they must be on the floor of the back seat, or maybe the trunk."

"I'll help you look." Maggie opened the back door and searched through what looked like the stuff from the drop-off table of the local thrift store, Granny's Attic. There were several coats, rubber boots, empty flower and plant containers, a clock, artist canvases, file folders, plus enough magazines and newspapers to make a substantial dent in mixed-paper recycling section at the dump. After a few minutes, Maggie found the grocery bags on a pile of old issues of *National Geographic* and handed them to Martha Jane.

"Thank you, dear." Martha Jane looped the bags over her arm. "Have you heard anything from Walter?" she asked.

"I just saw Jordan and he said Walter has hired him to be a helper and he'd be home early this afternoon."

"Well, that's good news." Martha Jane smiled. "Glad to hear it."

"When you're in the store, be sure and look for the halibut, it's on sale, I picked up some for dinner—Leslie's coming today."

"Leslie?" Martha Jane looked puzzled.

"My sister."

"Of course, Leslie...not a visit you were too excited about."

Maggie nodded. "I also picked up some groceries for Walter. I guess I feel sorry for him. But I was glad to run into Jordan and find out he was going to hire him. Walter had been acting like he didn't want any help from anyone."

"Walter got help for his drinking, Maggie. He went through the famous program in California, you know the one, the President's wife."

"Betty Ford."

"Yes, that's it. And he made a new start up here and I think it all took, because there certainly haven't been any incidents, at least none that I've heard of. I think you're quite right to help him with a little food in his fridge, dear."

"Maybe so. But I have to tell you, I'm dreading having to tell him about his agent."

"Well, you must do it, Maggie dear. And perhaps the food you're bringing will soften the blow."

After she got back from the store, Maggie unloaded her groceries and then carried the food she'd bought for Walter over to his place. He wasn't due home for a few hours, but Bill Bailey hadn't been out since after she'd fed him that morning. She'd take him out on the leash this time. Then she'd go back after Walter got settled, maybe around four when Jordan was coming, and she'd tell him about his agent.

Bill Bailey barked a few times when he heard her coming, but quieted immediately at the sound of Maggie's voice. As she opened the door, once again he greeted her with an abundance of dog slobber. Maggie put the grocery bags on the kitchen table and decided she'd unpack them after she took Bill out. She put him on the leash and when they got to the yard, Bill didn't seem to be in much of a hurry. He sniffed all around, rather choosy about picking his spot, and Maggie just wished he'd get on with it. Finally, he unloaded right by the drive and Maggie suddenly had visions of Walter stepping in it on his first day home from the hospital. She went back in the house and rummaged around Walter's kitchen for a plastic bag, went back out, bagged Bill Bailey's pile and put it in the metal garbage can by the side of the house. Walter better appreciate this, that's all I can say, she mumbled, slamming the top back on the can.

Maggie put the watermelon on the counter, and was putting the chicken, cheese, fruit and deli salads in the refrigerator when she heard a car in the drive. She went to the living room to see who it was and Bill trotted behind her and jumped on the couch, barking. Maggie stood behind him as he leaned forward with his paws on the windowsill. In the driveway they saw the Ride-On Vashon Cab with the back door open as Walter, with his arm and shoulder in a big, white sling, slowly climbed out. "Oh dear," she muttered. At the sight of Walter, Bill Bailey bounded from the couch, yelping with excitement and began leaping up and down against the door. Maggie scurried after him and grabbed his collar.

"Be careful, doggie, you'll knock him over," she said, trying to sound firm.

Walter opened the door as Maggie was bending over holding Bill, struggling to keep him from jumping on Walter.

"He's okay, just let him go."

"You're sure?" Maggie swallowed nervously.

"I'm sure."

Maggie let go and Bill leaped forward and then obediently sat down right in front of Walter. He reminded Maggie of a gymnast hurling over a vault and then nailing a landing, perfectly still— although Bill's tail swished the floor like an electric broom. But he didn't jump, just sat there with his head held high, staring at Walter. Maggie couldn't believe it.

"Hi old boy, did you miss me?" Walter scratched Bill's ears and bent down to receive one of Bill's big slobbery kisses. After practically making out with the dog, Walter seemed to remember that Maggie was still standing there.

"Hi Maggie. What are you doing here?"

"I came to let Bill out and left some food." She wanted to go home right then and there, but she knew if she waited any longer to tell him about his agent, it would only get worse. "I wasn't sure what you might want to eat—there's a roast chicken, some juice and some deli salads."

"You shouldn't have done that, Maggie. I'm perfectly capable of taking care of myself." He sounded quite firm, but he was smiling.

"You're welcome."

"What? Didn't I say 'thank-you'?"

Maggie shook her head, wishing she had shut up and not sounded like some persnickety Miss Manners.

"Thank you for taking care of Bill Bailey, and for your thoughtfulness about the food. It wasn't necessary, you know—"

"I know."

"But I appreciate it." Walter sighed, and looked over at his desk. "And I'm going to be able to manage just fine. I've hired some help, I called the Wigginses this morning and now Jordan has a summer job. He can help me around the place, and he's quite the whiz with the computers, so I'm going to dictate to him," Walter paused and glanced at the door. "Thank you again, Maggie."

She knew he was trying to get her to leave, and there was nothing she would have liked better, but it was the eleventh hour, and she'd run out of ways to rationalize not telling him about his agent.

"Would you like to sit down? Can I get you some tea or something?" Maggie asked.

"I told you I was fine. You're acting like a hostess and this is my house," Walter tried to make it sound like he was joking, but he couldn't hide the fact that he was starting to get a little annoyed.

"I know it's your house. I never said it wasn't. Oh God, this is ridiculous—"

"It *is* ridiculous—why are you hovering like—"

"Walter, I was trying to get you to sit down, because I have some bad news and I just—"

"Well, lay it on me. I'm a tough old fart."

"When I was here the first time feeding Bill, the phone rang. I wasn't sure what to do, but in case it was important I decided to answer it and tell the person you were out and ask them to call back and I wouldn't pick up so they could leave a message."

"Okay, okay—so what is it?" Walter was growing impatient.

Maggie spoke quickly, almost spitting out the words. "The call was from Jenny Schnieder and she didn't want to leave the news on a voice mail, and she wanted me to tell you personally that Madeline Gordon had died in Maine quite suddenly on that past Thursday, the Thursday before you went to the hospital. She'd had a heart attack and Jenny, the assistant, was calling all of her authors."

"No."

"I'm so sorry, Walter—I didn't know how to tell you—"

"No, God dammit!" Walter went to his desk and flung his left arm across the surface sending papers, the phone—everything crashing to the floor. Then he slumped in his chair, swiveled so his back was to her and held his head in his one hand, shoulders shaking.

The sound of a man weeping is heart wrenching and Bill Bailey and Maggie both went to him. Bill sat at his feet and Maggie laid her hand on his arm. "I'm so sorry for your loss...if there's anything I can—"

"Why the fuck didn't you tell me?" he shouted.

"You were about to have surgery—I thought it would be best to wait until—"

"You thought...*you thought*! How dare you make decisions for me and interfere in my life you! *Who the hell do you think you are?*"

"Walter, I just—"

"Get the hell out of here!" he roared. "Just leave me the hell alone!"

CHAPTER EIGHT

Maggie fled from the cabin and scurried across Walter's yard feeling like a whipped puppy. Tears filled her eyes and all she could think was what a fool she'd been to get involved with Walter Hathaway. What was wrong with her? Was she crazy? How could she possibly have thought that having anything to do with him could turn out well? Hadn't she learned anything from the disaster at Evergreen? And why hadn't she herself thought of Jordan Wiggins as soon as Walter went off in the aid car? She could have called him and hired him to take care of Bill Bailey. Then she wouldn't have had to deal with that dumb dog at all. Not only did Maggie feel hurt and angry and unappreciated, but she felt *really, really* stupid.

She put her hands in her pockets looking for a tissue, and not finding one, wiped her eyes with the back of her sleeve. As she neared the end of the path close to her drive, Maggie heard a car. She stepped back behind a large cedar and peeked around the trunk to see a shiny, black, luxury car pulling up, and behind the wheel in all her blonde, golden girl glory was her sister.

"Oh shit."

The car itself was very not-Vashon, which was known for a preponderance of unwashed vehicles, many covered with bumper stickers ("KEEP VASHON WEIRD" and "BE KIND TO ANIMALS, DON'T EAT THEM" were favorites. Maggie also liked "CATCH AND RELEASE BANANA SLUGS"). The island also had a large number of hybrids, Smart Cars, and assorted Rube Goldbergy types of transportation all designed with the laudatory goal of saving mother earth, definitely not Leslie's style. Leslie exited the big car wearing very high heels and a fawn-colored Armani pants suit. There were two diamond rings on her right hand: one on her pinky and one on her ring finger, while a teardrop diamond pendant dangled a few inches below her collarbone. Most people would probably assume a display like this had to be fake, but Maggie knew better. Leslie always had the diamond engagement and wedding rings from her previous marriages re-made into various pieces of jewelry, certain that this flash of bling signaled to all the world that she was *somebody*. Somebody very important: that she had worth. In one hand she carried a large leather travel bag, also fawn colored, and in the other, a small crate of some kind. Maggie couldn't be sure but it looked like the kind used to transport animals.

She had seen enough. Maggie pulled her head back behind the tree; and still reeling from Walter's rage, laid her forehead against the trunk of the big cedar and the tears that had filled her eyes spilled down her cheeks. Maggie was not a woman who wept easily. She had learned early on that no one would be there, so that on those occasions when she did cry it always was accompanied by an aching loneliness—and humiliation, another emotion that often accompanied her tears

Maggie felt trapped. There was no way she wanted to face Leslie. At least, certainly not yet. She needed some time to pull herself together, and the beach was the best place for that. If she could just get to the beach, she could take the kayak out for a bit and then come back to the house to greet Leslie and pretend she'd been out for a paddle and was just returning. Damn, she muttered, as she quickly realized she couldn't go down her own path without Leslie possibly seeing her. This left only one route: the path through Walter's yard. But the thought of going anywhere near Walter Hathaway was totally and completely unacceptable. A non-starter. Not an option at all. He'd probably come out on the porch to scream at her again. *Oh my Gawd…What are YOU doing here? I told you to get the hell away from me!* She could just hear him. Maybe with his good hand he'd grab a pitchfork and shake it at her. There was no getting around it, if she wanted to get to the beach, she'd just have to go through the woods where there was no trail.

Maggie set out through the thick growth of the woods. The ground was uneven, covered with huckleberry and salal and there were large sword ferns, dead logs, brambles and broken branches everywhere. Long vines choked the maples, alders and firs, but the worst were the blackberry bushes. They were vicious. Maggie broke off a long stick from a dead branch of an alder and used it to push the thorny rope-like stalks away. She was able to keep them away from her face but the thorns on some of the lower branches cut into her ankles. *Damn you Walter Hathaway. How dare you talk to me that way after the way I helped you with your dumb dog.* Every time she was stuck with a thorn Maggie got madder and by the time she reached the bank she was furious. *I hate that man!* she hissed through clenched teeth, as she grabbed the branch of a madrone and lowered herself down the bank. But even more— she hated that he could upset her so much—although she could admit that at least feeling angry was better than the hurt and humiliation she had felt at first. That had been pathetic.

Maggie got down to the water and realized Leslie might see her taking the kayak out of the boathouse and call to her. She'd have to go up to the house and face her and would never get the peace and quiet she needed to pull herself together. So instead, she walked quickly to the north end of the cove and continued walking beyond the point for about a quarter of a mile until she was completely out of sight of Baker's Beach. Everywhere the beach was littered with branches and twigs from the storm. Maggie made her way over the debris and when she saw a huge silver driftwood log that looked like it had been there for decades, she headed for it. She wanted to just sit there and think, hoping to clear her mind completely of the incident with Walter. Dealing with Leslie took a great deal of patience and fortitude and she didn't want to face her feeling so wobbly.

She could hear the motor of a powerboat some distance away, and several boats south of her were quietly trolling. Maggie looked out over the water, wishing she had a book with her. It would be the best way to stop thinking about that jerk Walter. Just immerse herself in a good novel.

Books had always helped her with just about anything she was struggling with. They gave her something to look forward to, offered comfort and a lovely escape that provided a hedge against loneliness. But after her father's death they'd become more: they kept her afloat. She was sixteen the year he died and Mrs. Nusbaum, the school librarian, made an arrangement with the school counselor to have Maggie be her assistant in the library. She hung out in the library before and after school and during every free period. She loved Mrs. Nusbaum. She was the reason Maggie decided to be a librarian. She was the person who told Maggie that there was such a thing as terminal depression. It was an enlightened view at a time when children were not only shielded from death, but especially from a death as difficult to comprehend as a death by one's own hand, to which her mother, in her despair and anger, had added her Catholic stamp of sin. Mrs. Nusbaum and books were an anchor. Maggie remembered coming home from school to find her mother in bed while Leslie sat on the steps of the front porch waiting for their father and she'd have to convince Leslie to come in by getting her to watch *Captain Kangaroo* on their black and white television. After fixing them both dinner—their mother never wanted to eat—Maggie would do her homework, read to Leslie and get her to bed, and then it would finally be her time: the best part of the day when she could be alone with her books. She especially loved *Nancy Drew Mystery Stories* and felt she had a lot in common with Nancy because neither of their mothers were in the story.

Maggie sighed and ran her hand along the smooth log. Time to get back. It had helped sitting by the water, it always did. She lifted her face to the sun and closed her eyes, relishing the warmth on her skin. She didn't feel wobbly anymore; the beach had worked its magic. Now all she felt was sad.

"Maggie!" Leslie called out with a joyful little yelp, throwing her arms wide. She emerged from the bathroom just as Maggie closed the front door.

"Hi Les." Maggie hugged her and the blonde fluff on top of her sister's head tickled her chin. It always surprised Maggie how small she was.

Maggie stood back and pointed at the crate sitting next to the suitcase. "Is this the surprise?" she asked, bending over to peer inside.

At the sight of Maggie's face, a Siamese cat let out a low wail and Maggie jumped. She loved most animals and would have had pets if George hadn't been allergic to them. She preferred dogs, although she liked cats, too. But she'd never taken to Siamese. Maggie found them a little creepy.

"Isn't he gorgeous!" Leslie pursed her lips in a coy little smile and whispered, "His name is Olivier for Sir Laurence Olivier. And I tell everyone that I'm sleeping with Olivier."

"I thought he was dead."

"That's awful. He just spoke to you. You can see he's perfectly fine, he did beautifully on the plane."

"I meant Sir Laurence. Maybe it's not so cute to insinuate you're sleeping with a dead guy."

"That's sick, Maggie." Leslie looked perturbed, then she inhaled dramatically. "Oh this air! It's so clean and fresh. What a wonderful place this is." She picked up her bag and the crate. "I'll take him to the guest room. And Olivier is only part of the surprise," she said, batting her eyes then winking, "I can't tell you the rest until tomorrow."

In the guest room, Leslie put her bag on the bed and then put the crate in the corner under the window. "Could you make sure all the doors and windows are closed? I'm just going to open the door to the crate so Olivier can come out when he feels he's ready."

"What about a litter box?"

"Oh, I'm glad you mentioned that. I'm going to go in town and pick one up. I didn't bring it because I didn't want to check bags at the airport." Leslie smiled sweetly. "But I brought a small amount of litter and if you have a roasting pan then he could use that temporarily until I get back from the store."

"I don't want cat shit in my roasting pan."

"If he uses it, I'll wash it. I'll pour boiling water on it, it'll be fine." Leslie opened her leather bag, which Maggie thought looked like it cost more than her own car, and pulled out a Ziploc bag filled with cat litter. She looked at Maggie expectantly. Maggie recognized that it was a "what-are-you-waiting-for?" kind of look, reflecting Leslie's certainty that she'd put any concerns Maggie had to rest about her cat using her roasting pan for a litter box. Leslie had a pleasant expression, without the slightest hint of doubt that she and her cat were entitled to the roasting pan.

You never asked me if you could bring that stupid cat! You never even asked me if it was a good time to come! All you ever think of is yourself and I'm sick and tired of it!

Maggie towered over her little sister. Using all her resolve to stay mute, she tried to focus on taking a deep, cleansing breath, pretending she was in her yoga class:

Ommmm...ommmmm...om...you   selfish....om...little   brat!... ommmm.

Maggie began to feel like a yo-yo, anything but centered. Mostly a little nuts.

Then she noticed that Leslie had gotten another face-lift. Her huge dark chocolate eyes had a wide, startled expression like Andrea Mitchell or Joan Rivers. They reminded Maggie of the eyes in a Keane painting, almost cartoon-like in the face of a waif, a motherless child, an orphan of the storm. Her sister, just like the paintings, had become kitschy. Trendy for a nanosecond, then a cliché trying to hang on long past its shelf life. Maggie sighed and went to the kitchen and came back with the roasting pan.

"Thanks." Leslie put the pan on the floor next to the crate and dumped in the litter. Her nails were a bright shade of pink, flawlessly manicured and matching her lipstick. It struck Maggie as an odd picture as she watched Leslie clad in her Armani suit carrying out this little domestic chore.

"Look, you're probably tired from the trip. I'll go into town and get a litter box—I have to pick some stuff up anyway," Maggie said. The house was getting stuffy with everything closed up to prevent Olivier's escape. But besides wanting her own escape, Maggie had a sudden craving for some serious carbs. A giant chocolate chip cookie from Café Luna and a mocha latte. Just for herself.

"Great." Leslie sat on the bed and took off her shoes. "Maybe I'll take a little nap. Oh, and could you pick up some cat food? And some more litter?"

"Yeah. Okay."

"I'll make a list. Do you have some paper and a pen I could use?" Leslie asked.

"Why do I need a list?"

"Olivier prefers Fancy Feast Grilled Tuna Feast, but there are a few others he'll eat if they don't have that, so I'll list them in order of his preference."

"You know the other night I saw a documentary on television about people in Haiti who were eating cracker type food they made from mud, because food was so scarce." Maggie glared at Olivier in the crate and then left the bedroom to get paper so Leslie could make the list of his preferred food. She knew it was a hit and run, a guilt-provoking maneuver meeting the gold standard of their mother before she got so depressed.

Leslie was sitting on the floor in front of the crate when Maggie came back with the pen and paper. She was stroking the cat. "You always make me feel bad, Maggie. I need Olivier, he's all I have. And he's been helping me get through a very bad time since everything ended with me and Leonard."

Then her lower lip trembled and her eyes filled with tears. She brought her knees to her chest and curled up, as she hid her face in her hands. Her thin shoulders were shaking slightly as she wept and as certain as the sun rises in the east, and blessed are they who mourn, for they shall be comforted, Maggie went to her sister and hugged her.

Maggie got home from the grocery store to discover three things: Leslie's black rental car was gone; there was a note on the kitchen table and a cat turd in the middle of her roasting pan. With the doors and windows shut, the house had been hot and stuffy; now it was hot, stuffy, and it stunk. Olivier was sitting in Maggie's favorite reading chair and let out an eerie meow as she came in the house. She wished a window had been left open to encourage his escape.

As she unpacked the groceries, Olivier stared at her and made another of his awful noises.

"Shut up, cat," Maggie said, glaring at him. As soon as she put the groceries away, she filled the new litter box with Tidy Cat (guaranteed odor control). Then, practically gagging, took her roasting pan graced with Olivier's turd outside by the deck and set it by the hose. When she returned, Maggie was a little slow in the closing the door, not terribly motivated to keep him in the house.

"You're going in that crate, cat," she said, firmly. "I can't stand this stuffy house another minute." Maggie enticed Olivier back into the crate with a little glob of Grilled Tuna Feast and as soon as she fastened the door, she ran around the house opening every window and both doors, then grabbed Leslie's note and went out to the deck to read it.

> Dear Maggie,
> I had to leave to meet someone and I should be back in about a couple of hours at the most. (It's part of the surprise!!!!) I'm sure you'll be back before I get there, so please feed Olivier and fix the new litter box. Thanks!
>
> Love you,
> Leslie

Please and thank you. At least she got that right, Maggie thought, but as far as she was concerned, her sister's request that she take care of her stupid cat reeked of her typical entitlement and Maggie scrunched up the note, went back in the house and threw it in the trash. She decided to feed Olivier the rest of his

Fancy Feast in his crate and leave him in there so the house could continue to air out. How had she gotten herself into the role of a pet caregiver? First Bill Bailey and now Olivier. What was with these names anyway? Even Martha Jane, bless her heart, named her cat a person's name. Maria Montessori was a lovely cat though, but whatever happened to Fido, Spot and Rover? Maggie shook her head and went to get the rest of the Fancy Feast food. Martha Jane was fond of a Quaker saying, "Be open to the leading." But Maggie thought that if she had been led to take care of Walter's neurotic dog and now Leslie's weird cat, it was a leading she'd prefer had been opened for someone else.

CHAPTER NINE

The itching began a few minutes after Maggie had shoved the can of Fancy Feast Grilled Tuna Feast into the crate for Olivier. At first she thought it was some mosquito bites—or maybe spider bites, but as she looked at her arms, then at her ankles and the top of her feet she saw what looked like a rash and the skin seemed to be starting to swell. Not bites. It had to be an allergic reaction of some sort and the only thing that had changed in her environment was that damn cat. That had to be it. Well, Leslie would just have to leave it outside, that was all there was to it. As she went to the medicine cabinet in the bathroom to get some Benadryl, Maggie thought more about the cat. She'd hardly touched it. Not only that, in her whole life she'd never been allergic to animals. She opened the medicine cabinet and took out the bottle of Benadryl and unscrewed the cap. And then it hit her. Maggie looked at her arms, which were itching even more and the redness and swelling was more pronounced and tiny pimples were forming. Poison oak. She had poison oak. *Damn you Walter Hathaway.* Those woods had been full of poison oak!

At least she knew what to do. Becky had gotten it one summer and Maggie was good at retaining this kind of information. She threw off her clothes, dumped them in the washing machine and jumped in the shower and scrubbed and scrubbed. Lather, rinse, repeat...she must have done it a dozen times. Then she picked up her sandals with a rag to avoid touching them and took them to the yard where she poured detergent on them and soaked them with the hose. Then she went to the kitchen for additional medicine. A vodka martini.

Sunlight could irritate the rash, so Maggie dragged her easy chair to the darkest corner of the living room and sipped the martini. The only thing she wasn't sure of was how alcohol would affect the urushiol, that oily stuff on the leaves that gets in your system, and frankly, at this point she didn't give a damn. Yes, she was certainly "self-medicating" with her martini and it seemed like a fine idea.

She was beginning to feel drowsy from the Benadryl and the drink when Leslie burst in, high heels clicking across the floor, car keys jangling and little out of breath.

"Oh Maggie!" She swooped into the living room and flounced down on the couch. "Are you ready?"

"Ready for what?" Maggie grumbled from the dark corner, already beginning to feel a little sloshed.

"The surprise...the surprise I've been telling you ab—" Then she sat up abruptly and looked around. "Where's Olivier?"

"In his crate."

"In the guestroom?" Leslie stood up.

Maggie nodded and sipped her drink. "Yes, he's in the guestroom in the crate."

"Oh poor Olivier." Leslie ran from the room. "Did you feed him? Did you get the food I asked?"

"I did. I got that friggin' Fancy Feast Grilled Tuna," Maggie growled. "Are you okay with that?"

Olivier meowed as Leslie carried him back to the living room and put him on her lap. She put her face against the crown of his head and closed her eyes and sighed. After a few minutes she sat back against the couch and stroked him, slowly moving her hand with her perfect pink nails back and forth across his back. "Is something wrong, Maggie?" she asked quietly.

"I have poison oak."

"Oh dear. That's terrible."

"Yes it is."

"Well, how did you get it."

"Gardening. I was doing a little yard work before you came."

"I'm really sorry about that. Is there anything I can do?"

Yes, you can leave and take that stupid cat with you. Maggie sipped her martini. She probably should offer Leslie something so she wouldn't be drinking alone, but she didn't want to.

"Maggie?"

"What?"

"Is there anything I can do?" Leslie asked again.

"No. It just has to run its course." Then after a minute, she muttered, "thanks."

"Well, that's really too bad."

"I'm not sure how bad it's going to be...it takes about twelve hours before it's completely in your system. I'll pick up some stuff at the pharmacy if I need to."

"Would you like to hear the surprise now?"

"The surprise?"

"The surprise I've been telling you about, Maggie." Leslie sounded hurt.

"Oh, the surprise. Yeah...sure."

"Well—" she paused dramatically, "I have made a major decision and I've kept it a secret so I wouldn't spoil the surprise." Another dramatic pause. "I've just come back from town where I've signed papers—"

"From where?" Maggie's speech was slurring a little.

"From town. The town of Vashon. The only town on the island—"

"There's Burton and Dockton—"

"I didn't think they were real towns, I mean—"

"Burton has a post office and its own zip code. And it has the art gallery and the gas station and the Quartermaster Inn and the grocery store—" Maggie closed her eyes and sipped the martini.

"Do you want to hear about the surprise or not?" Leslie said, becoming frustrated.

"Yeah. Lay it on me," Maggie muttered, her eyes still closed.

"I signed papers at the Fillinger real estate office making an offer on this wonderful house on Hormann Road just down from

Baker's Beach. Maggie," she paused, then announced, "I'm going to live on Vashon Island!"

Maggie sat up and opened her eyes and stared at Leslie. "You what?"

Tell me this isn't true. I'm dreaming. I've nodded off and I just had a little bad dream. A nightmare, I've had a nightmare.

Leslie leaned forward, beaming. "I'm going to live on the island. It's time I should be near family and that's you...and I've been looking at Vashon Island houses online ever since Leonard and I split up and today I went and saw the house that I was sure was the right one and it *was* and I just fell it love with it! I kept it a secret because you have such an influence on me and I wanted this to be all my own decision. Of course, I'll need to do a lot of remodeling but it will be a wonderful project to help me get over Leonard and I've gotten so much help from my realtor Betty Sue Schnitzer—"

"She's a crook."

"What?" Leslie cocked her head and opened her eyes quite wide.

"It's a terrible house. Everyone knows it. There are mudslides and the ground won't perk for a septic and you'll never get a permit to do anything without a septic that's up to code and it's known for termites and rats." Maggie recited this litany of defects with great authority.

"How do you know this?" Leslie frowned.

"Everyone knows this. It's a small town, everyone knows everything and if Betty Sue Schnitzer didn't tell you it's because she's a crook."

"Well, I'm not that stupid, I mean the offer is contingent on an inspection so I'm sure I'll find out any problems and then I can back out if I have to," Leslie said, quietly. "The owners have twenty-four hours to respond. But I offered full price and Betty Sue knows mine is the only offer and I don't have to get financing or anything so the deal is as good as done, unless the inspector finds stuff that for some reason is totally un-fixable. The inspection is scheduled first thing in the morning and so I'll be going over there again with Betty Sue. Want to come?"

"No."

Maggie sipped her martini and neither of them spoke. Outside they heard a car start up somewhere along Baker's Beach Road and the crowing of Howie and Mark's rooster.

"Maggie?"

"What?"

"I thought you'd be happy," Leslie's voice cracked and Maggie could hear her start to cry.

Maggie sighed. "Look, I feel lousy. I itch like hell and this damn rash is getting worse." Maggie looked at her arms, which now had little raised pimples that looked like they had fluid in them.

"I know you feel bad, I thought this might—"

"I'm sorry, it's just such a shock and it's not how I go about things. I'm cautious and deliberate and I research everything carefully and it's just hard for me to relate to...." Maggie sat back and closed her eyes.

"Wouldn't it be fun to live in the same place? We haven't lived in the same place since we were kids."

Good, let's keep it that way. Maggie sighed, finally she said, "I just don't think you'd like it here. It's not your kind of place, it's very quiet. There's no Nordstrom. No Gucci. No Armani. And the only jewelry store just went out of business." Maggie stared at Leslie, who had stopped crying but looked like a waif—face-lifted, botoxed, and bling-bearing but nevertheless a waif—and her heart softened. It happened every time. Maggie had a fierce sense of duty and she was incapable of abandoning someone who needed her. She knew too well what it felt like. Another deep sigh and then she said, "It'll be okay, Les. If you're here, we'll make it work."

"And we'd have fun, right?"

"Sure," Maggie said, with a sad smile. Then she stood up. "I'm going to get something to put on this rash and then I'm going to lie down." Maggie went to the kitchen and fixed herself another martini and then went to her bedroom and shut the door.

Maggie was not that much of a drinker and the combination of two martinis and the Benadryl completely zonked her. She slept until almost ten the next morning and when she finally struggled to the kitchen to make coffee, she saw that the big black car was gone and there was a note from Leslie next to the coffee maker.

> Dear Maggie,
>
> Betty Sue called me first thing this morning and the owners have accepted my offer! We're meeting with the inspector and then I'll be at her office and then she wants to take me to lunch. I've only been here a short time and I've already made a friend!
>
> I've fed Olivier and please remember to make sure he stays in the house if you leave. And I'd like him to feel at home outside of the crate, so please shut the windows.
>
> Hugs and kisses,
> Leslie of VASHON ISLAND!!!

It was too early for a martini. Besides, Maggie had a headache and she guessed this type of medicine really wasn't her thing. Leslie of Vashon Island…it didn't sound right. Not at all. A very sour note, discordant and screeching, like the irritating squeak of chalk on a blackboard or that awful noise the microphone made at a school assembly when she'd messed up turning it on. All she could hope for was that the inspector might find a lot of terrible things wrong with the house. It would be wonderful if there really were termites that had destroyed the foundation and the whole place was such a disaster that it couldn't be repaired and she'd have to look some more. Her new friend Betty Sue would have to find her something else and the whole process would drag on and on and Leslie would soon realize that island living after all really wasn't for her. Not her cup of imported $28 per pound exotic tea.

Maggie crumpled up the note, threw it in the recycle and made coffee. While she waited for the coffee to brew, she scratched her arms. In spite of her best efforts yesterday to wash off the exposure to poison oak, her rash was worse and she decided she'd better go to the pharmacy and get something to help with the itching. Hydrocortisone or zinc oxide was supposed to relieve it and she could get those over the counter. On the way she'd mail Ashley's birthday present. Maggie had found it increasingly difficult to know what to buy for her granddaughter. Between age nine and ten there had been some kind of leap and Ashley was concerned now with what was and what was not cool. At least that was a word Maggie understood, one that had held its meaning and use for a few generations even though she had no idea what Ashley thought would be a cool present. Even though it seemed impersonal, she'd decided to send a check and let her pick her own gift when she got home from camp. But she decided to send it with a pair of small pearl earrings. Ashley had gotten her ears pierced at the beginning of the summer and since her birthstone was pearl she thought maybe she'd like them.

Before she left, Maggie put on a long-sleeved shirt to discourage herself from scratching her arms and then went to check on the cat, with the intention of stuffing him in the crate. There was no way she was going to shut all the windows. No thank you. The whole house would get hot and stuffy and smell like a kennel. Maggie had little faith that the odor-free litter could fully live up to its claims. She found Olivier asleep, curled up on the bed in the guest room. And as she looked at him, she realized she didn't know what would happen if she tried to pick him up. It could end up that she'd have to chase him all over the house. Maggie was in no mood for that kind of hassle. Reluctantly, she decided to leave him where he was, close the windows and door and be on her way.

It had been four days since the storm but there were still a number of huge tree limbs that had been cleared to the side of Vashon Highway, and right before Burton, the beach was covered with branches that looked like they were too heavy to have been washed out with the tide. There wasn't much wind and Quartermaster Harbor was quite calm. A blue heron stood at the edge of the water, and it seemed to her that no matter what time of day she went to the post office and passed Burton Beach, there was a heron there fishing. It must be a prime spot for them and she was always impressed with their patience. It was a quality she admired and she hoped she could have the patience of a heron when it came to Leslie. There was no telling how long it would take her Vashon home-buying adventure to play itself out. Maggie just hoped she'd be able to be calm as she waited for it to end, as she was sure it ultimately would. Leslie never stuck with anything, and Maggie understood that her sister always looked for a geographical cure, a new place as well as a new person (always male) to fill the emptiness she carried around that no place or person could ever fill. She would move on, Maggie was certain. It was just a matter of when.

Maggie loved the Burton post office. It was very small with just one little counter and one postmaster on duty. There were several on the staff who rotated to Burton from the main island post office in Vashon and Maggie, like most people who had a box at the Burton office, was fond of them. There was rarely much of a line and when there was, everyone was friendly and relaxed. She couldn't remember ever hearing grumbling. Mickey was working today and she had put the check for Ashley and the earrings into a priority envelope so there was no need for him to weigh it. Maggie had the exact change and stayed a minute to get her receipt while they talked about the storm. Weather was always the most frequent topic of post office conversation, even when there hadn't been a storm.

As she was leaving the post office she saw a dark blue Toyota truck turn into the little parking area. Like many island trucks, it was well past its prime and covered with dust. The driver was blocked from view by the large, brown head on the passenger side. There was no mistaking the passenger: Bill Bailey. It was Walter's truck. Maggie put her head down and scurried to her car as if she had on blinders.

"Maggie...wait!" Out of the corner of her eye she saw Walter struggling to get out of the truck with his arm in the sling. "Maggie!"

She pretended she didn't see or hear him. Hear no evil, see no evil. Although she certainly was tempted to speak some evil. She slammed her car door shut. In her heart of hearts Maggie thought avoiding Walter Hathaway was juvenile and ridiculous. After all, the only thing she'd gotten from avoiding him yesterday was poison oak. But being ridiculous was preferable to having anything more to do with that man. She shoved the gear stick in reverse and peeled out like a crazed teenage show-off and sped down the highway not looking back.

CHAPTER TEN

By the time Maggie got home from the pharmacy, the rash was driving her crazy and she was convinced it had gotten worse because of the distress she felt when she ran into Walter. She dumped out the hydrocortisone and the zinc oxide from her purse and ripped open the boxes. Squishing the tube of hydrocortisone cream with a vengeance, she slathered the stuff all over her rash. Then she opened the zinc oxide and dabbed some of that on the itchiest parts for good measure.

Nothing took her mind off her troubles like a book and Maggie wanted to get back to Stephen Dedalus and his troubles. She found *Portrait of the Artist as a Young Man* on the coffee table under a bunch of newspapers. In the kitchen she got a tall glass of water, thinking it might help flush some of the poison from her system, and then went to her reading chair. She'd left off with Stephen Dedalus struggling with his conscience, and was just getting engaged in the story, now centered fully on Stephen's shame—when Olivier began to scratch on the guest room door and loudly meow. The sound was eerie, pathetic and almost human. She tried to read a few more paragraphs: Stephen Dedalus was now wallowing in guilt, but Joyce's words were accompanied by the creepy cry of the cat. *That's it!* No way am I staying in this house with that animal.

Maggie slammed the book shut and charged out the front door and down the porch steps. She felt a twinge of conscience leaving the cat crying and alone in the house—not a wave of Dedalusian guilt—but just a little twinge and certainly not enough to make her change her course as she headed straight for Martha Jane's house. Maggie always loved what Robert Frost said about home, that it was the place where, when you go there, they have to take you in. She supposed it had some validity when it came to her and Leslie. She always felt that she had to take her sister in whenever Leslie would show up on her doorstep, but the only place that came close to that kind of secure refuge for Maggie was Martha Jane's.

"Hi, Mrs. Lewis!" Jordan Wiggins called as he was crossing the road in front of Martha Jane's. Jordan's grandmother insisted that he never address adults by their first name and it always made Maggie feel like she was back in the library at Evergreen Elementary. She rather liked it. The kids never quite got the "Ms." part down, but that was fine with her.

"How are you, Jordan?"

"Good. I'm starting my job today."

"Your job?"

"Working for Mr. Hathaway. Remember?"

"Working for Mr. Hathaway. Right," Maggie nodded.

"And I'm not gonna lie, it's really great I'm working there actually, because it's like I have to get away from my grandmother. Know what I'm sayin'?"

"Well, can't say that I do—" Maggie hedged, hoping she had never indicated to Jordan that in truth she didn't think much of either of his grandparents. Sondra Wiggins made a career out of hassling Howie and Mark about their chickens, complaining they were too noisy. And when Martha Jane had hired a nice young man to help her stain her deck, Sondra Wiggins accused him of running over her rose bushes with his truck and insisted he replace them. Howie had seen her husband back over the bushes, but Sondra would have none of it. She said Carl denied it and of course, Sondra believed him. It was typical of Carl, who Maggie thought looked like an overweight Tucker Carlson, given to wearing shirts with little reptiles on them and plaid pants. He was smug and sanctimonious, and as Howie put it: Carl Wiggins was an arrogant prick who was more than capable of lying to his wife or anyone else if it served his interest. The situation with the bushes hadn't turned into the Hatfields and the McCoys, but the Wigginses' relationship with Howie and Mark was far from harmonious and Maggie always suspected there was more to it on Sondra's part than just her chicken issues. And there was also the time that the Wigginses had Martha Jane for dinner and Sondra had made some dessert that Martha Jane loved and when she asked for the recipe, Sondra Wiggins wouldn't give it to her.

"My grandmother's insane." Jordan shoved his hands in his pockets.

"What's happened?" Maggie tried not to sound too alarmed, especially since Jordan had made this pronouncement rather casually.

"Grandma Sondra and Grandpa Carl's house is on the garden tour and she wants it to be like perfect. She's insane about every little weed. Know what I'm sayin'? And Grandpa Carl goes to the golf course every day to get away, and then he's hangin' with Mr. McIntyre at the clubhouse until it's dark."

"And it doesn't get dark until pretty late." Maggie wanted to sound understanding but didn't want to bash his grandmother, even though she thought it was quite selfish of her to put her garden on the tour while Jordan was visiting.

"What's wrong with your arms?" Jordan peered at her arms, which were covered with white goo.

"I got poison oak." Maggie had to smile. She loved that about kids, they notice things and tell you. Not like many adults where you could have a black olive hanging from your front tooth for an entire evening and they'd pretend they didn't see it.

"That sucks."

"I agree." Maggie winced a little.

"Well, I gotta get to work. See you later, Mrs. Lewis."

Jordan's use of language seemed right in tune with the way the older kids at Evergreen spoke, even though he went to school in Oregon. She supposed it was television or all the Facebook and texting that contributed to a common teen language. Maggie didn't have a problem with it, but she never could get quite comfortable when they said something sucked. Especially when the younger kids picked it up. It sounded too crude to her, although she remembered one time when a second grader was upset because the cafeteria ran out of dessert and said, "That sucks, Mrs. Lewis—like lemons." Lemons. All to the good, if that's what kids thought. But the expression still grated a bit.

Martha Jane was in the kitchen and when she saw Maggie coming up the walk she waved and motioned for her to come in. She loved to have people drop by and Maggie knew her friend's routine pretty well. She was up early, especially in the summer, then she went to Fred Weiss's studio where she'd paint for a while. She often had lunch there and then came back and took a long nap. She professed to being a strong believer in naps and they were an important part of her daily routine. But Martha Jane was the kind of person who would drop everything if you needed her and never seemed to mind if things upset her routine. Elderly people were supposed to be set in their ways, and Maggie surmised that Martha Jane's concern for people was an aspect of her character that was set in stone and would trump any resistance she might have to altering her routine. There were glitches in Martha Jane's memory, but there were things she loved to quote that were hard-wired and one of them was a Japanese proverb: the bamboo that bends is stronger than the oak that resists. Maggie thought that Martha Jane was one of the most bamboo-like people she'd ever met.

"Aren't these just beautiful?" Martha Jane stood at the sink washing green beans. "I got them at the farmer's market this morning. And look at the cherries." She pointed to a paper bag on the counter. "I got those at the stand in front of The Hardware Store, they're the ones those folks bring over from Yakima." She popped one of the beans in her mouth. "It's odd isn't it that The Hardware Store is a restaurant now, and sometimes newcomers don't realize it really used to be a real hardware store."

"Sometimes, I forget that and I was even here when it was a hardware store." Maggie peeked in the bag. "Oh, Rainiers, the absolute best."

"Well, at least the restaurant kept the sign from the old hardware store that was out in front...'Today's Special'...and...then ...I seem to have forgotten the rest of it...how does it go again?"

"'Today's special—and so is tomorrow.'"

Martha Jane looked up from the sink and smiled, then she saw Maggie's arms. "Oh my, what's happened?"

"Poison oak, I'm afraid."

"Oh you poor dear. That's nasty stuff. I'm almost through here—there's still some iced tea left, help yourself and then let's sit in the living room and I'll be right there." Martha Jane dumped the cherries into a strainer and ran water over them. "The pitcher's in the fridge."

"That'll be lovely, thanks."

Maggie was not the kind of person that anyone addressed as "you poor dear." She supposed it was because she was too tall, and seemed too strong, too self-reliant. And even though she felt a little silly hearing it, she loved it coming from Martha Jane. It was exactly what she needed and exactly why she'd headed straight for Martha Jane's house the minute she realized that with those creepy cat noises, her usual method of coping—losing herself in a book—was simply not working.

Maggie poured tea for both of them and went in the living room where sunlight was streaming in the big bay window that faced the beach. The couch was farther back from the window and still in the shade and she sat there, sharing the space with Maria Montessori. Maggie sipped her tea and stroked the cat. "You are a very nice animal," she said. "I wouldn't mind a cat like you."

"What's that dear?" Martha Jane shuffled in from the kitchen and grimaced a bit as she slowly lowered herself into the chair across from Maggie. Martha Jane rarely complained about her arthritis, but Maggie knew it had to be painful and she was always amazed at Martha Jane's determination not to let it stop her.

"I just told Maria that I wouldn't mind a cat like her." She moved her hand slowly across the cat's back. "My sister arrived yesterday with a cat. It's a Siamese and for some reason it's about the only kind of cat that I don't warm up to. Although there's some kind of strange hairless cat that I've seen photos of that I don't suppose I'd care for. I can't remember what they're called but—"

"Sphynx!" Martha Jane said, triumphantly. "They're called sphynx!" Martha Jane leaned forward, "You know I just love it when I remember something like this, it's a little boost of confidence."

"Good for you!" Maggie grinned and gave her a thumbs-up.

"Now tell me, how did you get this poison oak? And is that stuff you've put on it helping?" Martha Jane took a long sip of her tea, and then with her hand shaking slightly set the glass on the end table. "Oh, and you know what I always say when I'm with folks and we start talking about our ailments. Everyone gets three minutes and I get out my egg timer, because there are so many more interesting things to talk about. Like the fawns! Have you seen the doe with the two babies, still with their spots...just precious! I saw them at the edge of Howie and Mark's lot right at the beginning of the woods."

"I haven't seen them, but I'd love to."

Martha Jane sat back and was quiet for a moment. "We weren't talking about the deer, were we?" She reached for her tea. "Oh yes, ailments. I remember now, well, I was just trying to say that since you never have ailments I think you should talk about your rash as long as you'd like."

"Thanks, but I don't want to bore you."

"It must be a problem though, Maggie, because you don't seem quite like yourself."

"It's my sister, her cat...and well, as much as I hate to admit it...Walter."

"What does Walter have to do with your sister and her hairless cat?" Martha Jane looked puzzled. "I'm afraid I must have missed something, I'm sorry, dear—"

"It's a Siamese cat that my sister brought and it makes this terrible sound. A creepy, whining cry and it's just so demanding, which is exactly how I feel about Leslie. And yesterday she dropped a real bombshell." Maggie took a deep breath and closed her eyes for a minute. "Leslie says she's buying that house that's been for sale on Hormann Road. She says she's moving here. Moving to Vashon and I feel like if she really goes through with this, I could just get eaten alive."

Martha Jane shook her head. "I'm so sorry."

"I told her the house was terrible and the realtor was a crook, but I just made it up. I really don't know if it's true...I've never heard of the realtor. I think she must be someone new. The truth is, I was feeling a little desperate and I wanted to discourage Leslie from this whole terrible idea. Everyone here knows it takes a certain kind of person to live on an island with no bridge, that you can only get to on a ferry. It can be so inconvenient and you just have to love quiet and nature and small town living. Leslie is absolutely *not* that kind of person."

"I see. And I don't suppose you could tell her you're concerned about your relationship, that it might be strained with her living so close?"

"Leslie just seems so fragile. I always end up feeling sorry for her."

"In my experience, Maggie, it's sometimes these so-called fragile people who are the ones who end up ruling everyone; they exercise a great deal of control and in their helplessness get everyone to do exactly as they want." Martha Jane looked out at the water, then turned back to Maggie. "I don't mean to say that there aren't people who genuinely need help, but I just think it's wise to have your eyes open. And I agree with you about the hairless cats, I don't think they're appealing at all. Of course, I don't mean to imply that all creatures without hair are unappealing. There are bald people certainly, bald men, I mean...although we women as we age lose our hair, too. But the point is that there are bald men who do have appeal, but on a cat I think it can be a little repulsive."

"Yes, repulsive." Maggie agreed. She always felt better when she talked to Martha Jane even when there were little conversational hiccups and snags. She'd learned to let the conversation flow around them like they were rocks in a river. Martha Jane was a generous listener, a quality that Maggie found to be increasingly rare. Maggie sometimes wondered how she would have gotten through all the bouncing around she'd done after her divorce from George if it hadn't been for Martha Jane. She never gave her any advice, but listened with her heart. Although this afternoon, Maggie thought she could do with some advice. She had yet to say anything about Walter, and felt a little awkward about how to bring up the subject. She took a big gulp of her tea, then continued to stroke Maria Montessori. Finally she said, "And you're right about bald men who have appeal, and then there's Walter who mostly seems to be losing hair at the crown."

"He still has a lovely head of hair. Beautifully snowy and silvery white."

"I ran away from him this morning at the post office."

Martha Jane couldn't hide her surprise. "He's such a recluse I can't imagine him chasing anyone and now with his arm and all."

"He wasn't chasing me," Maggie said. "I was coming out of the post office when he drove up and he called to me and I just ran to my car and pretended I didn't hear him. It was juvenile and ridiculous and I'm terribly embarrassed. But I'm so mad at him, I'd like to strangle him." Maggie sighed and leaned back against the couch. "There. I've said it. It isn't gracious or attractive but it is exactly how I feel."

"I know he can be cantankerous and grumpy but—"

"Martha Jane, when I told him that his agent died he went berserk. He was enraged and he attacked me—"

"Oh dear heaven!" Martha Jane put her hand over her mouth. "Were you hurt?"

"Verbally attacked, not physically although honestly, I think he looked like he wanted to hit me and he just lit into me and screamed at me to get the hell out."

"No wonder you want to avoid him!"

"Yes, no wonder!" Maggie couldn't bring herself to explain that was how she got poison oak. It was too humiliating.

"But you don't want to have to go around running away, like at the post office." Martha Jane folded her hands across her stomach.

"Exactly."

"I think he probably wants to apologize, Maggie."

Maggie shook her head. "I doubt that."

"No, I'm serious. I had my easel in front of the house this morning at the edge of the beach. I'm painting a seascape and

Walter and Bill Bailey came by and he stopped to talk, something he rarely does, and I just felt that he wanted to say something. He knows what good friends you and I are."

"Hmmph," Maggie snorted.

"No really, dear. He asked how everything was at Baker's Beach, and I'm quite sure now that he was asking about you. If you want any peace of mind, I think you'll just have to forgive him."

Maggie turned away and looked out the window and didn't say anything and Martha Jane continued, "I heard it said somewhere, or maybe I read it...well, no matter. But about forgiveness and men and women. It's that women forgive but never forget. And men forget but never forgive. I think there's some truth to it."

"Maybe. I don't think Walter ever forgave his wife for running off with the producer when they made the film of *The Adventures of Fric the Chick*."

"He was devastated, wasn't he...I remember hearing about it somewhere. And then of course, there's what Gandhi said about it all."

Gandhi? It was a rather significant Martha Jane neuron misfire and Maggie wasn't sure what she should say, so she continued stroking the cat and looked out the window as if she hadn't heard.

Martha Jane smiled. "Gandhi said, 'the weak can never forgive. Forgiveness is the attribute of the strong.' I'm sure you're strong enough to forgive him, Maggie, if you just put your mind to it. And then you won't have to scurry around to avoid him if you bump into him somewhere. Think of it as doing it for yourself, for your own peace of mind. And of course, you really don't need to have much to do with Walter. I would imagine it would just be enough to be civil."

Civil. Could she do that? She'd have to think about it. Maggie wasn't sure if civil constituted forgiveness, but she supposed it was more merciful than wanting to strangle him.

After she got home, Maggie was putting more hydrocortisone cream on the rash when she heard Leslie's car. Quickly wiping her hands, she hurried to the guest room to let Olivier out. He'd been whining and carrying on ever since she'd gotten back from Martha Jane's and she was actually relieved to have Leslie back so the thing would shut up. Earlier she had gone into the guest room to try to get it to settle down but it was no use. Their relationship was pretty well established: she didn't like the cat, and the cat didn't like her.

Leslie burst in jangling her car keys, flashing bling, juggling her huge leather purse and a paper bag. "Ta-da!" She set everything on the kitchen table, then whipped a bottle of champagne from the bag. "Dom Pérignon! Only the best for the Lewis sisters, right, Mag!"

Mag. She really hated to be called "Mag." It sounded too much like hag, and then there was "Magpie," the nickname her mother had for her when all Maggie was trying to do was engage her: talking to her, trying to find something, anything that might interest her mother to get her attention. Magpie...the chatterer. A nickname she despised. She looked at the champagne and shuddered, knowing full well what it meant. Olivier ran to Leslie and she scooped him up. "You're going to be an island cat, little guy!" She covered his head with kisses. "It's a done deal." Leslie beamed: a huge, wide, triumphant grin. "The inspector found a number of things, but it's all do-able. And Betty Sue has given me a list of contractors and I'm going to start interviewing them right away," she paused, breathless with excitement. "So let's get this opened and get some champagne glasses and let the celebration begin!"

The wake. Let the wake begin. Maggie went to the drawer where she kept the knives and cooking utensils and rummaged through it for a corkscrew. "I know I've got one here somewhere."

"Don't you have anything to say?" Leslie pulled Olivier close to her.

"I'm overwhelmed, that's all." Maggie gave her sister a weak smile. A weak smile for a weak sister as she tried to remind herself that this wasn't going to last. She'll be out of here by the end of the year. As soon as the rains come with long dreary gray days when the mountains disappear and the blue sparkle of the sky turns to clouds the color of cement, Leslie will vanish, she'll be gone like yesterday's news and so much flotsam with the outgoing tide.

Maggie found the corkscrew, set it on the counter and then went to the cupboard for some glasses.

Leslie peeled the foil off the bottle. "Oh, I guess I don't need the corkscrew, it just has a little wire thingy on it."

Maggie put two glasses on the counter and watched while Leslie tried to open the bottle. "This is kind of hard—I don't seem to be getting it." She looked at the jelly glasses. "Don't you have any champagne glasses?"

"Nope."

"Wine glasses, maybe?" Leslie grimaced, struggling with the cork. "Here, you do it—" She shoved the bottle at Maggie.

And this is how it will be. Here, you do it. Just like our whole lives. Maggie got a dishtowel and put it over the cork so it wouldn't explode out of the bottle and hit Leslie in the head. There was a big pop and the champagne fizzed over the side of the bottle.

"Good!" Leslie clapped her hands. "Surely, you must have wine glasses somewhere. It just won't taste right in these."

Maggie sighed and went to the cupboard next to the refrigerator and brought out two wine glasses, then poured them each a glass.

Leslie raised her glass. "You make the toast, Mag. You're always better with words."

Maggie could only think of toasting the day in the not-too-distant future when Leslie would leave. *Good riddance to bad rubbish...A rolling stone gathers no moss...So long sista...* But it was her father's Hebrew words that came with an image of Leslie's small hand tugging on her sleeve. *He won't wake up. He's asleep in the garage.*

"*L'chaim*," she toasted, and her eyes filled with tears.

CHAPTER ELEVEN

Howie and Mark's rooster woke Maggie up around five-thirty the next morning. She put the pillow over her head, hoping to muffle the sound and get a little more sleep. It usually worked. She'd fall back to sleep and it wouldn't be too long before the rooster would be silenced when Mark or Howie, both early risers, went out to feed their little flock. But this morning Olivier heard the rooster and he joined the crowing with his awful whiny meow. It was hopeless. Maggie pulled the pillow off her head and struggled out of bed. She was always a little stiff in the morning and it took her awhile to get the kinks out. This morning, she was feeling pretty tired; she hadn't slept all that well and her rash wasn't getting any better. After she showered, she itched like crazy. She couldn't help thinking that the stress of Leslie's news was making the whole thing worse—making it that much harder to heal. And of course, that awful encounter with Walter had unquestionably not been good for her health and well-being.

The morning was chilly and cloudy and she pulled on jeans and a sweatshirt. She rolled up the legs of her jeans and covered the rash with the hydrocortisone, then put the stuff on her arms. What a hassle, she thought, knowing the cream would end up sticking to the inside of her clothes. She went to the kitchen to put coffee on. Out the window she could see several fishermen trolling near shore. The clouds hung low over the Kitsap Peninsula covering the tops of the dark green hills. But to the north where the sun had burned through, she could see streaks of blue slicing through the clouds, giving the promise of a brighter day. It would have been a peaceful morning if it weren't for that stupid cat. Didn't Leslie hear him whining and carrying on? What was the matter with her?

Maggie heard the toilet flush and then the whining stopped and Leslie, wearing an ivory satin monogrammed nightgown, came in the kitchen carrying Olivier. "He's just like a little baby," she smiled, sleepily. "Won't even let Mommy go to the bathroom, will you Snookums?" Leslie held Olivier against her face, then put him down. "I always have to feed him first. He insists." Leslie went to the refrigerator where she'd put the can of Fancy Feast Grilled Tuna Feast he'd partially eaten yesterday.

Olivier followed Leslie back into the guest bedroom where she put the rest of the food in his dish, then came back to the kitchen. "Do you recycle these?" Leslie asked, as she rinsed out the can.

"There are bins by the back door. We have to separate paper, tin and plastic, and glass."

"Sounds complicated, but I guess I'll learn it all soon enough." She smiled, and carried the can to the back door. "I see you have them all labeled," she called, cheerily. "Always the librarian, so organized and everything."

Maggie peeled a banana and didn't say anything. It was usually about all she had for breakfast. Potassium for her heart. She chomped on the banana, wondering if having to deal with Leslie day in and day out would shorten her life.

Leslie got a mug from the cupboard and poured herself coffee. "I'll just help myself to breakfast, Maggie. I don't want to trouble you."

"Good," Maggie mumbled through a mouthful of banana.

"What?" Leslie laughed. "Remember how Mom always told us not to talk with our mouths full? Or maybe that was you, maybe you told me that."

"Well, someone said 'do as I say, not as I do.'" Maggie took another bite of the banana.

Leslie fixed herself a piece of toast, and sat at the table with her coffee. "I really want you to see the house, Maggie. I could hardly sleep last night thinking about how I'm going to remodel it. I wish I could start this minute, but I've got to go back to LA and get my house on the market. But don't worry, I'll come back as soon as I can and one of the first things I'm going to do is put in a pool. I've always had a pool and besides pools being beautiful, it's just the best exercise. And I think we should—"

"A pool!" Maggie stuffed the last of the banana in her mouth and threw the banana peel in the bowl under the sink for the compost pile. She wiped her hands on a dish towel and poured another cup of coffee, thinking a Bloody Mary might be a better way to start this day. Then she sat across from Leslie, trying to be patient. "Leslie," she paused for a deep breath, "does the house have its own well?"

"I don't know. I didn't ask about that."

"You'll need to find out before you get too far ahead of yourself. The houses here at Baker's Beach are all on one well. Howie and Mark keep it maintained and we all chip in for it. But I don't know the situation on Hormann Road and you really just can't jump ahead. If a number of people on Hormann Road are on one well, there are water shares and the number of shares are regulated and—"

"You sound like Eeyore," Leslie giggled.

"Who?"

"Eeyore the Donkey. Don't you remember reading me *Winnie the Pooh* when I was little?"

Maggie got up from the table. "Fine, Les. Whatever."

"You're mad."

Maggie sighed. "Just worried that you don't know what you're getting into. Permits, septics, water rights—it can be a huge hassle, that's all."

"Please come and look at the house. Won't you do that with me this morning? I told Betty Sue that I couldn't wait to bring you over and she told me where she'd leave the key." Leslie smiled, sweetly. "Please?"

Oh great, next she's going to say pretty please with sugar on top and of course I'm Eeyore the Donkey who says it looks like rain. Maggie, the one who rains on all her parades. Maggie looked out the window at the fisherman who were now trolling a little farther out, wishing she was out there, too, with nothing to think about but whether or not there would be a tug on the line. How patient they seemed, just sitting and barely moving along with hardly a wake. She bent down and scratched the top of the rash on her ankle where she'd missed a spot with the cream. "Sure, Les. Fine. Let's walk over and see your new house."

Maggie went to put more cream on her rash while Leslie went to get dressed. The rash seemed bigger and bumpier and she wondered if she ought to think about getting something stronger for it from her doctor. Maybe she'd wait another day. Everything just took so much longer to heal when you got older. Even a little bruise seemed to stay forever, months almost. She supposed she just needed to be more patient. Patience was something she could use in every aspect of her life these days, she thought. In the living room she picked up her book, but decided not to start reading if Leslie was almost ready. She went to the bathroom and knocked on the door.

"How long are you going to be?"

Leslie opened the door. "Not too much longer, I just have to get these on." Between her thumb and first finger Leslie held what looked to Maggie like a hairy insect.

"What's that?"

"Eyelashes." She turned to the mirror and with her mouth open, closed one eye and began carefully sticking the eyelashes on her eyelid. Maggie thought it looked like a black caterpillar and she also couldn't believe what had happened to the bathroom. There were so many little jars and tubes of who-knew-what and lipsticks, mascara, foundation, eye shadow, blush, and brushes that it looked like a department store make-up counter that had been rammed by a runaway truck.

"I'm going out to the road to get the paper."

"Okay, all I have left to do is my hair and then we can go." Leslie took the other strip of eyelashes from a little box and closed the other eye. "Oh, and be careful when you go out that you don't let Olivier out," she said, pleasantly.

Waiting for Leslie was nothing new, and for Maggie it always got old very fast. Her sister was the type that was chronically late. Not only had Leslie never learned to manage time, but she was so self-involved that considering the feelings of the people she kept waiting was never part of her equation. She wasn't unaware that she kept people waiting, however, and she always arrived with a breathless string of apologies that were an automatic part of her greeting, uttered with stagey enthusiasm but empty of remorse.

Maggie stopped at the bottom of the porch steps and looked out at the fishermen who were still trolling close to shore at the north end of the beach. Morning mist rose across the water and the clouds on this part of the island had yet to burn off. Again she had the thought that under different circumstances, it could have been a peaceful morning. It was cool and gray, a good morning for reading with a steamy cup of coffee, and instead here she was, wishing she was anywhere but at home, trying to stay upright, steady and patient in the face of Leslie's invasion.

When Maggie returned with the paper her house smelled terrible and she could hear Leslie spraying something in the bathroom. It was a cloying smell like a mixture of glue and cheap perfume. Maggie ran to open the kitchen window just as Leslie emerged from the bathroom, every blonde hair in place, her make-up perfect and polished and dressed in a fine-gauge pearl gray cashmere sweater and khaki twill slacks.

"What are you doing?" Leslie grabbed Olivier and scooped him up.

"Opening the window. I don't know what you were spraying but it stinks."

"It's Daniel Klein Salon Hair Mist. It's an exclusive product from the Daniel Klein Salon, they have their own line and it's the best salon in LA."

"Well, with all that smog they probably don't realize how bad it smells." Maggie went to the window by the back door and opened it.

"What about Olivier?" Leslie whined.

"What about him?"

"I'm afraid he'll jump out the window when we leave and—"

"Put him in the crate—I have to air out the house." Maggie said in her best Ms. Lewis–the–Librarian voice and went to the living room to open more windows.

"Too bad you don't have screens," Leslie said, as she took the cat to the crate in the guest room.

"I don't need them. It's quite common in the Northwest for people not to have screens, believe it or not." Maggie opened the window next to the front door.

Olivier began his awful moaning meow as soon as Leslie put him in the crate. "Well, I'm certainly going to have screens on my house." Leslie called from the guest room. She hurried to the living room, where Maggie was opening the last of the windows. "We should go. Let's hurry and leave now. I think he'll settle down when he realizes we've gone."

"Fine."

I was ready forty-five minutes ago, but you had to spend all that time in the bathroom as if you were getting ready for a photo shoot. And I don't want to see your dumb house anyway, was what Maggie thought as she wondered again how it was that she had ended up doing things she didn't want to do. Like taking care of Walter's dog and having to deal with him and now schlepping over to see Leslie's house when the last thing she wanted was to have her living here. I am sixty-five years old and she's fifty-five…isn't it time I get myself free? And what is retirement for, if it doesn't mean some kind of freedom?

Sondra Wiggins was in her yard as Maggie and Leslie came down Hormann Road. "Well, hello ladies!" she called, waving from the corner of her garden. "Is the rumor I hear about you true?" Sondra came over and stood next to the fence. Underneath her large-brimmed straw hat, her thin, auburn hair was tied back in a pony tail, and she smelled of Hawaiian Tropic sunscreen. She had a neat, trim figure and when she wasn't in her garden, Sondra was either playing golf or exercising with Greg Lovekin, her personal trainer. Sondra squinted and peered at Leslie. "Is this your sister, Maggie? Really? You don't look anything alike."

Right. Because I'm a peasant and she's a princess. Maggie tried to keep from snarling. Sondra's remark was one she'd heard most of her life and it never failed to piss her off. She curtly introduced Leslie, who smiled, and always the charmer, immediately said, "What a gorgeous garden! Those roses are not to be believed!"

"Thank you, and yes, they are doing wonderfully. They're David Austin and our designer really got us the most sensational varieties. We had the garden done by Terrance Plimkin-Jones, but I'm a little annoyed that he's not here with the tour coming up. He's out of the country, in England touring gardens. He's from London originally, and I can understand that he likes to go back, but I just wish he could have picked a better time with the tour and all. You've probably heard we're on the tour this year. Well, the storm destroyed some of our trees and the limbs crushed some of the Portuguese Laurel hedge and the Nelly Moser clematis had been winding through it and now there's quite a bare spot. I'm trying to add a few more plants to block out the bare spots or maybe move the day lilies with their brilliant color. I think eyes would naturally focus on them and away from the problem with the hedge." Sondra sighed and looked over the garden. "I just see the flaws right now and I keep calling and emailing Terrance and he hasn't gotten back to me."

"Well, it looks perfect to me," Leslie said encouragingly. "And I'd love to have the contact information for your designer. We're going to be neighbors soon and—"

"So, the rumor is true, is it?" Sondra raised her eyebrows.

"Yes, I've bought the Coghlan place and I'll be moving to the island and of course, I'll be landscaping. I want to begin on the landscape right away while there's still good weather. And I really would love to get in touch with your designer—you said it was Terrance something?"

"Yes, well I think he's much too busy and won't be taking on new clients for a while," Sondra said quickly.

Maggie saw that one coming. Sondra wouldn't even give Martha Jane a recipe, so there was no way she'd want Leslie to use her landscape architect. Vashon Island was a small pond and Sondra Wiggins intended to be the biggest fish possible. The talk was that Sondra and Carl had spent close to seventy-five thousand dollars on the garden. Maggie had to admit that with its sylvan setting—the lovely water feature, the elegant stone bench nestled in front of the towering firs and the rose garden—it was indeed stunning. Maggie watched Sondra scrutinizing Leslie, taking measure of her clothes, shoes, make-up, hair and trainer-toned body while they discussed the design of her garden and knew she'd see Leslie as competition.

"It will be lovely to have someone in that house," Sondra smiled. "It was so unfortunate the bank had to foreclose on the Coghlans. I suppose they practically had to give it away and you got a marvelous price?"

Why bother asking? Maggie wondered. Everyone would know soon enough what Leslie paid for the place. People always did. It was a matter of public record. All they had to do was go on the King County website and then news traveled fast. Maybe Sondra didn't want to wait until it was on the website and just wanted to be the first to know.

"We better get going." Maggie looked at her watch.

"Nice meeting you." Leslie gave her friendly little wave.

They continued walking on Hormann Road, Maggie moving quickly, taking long strides, wanting to get this house viewing over with, while Leslie, a head shorter, scurried to keep up. When they were out of earshot, Leslie said, "What a nice woman. I loved that garden and I'm sure she'll be a lovely neighbor to have."

If this thing went through and Leslie actually lived here she would have to come to her own conclusions about people. There was no way Maggie was going to tell her that the Wigginses weren't her favorites on the island. It wasn't just Sondra's constant complaints about Howie and Mark's chickens and the business with the hedge, and how irritating it was to have Carl try to impress everyone by broadcasting how much he spent for things. It went much farther back to when Carl Wiggins' son Sean, Sondra's stepson, was in high school. There was a rash of petty thefts from the farm stands all over the island and several times Sean Wiggins' silver Porsche had been seen at odd hours near some of the farm stands. Frank Glidden and Bill Overson, two guys on Orca Drive who had a small organic farm, also raised chickens and sold the eggs and had been having their eggs stolen. The farm and flower stands and the eggs on the island all were handled on an honor system with a locked cash box with a slot for money, and for the most part people were honest. But not that summer. Frank and Bill were tired of getting their eggs stolen and they staked out the area near the road where they kept their cooler with the eggs. Frank had a brother-in-law who worked in some electronics store and he fixed them up with a mini infrared video camera. The egg stealer turned out to be Sean Wiggins. Wealthy, preppie Sean Wiggins who went to a boarding school off-island. Carl got a lawyer and Sean got off with some community service, and Carl and Sondra thought it was rather amusing and called it kid stuff. And Sean Wiggins turned out just the way Sondra and Carl had hoped; after he graduated from Yale he got an MBA from Wharton and went on to New York, where he became an investment banker on Wall Street.

"Now don't judge it right now," Leslie said as they arrived at the house. "The land itself is just terrible but it's the first thing I'm going to tackle. I guess the Coghlans kept firing the real estate people when the house didn't sell and then after a while, they'd gone through everyone on the island and then got Betty Sue, who's from Seattle. And Betty Sue explained that with all those different realtors the yard just wasn't kept up."

"It's a jungle." Maggie looked over the tall grass and the blackberry bushes that were snarling everywhere and wondered if there'd ever been a yard. There were vines smothering the cedar and firs on the edge of the property and huge ferns in the middle of every kind of weed known in the Pacific Northwest. It looked a lot like the brush she'd climbed through between her property and Walter's. "I don't think we should walk anywhere in the yard, Les," Maggie said tersely, suddenly feeling her rash itch all up and down her legs.

"Why not? The path is cut back pretty well. Let's just take a tour around and I'll show you where I want to put the pool."

"I'm not going. I don't want to run into any poison oak."

"I'm sure there's not...I mean, Betty Sue would never have—"

"Look, I've got to get back, I need to put more cream on this rash so—"

"Okay, okay. We'll skip the yard and just go in the house and I can show you from the deck."

The house was very contemporary and stylish. The exterior siding was made from stone and cedar and there was lots of glass: huge windows with dove gray trim. Betty Sue had left a key under the mat for Leslie and she unlocked the front door and flung it open. "Ta-da!"

This was the second "ta-da" she'd trilled in two days and Maggie had yet to get into the spirit of it. She followed Leslie into the house, which Betty Sue had staged here and there with expensive tan leather furniture, a tall ficus tree, and smoky purple-gray glass end tables. A painting over the fireplace looked like one of Anne Kuroda Duppstadt's. She was a friend of Martha Jane's, who had also studied with Fred Weiss on the island. and her work was now getting international recognition. You had to hand it to this Betty Sue person, Maggie thought. With the white walls and pale oak floors, the custom fir cabinets and slate entry, the whole effect was like something out of *Architectural Digest*. The interior had a very LA feel to it and it was very not-Vashon. No wonder Leslie could picture herself here.

"Well, what do you think?" Leslie cocked her head. Her eyes were huge and Maggie thought she seemed to be almost wiggling, like a puppy eager for attention.

"Very nice."

"Nice. Is that all? I mean, come on—it's more than nice, I mean it's really beautiful don't you think?"

"It's beautiful. Of course, it's beautiful and I don't see what it needs. What would you remodel here?"

"Maybe not exactly remodel, but I might add an entertainment center and then I think I'll be turning one of the bedrooms into a gym. I don't think it will take much. It really is ready for me to move into right away. But the yard has to be worked on immediately—I guess the recession hit the Coghlans right after they'd built it. They'd torn down an old cabin that was here, built the house and then ran out of money so they couldn't landscape and then of course, they weren't able to live here and had to sell."

"Do you ever feel like a vulture?"

"How can you say that! I'm helping the economy! Think of all the workers I'll hire for the landscaping and Betty Sue gets her commission, of course."

"Of course."

Leslie crossed the great room to the wall of windows facing the beach. "And it's low bank waterfront which Betty Sue says is very special. I know it's a little hard to picture with all this brush and weeds and everything, but the steps from the deck will lead to a perfectly manicured lawn. All this will be cleared and then the pool will be a salt water pool with natural rocks edging it, large boulders of different sizes and shapes so it will look like it's always been here."

"I just hope you've checked into the water situation," Maggie said and then saw Leslie roll her eyes and decided not to go there. "Okay, fine. No advice. And you're right," she continued, deciding to try to be less snarky, "if you want to get a good chunk of this cleared away before winter, it's going to take a huge crew. And I agree, there are certainly folks on the island who need work."

"Betty Sue is helping me, she has a whole list that she's going to recommend and I'm going to get the property cleared while I'm in LA, because the clearing has to be done anyway, no matter who the garden and pool designer is. Then as soon as I can, I'll interview landscape architects."

Maggie was both relieved and a little annoyed. She was glad Leslie hadn't asked her for names; she didn't want to be involved in any of this. But as she bent down and pulled up her jeans to scratch her ankle, she bristled at the thought that she'd been coming to the island for almost twenty years, and this Betty Sue person didn't even live here, what did she know?

The itching had gotten worse and when they got home the first thing Maggie did was get out of her jeans to put on more of the hydrocortisone cream. She inspected the rash and saw no sign at all of any improvement. It was just as bad as the day she gotten it, and if anything, it both looked worse and felt worse. The gunk she was plastering all over it wasn't helping and she'd simply had enough. So much for DYI health care. Time for better living through chemistry. Drugs...that's what she needed, and she went to the phone and called the clinic. While she was on hold, she could hear Leslie on her cell phone in the guest room making a flurry of calls. Arranging one thing after the other: plane reservations for a trip back to LA, her realtor in LA, a house stager in LA, movers in LA, and Betty Sue Schnitzer.

She better not ask me to take care of that cat, Maggie thought, scratching her arm. Then the nurse came on the line and after Maggie described her rash and symptoms, she was put through to appointments and given one at ten the next morning.

"Let's go out for dinner," Maggie suggested, when Leslie was through with her calls and announced she'd be leaving first thing in the morning. "I'm not up to cooking."

"Great, you know I've never been much of a cook. Leonard and I ate out most of the time and then for parties or when we had guests, I always had caterers," she paused and absently twirled her diamond ring, "I suppose Betty Sue will know some caterers on the island."

"If she doesn't know, I'm sure she'll find out," Maggie said, feeling a little more pleasant since it was definite that Leslie, who always flew first class, hadn't had any trouble getting reservations.

At The Hardware Store restaurant, Maggie ordered buttermilk fried chicken with Yukon mashed potatoes, homemade gravy and veggies. Leslie ordered a Caesar salad and then proceeded to pick out all the croutons and leave them in a pile on the side of the plate. "Too bad the island doesn't have a gourmet restaurant," Leslie lamented, taking a tiny bite of lettuce.

"This is plenty gourmet for me," Maggie said, opening her mouth wide and shoveling in a big forkful of gravy-drenched mashed potatoes. "Besides, there used to be a couple of gourmet restaurants and they never made it." Why was it, she wondered, that people could be on the island all of five minutes and would begin touting what the island needed? But she was determined to keep things pleasant, so she kept quiet and took a big bite of chicken. She liked The Hardware Store. It was in the oldest commercial building on the island, well over a hundred years old. It was even on the National Register of Historic Places. It had an espresso bar, an art gallery in the back, and called itself "the heartbeat of the island." But Maggie knew it wasn't up to the LA and New York style Leslie had been accustomed to most of her adult life. Or at least ever since she became the Perky Sweet Prune Lady—and Maggie was sure the ferry ride into Seattle for a fancy dinner would lose its charm for her sister in about a New York minute. She smiled to herself as she chewed her chicken.

It was still quite light when they got home and Maggie made decaf coffee and they took it out to the deck. Leslie babbled on about her new house and all the entertaining she planned to do. "You know, I've always been very civic-minded," she said, stroking Olivier, whose purring Maggie even found annoying.

"I didn't know that."

"Well, I have been. Everywhere I've lived I've tried to make a contribution. Usually to arts organizations and I'm sure I'll do the same here. There seems to be quite a bit going on here in the arts for such a small place."

"I suppose so." Maggie's rash had itched less when she'd had wine with dinner, but now it was bothering her again.

"I've been meaning to ask you, Maggie—" Leslie smiled sweetly. "Would it be too much trouble to take care of Olivier while I'm in LA?"

"Yes it would."

Leslie bit her lip, then sipped her coffee. "He's a good cat, Maggie...really he is," she said softly. "He's no trouble, and I won't be gone long and I just don't see why—" her voice trailed off and she looked down at the floor.

"I'm sure he'd be happier with you and he'd like another plane ride." Maggie got up from her chair and walked toward the door.

"Where are you going?" Leslie looked worried.

"Just getting more coffee." Maggie went back in the house, letting the door slam behind her. In the kitchen she opened the liquor cabinet and took down a bottle of brandy and dumped it in her coffee cup. A coffee nudge was supposed to have crème de cacao and whipped cream, she thought, stirring it a little. This would be a pared-down version, just the basic recipe. Maggie took a big swig of the coffee-flavored brandy and went back to the deck.

She sat down and sipped the brandy and watched a tugboat going north along Colvos Passage, the wide channel between the west side of the island and the Kitsap Peninsula. It was pushing a barge piled high with huge crates.

"I'll be able to watch all these boats and things, too. From my new house. I think it's so romantic and I suppose a lot of them are heading for Alaska."

"I suppose so," Maggie mumbled and sipped her brandy-coffee.

"Would you just think about it? About Olivier? Travel is very hard on little animals. It would make it so much easier for me and then I'll be able to—"

"Okay," Maggie sighed, as the warmth of the brandy mellowed her resistance.

"Okay what?"

"Okay you can leave him."

"Oh, Maggie! Thank you so much," Leslie gushed. Then she sat forward and scowled. "What's that noise?"

Maggie closed her eyes and swigged the brandy. Walter was "calling" Bill Bailey.

"*Won't you come home, Bill Bailey? Won't you come home?*" His voice boomed out over the water. Maggie gritted her teeth. Well, at least *he* must be feeling better.

"Someone's singing. A man. A man's singing somewhere." Leslie seemed quite excited. "Don't you hear him?"

"Of course." Maggie's jaw clenched, as she muttered, "It's just Walter, my neighbor. That's how he calls his dog."

"That's kind of weird."

Maggie nodded. "This is Vashon."

Leslie sat forward, listening. "But he does have a nice voice—does he do this a lot?…call his dog like this often?"

"A lot."

"What does his wife think?" Leslie asked.

"He's single."

"You know it is really quite a nice voice." Leslie smiled. "How old is he?"

"Who? Walter or Bill Bailey?"

"Who's Bill Bailey?"

"The dog."

"Oh I get it, that's why the song. Ha-ha." Leslie beamed. "How clever!"

"It gets old fast." Maggie's jaw tightened.

"So about this Walter—how old is he?"

"In his sixties at least, I think. He's kind of a hermit, actually. And can be rather unpleasant from what I've been told." Maggie abruptly stood up. "More coffee?"

"No thanks, I'm fine."

In kitchen Maggie made another basic Coffee Nudge, this time with even less coffee. There was no way she was going to tell Leslie anything about Walter. She'd find out anyway soon enough if she actually ended up living here. And then Maggie realized that the train had left the station—it wasn't going to be *if* Leslie ended up living here—but *when*. She gave her coffee another big splash of brandy. This whole ridiculous situation was really going to happen, and in the meantime here she was stuck with Olivier with no one to blame but herself. At least there was that crate. Without it, even if she was a little tipsy, she was quite sure she would never have agreed to let that whiny animal stay.

CHAPTER TWELVE

Maggie thumbed through an old issue of *Family Circle* but didn't find much that interested her. She usually brought a book whenever she went anywhere, but stuffing Olivier in the crate took longer than she expected and she'd rushed off to the clinic without one. She felt frustrated; she hadn't been able to read any of *Portrait of the Artist as a Young Man* during Leslie's visit and wanted to get back to it.

The waiting room wasn't very full and Maggie had taken a seat across from the reception desk in a row where all the chairs were empty. A white-haired couple, who looked like they were in their eighties, sat near the door to the examining rooms. Down from them at the end of their row, a mother sat with a squirmy toddler on her lap. With just these few ahead of her, Maggie thought she probably wouldn't have to wait too long

She'd never found *Family Circle* particularly stimulating and this issue was no different...*Walk the Weight off in 12 Weeks...The Best Shoes for a Walking Workout...How to Wear Short Hairstyles... Slim Down Suppers*...well, maybe that one. She turned to the page with the *Slim Down Suppers*. They certainly made the food look delicious in the pictures, but she really didn't think there was anything she'd want to make except maybe the "Chicken and Corn Chili" or the "Shrimp Stir-Fry." Although the photo of the "Plum Glazed Pork Loin" did look pretty good. Maggie thought about Howie and Mark's plum trees. In August they'd be picking the plums, maybe she'd copy the recipe for them. She took a pen and the little notebook she always carried in her bag and turned to the page in the back of the magazine where the recipe would be found only to see it had been torn out. She really, really hated that. Some people were so selfish. In the library it was absolutely one of her pet peeves: people who marked up books or tore out pages. It didn't take much for her to swing into a major rant about it. Maggie looked at her watch. They seemed to be running slower than she'd expected with so few people here. Half-heartedly, she went back to leafing through the magazine...*Walk the Weight off in 12 Weeks*...well, maybe she'd look at that. She was turning to the article when the main door from the parking lot opened and she glanced up...*Oh no*...She froze for a minute—then pretended to cough, and quickly buried herself in the walk-the-weight-off article. Maggie held her head down and the magazine up, literally burying her nose in it. Her impulse was to flee from the clinic with the magazine over her face, hoping that Walter, who was now walking toward the reception desk, hadn't seen her. At the post office she'd been able to make a quick getaway, but now she was trapped. It was poison oak all over again. She'd gotten the damn stuff trying to avoid him and now if she ran out and avoided him, she wouldn't get the medicine for it.

"Walter Hathaway," Walter gave his name to the receptionist, who asked for his insurance card and then told him to take a seat.

Maggie held the walk-the-weight-off article inches from her face. This is really stupid, she thought, I've got to remember what Martha Jane said about this. Something about Gandhi and forgiveness, the weak can't do it or something like that, only the strong, and that it would be enough to be civil. That's it. Civil. All she had to do was sit there and be civil.

"Maggie? Is that you?" Walter adjusted the sling on his arm as he turned from the receptionist desk.

Maggie put the magazine down, trying to appear casual. "Hello, Walter." Her rash itched like crazy and she wanted to whip up her pants legs to scratch her ankles and shins, but instead she sat perfectly still trying to project a little dignity.

"Mind if I sit down?" He motioned to the chair next to hers.

"There's plenty of other seats," Maggie said reasonably, giving him a fake half-smile, trying not to sound snippy. She waved her hand, gesturing to the waiting room where now, only the older couple remained. The mother and toddler had gone in to see the doctor.

"Maggie, please—"

"Shhh," she shhuusshed. A strong shhuussh that had been perfected from years in the library, and she nodded toward the receptionist and the older couple who had perked up and seemed quite interested in the two of them.

"I just wanted to—" Walter tried to lower his voice.

"Fine," she hissed, "then just sit down."

Maggie picks up the magazine and starts to pretend to read. Walter puts his good hand on her arm and leans close to her. "I'm so sorry. I don't like to make excuses, but I was loaded on pain meds that day and when you told me about Madeline I took it all out on you. It was unforgivable, but I hope you can forgive me."

Walter's face is inches from hers and Maggie's heart starts to race. What is wrong with me? she thinks. Am I mad, scared, or what? Maggie swallows, and takes a deep breath. The receptionist and the older couple look at them intently and all she wants is to get some medicine for her damn rash and get the hell out of there.

"Maggie, can you?" Walter asks, more insistent and he forgets to whisper.

"Shhh."

"Sorry," he whispers. "Can you?"

Maggie bites her lip. Her rash feels like a million mosquito bites and it's all she can do to keep from ripping at her pants legs to scratch the hell out of it. She licks her lip and takes another deep breath and says quietly, "Walter, Gandhi once said 'the weak can never forgive. Forgiveness is the attribute of the strong.'"

"So are you weak or strong?" he asks with a smile.

"You decide," she whispers.

"Strong."

"So be it." She can't help smiling but she also remembers that Martha Jane said "women forgive but never forget" and she decides that she has forgiven enough to be civil and that would be it. Maggie picks up the magazine and this time pretends to read the article about the best shoes for walking. While the words blur in front of her, she is thinking about a portrait of an artist as an old man, one whose conscience has been giving him quite a bit of trouble, which is just fine with her.

After stopping at the Vashon Pharmacy to get the prescription for prednisone filled, where she also picked up a pair of earplugs to deal with Olivier's nocturnal meowing, Maggie was eager to get home. Ever since the storm, she felt as if her life had been torpedoed. Between taking care of Bill Bailey when Walter was in the hospital, and Leslie's visit with her disturbing announcement, intense memories and the conflicts that accompanied them had sprouted like weeds whose roots she'd never been able to get rid of. Leslie said she'd be gone at least three days and Maggie had almost cheered when she left for the airport that morning. It would be a lovely little hiatus and to celebrate, after she was through at the pharmacy, Maggie stopped at Thriftway to pick up a nice little box of Fran's chocolates. Next, she stopped at the flower stand across from the Burton store, where she put $5.00 in the slot of the cash box and picked out a lovely bouquet. Over the years, Maggie had perfected the ability to give herself treats: a good book, fresh flowers, and chocolate were staples.

Olivier began his miserable meow the minute she got in the house, so she checked that the windows were shut and then let him out of his crate. Maggie cringed, thinking of how Leslie would decompensate if the cat got lost. Even though she found Olivier extremely annoying, when it came right down to it, she didn't wish the thing harm. She liked most animals and in fact, had been thinking about getting a dog now that she was retired. All the years when she was working, it hadn't seemed fair to leave a dog alone all day. And then of course, when she was married to

George, he'd claimed he was allergic to dogs. He sneezed a bit, she supposed, but she knew he had been a little afraid of them and saying he was allergic gave a more manly spin to it. Poor George. As their marriage wore on, Maggie wasn't sure if he was one of those asexual people, or just someone without much libido. Or perhaps gay and had just been born in the wrong decade. It was hard to even remember what the sex had been like—what there was of it, except kind of bland, like oatmeal—even in the early years. In fact, everything about George was bland. His father, Simon Tuller, was a prominent attorney and George was programmed to go into law, just as he was programmed to find the right sort of wife. Someone not too flashy: a responsible type, and most importantly, someone who would not be a threat to his very authoritarian mother. Maggie fit the bill perfectly and for her part of it, she had to admit, it was his very oatmealness that appealed to her. He would never have to worry about being unemployed—there would always be a job in his father's firm. His range of emotion was restricted and narrow, he wasn't unpleasant and there would be no surprises. After the angst and turmoil of life with her bipolar father and beautiful rag-doll sometimes-zombie mother, George Tuller looked pretty good.

It may have been a delayed adolescence, but whatever it was, Maggie could trace the little upheaval that ended their marriage to the death of George's mother. His father had Alzheimer's and had been living in a nursing home for two years when Marjorie Tuller died. It seemed to uncork George, because within six months, he took early retirement and left the firm. He had been involved in a huge maritime shipping case and when it settled after six years of litigation, he received a considerable chunk of money and left to pursue the one thing that was close to his heart: golf. Their marriage—a polite, passionless relationship where they were like roommates with separate lives who checked in with one another and occasionally did things together—had been dwindling for years. The death of his mother seemed to give him a little zing, some oomph to pursue what he truly cared about. When Maggie said she had no interest in moving to Carmel to satisfy his longing to be where the golf courses were bathed in sun all year, the marriage sputtered, fizzled and died.

But the divorce had thrown Maggie much more than she had anticipated it would. Not that she felt deeply injured or experienced a particularly painful loss, it was just that it discombobulated her. She felt off balance and out of whack. It was difficult to focus and get her head around the idea that she was a divorced woman, which also meant she was single.

Sometimes Maggie wondered what her life would have been like if she'd married for love instead of security, but it was hard to say she had any regrets. Her marriage had given her a wonderful daughter and although she and Becky didn't always understand each other—Becky was much more like George in terms of her temperament and constitution—she and her granddaughter had such a natural affinity that at times it astonished Maggie. So, no regrets. Without George: no Becky. And without Becky: no Ashley.

Ashley would be home from camp soon and they'd take up their weekly Skype talks again. Even though Maggie had first balked at mastering the technology that was now required of librarians, she was certainly no Luddite. The Skype machine, as she liked to call it, had brought the great joy of these wonderful weekly encounters with her precious granddaughter. They laughed themselves silly at their distorted funhouse faces and Maggie thought when they talked at the end of the week she'd even pick up Olivier to show Ashley. Skype would undoubtedly make him look quite weird and she knew Ashley would get a kick out of seeing him.

Either the prednisone had kicked in, or the calm she felt without Leslie around (or perhaps both) had a good effect on Maggie's rash. The itching seemed to stop that evening. After a light supper of some frozen lasagna that she'd popped into the microwave, a little green salad and nice glass of burgundy, Maggie settled into her reading chair. First she carefully unwrapped one of the chocolates from its gold foil. The chocolate glistened like a black sapphire and she gazed at it for a moment before opening her mouth and slowly inserting it. She savored it, hardly chewing, letting the chocolate melt, and then opened her book. She was so content that when Olivier jumped into her lap later in the evening, she slid over in her chair to accommodate him and absently stroked his back while continuing to read her book.

Two nights later when Leslie called, she could honestly tell her that he was doing fine. The earplugs had done the trick and Maggie was able to sleep in peace and woke up to feed him on her morning schedule and not his timetable. In fact, to her surprise, Maggie realized that she had adapted to having Olivier around and she hoped it was an omen, a sign that eventually she'd be able to adapt to having Leslie living nearby.

"Betty Sue has been just fantastic," Leslie gushed. "They're going to begin clearing my land this week. And you'll never guess who's going to do the work—" Then she giggled, her breathy, little girl giggle. "You'll never guess!"

"Then I guess you'll have to tell me." Maggie held the phone to her ear with her shoulder and unwrapped another piece of chocolate.

"Goats!" Leslie giggled with glee.

"Goats? Oh you must mean Rent-a-Ruminant. They've been in business for quite a while. I think they have over a hundred goats now and they clear land by eating ivy, blackberries and all kinds of invasive species like—"

"Well, it's not them," she said, somewhat deflated. "Betty Sue tried them but they're booked so she found a brand new vegetation management company on Orcas Island and they'll be coming over with sixty goats. She says the guy who started the business is a very enterprising young man. Want to know what it's called?" she asked, perking up.

"Sure."

"'Got Goat.' Isn't that the cutest thing?"

"Very cute."

"And it's only going to take them about three days, they'll be spending the night and Betty Sue says they'll be coming in a forty-foot goat trailer. I just think it's so exciting. I only wish I could be there to see the whole thing, but I have to stay down here. Leonard doesn't agree on the price for the house and the lawyers are talking—"

"Leonard?"

"Leonard—my soon to be ex-husband—"

"Oh, right. Leonard."

"And his lawyer is on vacation, so it's going to be at least another week or more before I can come back. I gave Betty Sue your name in case anything comes up, hope that's all right."

Maggie stuffed the chocolate in her mouth and immediately unwrapped another piece.

"Maggie?"

"What?"

"I was sure it'd be all right when Betty Sue mentioned it."

"Fine. Whatever." She actually didn't mind all that much; this Betty Sue person probably wouldn't need anything since she was in contact with Leslie all the time. Besides, having more time without Leslie had great appeal. The cat even seemed less intrusive and needy, especially early in the morning thanks to the earplugs.

In the days that followed Maggie took her kayak out first thing every morning not long after sunrise. She paddled close to the shore where she could manage the currents and after she got beyond Baker's Beach she fell into an easy rhythm. There were times it became almost meditative with the strokes slicing the sea, as if her arms and the paddle were connected to each other but detached from her will and conscious mind. She treasured those mornings with an exquisite regard for them driven by the knowledge that they weren't going to last. Not only because soon her sister would arrive, but because summer would end. Fall would arrive and with it the blank slate of her life without Evergreen Elementary. Maggie had deliberately put off making any plans; she'd wanted the summer to unfold as a time to contemplate and give careful thought to what she would do with the rest of her life. Her desk was piled with pamphlets about the Peace Corps, Senior Adventure Travel, Habitat for Humanity, and Elder University.

She often envied Martha Jane with her passion for art, and even Sondra Wiggins with her love of gardening. Maggie had no clear idea of what she wanted to do beyond see Becky—and especially Ashley—when she could, and spend time with her friends. At the moment, the only thing she was sure she wanted to do was savor life on the island, knowing she didn't have to leave. But Maggie also knew that as the months went by, she'd need to be involved in something that would give her a sense of purpose, something to commit to beyond her weekly Skype visits with Ashley. They were wonderful, but they wouldn't be enough.

For the first time since her father died, Maggie didn't have responsibility for other people. She'd had almost fifty years of having to be someplace at a certain time: at home for Leslie, at home for Becky and George, at Evergreen for her work. Now with retirement, the freedom and the lack of structure in her life felt a little confusing. Hard to comprehend, really. Maggie was well versed in many homilies about using time...*in life there aren't any dress rehearsals...it is the first day of the rest of your life...we have only this moment, sparkling like a star in our hand and melting like a snowflake—let us use it before it is too late*...All very nice. She indeed knew she wasn't going to live forever. No one gets out of this life alive. Of course, she knew that. And she certainly wanted to make the most of whatever time she'd have left on this planet. That wasn't the problem: it was just how to best do it that sometimes left her feeling muddled.

CHAPTER THIRTEEN

Maggie was awakened by a high-pitched, wailing noise that sounded almost like a scream. Groggily, she sat up. *Portrait of the Artist as a Young Man* lay face down on the bed with her reading glasses on top of it. The gray light of dawn filtered through the curtains and with her heart racing, she scrambled out from under the covers and swung her legs over the side of the bed. Hurrying through the house, she was fearful that the sound could be coming from Olivier. She'd left a window open. He'd gotten out. He'd been attacked by a vicious raccoon. But when she got to the living room, Olivier was sitting quietly on the windowsill, peering out at the yard. Still feeling fuzzy, she realized she hadn't taken the earplugs out. She pulled them out of one ear, then the other, and immediately recognized that the sound she was hearing was an actual siren.

Oh no...Martha Jane. Maggie knew there would be a time when it would come. Her dear friend was in her nineties and it was inevitable that she would lose her one of these days. One of these days. But not this day...not now, please...*not now*. Maggie ran back to the bedroom and grabbed her jeans and shirt where she had left them on the chair. She dressed quickly and tore out of the house, running toward the siren, which sounded like it was coming along Hormann Road heading in the direction of Baker's Beach. As she ran across her yard, she saw Howie and Mark running from their house and just as she got to them, Martha Jane appeared on her deck in her old blue bathrobe, carrying Maria Montessori and looking perfectly healthy.

Howie and Mark saw Martha Jane at the same time and the three of them just fell into each other, both laughing and crying. "You thought the same thing—" Howie wiped his eyes and then hugged Maggie tightly, who reached for Mark and the three of them huddled in front of Howie and Mark's front porch, clinging to each other in a hug worthy of any Esalen encounter group.

"Yoo-hoo!" Martha Jane waved to them. "I'm not dressed yet—can you go over to Hormann Road and tell me what's going on? It sounds like the Medics and I just hope no one's hurt over there."

"We're on our way," Mark called to Martha Jane and the three of them trooped past her house heading for Hormann Road. By the time they came to the end of the path behind Martha Jane's house, the siren had stopped and they could see then that it wasn't the Medics. A King County Police car was parked in front of the Wiggins' house and they heard Sondra Wiggins shrieking incoherently and Jordan gleefully yelling "Yippee-kai-yah! Yippee-kai-yoo!" They couldn't see what was going on because of the tall hedge that screened the Wiggins' yard. Next to the path there was a small hill covered with firs and cedar trees. Howie pointed to it and Maggie and Mark nodded. With Howie in the lead, followed by Maggie, then Mark, they traipsed up the hill. At the top, they stood behind the trees where they had a perfect view down into the yard.

To their amazement they saw a large herd of goats—at least fifty or more—quietly and contentedly munching and grazing, all helping themselves to the splendid smorgasbord of Sondra Wiggins' spectacular garden.

"Karmic retribution?" Howie whispered.

"Oh my!" Maggie peered around a tree and watched Jordan, who was wearing green-striped pajamas, arms flailing, grinning and whooping, trying to chase the goats, who paid him no more attention than if he were a little fly buzzing about. Frozen in the middle of yard, unable to move and wearing a red tee shirt with white letters that said "Got Goat" was a tall, terrified young man who looked like he was in his early twenties. Sondra stood in a mauve satin nightgown in the middle of the David Austin rose garden continuing to shriek incoherently, and Carl, with his considerable belly bulging over the top of his orange and brown plaid boxer shorts, was bellowing at the sheriff, who seemed more than a little annoyed. "No one died here, mister," he snarled. This is not a life-threatening emergency or any kind of injury to a person, and yes, I can see that you have some property damage, however—"

"God dammit, then if you're not going to do anything about this, you better believe I am! I'm going to sue the little bastard!" Carl, looking like a rhinoceros about to charge, turned on the young man. "You! You stupid sonofabitch, you'll be sorry you ever set foot on this island!"

"Set hoof," Maggie whispered.

"I wish I had popcorn," Mark added.

"Too bad we didn't bring lawn chairs and a cooler," Howie whispered. "Maybe we should place bets on which one will be the last goat standing."

"I think the ones with the floppy ears are really adorable. I wish I had my camera, I'd love to have pictures to show Ashley." Maggie looked back toward Martha Jane's house. "Maybe I better go tell Martha Jane, I'm sure she's worried that someone's really been hurt."

Jordan had stopped running around wildly after the goats and was now approaching them more purposefully. He snuck up behind a black and white goat with eyes like blue marbles that was calmly eating the ornamental poppies. Jordan happened to glance up the hill and when he saw Maggie, Howie and Mark peering through the trees, he waved.

"Hi, Mrs. Lewis," he called. "Pretty exciting, huh?" He left the goat eating the poppies and trotted over to the hill to tell them what had happened.

"Last night the Got Goat guy forgot to plug in the electric fence that he put all around the Coghlan's yard where the goats were and they ate through the fence and moved over to Grandpa Carl and Grandma Sondra's garden," Jordan explained, quite pleased to be able to give them the report.

"But isn't your grandparents' yard fenced, to keep out the deer?" Mark asked. "Wouldn't that keep out goats?"

"Oh sure, the yard has this fence and a huge hedge all around it to kind of disguise the fence. Grandma Sondra doesn't like the yard to look like it's fenced—even though it really is, and the goats just ate a hole in it. The only thing that keeps them out is an electric fence," he explained, enjoying imparting his knowledge. "The goats were all very quiet and we didn't even know they were in the yard until Grandpa Carl got up. He had an early golf game and he was brushing his teeth and he looked out the bathroom window and the garden was full of goats."

"Quite a lot of goats," Maggie said, looking at what was left of the garden.

"There's almost sixty and almost all of them left the yard next door where they were supposed to be eating the blackberries and weeds."

"I imagine your grandparents' garden was tastier," Maggie said.

"Probably like being stuck eating Spam and then you look over and see roast duck and fingerling potatoes—" Howie said.

"With green beans almandine, and maybe chocolate gelato for desert—" Mark chimed in.

"Or a beautiful cheese tray with lovely fresh grapes," Maggie added.

"Right. The weeds next door wouldn't look so hot—I'd say kind of like leaving school cafeteria food for Burger King," Jordan agreed.

"But I do wonder why it is that thorns and metal wire and things like that don't bother them?" Maggie asked, "maybe we should look that up sometime, Jordan."

"Sure. I'll google 'goat.'"

Carl Wiggins saw Jordan talking to Maggie and spun around from the sheriff to glare at her. "You tell that sister of yours that she better get a lawyer—how the hell could she hire this idiot, who doesn't know his ass from a hole in the ground! You better believe she's responsible for this!"

Howie put his arm around Maggie. "We'll go back to Martha Jane's with you."

"Right. Don't even talk to Wiggins," Mark whispered, "the guy has guns and I'm surprised he hasn't started shooting the goats. He could get really crazy."

"I don't think he would with Jordan there," Maggie said, "but you're right, I think we'd better be going."

Martha Jane was relieved to hear that no one was hurt but she felt very sorry for Sondra Wiggins. "It was so important to her being on that tour, she must be devastated." Martha Jane stroked Maria Montessori. "I'm sure it's some kind of lesson not to get too attached to things, too attached to the outcome. It will be hard for Sondra to keep in mind the pleasure she had creating the garden, the joy of the journey. Maggie what was the poster in someone's room at Evergreen? About failure?"

Maggie smiled. "Gretchen's fifth grade room, 'Failure is an opportunity to begin again.'"

"Yes, that was it. But I don't suppose that would mean anything to Sondra right now."

Howie rolled his eyes. "Hardly."

Mark put his hand on Howie's arm. "I need coffee. This was not how I planned to start the day."

"I just put on a fresh pot, would you like to come in?" Martha Jane asked.

Howie shook his head. "We've got chickens to feed, but thanks. We'll see you later."

"I'll take you up on it," Maggie said. "I'll have to call Leslie and this Betty Sue person and I'm not quite ready to deal with them."

Maggie followed Martha Jane into her house. She thought about Olivier waiting back at her house, wanting food. Well, it won't kill him to wait just a bit. He won't starve, she told herself, trying not to feel guilty.

"Help yourself in the kitchen, Maggie. There's cream and milk in the fridge and sugar on the counter next to the coffee pot. I'll be on the deck."

Maggie got her coffee and sat across from Martha Jane, whose blue terrycloth bathrobe had spots of food and little shredded patches where it looked like Maria Montessori had been kneading with her claws.

"This is not how I imagined my summer, I have to say." Maggie sipped her coffee. She looked out at the water where small waves brushed the shore as the tide slowly came in.

"Not quite like the phrase from one of the Shakespeare sonnets...now what is it...it's a phrase I loved so much—" Martha Jane paused, and pursed her lips, then sighed. "You know I do try to accept that there are things I don't remember, but it's a frustration."

"You remember what's important."

"I don't know about that some days."

"You remember how to love." Maggie looked at her friend with tenderness.

Martha Jane reached for Maggie and patted her hand. "You're a dear. Thank you for that." Then she smiled. "I remember now, it's 'summer's honey breath'...the phrase from the sonnet. Beautiful isn't it...'summer's honey breath.'"

Maggie nodded. "So far it's been summer's halitosis for me. I can't believe my sister has already made a mess and she hasn't even moved here yet. And Carl wasn't kidding, he's the type that will sue and Leslie will be a wreck."

"And you'll have to pick up the pieces, I suppose." Martha Jane reached for her coffee cup and held it with both hands.

"Without a doubt," Maggie muttered gloomily. "It's so different from what I'd imagined all last year as my work at Evergreen came to a close. I looked to this summer as a time for me to be quiet and just live in this place. I haven't wanted to hurry a decision about what to do next, but to just let the possibilities unfold and give myself the summer or even longer if I needed it for a decision to ripen." Maggie looked away from the shore and turned to her friend. "How do you do it?"

"Do what, dear?"

"Be old. How do you be old?"

"Every day I wake at dawn to watch the sun rise. I wait like a child to see what nature will offer. Then I have a lovely breakfast with eggs from Howie and Mark's chickens and toast with Margaret Buckman's jam...do you know her? She lives on Maury Island and grows wonderful strawberries and blueberries and the jam is just out of this world. I'll ask her for a jar for you the next time I see her."

"And then what?"

"And what, dear?"

"About being old."

"Oh, well, I try to do each thing with absolute concentration. So I won't get discombobulated. After breakfast I sit quietly with Maria Montessori. She eats when I do and I think about this world and my gratitude for it. Then I'm off to Fred Weiss's studio to work at my painting, and then home for a nap, and then often I see friends for dinner and then in the evening there's music and reading. You see, I think my existence is much like my cat's. Maria Montessori doesn't have to do anything. She doesn't even get the mice anymore, which is fine. Just her company gives me pleasure and comfort. My friends and family tell me they enjoy the pleasure of my company and I suppose that connection is enough of a purpose for me now. So I see myself like her—just an old cat that doesn't catch mice anymore, and that will have to do.

"But of course, I didn't always feel this way. I used to see my worth mainly through what I accomplished for other people. I think being a teacher and being useful to my students was the strongest part of my idea of who I was. It took me a long time to understand that just being with someone and making a connection was doing something." Martha Jane paused. Then she put her hand on Maggie's arm. "Now don't get me wrong, Maggie dear. I'm not indifferent to the pain and suffering in this world, on the contrary, sometimes it feels as though my heart will break.

But in terms of doing much about it, I've accepted my mediocrity, my very ordinariness and it took a bit of doing because it's not a popular concept in our culture. I wasn't endowed with heroic attributes, to lead the fight for great social change. I've only done my little bit, I hope to love the part of the world that touches me and beyond that, well, it's things like contributing a small check to the Red Cross and other things like that," she said quietly, closing her eyes for a minute. "Oh, and I sign petitions and that sort of thing." Then she looked again at Maggie. "But mostly, it all comes down to trying to be a good neighbor. I've had a small life if measured in how one impacts the world, but it couldn't have been larger in joy and appreciation. I'd say that old age is our final flowering and what direction the flowering takes will reflect what has always been the essence of each person."

It had been good to talk with Martha Jane and Maggie was eager to take a long walk to think about her friend's observations on growing old. She wanted to think about what she'd said about making human connections being enough of a purpose. She could see that when it came to Martha Jane, but wasn't so sure it could be true for her. But first she'd better feed Olivier and call Leslie and get that over with. And then Leslie herself could call Betty Sue. Maggie wanted to have as little to do with this galloping goat fiasco as possible

Leslie answered her cell on the first ring. "Maggie, is everything all right? Oh no…it must be Olivier—something's happened to him!"

Maggie realized she never called Leslie just to chat, so she'd quite rightly jumped to the conclusion that all was not well. "It's not Olivier, Leslie, calm down. It's goats."

"Goats? What goats?"

"The goats that you hired to clear your yard."

Leslie let out a deep sigh. "Oh well, thank God it's not Olivier. What about the goats?"

"They got out and ate the neighbors' garden."

"You don't mean the lady we met who had those beautiful roses and everything?" Leslie asked, with a note of alarm.

"Sondra Wiggins. They destroyed her garden."

"That's terrible!" Leslie said with a gasp. "Oh, what a shame!" Then she paused. "That Got Goat guy should replace everything of course—"

"He's going to sue you."

"Why should the goat guy sue me, I didn't let the goats out."

"Not him. Carl. Carl Wiggins is going to sue you."

"Oh Maggie...this is awful." Leslie's voice cracked as she sniffled and began to cry. "I don't know what to do, what should I do?"

"Get a lawyer," Maggie said, thinking about Sondra Wiggins bleating and shrieking and now Leslie coming undone. What a mess.

"Oh, yes, of course, well, I'll ask Eli, my lawyer here, for the name of someone who handles this sort of thing and they can send someone up," Leslie said, sniffling.

Maggie took a deep breath. "Leslie, I want to give you some advice."

"Yes, please. I know I can count on you."

"Don't get some out-of-town big shot lawyer. I just don't think it would sit well with the local judge, if this thing can't get settled out of court. And I think you're a lot better off if you can find someone on the island."

"Oh, I see," she said, her little-girl voice breathy as she perked up a bit. "Yes, I can see that makes sense. I'll ask Betty Sue for the name of a lawyer—." Then she paused for a minute. "Of course, maybe that's not the best idea since she found the goat guy and that didn't turn out so well. Can you find someone for me, Maggie?"

Maggie looked at Olivier happily eating his Fancy Feast Tuna. "Oh, I'm sure you can find someone. I know how resourceful you can be."

CHAPTER FOURTEEN

The following Wednesday morning when Maggie went out to the road to get the paper, she opened the *Beachcomber* to be greeted by the headline: *GOATS GOT PREMIER GARDEN*. Maggie sighed and shook her head in disgust. Oh great, Leslie's in the news. Notorious already. Her sister's life had always seemed to Maggie to be something of an Italian opera, but she had never expected the latest act to open on Vashon. And so soon. Maggie heaved another great sigh, then took the paper in the house, got her glasses, poured a cup of coffee and sat down to read all the gory details. The story quoted both Carl and Sondra Wiggins, Betty Sue Schnitzer and the King County Deputy Sheriff. But Ernie Olson, the owner of Got Goat, had not responded to the *Beachcomber*'s repeated efforts to contact him and the story reported that the Got Goat phone had been disconnected. Betty Sue Schnitzer told the paper that she had arranged for Got Goat to clear the property on Hormann Road on behalf of Leslie Lewis of Los Angeles, who had recently purchased the prime waterfront home and would be moving to the island later next month.

Later? *Never* would be a lot better. Maggie threw the paper down on the kitchen table. It wasn't surprising the goat incident had made the paper, after all the Sheriff had been called. She only wished there had been more news on the island last week so the story might have just been a little item in the Sheriff's Report. The report regularly appeared on one of the back pages of the paper, listing all the incidents when the King County Sheriff's office on the island had been called. But it wasn't unusual for this sort of thing to make the front page. Maggie remembered a big brouhaha awhile back when otters were getting into a boat on Sylvan Beach and the owner of the boat hired a trapper who shot them. The paper reported that People for the Ethical Treatment of Animals, PETA, based in Virginia, had been contacted about the killing of the otters. Maggie picked up the paper, folded it, and carried it out to the recycle. Well, at least Carl Wiggins hadn't shot the goats. Maggie didn't want to begin to imagine how big this thing could have gotten then.

She'd set aside the day for chores: changing the sheets, new litter in the box for Olivier, emptying the wastebaskets, taking the recycle and the trash to the dump, and doing the laundry. In the afternoon she picked up the mail at the post office and went to Thriftway to get food for dinner. She had planned to just get something from the deli, but they had some beautiful king salmon on sale and she snapped it up, then got a few ears of Yakima corn and the first of the local heirloom tomatoes. Beautiful. She had some lovely greens Howie and Mark had given her from their garden. She'd have a fresh, crisp salad, and with a nice glass of white wine—she thought she had a bottle of pinot gris open—it would be a perfect summer dinner. Oh yes, and a few chocolates for dessert.

To her surprise, Maggie was beginning to enjoy cooking for herself. She'd had to do all of it when her mother became so despondent after the death of her father, and it set the foundation for the way she'd experienced cooking throughout her life: a burden. A big pain in the butt. Having to cook was always associated with having to be the adult. With not having any mothering, and it always made her feel alone. There was sadness attached to it, and anger as well. But with all the organic farms on the island, fresh vegetables and fruit were bountiful. The wonderful local food was an inspiration and without any kind of conscious resolve, she found herself more and more often wanting to create a nice, simple little dinner for herself.

Maggie fed Olivier, then put on the Chamber Orchestra of Europe's recording of Rossini's *The Barber of Seville* with Kathleen Battle and Placido Domingo. The overture alone was so cheerful and charming, it always lifted her spirits. She hummed to the music as she grilled the salmon, sliced the tomatoes and tossed the salad. The corn only took a few minutes to boil and when it was ready, she slathered an ear with butter and took her plate and the wine to her table on the little terrace near the path to the beach. Heaven.

It was a lovely evening. The light purple blue of the water reminded her of the first buds of lavender and she decided to take a walk after dinner to see the sunset from the beach. Then when she got back, she'd put decaf coffee on and settle into the evening with her book. Her book and a chocolate. Or two...or three.

Maggie checked the tide book to make sure she wouldn't get stuck against the bank if the tide was on its way in and saw it was several hours before high tide. The beach would be narrow, but if she headed home just after sunset she wouldn't have a problem. She grabbed a sweater and as she slipped her arms in the sleeves, she realized that she hardly thought about her rash anymore. Thanks to the prednisone, it had almost completely cleared up. A relief in more ways than one: the rash had been a constant reminder of what a fool she'd been to go through the forest to avoid both Leslie and Walter: something she was very glad not to remember with each itch.

Maggie had several sturdy driftwood sticks that she kept near her boathouse. The beach was rocky and if the tide had just gone out, the wet rocks could be covered in slimy green seaweed and it was easy to slip. But even if the rocks weren't all that wet, you had to be careful not to twist an ankle. Maggie picked up one of her walking sticks and headed north from Baker's Beach where she could have the best view of the sun setting behind the Olympics.

It was a quiet evening and as she made her way along the rocky beach, the color of the water changed minute by minute. Light and dark blue, lavender with streaks of pink, the sea in Colvos

Passage mirrored banks of clouds in every shade of pink. Closer to the setting sun, some were edged in crimson. Against the sky, the Olympic Mountains with their jagged edges were deep purple and Maggie decided that when she got to Peter Point, she'd sit and watch the sun as it sank behind the mountains.

When she got to the point, she spotted the perfect log back against the bank. At least four feet in diameter, it was a soft silver gray and had another smaller piece of driftwood lodged behind it, making a wonderful natural bench with a backrest. Perfect. Perfect...except for what she saw next which completely ruined it. At the end of this lovely half-moon of beach, Maggie spotted someone whose presence was guaranteed to spoil the whole sunset: Walter. He and Bill Bailey were about 30 yards north of her at the water's edge. He had his back to her but she could see that his arm was still in the sling. With his free hand he threw a stick for Bill, who charged into the water, quickly retrieved it and swam back to Walter, where he dropped it at his feet. Then Bill began barking, while he jumped and leaped all around Walter, eager for him to throw it again.

Why does *he* have to be here? Maggie bristled. Why come all the way up here where there's the best view of the mountains just to throw a stick? Why can't he throw the stick for the dog in front of his own house? The last thing she wanted was to have some pathetically stiff little conversation with him. Running into him at the doctor's office had been quite enough, and Maggie's first impulse was to turn and go back home. Walter was focused on Bill and with all that barking and jumping around, she could just leave without him ever seeing her.

She stood with her arms folded across her chest, glaring at Walter's backside, and started to turn around and head toward home. Then she stopped, gritting her teeth. *Dammit. Why should I let him ruin the sunset for me?* It was such a beautiful evening and she'd looked forward all during her lovely dinner to seeing the sun set behind the mountains. Why let Walter Hathaway deprive her of this pleasure? Besides, the sun would be setting behind the mountains in just a few minutes and she could watch it and then leave without Walter ever knowing she'd been there.

Maggie walked carefully to the log and quietly sat down. Everything was pink, lavender, purple and silver, with the trees across the water on the Kitsap Peninsula the deepest green, almost black. It was quiet when Bill was swimming for the stick, although as soon as he'd retrieved it and came back to shore, the jumping and barking started up again. It was certainly not as peaceful and meditative as she'd envisioned, but she was determined not to leave until the sun set. She would block out Walter and Bill Bailey and be mindful only of the exquisite picture in front of her eyes.

A rhythm developed of quiet, as Bill swam out for the stick and swam back, followed by barking, while he waited on shore for Walter to throw the stick again. Walter was throwing the stick about the same distance each time, so the stretches of quiet and the intervals of barking had developed into a predictable pattern. Without realizing it, Maggie was tuning into this rhythm. When it changed and the quiet lasted much longer...too long...she looked for Bill Bailey and saw him out in the water where he seemed to be stuck. Bill was paddling in place and not making any headway. His paws moved furiously but he went nowhere as if he were on some underwater treadmill. His head bobbed, he seemed frantic and Maggie saw Walter shout to Bill and start into the water.

As if in a dream she is off the log and within seconds in front of Bill where she runs into the water. The shock of cold numbs her but she is oblivious to it and she half swims, half walks, churning through the icy water until it drops off suddenly and she swims several yards toward Bill and grabs his collar. He is entangled in a piece of fishing net, enmeshed in the middle of a kelp bed and both the net and the long rubbery ribbons are wrapped around his legs. She swims, pulling him, dragging kelp until her feet touch bottom and she half swims, crawls and climbs up the sharp drop-off, holding Bill with one hand until she stumbles on the shore. Her sneakers feel like blocks of ice and her wet clothes are leaden, sopping with freezing salt water. Walter kneels next to her and puts his arm around her. He holds her, wet and shaking against him, as Bill shakes water everywhere and licks her face.

"Maggie—" Walter lays his cheek against her forehead and then smoothes her wet hair. "Put this on." He tries to take off his jacket and struggles one-handed to get it off. "Christ, I hate this friggin' sling—"

"Don't worry," she says, gasping for breath. "I—I just need to get home to a fire."

"Can you stand? Let me help you." He pulls her up with his free hand and she leans against him.

"I guess I'm a little wobbly," she says through chattering teeth.

"We're going to my house. Come on." He holds her around her waist and slowly they make their way along the shore.

Bill Bailey trots ahead—he is panting and every few minutes he looks back to make sure Walter and Maggie are there. They walk slowly—she is exhausted and freezing. The sun has disappeared and Maggie shudders in the night air. Her mind feels as damp and wet as her heavy clothes and she's a little dazed. Her shoes squish with water with each step and Walter walks carefully, sure-footed in his hiking boots as they move across the rocks.

"We're almost there," Walter says minutes later as they round a bend. He nods toward his cabin, which sits nestled against the forest at the edge of Baker's Beach. The lights from the front window give out an amber glow in the evening sky. Bill Bailey runs ahead of them, bounding along the path and up to the front porch, where he turns and looks back at them. He is panting heavily, and still wet, again he shakes the water off his coat.

Walter turns toward the path to his house and she stops and points south toward her house. "Really, I can make it—"

"Bullshit. You're coming with me." He holds her firmly with his free hand and she doesn't have the energy to resist.

In the house, Walter took her straight to the bathroom and turned on the shower. "Let it be just lukewarm at first, then as you get used to it, make it hotter and hotter. It will be too much of a shock if it starts out hot. I'll get some clean towels and you can wear my sweats—I think I have some that aren't too raunchy." He left her in the bathroom and Maggie looked at herself in the mirror. Her hair was sopping wet. It looked like an old-fashioned rope mop ready for the wringer and her face was bright red and her lips were blue. How odd, she thought. I look kind of patriotic: red, white and blue. She was still staring at the mirror when he came in with towels and a clean sweatshirt, sweatpants and a pair of wool socks. "Do you want cocoa, coffee, or tea?" he asked. "Sorry I don't have any brandy, but I don't keep that stuff anymore."

"You choose," Maggie shook her head. She still felt dazed and confused and quite undone trying to accept that she was standing shaking in Walter's bathroom, looking at her flag face in the mirror about to take a shower and put on his clothes.

"Cocoa," he said, "and remember, just lukewarm at first. And only when you're used to it, slowly increase the hot water." Then he left.

Maggie sat on the toilet seat and tried to untie her shoes. Her fingers were numb and her hands were shaking. She always tied her laces in a double bow so she wouldn't trip, and they were soaked and hard to untie. The bathroom filled up with steam as she struggled with the laces, and after what seemed like a very long time she finally got them loose. Slowly, she pulled off the wet shoes and sopping wet socks and felt her feet. They were bright red and reminded her of a lobster, but her fingers were so numb she couldn't feel anything. She struggled out of her wet clothes and then pulled back the shower curtain to feel the water. Even though it was lukewarm at the most, it felt very hot and she let it run over her hand for a while until she got used to it before climbing in. She stood away from the shower head letting the water run over both hands, then over her arms before she moved under it and rinsed the salt water from her hair. Maggie had no idea how long she'd been there before it felt like she could stand to make it hotter, but she gradually turned up more and more hot water until the feeling began to come back to her numb hands and feet.

She still felt quite disoriented in the steamy bathroom when she got out of the shower, but she grabbed the towels, dried her hair the best she could, then dried her face and body, which remained very red. Maggie wrapped her wet clothes and shoes in one of the large towels and got dressed in Walter's sweatpants and sweatshirt. They were dark purple and the sweatshirt had a big gold "W" on the front. She hadn't known Walter was a Husky fan, and realized that in spite of the little snooping episode when she'd stayed here, there were all kinds of things about him that she didn't know. After she put on Walter's socks, she looked in the mirror and ran her hands through her hair trying to make it less mop-like. It felt weird not to have any underwear, but at least the sweatshirt and sweatpants were big on her and also being a dark color would obscure her saggy old body a bit.

The socks were also too big and she shuffled out of the bathroom, hoping she wouldn't slip on the wood floor. Walter was waiting in his bedroom and when the bathroom door opened, he handed her a mug of hot cocoa. He put his hand against her cheek. "Your head is still like a block of ice. Come on." He pulled back the comforter of his bed. "Crawl in here and have your cocoa, you'll warm up faster than in front of the fire."

Maggie thanked him and took the mug. Standing next to his bed, she held the mug with both hands, warming them before she took a sip. She didn't know what to say. The hot cocoa was delicious, smooth and chocolatey. "I'll just finish this and then go."

"You probably saved Bill's life you know."

"I don't know. Maybe, maybe not...he might have gotten free on his own."

"I didn't know you were there."

"Well, I wasn't following you or sneaking up on you." Her voice was tired and edgy. "I wasn't accusing you. I'm grateful, Maggie."

"I wanted to see the sunset and that stretch of beach has a beautiful view of the mountains. Then I saw you and Bill, but the sun was about to set so I sat on a log near the bank, you didn't see me—that's all. And then Bill was in trouble and you only have one arm and well, I just didn't think, the next thing I knew I was swimming to him."

"You're a good swimmer."

"Thank you."

"I didn't know that about you."

"Well, now you do."

Walter put his arm around her. "Just get under the covers, Maggie. I'll put your clothes in the dryer. And when you're really warm enough, I'll walk you home."

"Well, okay, I guess. I'm still freezing." Maggie put the mug on the nightstand and got in his bed. She sat up leaning against the headboard and pulled the comforter up to her chin.

"I'll be back in a minute." Walter went in the bathroom and came out carrying the bundle of her wet clothes with his free arm. "Need any more cocoa?"

"Not yet, thanks."

Maggie pulled the comforter tighter around her and reached for the mug on the nightstand. What the hell happened here, she wondered. What was she thinking, going after the dog that way, maybe she had grown more attached to Bill Bailey than she realized. Had she really saved his life? Maggie never thought of herself as brave, and couldn't quite believe she had gone in after the dog. She understood now, in a way she never had before, what people meant when they said, "I didn't think." People who jumped in water to save someone or went into a burning building. It was like that, she really hadn't thought, it had all been automatic. Something just took over. And now here she was freezing to death in Walter Hathaway's bed. And then she had another thought and her eyes filled with tears. Was it a do-over? She hadn't been able to save her father; could she at least save a dog?

When Walter came back, tears were streaming down her face. She stared into space, oblivious to them, holding her mug with both hands.

"Oh Maggie, you must be exhausted." Walter sat next to her and gently took the mug from her hands and set it on the night-stand. Then he put his arm around her and she leaned forward resting her head against his shoulder while he stroked her back and she wept.

"I'm so sorry," she said after a few minutes, "I don't know what happened—"

"Shhh, it's all right. Everything's all right."

Maggie felt herself relax and melt into his shoulder, she closed her eyes as he caressed her back, then slowly opened them and lifted her head to kiss his cheek. Walter bent down and kissed her lips and she wrapped her arms around his neck and he kicked off his shoes and slid under the covers next to her. At first they just held each other and the warmth of his body was comforting as it warmed hers, but then the warmth slowly spread and became the heat of longing, and a part of her that she was sure had died had only been dormant and she knew then what parched leaves felt at the arrival of a summer rain.

CHAPTER FIFTEEN

Maggie woke to the crowing of Howie and Mark's roosters. Outside a pale mist rose from the water softening everything, and she looked over at Bill Bailey lying between them, then at Walter, sleeping quietly on his back with his arm in the sling. She watched his chest rise and fall and wanted to touch him. This was a bit more than civil discourse, she thought with a sad smile, remembering his warmth taking away the cold, their breathing together, breathing each other through the night in a sweet miracle of tenderness. She had tasted what it was to feel protected and cherished and now she lay on his bed, wide awake, cracked open and afraid there could be no going back. She knew his loneliness. It was hers.

She saw his sweatpants and sweatshirt and slipped out of bed and pulled them on. She went to the bathroom, trying not to disturb him, but when she came out he was awake.

"Mornin' Maggie," he said, a slow smile spreading across his face. "I'll put coffee on for us." Bill Bailey jumped down from the bed, tail wagging, and went to her and licked her hand.

It was too domestic, too dear and she had to tell herself to take it in, not to bolt. She bit her lip and ran a hand through her hair. "That would be great," she said, trying to sound relaxed. "I'll go get my clothes out of the dryer."

In the bathroom, Maggie pulled off his sweats and as she changed into her clothes, she wondered if they'd talk about last night. Or would it be all friendly and chummy, but without any acknowledgment of the way they'd been together?

"The coffee will be ready in a minute," he said, as she came in the kitchen. "I've got one of those coffee makers that stops dripping when you remove the pot so you don't have to wait for the whole thing to finish."

"It smells good." Maggie leaned against the counter.

"I'm making us breakfast. Sit down, relax." He went to her and put his arm around her, then kissed her. "Mornin' Maggie," he whispered. "I like the sound of that. Now, how do you like your eggs? I thought I'd make us an omelet, that okay?"

"Can I help?" she asked.

"Nope."

She laid her hand on his cheek and closed her eyes for a minute. "Pat the bunny." She smiled.

"Bunny?"

"I suppose it's an occupational hazard, being a children's librarian. Your face, well it just reminded me of *Pat the Bunny* and there's a page where it says 'Pat Daddy's Face' and it has a cut-out with a piece of sandpaper for his face. It's called a touch and feel book, that's all, it's silly, it's been around since the forties, and yes, I'd love an omelet."

"I didn't shave, maybe I should have—"

"No." Maggie put her hand on his cheek again, then kissed it. "You feel like a man."

"A touch and feel book?" He pulled her to him with his one hand. "How 'bout us having some of that?" He slipped his hand under her shirt.

Maggie laughed and moved away. "How 'bout some of that coffee you promised?" She was still trying to digest what had happened and couldn't handle anything that would lead back to the bedroom.

"Okay, here you go." Walter went to the pot, poured coffee and brought a mug to the kitchen table. "Take anything in it?"

"No, just black."

From the refrigerator, he got eggs, butter, milk, and cheddar cheese and cracked the eggs into a bowl and melted butter in a skillet. He whipped the eggs with a little milk and grated some cheese. "Cheese okay in the omelet?"

"Sounds delicious. Do you get your eggs from Howie and Mark?"

Walter nodded. "It's convenient and you can't get 'em any fresher."

Maggie watched him cook and drank her coffee. "You know I feel uncomfortable just sitting here getting waited on—while a person who just had surgery and can only use one arm is doing all the work."

"Well don't." Walter didn't say anymore and when the omelet was ready, he took some red grapes from the refrigerator and put them on the plates and came to the table.

"Thank you. This looks delicious." Maggie cut a piece off the omelet and took a bite. "Mmm...it *is* delicious."

Walter took a bite, then he drank some coffee. Finally he said, "I didn't plan this you know."

"It's lovely how you just threw it together." Maggie pulled off a grape from the stem.

"I wasn't talking about the breakfast. When I insisted you come to my house to get dry, to get warm...well, it wasn't some Machiavellian scheme. I didn't want you to go home alone soaking wet and shivering after you saved my dog. I'm not sorry this happened and I hope you're not. But if you are sorry—"

"I'm not."

Walter sighed, shaking his head. "Ever since I found you here on this island, seems like all I've been doing is apologizing."

"Oh no! Olivier!" Maggie put her fork down and pushed her chair back. "Where are my shoes? I've got to go—"

"Who's Olivier? Walter looked hurt. "Or maybe I shouldn't have asked—" He glanced down at his plate, then muttered, "Your breakfast will get cold."

"My sister's cat. I forgot all about him!" Maggie ran to the hearth where Walter had put her shoes, and quickly pulled them on and tied the shoelaces. "I have to go feed him and then I'll be back. I can just heat up the omelet, can't I?"

Walter brightened. "Sure, I'll pop it in the microwave."

"Great. Thanks, I'll be back in just a couple of minutes."

Maggie walked quickly across Walter's lot to the path in the woods, aware of her own pulse, which seemed to be racing. The morning mist had burned off and on the way to her house the sun was too bright, the water too blue, and the ground beneath her feet so rich and teeming with life that her heart ached.

Olivier greeted her with a loud aria of meows and rubbed back and forth against her legs, while she opened a can of Grilled Tuna Feast. She dumped it in his dish and he ate greedily and Maggie felt bad he'd had to wait so long.

The light on her phone was blinking and while Olivier ate she listened to the message.

"Maggie, I was wondering—" Leslie's voice was so soft and breathy it was hard to hear her, and Maggie turned up the volume on the phone. "—have you found a lawyer yet? Please let me know right away, and I just wanted you to know that I've talked with Betty Sue and she told me about the newspaper. On the front page and everything and I want you to know that I want to have a better start in this community and I'm going to make a large donation to an island arts organization. Betty Sue has been advising me and I think it will help introduce myself to the community in a good way and I'm not going to tell about it right now, it's going to be a wonderful surprise."

Maggie hung up the phone. Another surprise. Yippee. She's going to throw her money around so she can be a big fish in this little puddle. Who cares. Maggie sighed. But she supposed she could ask around about a lawyer. Maybe something about being with Walter made her feel more generous. But not this second. She wasn't going to drop her life, she smiled to herself, especially now that it had taken an astonishing, wonderful and frightening turn.

Olivier finished the last of his Fancy Feast and came to her, rubbed against her leg and purred. Maggie picked him up and stroked him. "You're not that bad, cat. You could use a vocal coach and some voice lessons, but I guess you're not that ugly." Still holding Olivier, Maggie looked out the window toward Walter's house and her mind jumped to what she'd seen snooping: the business cards from the women, all those librarians and booksellers and then that letter from Charlotte, whoever she was. Maggie could only think of bracing herself against rejection, how brutal it always was. How she could get bulldozed and this was supposed to be a peaceful summer. She turned away from the window. She'd call him with some excuse about why she couldn't come back.

Carrying Olivier and holding him close to her, she went to the desk and stared at the phone. The cat was warm in her arms. She could feel the beating of his little heart against hers and remembering how cold she'd been last night and the warmth of Walter's skin against hers, his calloused gentle hands, she put the cat down and went back to Walter's to finish her breakfast.

"Is the cat all right?" Walter took her plate from the microwave and put in front of her. "More coffee? It's gotten cold."

Maggie nodded. "He's fine. And I can get the coffee...you don't have to wait on me."

"I want to. I can never repay you. I don't know if you have any idea of what Bill Bailey means to me, Maggie." Walter went to the sink and dumped out her cold coffee and poured her a fresh cup, then he sat across from her. "Sometimes this dog seems like the only thing I can count on."

Maggie didn't know what to say, so she listened with a hushed politeness, quietly finishing the omelet. It had gotten a little rubbery in the microwave but she ate it anyway.

"Now you can say that a dog just loves you because you feed it, and I don't dispute that, but that's not all of it. Sometimes when Bill Bailey looks at me, I can feel how he's bonded to me and he stays right with me so I know he thinks 'you're okay, Walter. You're an okay guy.'"

Walter Hathaway? Needing reassurance? Maggie had trouble hiding her surprise. "You've been admired by so many people, Walter, think of the millions of children who love your books. That must count for a lot." She took her plate to the sink, rinsed it and came back to the table.

"Joan Baez got it right when she said the easiest kind of relationship is with ten thousand people, the hardest is with one." His gaze was steady on hers. "What about you?"

"About what?" Maggie looked at Bill Bailey who lay on the floor at Walter's feet.

"Don't be coy." He smiled. "About relationships? You're a wonderful woman—there must have been or are there?...you know?"

"I never remarried after George and I divorced—I did have one serious relationship but he had two daughters and their mother, his ex-wife, resented me and the kids just could never accept I was in their father's life...the tension finally just got to be too much." Maggie smiled, "I've been doing fine on my own, you know."

"Obviously. You seem to be thriving," he looked at her appreciatively.

"And you?"

"I was finding the city just too distracting and I wanted a simpler life and one where I could focus more on my writing."

Maggie wanted to call "foul." He expected her to tell him about her love life, but in return he was going to tell her about his work. How fair was that? But she decided not to push it, maybe she didn't want to know. Sometimes it was true that what you didn't know couldn't hurt you.

"And it was going okay until this happened." He pointed to the sling. "And then of course, losing Madeline. I'm still reeling from that, and about Madeline, well you know how sorry I am about—"

"You already apologized and there's no need—"

"You're sure?"

If she was still mad at him what did he think happened last night? What did he think she was doing there this morning? Was he really that insecure? "Walter—" she leaned forward, her eyes wide, "do I act like I'm holding a grudge?"

"No, not at all, I guess I'm just gun-shy." He looked down and patted Bill Bailey. "Madeline was a friend, she'd been my agent for years and it's been like losing family. She didn't have any children; everything was left to a nephew and his wife and they are making immediate arrangements to sell the agency. They're growing grapes in upstate New York. I suppose they need money, because they haven't wasted any time in selling. And I never knew this, but they were listed as co-owners of her business so there could be a quick sale if anything happened to Madeline. I'm supposed to get word about the sale soon. And in the meantime, I'm chugging along with a new book."

"So Jordan must be a big help, are you dictating to him?"

Walter leaned back in his chair. "I like the kid, you know."

"He is a great kid. And—"

"Well, I can't really say it's working out."

"He's showing up, isn't he?" she asked.

"Oh yeah, he comes on time, very reliable—"

"But he doesn't get down to business, is that it?"

"Sometimes while I'm organizing my thinking, he'll sit there with his cell phone and send text messages to his friends. But that's not really the problem, he does it so fast. I can't believe how fast those thumbs and fingers fly on that little phone, and the minute I begin to talk he puts it down, puts his hands on the keyboard of my computer and he never misses a beat." Walter stood up and cleared off his plate. "Can I get you anything else? Did you get enough to eat?"

"I'm fine, it was great—thanks."

"I guess I haven't really been quite ready to face this about Jordan, but the reason it's not working is that he wants to put his ideas into my book. I'll start dictating a scene and he'll say, 'Mr. Hathaway, maybe a guy from space could come down, or see, like there's this kid who has a meth lab and it blows up and then there's this other kid who has special powers and everyone thought he was dead, but he isn't because he's disguised as one of the regular kids.' You get the picture," Walter half-sighed and half-snorted and went over to his desk. "And then there are jokes. He wants me to put in these jokes." Walter picked up a sheet of paper next to the computer. "What did one flea say to the other as they were leaving to go to the movies?"

"What?"

"Shall we walk or take the dog."

"Oh, well, I see what you mean."

"And that's one of the better ones, 'Why did the cat family move next door to the mouse family?...so they could have the neighbors for dinner,' and then 'why did the vampire's girlfriend dump him?...because the relationship was too draining.' Get the picture? There's a whole list of these things—I could go on and on."

"No need." Maggie laughed. "I get the idea."

"You think they're funny?" Walter threw the paper down on the desk.

"Not that funny, it's just that Jordan reminds me of the kids at Evergreen, all the stuff they do and say—kids, that's all, they just make me laugh."

"Don't get me wrong. I like Jordan. It's just that we're not getting anywhere."

"I can see that." And then without thinking, with words that just seemed to fly out of her mouth, she said, "I'd be happy to give you a hand, if you'd like." Then she laughed. "No pun intended.

"I don't know, Maggie, I can do it myself, hunt and peck with one hand. It's damn frustrating but I can manage."

"Okay then, but if you change your—"

"You'd really...?" Walter walked to the table and sat down again across from her. "I don't think it'd be that interesting, you know—just typing what I dictate. I can't stand the idea of burdening anyone."

"Of course I'd do it." Maggie put her hand over his. "I love your books, Walter. I'd be happy to help you."

"You're really serious?"

"That's what I just said." Her smiled faded. "Do I seem like someone who's insincere?"

"No, not at all. I just want to make sure you mean it and of course, we'll have to have some kind of arrangement, I was paying Jordan and—"

"I wouldn't hear of it. I consider myself a volunteer for children's literature and all I'd want is that when it's published, maybe you'd give me a little stash of books."

"Well, sure. Of course. But what if I throw in cooking us dinner sometimes, or maybe I could buy you dinner at The Hardware Store, or even—maybe go into Seattle to a play or dinner or something. Would that be all right?"

Maggie blinked and looked away. Then her eyes met his gaze and she said, "That would be all right."

CHAPTER SIXTEEN

They were golden summer days, those last weeks of July, and Maggie couldn't remember a happier time. Not in years anyway. She woke at dawn, greeting each day as an unopened gift as she watched the sun rise. The grass glistened with dew, the spider webs on her deck sparkled with tiny dots like little crystal beads, and the kingfisher on a low branch over the water sat poised to dive. The air was fragrant with salt and seaweed and the wild sweet peas that had begun to bloom, their bright fuchsia blossoms vivid even in the morning haze. What brought joy was being needed. Around ten each morning, she went to Walter's. He had a fresh pot of coffee waiting and she would get a cup, then take her place at his computer, drinking coffee when he paused during the dictation. Wearing his horn-rimmed readers and dressed in jeans and an old gray sweatshirt, Walter sat in a big overstuffed chair in front of the fireplace. On his lap he had pages of the work he had dictated the day before and would begin by going back over them to make revisions. Sometimes he would change just a few words, other times he added new pages and deleted large sections. Maggie offered no comments or suggestions. She liked to think of herself as an extension of the author and she found it fascinating to get this glimpse into how his mind worked. But Maggie couldn't help getting engaged in the story. She knew many writers did not like their work to be compared to other writers, so she would never tell Walter what she was thinking, but there was something about *A Goose Called Hope* that reminded Maggie of E.B. White's *Charlotte's Web*. Both books had a life and death struggle. Mr. Arable wanted to kill Wilbur, the pig in White's book, and in Walter's the entire community, led by Mr. Hedgehopper, want to kill Hope and the whole flock of Canada geese. Walter's big hit *The Adventures of Fric the Chick* had a similar theme as Fric was short for Fricassee, the name given the protagonist, which foretold what was to be her future. In the story, to keep any child from becoming too attached to the chickens on the farm, they were all given names like "Fried," "Nuggets," "Roast," and so forth.

Maggie wondered how Walter's themes reflected his personality, but she only stopped typing to talk to him if she needed a word clarified or to ask about punctuation. They developed an easy rhythm, where she could anticipate paragraph breaks and when sentences ended without Walter having to say "full stop" or "new paragraph." When they'd finished for the day, usually at the end of a chapter, Maggie would print it out for him and that's when they'd talk for a while. And she did learn more about him.

Walter was in his last year of college at the University of Oregon majoring in English Literature when his name came up in the draft lottery for Vietnam. When he got out of the army, he finished college, got a teaching certificate and a job teaching high school English. He'd always wanted to be a writer so while he was teaching, he began what he hoped would be a Great American war novel. "The only problem," he told Maggie, "is that the thing was total crap. I struggled with it for quite a few years, and maybe it did serve some purpose to me personally—I avoided a lot of nightmares, the horror just came out in the writing and it was one big, wretched vomit of violence and pain."

"How did you get from a Vietnam novel to *The Adventures of Fric the Chick*?"

"We had chickens when I was a kid. I grew up on a farm in Aurora, Oregon, a little town southwest of Portland. And my mother did give them those names so we wouldn't get attached. I couldn't save anyone in Nam, I guess I wanted to be God and save someone or something and there was Fric, doomed from the start with a name like Fricassee."

"Your mother must have understood kids." Maggie went to the kitchen to get more coffee.

"She did." Walter leaned down and patted Bill Bailey. "But she wasn't here long enough. She died when I was eleven. Leukemia. We had housekeepers after that, some were nice enough, and loving you could say—but I always thought they were paid to care about me. I saw a shrink after my divorce and I always thought he was paid to care about me, too."

At first he didn't ask about her life. She didn't take it for a lack of interest; she had sensed his fear of letting her be too important, too real in his life. She understood it, because it was the same for her. The days unfolded, those sweet summer days, but underneath ran a current of anxiety, a little hum, unspoken but with an unmistakable message...not too close...don't get hurt. But after they'd been working together for a little while, after he'd told her about the death of his mother, he wanted to know more of her and she opened up to him.

"My father was bipolar, although when I was a kid I never saw his depression. He would just seem tired and then he'd sleep a lot. Our lives were a big trampoline, he'd be way up and then come straight down only to fly up again. He went from one scheme to another—he was charming and charismatic and had a succession of sales jobs. He'd do extremely well, get a big bonus and go on a spending spree. He was a secular Jew and my mother was Irish Catholic, I'm sure she rebelled against her very strict mother and I'm also sure he swept her off her feet.

"My mother was very beautiful, but very self-contained. I think her role was to put the brakes on him, he was like a roomful of sparklers and she was the bucket brigade, dousing everything. But in spite of his volatility, I think he may have been the stronger of the two. She simply couldn't go on without him.

"When I was sixteen, he committed suicide; my little sister found him in the garage, in the car with the engine running. My mother only lived three years after that. She died of a heart attack and people said it was like a broken heart. But I never saw it that way. I thought it was an empty heart and it just quit. He had always filled her up and without him there wasn't anything there. With her I suppose it was a lot like the long goodbye—the way they characterize Alzheimer's. People with depression abandon you, so we lost them both after he died. I could hardly stand the pain. After a while I had no tears left. And books, well, they were my salvation."

"Mine, too."

There was an intimacy growing between them but in spite of it, they didn't make love again. It was as if they wanted the emotional closeness to catch up to where they had been physically. He would make dinner for her, sometimes read aloud to her what he'd written that day, and mark passages with his good hand. And then she'd leave. They did kiss goodbye. It was sweet and lingering, but a kiss that meant goodbye or 'til tomorrow.

One morning Walter got a chair from the kitchen, lifted it with his good hand and carried it to the living room, setting it down across from the desk where she was working. He straddled it and rested his good arm on the back, learning forward as he dictated. He was only a few feet from her and he dictated revisions from the previous day's work and then began a new scene.

"New paragraph. 'Just as Hope and the flock gathered in the woods behind the Hedgehopper's Bicycle Shop—'" Walter paused and Maggie looked up from the computer to see him staring at her. "God, you have beautiful eyes."

She didn't know what to say and laughed uncomfortably. "Is that dialog? Who's speaking?"

"Walter."

"To *moi*, said Miss Piggy?" Maggie made a goofy, sweeping gesture toward herself. There was laughter, then tenseness on her face.

"*Oui*." Then he looked away and there was an awkward silence. "Well, back to work I guess."

Maggie wondered what would have happened if she had come out from behind the desk and gone to him. Of course, he could have gotten up from that chair and come to her, but he didn't. Neither of them moved and they went back to Hope and the flock of geese behind the Hedgehopper Bicycle Shop and later to what had now become a ritual: the goodbye kiss at the door.

As the weeks wore on, she started to wonder why there wasn't anything happening beyond that kiss goodbye. Maggie had lived very comfortably without a man, without sex. When she'd thought about this summer and how she wanted it to unfurl in a leisurely way, she had certainly not seen having a romantic relationship as one of those possibilities. And just what was going on with her and Walter anyway? It was a friendship. A kissing friendship, she supposed. They seemed to have struck a bargain where they provided each other with some male-female companionship that had a little spark to it, where he got some help that he needed, and where she got to be needed. That was the deal, and it ought to have been enough except that Maggie had loved that night in his bed. It was exhilarating to have that part of herself seem so alive and vibrant after all these years, but it hadn't awakened a craving for sex, as wonderful as it had been. Not that she'd object if they went to bed again, she'd probably love it, but the longing she felt was to be held.

Maggie knew her sister would never have settled for goodbye kisses if she were in this situation. Leslie would seduce him. But Maggie didn't see herself as the seductive type. Far from it. She'd been typecast pretty early in life and had never forgotten how her father called her "my big sturdy girl" and Leslie "my little kitten." She was tall, big-boned, womanly and round. During her Bohemian phase, before she met George, she was an earth mother hippie chick type. She was sensual, she knew that…but not seductive and at sixty-five, it all seemed a little silly anyway. Except when she thought about how it felt to be in Walter's arms, and in his bed. Maybe he just needed a little encouragement. She thought she might be able to get up the nerve to figure that much out.

It took Maggie another week but she finally decided it was time to give Walter that encouragement. She thought the weather had something to do with it when she woke one morning to a bleak sky threatening rain. By the time she left for Walter's, it had started. Not a soft summer rain either; it was a downpour. A day meant for staying inside: cozy, warm, cuddled up and maybe…?

The minute Walter opened the door she knew something had happened. His face was red, his blue eyes hard, and his jaw was clenched. It seemed all he could do was to say hello in a civil tone.

"Walter, what's wrong?" She started to take off her rain parka, then stopped. "Would you rather not work today?"

"Something's come up," he growled.

"Was there something I—"

"No, for God's sake. It's not you. Just look at this—I got this email just a few minutes ago. What the hell is wrong with these people!" Walter went to his desk and stood over his computer, glaring.

She took off her parka, put it on the hook next to the door and then stood next to him and looked at the email. It took up the whole screen.

Dear Mr. Hathaway:

I am a literary agent at International Writers Management and as you may know, the Madeline Gordon Literary Agency has just been purchased by IWM. As I handle children's and young adult writers, Ms. Gordon's clients who write for this market have been assigned to me.

I have recently read your file and the partial manuscript of A GOOSE CALLED HOPE and unfortunately, although it has some nice moments, it has a rather old-fashioned feel and I'm sorry to say I don't think I'd be successful in finding a publisher for it in today's difficult market.

I'm aware of your success with The Adventures of Fric the Chick, but in my judgment that is not enough of a platform to build on. It may be wise to try and build a strong presence in social media, perhaps writing a blog, using Facebook and Twitter so you can develop the kind of platform you'd need to market this kind of material. I'd be happy to look at any other projects you might develop.

Sincerely,

Beverly Hrones
IWM
249 E. 48th Street
New York, NY 10012

Maggie finished reading and turned to him. "Walter, I am a children's librarian. I know something about children's books and your book is wonderful. I don't know who this woman is, but she is a complete idiot."

"I'm a writer for God's sake not a snake oil salesman, what is this crap about Twitter!"

"The agents only think about what the editors will buy and I've met a lot of these editors at ALA meetings over the years and I know they're overworked and under tremendous pressure to make money for the corporations and—"

"You're taking her side!" he bellowed.

"Of course not," Maggie tried to explain, "I'm just saying that it's all about the money. Whether they think they'll make money. I'm of the school that doesn't mind if what kids are reading isn't great literature because it's so important that they read. But I think your book is wonderful from a literary standpoint *and* I think kids will love it—how many times do I have to say it?"

"A lot." Then he smiled. "Sorry about my little outburst. There it is again, Maggie, another apology. That's me, sorry-ass Walter."

"Look. The woman's an idiot, like I said, and of course, you'd be pissed—who wouldn't be?"

"You don't think I have a thin skin?'

"No way. I think writers and people in the arts are extremely strong just to be able to put their stuff out there. You're quite brave. Stand-up comedians are exceptionally brave, I think—the way they get heckled—I don't know how they can do it, frankly. But getting bad reviews is terrible, too. Especially the way they live forever now on the Internet. Everyone in the arts— musicians, singers, actors, writers, painters—they're all a tough bunch."

"I don't know what to do now, that's all."

"Keep going. The book is wonderful, and Madeline Gordon thought so—" Oops. She stopped in mid-sentence, not wanting to let on that she'd been snooping in his stuff.

"Madeline? What about Madeline?"

"I'm sure she must have loved it, didn't she?"

"Well, yes. Yes, she did, although she said it would be hard to sell but she'd do everything she could."

"So there must be another agent out there who would love it and give it her all. Or his all. A man who'd give it his all."

"Maybe."

"Would you like me to type a response for you? To this um—" Maggie looked back at the screen. "Beverly Hrones."

"I already did. I pecked it out with one hand."

"Oh."

"Here, I'll show you." Walter bent over the computer and went to the file on his email program that showed the messages he'd sent. He clicked on the last message and Maggie put her hand on his shoulder and leaned toward the computer.

Dear Ms. Hrones:

Tweet you, you twit.

Sincerely,
Walter Hathaway

CHAPTER SEVENTEEN

Walter wanted to take a break from dictating the novel for a few days. He said he had a doctor's appointment and some other things to attend to and he'd give Maggie a call when he could start in again. It sounded plausible, but Maggie suspected he'd been devastated by the response of that agent, that dreadful Beverly person, and just couldn't face the book right now. Creativity was a life-affirming, active endeavor; it took stamina and a very determined resolve to bring a story into the world. Maggie could understand how difficult it would be after getting the rejection from that idiot. What an arrogant, self-important, little airhead...what a moron! How dare she treat him with such disrespect! Well, they could just show *her*. She'd be sorry when Walter found a new agent and *A Goose Called Hope* won the Newbery. Eat your heart out, you twit! Although Maggie had to admit she thought it probably hadn't been such a good idea for Walter to send that email about tweeting and so forth. But who could blame him?

She decided she would get to work right away to help Walter find a new agent. She began googling around on the Internet and was delighted to find a wonderful free website that listed literary agents. It was a gold mine of information: a link to the agent's website, a list of who their clients were, whether they wanted email submissions or snail mail, and the books they had sold. Some of the listings for agents who represented very well-known children's writers said, "This agent does not currently accept unsolicited queries." Surely they didn't mean Walter Hathaway. Why any agent worth her salt (or his—although she didn't see too many men listed for children's books) well, they would undoubtedly jump at the chance to sell a new book by Walter Hathaway!

Maggie spent most of the morning on it and compiled a good list of agents who represented authors whose books she knew very well. They represented the very top writers: the ones she thought were in the same league with Walter. Or close to him anyway, as she thought Walter was simply one of the very best. The top brick on the chimney as the Brits say, that was Walter.

As she printed out the list, Maggie watched the sheets piling up on printer tray and suddenly she froze. *What the hell am I doing?* It was one thing to type his manuscript—that was only temporary. When he regained the use of his hand, her secretarial services would be like crutches discarded when they were no longer needed. But this? This upped the ante. This meant helping him in a new way: becoming more involved. True, she had been thinking about how to offer him more encouragement to move things along beyond that goodbye kissing business at the door. But did she really want this? Did he? And what about the dream she'd had last night? All morning she'd tried to forget it. But as the printer stopped and she saw the agent list she'd made to help him, the images flooded her mind with such intensity that she literally felt off balance and had to sit down.

Walter is standing on the beach holding his ukulele. He wades out into the water, turns and belts out "When a Man Loves a Woman," singing with all the passion and heart of Percy Sledge in the original version. He leaves the water, sits on a big driftwood log and the song turns into "Memory," the theme from Cats. *Then a human female in a cat costume, like in the Broadway show, comes out of the woods and purrs and cuddles up to Walter. It has yellow fur and huge dark chocolate eyes.*

The main thing that was obvious to her, and why the dream was disturbing, was that she, Maggie, was nowhere to be seen. She wasn't in the picture. And it sure wasn't too obscure having Leslie show up in the cat outfit, or did she represent some generic female Walter was involved with—or maybe that, that *Charlotte*? She looked at the agent list on the printer again. Exactly what *was* she doing with Walter Hathaway?

Maggie needed to think and she often did her best thinking when she was out on the water in her kayak. It was quiet and peaceful, with so few distractions, that things almost always became more clear. But before she left for the boathouse, she went to her computer and sent an email to her granddaughter. She wished she'd had a picture of the goats to attach to it. The goat episode was certainly one of the biggest things that had happened this summer and Ashley would no doubt find it very interesting. Writing Ashley always grounded her, connecting her with something very real and good in her life. There was no ambivalence when it came to Maggie's relationship with her granddaughter. Unlike this thing with Walter—whatever it was.

On her way to her boathouse, Maggie stopped at Martha Jane's to tell her she'd be going out for a little paddle. "Iced tea when you get back?" Martha Jane was painting on her deck. "I'll need a break soon."

"Wonderful, I should be back in about an hour."

As Maggie was getting into her kayak, Jordan Wiggins came around the south end of the beach. He was dressed in shorts and a tee shirt that said "HOMEWORK KILLS TREES," and there were earphones in his ears. His head was bobbing from side to side and he seemed to be jumping and moving with an air guitar that he stopped "playing" when he saw Maggie. He waved and when he got closer, he took his earphones out. "Hi, Mrs. Lewis, goin' out, huh?"

"Thought I would. How are you, Jordan? I haven't seen you for a while."

"My grandmother is paying me to plant stuff in the yard, so when Mr. Hathaway thought we should take a break, it worked out good because I didn't have to quit him to do my grandmother's stuff."

"Glad it worked out for you. How is your grandmother doing?"

"She's still insane."

"Oh."

"She can't find the man who designed her garden, so she hires people on the island and then she fires them. So now she's trying to choose new stuff and plant it herself. When she acts like a crazy person, I come to the beach to get some space, if you know what I mean."

"I do know. The beach is a good place to get space."

"Well, see you later, Mrs. Lewis." Jordan stuck the earphones in his ears, waved to her and continued bopping down the beach.

There was a slight breeze and Maggie decided to paddle north so when she returned she'd have the wind at her back. Audrey Katovsky, who lived on Hormann Road, was beachcombing with her two granddaughters and they all waved as Maggie paddled by. She couldn't help but envy Audrey Katovsky. Her grandchildren lived in Seattle and they were often on the island, especially in the summer, and Audrey did a lot of babysitting in town for them as well. Maggie sighed. There had never been a day that she didn't wish she lived closer to Ashley. Skype helped, but her visits, whether it was when she went to California, or when Ashley came there, were just too short and too far between. It was never enough. Maggie glanced back at Audrey and the kids who were now skipping stones and wondered if Audrey knew how lucky she was.

It was lovely to kayak, it always was. But that afternoon it didn't work its magic to clear her mind. She was still in a muddle, the sun was getting hot, and having iced tea with Martha Jane sooner rather than later seemed like a good idea. She turned back before she got to Peter Point.

When Maggie came up from the boat house, Martha Jane was slouched in the wicker chair with her feet up on an ottoman. She held a glass of iced tea, balancing it on her stomach like a table. "Hi, Maggie. Help yourself." Martha Jane pointed to the pitcher on the picnic table. Then she pointed to her easel, which was turned so you couldn't see the painting. "I can't look at it when I'm taking a break, because I can't leave it alone. Then I start fooling with it and when I do that...when I'm tired...I just make a mess."

"Thanks, tea's perfect." Maggie poured herself a glass and sat next to Martha Jane. She looked at the back of the easel. "Most things are like that when we get tired, I think. I have to be careful when I kayak not to get carried away and go too far, to make sure I have enough energy to get back. Although I came back a little earlier than usual today."

"How've you been, Maggie?" Martha Jane shaded her eyes to look at her. "I haven't seen too much of you the last few days."

"I've been helping Walter," she said, trying to sound casual.

"Really!"

"I ran into him on the beach and it wasn't working out with Jordan helping him and before I knew it I'd volunteered." Maggie decided to omit a few little details. "He's dictating his new book and I just type it for him."

"How's the book?"

"Wonderful."

"Well, that must be very satisfying."

"That, and confusing, too. I've always thought of myself as something of a feminist. I don't mean that I dislike men, but I've always had my own career, my own interests and frankly, I don't know what I'm doing with him. I don't know what it's about."

"What's wrong with helping him? Helping a friend?"

"Nothing, I suppose."

"Maggie dear, would you be questioning this if you were helping a woman writer? Or helping a young person, a child?"

Maggie shook her head. "No, I guess not."

"Walter's a human being, last time I checked," she said, chuckling. "You're just helping another human being."

"But it seems like I've fallen into this subservient role, kind of one-down and everything is revolving around the man, around Walter. Typing and all—"

"Do you bring the coffee?"

"He makes coffee, and sometimes he fixes dinner."

"He must be grateful for your help, then."

"But it's more complicated—because it seems to be more than a platonic friendship and I know this sounds ridiculous, but I've been so happy."

Martha Jane chuckled.

Maggie smiled. "I told you it sounded ridiculous. Complaining because I'm happy...it must seem like I've got a screw loose or something. But I don't want to rely on a man to make me happy. I want to find my own happiness myself."

"I guess I don't understand why finding your own happiness can't include having a close relationship?"

"I don't know, maybe it can, I know that it's meant a lot to me to be useful—but then I also worry that I'm rescuing him. And that doesn't seem very healthy."

"I doubt Walter needs no more rescuing than any of us. Don't we all need rescuing?" Her voice trailed off and Martha Jane closed her eyes for a moment.

"Rescuing from what?"

"From loneliness." Martha Jane put her glass on the table and folded her hands and rested them on her stomach. She looked out toward the water, then closed her eyes and her head nodded and it looked to Maggie like she'd begun to doze.

Maggie went to the picnic table and poured herself another glass. She didn't ask Martha Jane if she wanted more. On the table next to her, her glass was still almost full.

"...and then there's always Will Rogers," Martha Jane said, smiling and lifting her chin.

"Will Rogers?" Maggie sat down next to her.

"Yes, he said, 'we can't all be heroes, because somebody has to sit on the curb and applaud when they go by.'"

"But it seems like the women have done most of the applauding, don't you think?"

Martha Jane nodded. "I can't argue with that, dear, but I still think there's not enough value given to those who appreciate and encourage others…as if everyone is supposed to be the star of the show, if you get my drift. And what about being a grandparent—" Then her voice trailed off and she closed her eyes again.

Maggie didn't know how being a grandparent could be connected to her and Walter. She adored Ashley, it was probably the sweetest, least conflicted relationship she'd had in her life. But that had nothing to do with whether she was going to get more involved with Walter. And what about sleeping with him without having to throw herself into Puget Sound to save his dog?

"And weren't you the one who asked me the other day about how to be old?"

"I did." Maggie nodded.

"What I know is that my body is the house I live in and it's fading away, quietly collapsing and will turn to dust, but *I'm* quite alive and there are two things that keep me that way. I thought about this after you left. Curiosity is one."

"You are very curious." Maggie reached over and patted her hand. "I love that about you. And the other?"

"What other?"

"The other thing that keeps you going?"

Martha Jane pursed her lips and tucked a wisp of her white hair behind her ear. There was a silence, then she said, "I think I forgot."

"Oh well, that's okay. Curiosity is a good one."

She leaned back with her hands folded across her stomach. Then she smiled and sat up straighter. "Oh, now I know and it's related to curiosity, it's having a project. It doesn't matter what it is. And the project for a grandparent can be helping out…you're not the star or the center of anything. Your main thing is to be like Will Rogers said, you're the ones who applaud, who support and encourage and that's being useful. The folks on the curb— they're needed." Martha Jane put her hand on Maggie's arm. "Walter Hathaway has a gift and it seems to me that helping him to use it would be a good project."

"I'll guess I'll have to think about that." Maggie yawned. "I just wish I weren't so tired. The truth is I've been literally losing sleep over this."

"Well, I suggest you go home and take a nap. Naps are good for you," Martha Jane said with authority. "They're very important."

When she got home, Maggie decided to take Martha Jane's advice. But before she went to her bedroom, she looked at the phone, realizing that she was hoping to see the message light blinking, hoping there was a message from Walter. Olivier meowed and rubbed up against her and she bent down and picked up him. "This is pathetic, cat. Like I'm some teenager waiting for the phone to ring, hoping the boy will call. I can't stand how ridiculous this is. How ridiculous *I* am! *At sixty-five!*"

Maggie carried Olivier to the bedroom, pulled the drapes closed and curled up on her bed with him. He purred and snuggled into the crook of her arm and she lay there staring at the ceiling. She was getting rather attached to Olivier. The things that she'd found annoying didn't seem to matter so much. Did proximity lead to attachment? By just hanging around with Walter would she get more and more attached to him? And what about his attachment to her? And who was Charlotte? For a while Maggie had decided it was a name from his past and didn't matter. And from time to time she'd had some success in forgetting what she'd seen. But then it would pop back up and when it did, it was like a beeping little alarm that she couldn't shut off. Maggie suspected the dream she'd had was connected to this woman, whoever she was. Also, she hadn't managed to mention her to Martha Jane. So when Martha Jane encouraged her to stay involved with Walter, she didn't have the full picture. There hadn't seemed to be any good way to mention it without letting on that she'd been snooping. Maggie wanted Martha Jane to think well of her. She didn't want her to think she was the kind of person who went snooping around into people's private stuff, even though she was. But of course, she had been taking care of his dog. Maggie began to doze off as she had an imaginary conversation with Martha Jane where she tried to explain why she'd looked into Walter's papers.

She didn't know how long she'd been asleep when she woke to the phone ringing.

She jumped off the bed and raced to the desk in the living room and stopped when she saw the name of the caller ID.

"Leslie Lewis 310-879-9654"

Not Walter.

She had a thought of letting it ring and take a message, but she'd done that the last time Leslie called, so reluctantly she picked up.

"Maggie!" Leslie gushed. "I'm so glad I found you at home—you sure have been out a lot."

"Hi Les." Maggie sat at the desk. Olivier came out from the bedroom and rubbed against her leg.

"Well, I just want you to know that Betty Sue found me a lawyer on the island. His name is Kirk Shanaman and I've talked with him and he thinks we'll be able to settle out of court with the Wigginses."

"Glad to hear that." Maggie yawned.

"Do you know much about him?"

"About who?"

"The lawyer? I've gotten to know him through emails and on the phone and he seems very nice."

"Name sounds familiar." Maggie reached down to pet Olivier.

"Do you happen to know if he's single?"

"I have no idea." Maggie yawned again.

"I wonder how old he is, of course that really shouldn't matter. Age is nothin' but a number, right?" Leslie laughed and Maggie yawned again. "Well, anyway," Leslie continued, "I have a wonderful surprise that I think will be like my gift to the island—although I don't have everything in place yet. So I don't want anyone to get their hopes up until it's a done deal and I can announce it. And I want to surprise you, too Maggie. But I'll give you one little hint."

"Oh please do," she said.

"Are you being sarcastic?"

How could you possibly think such a thing? Maggie muttered to herself and leaned down to pat Olivier again. "What's the hint?" she asked, trying to sound more pleasant.

"It has to do with your name!" Leslie giggled.

"My name?"

"Yes, it has to do with the name 'Maggie' and that's all I'm going to say."

"I don't want to be involved in the surprise."

"Don't worry, it's just in the name. I bet you're dying to know."

"I've gotta go. Olivier needs to be fed."

"Oh, my little darling boy. How's he doing? I bet he misses me, I hope you're giving him enough attention."

"We're getting along well," Maggie said. "Sometimes he sleeps with me. He purrs a lot."

"Oh, well good," she said, sounding not that happy.

When she got off the phone, Maggie went to the kitchen to fix something for her dinner and feed Olivier. She looked in the refrigerator. There was some leftover chicken and a bag of lettuce and mixed greens, but she didn't have the energy to even fix a salad. Instead she took a Lean Cuisine from the freezer and plopped it in the microwave. When it was ready, she decided it looked a little puny, so she put a piece of bread in the toaster. Maggie looked at her reflection mirrored on the side of the toaster. Everything was too big: her eyes, nose, mouth and the big creases in the corner of her eyes and on either side of her mouth. All too big. A big sturdy girl. Maybe the whole thing in his bed when she was freezing to death had been a fluke. Maybe the goodbye kisses each day had been a kind of courtesy thing. Maybe he didn't find her attractive. She was sixty-five. Who was she kidding?

Maggie took her dinner to the living room to eat in front of the television. As Gwen Ifill was discussing the deficit with some economist from Berkeley, Maggie heard Walter calling Bill Bailey.

"Won't you come home, Bill Bailey, won't you come home?"

Maggie put down her fork to listen. Walter's voice boomed out over the water, echoing in the woods.

"She moans the whole day lo—ong. I'll do the cooking darling, I'll pay the rent—"

Maggie smiled. The song. The dog. It was all so wacky. She kept smiling and closed her eyes, listening to Walter. Then after a minute, she looked at Olivier, who had finished his dinner and was sitting on the couch. "Hard not to love a guy like that, cat."

CHAPTER EIGHTEEN

"Maggie...." Walter's voice was low and croaky as if he'd just woken up. "I was wondering if um, well...if—"

"Yes?" Maggie held the phone, leaning against the desk with her legs tightly crossed. She'd jumped out of bed the minute it rang and now her full bladder was making her uncomfortable. She should probably ask if she could call him back, but he sounded so tentative and unsure of himself that she was afraid to get off the phone. Walter cleared his throat, but didn't say anything. She tried a Kegel exercise. Great. Walter finally calls and I pee in my pants. "Walter? Are you there?"

He cleared his throat again. "I was um wondering if you could come and help and um, type my book again?"

"Of course, I'd be happy to."

"I tried myself—hunt and pecking. Pretty slow going and I got frustrated. But I can do it if I have to, it's not like I'm an invalid or anything."

"Of course you're not. When do you want me to come?"

"How 'bout now," he said, then sounded embarrassed. "I mean, this morning, that is, if you don't have anything planned, of course it could be later and—"

"I'll be over in a half hour."

"Thank you, Maggie."

"Sure. See you soon." Whew. Maggie hung up and tore to the bathroom. Why is it so hard for men to ask for help? But her question was rhetorical: she knew the answer. They'd been socialized to be in charge, not to be needy. She understood that, but she still was always struck by it. Although, when she really thought about it, she supposed she and Walter weren't all that different in that regard. She also found it difficult to ask for help. There was always the fear that if she did and no one came through, it would be worse than if she had never asked at all. Guess it's not always just a gender thing, she decided, and besides, too much of a stereotype.

When she was through in the bathroom, Maggie ran to the kitchen and grabbed a banana and put on water to boil for a cup of Starbucks instant coffee. Then she stopped. Why was she in such a hurry? Why not make a pot? She should take her time. Not rush and bound over to Walter's house like a puppy eager to be fed. She turned off the kettle and made a pot instead, and then went to shower.

She lingered in the shower, letting the water hit her shoulders and neck. They'd felt knotted and tight ever since Walter had called and it bothered her that she wasn't able to control the way her body was expressing the tension she felt. Why was she letting him get to her like this? After she got out of the shower and was drying herself she thought, "Well, at least the rash from the poison oak is almost gone. That's some kind of progress." She dressed quickly in a blue tee shirt, khaki pants and sandals, resisting the temptation to put too much thought into how she looked (although she wasn't unaware that blue was a good color on her).

When she arrived at Walter's, Bill Bailey greeted her with kisses, unlike Walter who seemed a little shy and almost sheepish. "Are you sure you don't mind coming on such short notice?" he asked, as she went to the desk and sat down at the computer. "Can I get you some coffee? Or tea? Or maybe would you like something to eat?"

"I'm fine. I've had breakfast. Shall we get to work?'

"Okay, but let me know if you change your mind. I have a fresh pot of coffee."

"I will." Maggie looked at the screen and Walter's email was open. It looked like a reply to an email that hadn't been sent. Of course, she read it.

Greetings,

I am the account manager at Skye Bank for the late Harry Peters. On the 3rd of October 2006 his wife and only child were involved in a ghastly motor accident along Abuja express where all occupants of the vehicle unfortunately lost their lives.

Maggie read through the rest of it, which went on to offer 30% of the money in the late Harry Peters' 1.2 million dollar estate for transferring the money to a US Bank. Underneath was Walter's reply.

Dear Mr. Wilson:
Take the millions and shove
'em where the sun don't shine.
There's a sucker born every minute and
I'm not one of them. Get a job, fool!

Maggie looked up from the computer. "There's an email here that hasn't been sent yet—" "Oh, right. I was just about to send that when you came. Just go ahead and send it."

Walter saw that she hesitated and he came to the desk and stood close to her. He leaned over her and hit send. He smelled like Old Spice and she wanted to brush his cheek with the back of her fingers.

"Don't you worry that replying to the spammers encourages them?" she asked. "I think you're just supposed to report it to your email provider."

"Probably. But I've kind of been on a roll. I've been replying to quite a few of them. There's the woman in the hospital in Switzerland who has only a few months to live and wants to give me ten million dollars and wants me as a God fearing person to invest the money to fund churches, orphanages and charities for widows before she dies. I told her that I hated orphans and widows, so she might as well just die."

"Really? You really wrote that?"

"And about a dozen others. It's amazing the amount of this stuff that's sent, it makes me wonder who could be dumb enough to fall for this crap." Walter sighed. "Of course, I've been dumb enough to waste time replying to all this crap. But it has given me some satisfaction. It's cathartic and it's served the purpose of helping me avoid finishing the book."

Maggie looked up at him. "It's a wonderful book, why avoid finishing it?"

"I suppose because then I really will have to face this whole agent thing." Walter went to the kitchen and poured a cup of coffee. "Well, let's get to work, shall we?" He sat in the chair in front of the fireplace and after a few minutes, picked up the pages from where they had left off.

"Just so you know, I've made a list of agents that you might want to consider contacting." Walter just stared at her, so she continued, "I don't want to be presumptuous—I was just trying to well, you know—" Walter still didn't say anything. "You don't have to do anything with it, don't even have to see it, if—"

Walter stood up. Then he walked behind the desk, bent down and kissed her cheek. "It would be a big help. Thank you."

"I have the list at home, I can get it now if you'd like." Maggie put her hands on the desk, starting to get up.

He rested his hand lightly on her shoulder. "Let's work on the book this morning. I have to use my old brain before it fizzles and it seems to do a little better in the morning."

"Sure. That's fine." Maggie placed her hands on the keyboard, poised to type as Walter went to the chair in front of the fireplace.

"It's humiliating you know." He picked up the manuscript pages.

"What is?"

"This whole agent business. Having to sell myself—I don't even know what to say to these people."

"I can help you with that."

"Maybe at dinner?" He put the manuscript down and leaned forward. "Can you come for dinner tonight?"

"Dinner, oh well, um—" Maggie hesitated. Maybe she shouldn't be so agreeable, so accessible...maybe play a little hard to get...She felt herself cringe...and how silly is this? Like high school again, for God's sake, like when she waited for him to call.

Walter sat back and coughed. "Or some other night this week, if it's not good tonight."

"Oh no, I just had to think a minute. It's fine. Sure, I'd love to." She smiled, then quickly looked at the computer screen, trying to seem nonchalant as she waited while he read through the last few pages of the manuscript.

After a few minutes, he looked up and said, "Okay, this will be the last chapter."

"I'm ready when you are."

Walter talked quickly, dictating faster than he had before and it seemed to Maggie that he was like a long distance runner who had a kick at the finish. Several times he had gotten too far ahead of her and she had to ask him to slow down. They worked for about a half-hour, but it felt to Maggie that it flew by in just minutes.

The story was winding down. The conflict between the geese and the townspeople had been resolved, and Walter was about to dictate the ending. He stood up. "I need some more coffee. Can I get some for you, Maggie?"

"No, I'm fine, thanks."

"I guess I always get rattled when I get to the end."

"Have you felt that way with most of your books?" she asked.

"I think so. I've been living with these geese for quite a while and I guess I'm sad to see them go. I suppose I'll miss them. Does that sound nuts?"

"No, I think most authors probably feel that way. And when an author cares about the characters, the readers will, too. And it's the characters that seem real that live." She was about to say, "like Fern and Wilbur and Charlotte" but immediately thought better of it. Don't be an idiot, she told herself. The last thing he needs now is to be compared to E.B. White, being reminded not only of another author's book, but one of the great classics in children's literature. Maggie waited quietly while Walter came back in the living room and set his coffee on the fireplace mantel. Then he walked back and forth in front of the desk. He cleared his throat and started to dictate, then he stopped and went to the mantel and took a sip of his coffee. Then he cleared his throat again, and after a long pause he dictated the ending.

A young mother goose decided it was time to tell her gosling the story of Hope. "She was an amazing goose," the mother said. "She taught us not to give up when things looked bleak. We are alive today because of her."

"Is that why you named me 'Hope'?" the gosling asked.

"Yes, to honor her. And when you have a daughter you must promise to name her 'Hope,' too."

"I promise."

"Good, then our flock will always have a Hope."

Then, as the sun began to set, the young mother and the little goose, Hope, waddled into the water and swam out into the lake to join the flock swimming past the town dock. The sky was bright gold and streaked with lavender and pink clouds. Nearby a paddleboat churned through the water. It was filled with many townspeople who were out on a sunset cruise. When they saw the geese, all the people on the boat said "good evening" and waved. Mr. Hedgehopper waved and waved. And as the geese glided by, the young mother and Hope and all the geese in the flock honked "good evening" back to the people of the town.

The sun set and sank behind the hills and all the geese swam around the bend out of sight, leaving behind them tiny little ripples on the silver surface of the lake.

Walter had finished dictating the ending with a soothing, gentle tenderness in his voice, as if he'd been reading to a small child.

He turned away from Maggie, leaned against the mantel, and squeezed the bridge of his nose.

Maggie finished typing and then sat back with tears in her eyes. She sighed and watched Walter, who went toward the door.

"I think I'll get a little air."

"Should I type 'The End?'" she asked.

"Might as well," he muttered.

Maggie started to type, but then sat back and sighed. "It's beautiful, Walter."

"Hmmmph."

Walter went out on the porch and Bill Bailey followed him. Maggie watched them walk toward the edge of the yard where Walter looked out at the beach, then leaned down and patted Bill. She wasn't sure what she was supposed to do. Since the book was done maybe she should just leave? But it was only a few minutes before they came back in. Walter leaned against the fireplace and scratched his head. "I think it would be good to print out this last chapter, and then, Maggie, I'm not going to look at it for a little while. To get some distance. After a while I'll read over the whole book and see what it needs, see if I can improve it. Find any sour notes."

"I think it's perfect."

"Thank you, but I suspect you've gotten too close to it as well. Might even be biased," he said with a shy smile.

Maggie stood up. "What time tonight? And can I bring anything?"

"Just bring yourself. About seven?"

"Seven's fine, and you're sure?"

"About what?" He looked puzzled.

"That I can't bring anything?"

Walter went to her and put his arm around her; he closed his eyes and kissed the top of her head. "Thank you, Maggie," he mumbled. "And you must only bring your good self."

She was exhausted when she got back to her house, and decided to take a nap. She certainly seemed to be doing it a lot lately. But Martha Jane's attitude toward naps was a help, as Maggie always felt slightly guilty whenever she did lie down in the afternoon. It reminded her of her mother and it was an association that she didn't like. A prime example of how *not* to be. To be or not to be? Not like her that was for sure. It wasn't that she didn't have some compassion for her mother's depression and her limitations, but it was trumped by the abandonment she'd felt at losing not just one parent, but two. She remembered having the terrible thought that it would have been easier if her mother had died when her father did, rather than turn into such a zombie. She wondered if there was anything lonelier than being trapped with someone who was only there in body, who was completely disconnected from you, so you felt like you didn't exist.

Maggie lay down with Olivier and wondered why she'd started thinking about her mother and about her father's death. Leslie always seemed to stir up memories, but it had been almost fifty years, wasn't it time to stop feeling like an orphan?

She fell asleep almost the minute she stretched out on her bed, oblivious to everything, even to Olivier who was snuggled next to her hip, purring loudly. She slept soundly, and not the half-hour that was the usual duration of her occasional nap, but for several hours. It was finally the bleating sound of some loud horn that woke her. For a minute she thought she was back in her condo in the city. Slowly she opened her eyes and sat up, and realized it was a boat horn. Maggie looked at the clock. It was 6:40! She tore into the bathroom and showered in ten minutes, then dressed in her good jeans and a blue cotton sweater. As she was drying her hair, she looked around the bathroom. Maybe Leslie had left some product, something to put on her hair to make it look shiny and nice. Less of a gray mop. And lipstick, she must have some around somewhere. Something with a little color, a little jazzier than the Burt's Bees lip balm she always wore. She finished drying her hair and began madly pawing through the drawer next to the sink. Then she glanced in the mirror.

Stop. Just stop, she told herself in her best Ms. Lewis voice. *Get the list you made of agents and just go over there. You are too old for this.*

When Maggie arrived at Walter's, it was obvious he had picked up the house. And instead of his usual gray, rather ratty sweatshirt, he had on a nice plaid short-sleeved shirt. It was tucked into his jeans and he was wearing a black leather belt. She thought maybe she was imagining it, but even Bill Bailey seemed like he'd spruced up a bit.

"Hi Maggie, come in…come in. Please sit down—um, would you like a something to drink? I have sparkling water, or a tomato juice cocktail. I can make a Virgin Mary, I have olives and everything and celery and—"

"Thanks." He sounded so nervous; she forgot her own awkwardness and tried to put him at ease. "I'd love a Virgin Mary, can I help you?"

"No need. I do better in the kitchen with one hand than I do at the computer."

Maggie sat on the couch and put the list of agents on the coffee table. "I have the list here, should we go over it now?"

Walter brought her drink. "Hope this isn't too spicy." He went back to the kitchen for his drink, then made another trip for a bowl of peanuts. "How many are there?" He put the peanuts on the coffee table and sat across from her by the fireplace. Bill Bailey lay down next to him.

"I made a list of a dozen to start with."

"A dozen!"

"We don't have to contact all of them, if you think that's too many."

"I didn't think I'd have to go through so many to find someone." He sighed. "But I suppose there could be more out there like that twit from the agency that bought Madeline's agency." Walter sipped his drink. "I haven't had to do anything like this for so long, I admit I find it rather daunting."

"Walter, I have an idea." She put the list in her lap and leaned forward. "What if I write these people for you?"

"You mean, pretend to be me?"

"No, as myself. I can do it on your email and ask that they reply to your email address."

"Don't they want letters?"

"The ones on this list said they all preferred email."

"I see." Walter got a handful of peanuts, then went back to the chair. He stuffed a bunch of peanuts in his mouth. "Well, what would you say to these people?"

"I didn't quite understand. What did you say?"

"Oh, sorry." He chewed for a minute, then swallowed and took a sip of his drink. "I do know better, my mother always told me not talk with my mouth full." He smiled. "I was saying that I wondered what you'd say in your email?"

"I'd say that I was writing on behalf of Walter Hathaway and I'd say that your agent passed away and—"

"Why do you think people don't just say 'died' much anymore?" He went to the coffee table and got another handful of peanuts. "Didn't mean to get off track here. So what is it you'd write?"

"Just that you were looking for representation and have a new book for children. And then I'd briefly describe the book. The ones on the list all wanted to see sample chapters, so I'd attach the first three chapters. And I'd mention your distinguished career, and of course refer to *Fric*, which is a classic in children's literature."

"So how would you sign it? I mean who would you say you are to me?"

Maggie laughed and under her breath mumbled, "Wish I knew."

"What?"

"Nothing. Look, I'd just sign it Margaret Lewis, Children's Librarian, Evergreen Elementary School, ret." Maggie took a handful of peanuts and sat back. She held them in her left hand and picked them up one at time, chewing each one slowly. "Walter, *A Goose Called Hope* is a wonderful story and it also has the toilet humor element which is very popular with children."

"The what?"

"Toilet humor. The fact that the issue is the goose poop. Kids will love that. Some of the biggest kids' books have that."

"They do? Like what?"

"*Captain Underpants and the Attack of the Talking Toilets*, and then for younger children there's *Everyone Poops*, and *Farley Farts*—that's a board book where you push the button for a farting sound."

"Oh my God."

"And there's also *Walter the Farting Dog*."

"I don't think that's funny, Maggie."

"I didn't make that up—it's a real book and very, very popular." Maggie put another peanut in her mouth. "All I'm trying to say is that the fact that your book has poop in it is a selling point."

Walter went to the kitchen. "Can I get you another drink? I'll get going on our dinner."

"Can I help?"

"Nope."

"Well then, why don't I send the query letters to the agents while you're in the kitchen?"

"You were supposed to let me take care of you tonight."

"I think we should send these off and just get it over with, Walter, I really do."

"Well, I don't want to argue about it."

"Good, then it's settled." Maggie went to his desk and sat in front of the computer.

"I picked up a chicken casserole from Thriftway, and I'm just warming it up. It's easy with one hand," he said. "And Bill gets anything I drop on the floor. Don't you, boy?"

Maggie heard Bill's tail thump on the floor. She put the agent list next to the computer, then proceeded to make a file of the first three chapters of the book. It didn't take her long to draft the query. She knew it would be best to keep it short. Walter had the radio tuned to KPLU, the NPR station that played jazz. It was the station Maggie always listened to and as she wrote the queries, she could smell the chicken casserole warming in the oven. And it was too much: the music, Walter in the kitchen cooking for her, the dog at his feet. It felt like a home and she got a lump in her throat.

When the dinner was ready, Walter pulled out the chair for her with his one hand. He lit candles with his automatic fire starter wand, and she noticed that there was a jelly glass on the table that held a bouquet of wild sweet peas she thought he'd probably picked from his yard.

"This looks wonderful."

"When I can use both arms, I'll make my own dinner for you and not always the Thriftway dinners we've had. I like to cook."

"You don't mind cooking for one?"

"I've had a lot of practice. Been on my own quite awhile."

Maggie took a bite of the casserole. "This is good. It tastes better than when I've had it. Did you add something?"

"Extra bread crumbs with parmesan and sage. I toss them in a little olive oil."

"Hmmm," Maggie nodded appreciatively. "I guess it shouldn't surprise me that you like to cook since you're so creative."

"Cooking was the only creative thing I was able to do for a while. It's been a long road back. Trying to get back into writing. *A Goose Called Hope* is the first thing I've been able to finish. I've had a lot of false starts. Bread?" He passed a basket with garlic bread to her.

"Thanks." Maggie broke off a piece and put it on the edge of her plate. "This salad is lovely by the way."

"I like grapes in a salad." Walter took a little more of the casserole. "Everything went to hell in a hand basket after they made the movie. My wife got involved with the producer. And I went berserk and went after him. Beat the crap out of him, but he didn't press charges. He didn't want the bad publicity, since it was a kids' film. I almost killed the guy, but as it turned out after Lorna left with him, I ended up almost killing myself."

"You were suicidal?" Maggie tried to keep the alarm from her voice.

"The long slow kind. Booze. You saw one of my great perfor-mances, as you know." Walter finished eating and pushed his plate away. "You'll never know how sorry I am about what happened at your school, Maggie." He eyes met hers. "I went haywire. I was like a sailor on shore leave, a leave that lasted for years and I lost the plot of my own life. Not needing money can be a bad thing, believe me. At least it was for me. I didn't really have to work because of the income from *Fric*. And I didn't start writing again after I'd finished going through the SATT, the Substance Abuse Treatment Team Program at the VA Hospital. And then Char-lotte—" He stopped. "Look you don't want to hear this whole long dirge. I didn't mean to turn this dinner into an AA meeting."

Her heart began to beat as though it were tapping out a faint signal of distress...Charlotte?...Charlotte who?...She looked at the sweet peas in the vase, trying to find a way to ask without asking. Finally she said, "Walter, I think I should make some-thing clear—"

"That sounds ominous."

"I just wanted to say that you've probably noticed that I care about you. And that means that I care about what happens to you and what has happened to you. Which I don't see as a bad thing, do you?"

He chuckled, "Hardly." Walter went to the kitchen and put coffee on. "I have some blueberries and vanilla ice cream for dessert. Would you like that? And decaf?"

"Sounds great." That was it. If he didn't want to tell her, she'd just have to deal with it. She wasn't going to say any more, start badgering him to tell her.

After dessert and coffee they decided to take Bill Bailey for a walk on the beach. Walter got a windbreaker and loaned Maggie his tan corduroy jacket. It was big on her and he helped her into it with his one arm and then pulled her to him and kissed her.

On the beach, Bill Bailey bounded ahead and Walter took her hand, holding it as they walked over the rocky shore. "It wasn't that long after I finished the SATT that Charlotte died and—"

She looked at him, still holding his hand. "Charlotte?"

"My sister," he continued, quickly. "She had colon cancer."

Maggie felt weird, she had such a mix of feelings. First there was immediate relief that Charlotte wasn't someone he was having an affair with: a long-distance, same-time-next-year was what she'd imagined. But she felt sad for his sister and for Walter, and then she felt guilty for snooping in his stuff. The relief and the sadness were the strongest and Maggie wanted to say something about being sorry about his sister, but her voice caught in her throat and she began coughing.

"Are you okay?"

"Yeah, fine. Just chilly night air."

"Let's walk to that big rock and then head back." Walter put his arm around her.

"Okay."

"Charlotte loved Canada geese. A lot of people call them Canadian geese, but the correct name is Canada Goose. Charlotte was a stickler for that. She always corrected me—she wanted them spoken of properly." Walter was quiet for a minute, and he pulled Maggie a little closer. "She had a waterfront condo on the eastside of Lake Washington and she was incensed that people wanted to round them up and kill them. That's where *A Goose Named Hope* came from."

"I'm sorry about your sister, Walter. What you said about her reminds me of Martha Jane, she gets upset when people on the island talk about 'thinning' the deer. She thinks the people should be thinned."

Walter laughed. "Martha Jane was the one who suggested Vashon might be a good place for me. After I moved here last summer, I had to spend a lot of time fixing up my cabin. It was pretty run down and it took me most of the year to get it into shape. But this summer I've been able to write again. I had quite a bit of the book done when that damn windmill fell on me. And then Madeline's death."

Walter continued to talk about the island and what a good move it had been for him. He didn't say anything about asking Maggie to stay, so when they got back to the cabin, she thanked him for dinner and asked if she could bring his coat back in the morning.

"Sure, that's fine. And thanks for writing the emails to the agents." Walter bent his head down and started to kiss her. But she put her hands on his chest and leaned her head back.

"Walter, why don't you ever ask me to stay?"

He shook his head and gave her a sad smile. "I thought it was kind of a miracle that it worked that night after you saved Bill and I've been afraid it wouldn't work again if I was planning it. I'm not a young man, and I'm very out of practice. Also, Maggie, I feel like you've been giving me so much I didn't want to ask for more."

"I've just been typing your book."

"More than that. You saved Bill's life and I think you're sav—"

"Shh." Maggie put her hands over his lips. "Walter, just ask me to stay."

"Will you stay?"

Maggie put her cheek against his and whispered in his ear, "Yes."

CHAPTER NINETEEN

Olivier greeted her with great affection when Maggie got home the next morning. She thought it was sweet the way he rubbed against her legs. Even his loud meows, demanding to be fed, sounded less creepy to her. She opened a can of Fancy Feast and as Olivier scarfed it down, Maggie realized it was the last can. Leslie was still settling things in LA so she'd need to stock up on more. Maybe better get some more litter, too. And maybe a little toy, a little squeaky mouse or something. Maggie made a grocery list and then called Martha Jane to see if there was anything she wanted her to pick up.

"I was just going to call you, Maggie dear. Howie and Mark are coming over for dinner tonight, why don't you join us?"

"Great. Love to. What can I bring?" What she really wanted to bring for dinner was Walter. Maggie knew Martha Jane would be delighted to have him come, but Walter might think she was getting pushy, trying to parade him around to the neighbors. Besides, they were going to get together that afternoon so she could type the revisions for him. Maggie didn't want to play games, but it occurred to her that altogether it probably wouldn't be a bad thing for her to have plans tonight. Plans that didn't include him, so he'd see she hadn't just dropped her whole life to be with him.

"It's just going to be a simple supper," Martha Jane told her. "I'm roasting a chicken and Howie and Mark wanted to bring corn from their garden, which is lovely, but I have trouble with it.

My teeth, you know. But I told them to bring it anyway...I don't have to eat it on the cob... although there is something about it on the cob when it's slathered in butter that just tastes better... don't you think?"

"It is good that way," Maggie agreed.

"And when it's cut off the cob, I feel like it's baby food, if you know what I mean, although that is the cycle of life, I suppose, as our world gets smaller and eating and sleeping is about it. Like babies...but at least I can still paint...although the seascape I've been working on just isn't coming together. Fred says I may need to put it away and try something else and then get back to it with a fresh eye. Fred is often right about these things. I feel so blessed to have Fred Weiss as my teacher, a man of his experience and right here on the island." Martha Jane paused. "What were we discussing, Maggie dear?"

"The food, for dinner. I asked what I could bring."

"Oh, yes. Well, maybe some fruit for dessert. That would be lovely. And come on over about six."

Maggie picked up Olivier and kissed the top of his head and told him she was going to the store to get some nice food for him. She hummed on her way out to the car and all the way along Baker's Beach Road and Cove Road and Vashon Highway. At first she wasn't sure what the tune was that she was humming, or why it was stuck in her head. Then she remembered. Walter had it on last night before dinner. Old music for old people. It was Joe Cocker, "You Are So Beautiful." *You're everything I hoped for...You're everything I need...You are so beautiful to me...* Maggie sang the words as she came up to Bank Road. The people from Yakima with the fruit stand were out in front of The Hardware Store restaurant. She found a space to park in front of the Land Trust building and went to the stand, where she got some beautiful blueberries for dessert.

When she got back, she stopped at her mailbox at the end of Baker's Beach Road. She prided herself on being able to drive within inches of the mailbox without hitting it with her side mirror, then reach in for the mail from the car. When she put the window down, she saw the bright flash of a goldfinch, canary yellow against the dark green fir trees. What a lovely sight. What a lovely day. Maggie smiled as she reached in for the mail and then drove to the house. After she carried in the groceries, she sat at the kitchen table to go through the mail. A couple of bills, two solicitations from non-profits, *The New Yorker*, and an envelope without a stamp with just her first name on it—'Maggie' in oddly shaped letters, and she knew immediately it had to be from Walter, writing with his left hand. She opened the letter, thinking it was probably something to do with the revision of his book. But when she saw what he had photocopied and pasted on the note, she was speechless.

MAGGIE I CAN'T IMPROVE ON MILTON.
—W.

With thee conversing I forget all time,
All seasons and their change, all please alike.
Sweet is the breath of morn, her rising sweet,
With charm of earliest birds; pleasant the sun
When first on this delightful land he spreads
His orient beams, on herb, tree, fruit, and flower,
Glistering with dew; fragrant the fertile earth
After soft showers; and sweet the coming on
Of grateful evening mild, then silent night
With this her solemn bird and this fair moon,
And these the gems of heav'n, her starry train:
But neither breath of morn when she ascends
With charm of earliest birds, nor rising sun
On this delightful land, nor herb, fruit, flower,
Glistring with dew, nor fragrance after showers,
Nor grateful evening mild, nor silent night
With this her solemn bird, nor walk by moon,
Or glittering starlight without thee is sweet.

It was a copy of the passage where Eve speaks to Adam from *Paradise Lost* that Walter had pasted to his note and she sat in her kitchen reading it over and over until it finally and completely sank in that Walter was trying to tell her that nothing was much good without her.

At first she thought about putting a poem in his mailbox. *Paradise Regained* was the obvious choice, except the whole thing really did have to do with religion and she knew that Walter had not sent this poem to her for religious reasons. And she couldn't just ignore receiving a poem like this. You really couldn't do that. But to respond with Browning's *How Do I Love Thee* seemed excessive and Shakespeare's love sonnets were from a man to a woman and they seemed a bit over the top as well. Maggie decided to call him. She went to her desk and Olivier jumped in her lap. Nervously, she picked up the phone and after the fourth ring she was about to hang up when Walter answered.

"Hello." He sounded out of breath.

"Walter, I picked up my mail."

"Oh, well, good." He was breathing heavily.

"Are you all right? You sound out of breath."

"You take my breath away, Maggie." Walter laughed. "Actually, I was outside with Bill Bailey when I heard the phone."

"Well, I just had to tell you that I loved what you wrote."

"I didn't write it. John Milton did."

"I know that."

'I know you know that," he said, sounding a little embarrassed. "I wanted you to know how...well, how I...you know."

"Thank you, and I just want you to know that I loved that you did that. I guess I already said that—"

"So, I'll see you this afternoon?"

"Do you think we'll get work done?" she teased.

"I hope not," he said.

She smiled and hung up. She stroked Olivier, who purred, and Maggie thought that if she were a cat she'd be purring, too. "Who would have thought, cat? It looks like I have a boyfriend, and at my age. But isn't that a dumb word? Boyfriend. We're

both on the seventy side of sixty. There has to be a better word."
Maggie grinned and put the palm of her hand over her heart.
"Oh, my. Who would've thought?"

It made her laugh thinking about Walter saying that he hoped
they wouldn't get any work done. And the revisions probably
could wait, although not too long because she was sure in a week
or two he'd be hearing from the agents and would probably want
to talk over their responses, which she was sure would be positive. The reply he'd gotten from that moron who took over for
Madeline Gordon was an aberration. A dreadful mistake where
some know-nothing assistant in that huge agency had most likely
assigned Walter to her equally know-nothing pal. Certain that
the agents she'd selected would all want to represent Walter,
Maggie pictured the two of them walking on the beach, carefully
considering all the possibilities, weighing the tone and tenor of
each agent's letter. Then Walter, with her advice, would choose
the person who would be the best fit. He might narrow it down
and want to chat with them on the phone, which might take a
bit longer. But without a doubt, Walter would have a new agent
within a few weeks.

This scenario was so firmly fixed in her mind that she was
completely caught off guard when she went to help him that
afternoon. She was very much looking forward to working on
the revisions. And especially to whatever else he had in mind.
It was an interesting thing about sex, Maggie thought, as she
walked briskly on the path to Walter's house. If making love
wasn't available, people sort of shut down and lost interest. Then
if it suddenly became part of your life, the appetite just woke up
as if some switch had been turned on with a big, zingy jolt. She
was sure it was something they were both experiencing. When
she'd left Walter that morning he practically glowed. His blue
eyes were clear and vivid and he'd bounced around the kitchen
whistling while making coffee and toast. They ate cantaloupe
together, relishing the moist flesh, each shaving it down with a
spoon to where the tender, pale green skin shone through. After
breakfast, when he kissed her goodbye, it was with such vigor and

passion that she felt decades melt away as surely as she melted into his arms.

Maggie went up the steps to his cabin, so spry she felt like a spring chicken. Walter opened the door and at the sight of him, she was so startled that she just stood on the porch staring. His face was drained of color, his eyes were blank and veiled, his shoulders slumped and his chest sagged as if he'd had the wind knocked out of him.

"Walter, what happened?"

He didn't say anything and she became frightened that he'd fallen and reinjured his arm, or had another small stroke. "Are you hurt? Are you all right?"

"I don't think I can do this," he mumbled.

Maggie didn't know what to say. Walter just looked at her and didn't speak. Time seemed as slow as the hands of a schoolroom clock. She felt as if she was standing on the porch like some eager Campfire Girl poised to sell mints only to find a wasted old geezer who barely had the strength to open the door. "Can I come in? Can you tell me what's going on?"

Walter took a few steps back from the door and Maggie assumed he meant for her to follow. She closed the door and patted Bill Bailey, who wagged his tail as he licked her hand.

"At least somebody here's glad to see me," she said.

"It's not you."

"What is it, Walter?"

He ran a hand through his hair, making it stick up like white puffs of dandelions gone to seed. He pointed to the computer. "I've heard."

"Heard what?"

He pointed again to the computer.

"Oh, you want me to look at something. I feel like we're playing charades." She went to his desk where three emails had been printed out. Maggie couldn't believe it. They were form rejections from three of the agents on Maggie's list. They didn't even have the courtesy to write a personal reply! They get thousands of queries, she knew that. And she could understand that they couldn't reply personally to each one. But to reply like this to a respected author like Walter Hathaway, well, it was simply outrageous. The worst was one from a Luke Atwater promising face time with editors at the Atwater Writers Conference. "We will host over 50 editors where each author will have 3 minutes to pitch their work, be it fiction or non-fiction. In the first 90 seconds of each session, the author will make his or her pitch and the remaining 90 seconds they will receive immediate feedback along with invaluable suggestions for improving it. The low registration fee of $399.00 also includes Luke Atwater's book, *Perfecting Your Pitch: How to Make your Work More Marketable!*"

"I don't know what to say." Maggie bit her lip.

"Did you see the part about the *Ten Tools for Effective Blogging*? What am I supposed to write on a blog? 'Today I took my dog out and he peed on the rosebush.' Who cares what I do? Has the world gone mad?"

"I just don't know what to tell you...."

Well, I ignored the first two, but I replied to Atwater. Have a look."

Maggie went to Walter's email and clicked on the "sent" messages. At the top of the list was the reply.

Pitch you, you prick.

Sincerely,
Walter Hathaway.

"Good. He deserved that. But the others on the list can't all be this bad, I'm just sure of it. These early ones are just bound to be ones who, for whatever reason, didn't even give your query serious consideration. I'm sure the—"

"I don't think so."

"Well, let's just wait and not jump to conclusions. Have you made the changes you want in the book? I'd love to get those on the file for you." Maggie said, starting to sit down.

"I can't do this, Maggie."

"You weren't able to work on the book?"

He just shook his head.

"You can't let these idiots win! It's a wonderful book, someone will—"

"Publishing is no country for old men, Maggie." Walter sat slumped in the chair by the fireplace. "At some point you have to know when to quit, and it's clear to me it's my time. I had my run. I had a few good seasons, and I can look back at that."

Maggie went to him. She sat on the arm of the chair and put her arms around his neck; she started to kiss him but he hardly moved, sitting slumped and passive, immobilized with defeat.

"I'm sorry." Walter shut his eyes for a minute, then looked at the floor. "Maybe you better go. I'm no good to anybody like this. At least when I'm alone, I can't fail anyone."

CHAPTER TWENTY

Martha Jane's kitchen was filled with smoke when Maggie arrived for dinner with her bowl of blueberries. Howie was opening all the windows and Mark and Martha Jane were conferring over a roast chicken as black as asphalt.

"We have a little problem here," Mark said, as he hugged Maggie. "We're trying to see if anything can be salvaged."

Martha Jane kissed her cheek. "Those blueberries are lovely, Maggie dear. It's beginning to look like we'll be vegetarians tonight."

Howie came in from the living room and gave Maggie a hug. "Blueberries, salad, and corn are a perfectly good dinner, don't you think?"

"Absolutely." Maggie smiled. It was good to be with her friends.

"I just don't know what happened here." Martha Jane stared at the chicken. "I can't remember if I put it in much earlier than I should have and then forgot about it, or if the temperature was wrong...much too high. I haven't done one of these in ages. I use the microwave most of the time...I have to say, it's discouraging to feel less capable."

"I'll just cut into it. Maybe underneath the burned skin it will be okay," Mark tried to reassure her.

"Yes, if you like eating tree bark." Martha Jane smiled. "The deer do, you know...of course they don't eat it so much in the summer when so many things are in bloom. Did you see the darling little fawn the other day? I'm so glad your dog doesn't chase them...it's so terrible for the little ones when they do."

"Tanner is mostly interested in ducks." Howie looked at the juiceless chicken that Mark had sliced into. "Why don't I get some eggs from our house and make an omelet?"

"Lovely, Howie dear. Wonderful. I think Maria Montessori would enjoy some of this chicken, don't you?"

"And Olivier," Maggie added.

"Who's Olivier again?" Martha Jane looked confused. "You know when I forget names, I've just had to learn to ask."

"I'm not sure I ever told you his name. Olivier's my sister's cat. Leslie's in LA, getting things settled before she moves here."

Maggie got the plates and silverware while Howie came back with the eggs. He had cut some chives from their garden to put in the omelet along with some goat cheese. Mark was carving the chicken into little pieces for cat food and Martha Jane arranged a bunch of daisies in a blue pitcher for a centerpiece.

"There's a blue and white checked tablecloth in there." Martha Jane pointed to the chest of drawers by the door. "It should be in the top drawer." Then she chuckled. "Isn't that us, top drawer!"

Maggie smiled as she covered the paint-splattered picnic table with the tablecloth. It felt like they were a family and she wished Walter could be part of it.

They carried the plates out to the deck and Mark went back in and brought out water glasses, then wine and poured some for everyone. "We like this white burgundy. Even though it was meant to go with chicken, it'll be good with eggs."

"Which came first, do you suppose?" Martha Jane slowly sat down next to Maggie. "The chicken or the egg?"

"The big bang." Howie pointed to the sky and Martha Jane chuckled.

"So, what have you two been up to lately?" Maggie asked, unfolding her napkin.

"We went to a revival of *West Side Story* in Tacoma, and it was great, even Howie thought so." Mark looked at him and raised his eyebrows.

"I'm not that bad." Howie took a sip of wine.

"Yes, you are. Every production we go to gets an in-depth critique with every single detail scrutinized," Mark explained good-naturedly. "And if it's a play you know well, you always whisper when an actor drops a line, or flubs it or starts making things up."

Martha Jane smiled at Howie. "This omelet is simply delicious."

"Thank you." Howie smiled. "How I react to theater? It's just an occupational hazard, I suppose I can't help it. But this production we saw the other night was awfully well done, and the story, which is basically Romeo and Juliet, will always be relevant in any age, any culture."

"Like us," Mark said, taking a bite of salad. "Not exactly, but close."

"Like you?" Martha Jane asked.

"There's going to be a big family bash for his father. The good Admiral will be ninety next month, but I'm not invited. Mark and I have been together for almost thirty years and his father still acts like I don't exist. You'd think I'd get used to it, but I don't." Howie didn't sound bitter to Maggie, just sad.

"Well, it's his loss," Martha Jane said. "I'd be very proud to have you as a son and son-in-law. Could you pass those lovely blueberries, Maggie? You know, I don't see why fruit has to be thought of as a dessert when I think it's perfectly fine to have it with our main course. Did you get these at the farmer's market?"

"At the stand on the corner of Bank Road in front of the restaurant."

"What about you, Maggie?" Howie asked.

"Me?"

"What have you been up to?"

Maggie looked to the south towards Walter's house. She took a sip of her wine. "I've been helping Walter."

"Really?" Mark and Howie said, almost in unison.

"After the wind turbine fell on him in the storm and he had surgery, he couldn't use his arm."

"I thought Jordan was helping him." Howie spread butter on his corn.

"He was. Walter was dictating and Jordan would enter it on the computer, but that didn't work out too well, so I'm helping. But you see his agent died and he's had to find a new one." Maggie told them about the rejections and the effect it'd had on him. She put her fork down and sat back. "He's just devastated."

"I can understand that. You see it in the theater with older actors auditioning for part after part, and getting turned down. It's terribly wounding, on top of the injury of aging itself."

"I don't feel injured." Martha Jane took a spoonful of blueberries. "Certainly frustrated, like tonight with the chicken. But not injured. I'm still me. Not what I was at fifty, but my essence is intact."

"I wish Walter could feel that way," Maggie said.

"Fred Weiss told me once that art is often driven by injury. He said the creative act is an attempt to repair a sense of helplessness in the face of hurt by generating the art, making something happen that is all the artist's own. That no one can interfere with or take away." Martha Jane picked at her teeth. "Do I have blueberries stuck on my teeth?" She turned to Maggie.

"Nope. Looks fine."

Martha Jane picked at her teeth again, then ate another spoonful of blueberries. She chewed slowly, then said, "So the creative act is always life-affirming." Martha Jane scowled "At least I think that's what he said," she paused, still scowling, "or maybe I read that somewhere. Or one of you said it to me."

"I think it's true," Howie agreed.

"Not for me though, I don't think," Martha Jane continued. "I mean, I paint because I love it, not to repair some injury but I suppose it's life affirming because it gives me a reason to get up in the morning. But then I've never tried to get into big galleries and juried shows, the sort of thing where people say aye or nay about whether they think I'm any good."

"Theater is a huge risk. You can play to an empty house or see people in the audience walk out. It's a high wire act, being in the arts, that's for sure." Howie helped himself to more salad. "I've always thought the most vulnerable people are stand-up comics or actors who do a one-person show that they wrote themselves. They can't blame the playwright or the director or anybody if it flops."

"Is Walter's book good?" Mark asked her, taking another helping of omelet. "As good as his others? Like the one they made into the movie?"

"I think so. I think it's wonderful. And to keep it from readers, from an audience because it's not about vampires and edgy, gritty things seems like a waste to me. But that's mostly what the publishers seem to want."

"Why doesn't he publish it himself?" Howie asked. "There are a lot of companies that are set up to do that. I know quite a number of playwrights going that route."

Maggie reached for the wine bottle. "They used to call those 'vanity presses' and that term said it all—more wine, anybody?"

"Just a tad." Martha Jane smiled as Maggie poured some in her glass.

Maggie filled her own glass and took a sip. "There's still a stigma against it in the literary world, although it's beginning to change. But I wouldn't dare suggest it to Walter, I don't think he could ever overcome the stigma in his mind."

"Didn't he write the screenplay for *Fric*?" Howie asked.

Maggie nodded. "He did."

Mark looked at Howie and smiled. "I know where you're going with that. We should do it." He grinned. "Let's put on a show, as they say."

"What show? What are you talking about?" Maggie put her glass down and sat forward, resting her elbows on the table.

"Of course you should do it," Martha Jane said. "I know exactly what Mark means. Walter can write an adaptation to make his book into a play and Howie can direct it. It's perfectly obvious. Could you pass the blueberries again, Maggie?"

Maggie helped herself to more blueberries, then handed the bowl to Martha Jane. She glanced again toward Walter's house and didn't say anything for a while. Then she looked at Howie. "What do you think?"

He sat back in his chair and folded his arms behind his head. "Maybe we could give it a shot." Then he sat forward and laughed. "Can't hurt to try."

"Wonderful!" Martha Jane clapped her hands. Then she picked up her glass. "Here's to Walter's play. What's the name of it, Maggie?"

"*A Goose Called Hope*."

"Goose? Like Mother Goose?" she asked.

"Yes, goose. But it's about Canadian, I mean Canada Geese."

"I see. Well, here's to *A Goose Called Hope* by Walter Hathaway, directed by Howie Frankel!" Martha Jane lifted her glass.

While they clinked their glasses, Maggie wondered if Walter would even like this idea. What if he was too depressed and didn't want to work on adapting the book? She listened as Howie and Mark, encouraged by Martha Jane, got more and more energized about it and she began to worry. She was afraid that not only would Walter *not* want to write a script, but he'd be angry that she had talked about his situation and got their neighbors involved.

But Howie was on a roll. *We can use that new venue on the island run by ICA, Island Community for the Arts...It's a great theater space that would be perfect...Harvey Rubin's the artistic director...he's an old friend of mine...I'll call him to see if we can rent it for a weekend run... if we don't charge for tickets...Harvey will probably give us the space for next to nothing...once the script's done, I'm sure we can pull together a little production in three or four weeks...*

"Everyone wants tea, right?" Maggie got up to go in the kitchen.

"Thank you, Maggie dear. The cups are in the cupboard next to the stove."

"We'll have to get going on the script right away," Howie stood and began picking up the plates. "We'll have to give him a call first thing in the morning to see when we can meet. It'll save some time if I have input into the adaptation."

Mark and Howie cleared the plates and were taking them to the kitchen when Maggie came back in. "Look, I really love the idea of a play. But I think we have to give Walter some time to get used to the idea."

"We don't have a deadline do we, Howie?" Martha Jane asked.

"No, I suppose not. There's bound to be some free weekends that we can book the theater, but I think the sooner we can reserve it the better. But no, technically we could put something together anytime, even next summer if we wanted to wait."

"I don't like to wait for things." Martha Jane folded her napkin and put it on the table. "I don't know if I'll be here one day to the next."

"None of us knows when it's our time," Mark patted her shoulder as he reached to clear her plate.

"True, but the odds at ninety are quite different and if I have a vote, I'd like to be on record as stating a preference that we move ahead as soon as we can."

Maggie smiled. "Okay, I'll talk to Walter but I feel like I really can't push him. He was so down when he got these form letter rejections and I just don't know how fast he can bounce back. Or if he can. I just think it's harder when you're older. It's hard to keep fighting when things seem to be slipping away."

Howie went to the kitchen to help Maggie get the tea and brought out a cup for Martha Jane. He stood behind her, put his hands on her shoulders and looked out toward the water. "Do not go gentle into that good night," his deep voice rang out, "Old age should burn and rave at close of day. Rage, rage against the dying of the light..."

"Thank you, Howie dear." Martha Jane patted his hands. "What a grand voice you have, a great tribute to Mr. Thomas."

"Dylan Thomas drank himself to death, didn't he?" Mark asked.

Maggie nodded. "Like a lot of writers." She thought about Walter. At least he'd fought back from that fate. He conquered that demon, which took tremendous strength and resolve. Maybe he could draw on that same tenacity to keep writing. At least she hoped so.

When she got home from Martha Jane's, Maggie was disappointed not to find a voice message from Walter. She didn't truly expect it, but she'd been hoping. Just as she'd hoped all through dinner that she'd hear him calling Bill Bailey, singing the song, a sure sign that he was perking up. Maybe he had done it, and she just hadn't heard it over the dinner table conversation, but she didn't really think so.

What worried her was when he said "when he was alone he couldn't fail anyone." Did he mean that he wanted her to leave temporarily, meaning just that morning? Or was he bailing out altogether? Well, she certainly wasn't about to ask him. At least not tonight. But on her way home from Martha Jane's, she had an idea that she thought might help.

Maggie went to her computer and googled "rejections famous authors" and up popped quite a number of links. She found what she was looking for, read through them, then made a list; copying the ones she especially liked. She printed it out and read it over. Then she grabbed a pen and scribbled a note to Walter and left for his mailbox. She wanted him to find it first thing in the morning.

Walter·

A Goose Called Hope is a wonderful book. Don't give up. Here's what some other writers faced—

Twenty publishers rejected Dr. Seuss before it was published and one said his work was "too different from other juveniles on the market to warrant its selling."

The Tale of Peter Rabbit was turned down so many times, Beatrix Potter initially self-published it.

Sixteen publishers rejected *The Diary of Anne Frank* and one said, "The girl doesn't, it seems to me, have a special perception or feeling which would lift the book above the "curiosity" level."

A Wrinkle in Time by Madeleine L'Engle was turned down twenty-nine times.

One of the rejections of *Animal Farm* by George Orwell said, "It is impossible to sell animal stories in the USA."

There's tons more, but you get the idea—

Love,

Maggie

CHAPTER TWENTY-ONE

Maggie sat in line at the ferry dock waiting for the boat to Seattle. There were about thirty cars in front of her and while she waited, she looked over at the Highway Haiku. On the edge of Vashon Highway, three Burma Shave–type signs were placed a few yards apart where the road sloped down to the ferry terminal. Written in beautiful calligraphy, each sign held a line from a haiku poem. The haikus changed frequently and often reflected the spirit of the season. It was one of her favorite things on the island and this one said:

Atop the pine

A white crowned sparrow

Sings the sun down

As Maggie read the lovely poem, she thought about the poets who produced them and how much pleasure they gave her and so many others on the island. Probably tourists and other visitors, too. Who wouldn't find them charming? Those poets didn't create the poems, write them in the beautiful letters, and place them on the signs for fame and fortune. If they were signed, the poet's name was so small Maggie couldn't even see it from where she sat in the car. They were obviously not after recognition: it had to be about the joy of creating the poems and then sharing them. Maggie sighed, wishing she could get Walter to recognize that his writing would give pleasure like this. It had been two days...but who was counting? she smiled to herself....Still, two days since she'd heard from him and she was starting to wonder if she would. It was hard for her to admit how attached she'd become to him. If he didn't surface, it would take some doing for her to delete him from her psyche. Easy-come-easy-go was not for her, at least when it came to Walter. Or probably when it came to much of anything she cared about. It just wasn't her nature.

Once on the boat, Maggie went upstairs to the passenger deck for coffee. Across from the food service area, she spotted Mark, who waved and motioned for her to join him. She was pleased to see him. "Be there in minute," she said, with a nod. What an incredible day it was. While she waited in line, through the windows that faced south, she saw Mt. Rainier. It was glorious against the bright morning sky, and the water of Puget Sound stretched out from the ferry like acres of blue satin. Not only another dazzling summer day, but a warm one at that. Mark was dressed for it, in khaki shorts, a tee shirt with a logo she recognized even from across the boat. Habitat for Humanity. He and Howie had helped build a house near White Center last fall. He also had on sandals and she wished she'd thought to wear hers instead of sneakers. She was already getting warm in her jeans and it wasn't even noon.

"Whew, sure is hot," she said, as she sat across from him. "What are you up to today?"

"Sears. We need new tires for the truck. Howie and I try to buy local whenever we can, but they're a lot cheaper off-island." He took a sip of his coffee. "How 'bout you?"

"Just a Costco run. I called Martha Jane before I left, but she said she didn't need anything. Anything I can pick up for you?"

"We're set, thanks. Howie went last week." Mark leaned forward and smiled. "You know he's gotten quite a charge out of this play idea."

"Really?" She pulled a tissue from her purse and dabbed the little beads of sweat from above her upper lip. "I thought Howie seemed excited, but then I wondered if maybe he was just being kind."

"No, he's really pumped about it. He hasn't done a show since he retired two years ago and he misses it. Not that he wasn't ready to retire. He was more than ready to give up teaching classes, freshmen especially. And grading, writing evaluations and all the paperwork he had to hassle with. To say nothing of the department meetings and faculty meetings, the committee work. He was happy to say goodbye to all that. But giving up the shows was hard. Howie loves directing."

"Couldn't he have just kept his hand in and worked part time or something, so he could direct?" Maggie asked.

"In order to direct, he would have had to continue to teach a full load. There may be some schools where that isn't the case, but that's how they set it up at Pacific." Howie leaned back against the bench. "I think he was eventually going to try and find something. Although it would be hard to do it off island since it would mean commuting again and believe me, he was more than ready to give that up. And his friend Harv Rubin directs most everything that's produced on the island so he hadn't thought he'd have much of an opportunity. The idea of adapting Walter's book and putting a production together has gotten him really excited."

"That's wonderful." Maggie finished her coffee, took it to the trash container and came back to join Mark. "Now all we need is to get Walter on board."

"Are you worried he won't go for it?"

"A little. I just don't know how to predict what Walter might do. But I'm going to give it my best shot."

"I'm betting you're very persuasive."

"I'd suggest not betting the farm." Maggie laughed "But I'll keep you posted."

There was still no word from Walter when Maggie got back to the island. Nothing in her mailbox and no phone message. Olivier greeted her with his usual leg rubbing when she came in and she decided to give him a treat. When she was at Costco she debated about getting a case of cat food, but Leslie would be back soon and he'd be living with her and she'd be buying it. But she had picked up a box of Feline Greenies Cat Treats in the Savory Salmon flavor. The box said, "Keep kitty clean and fresh with the original green smart treat!" Then it described all the minerals and things in this natural treat and how it would help reduce tartar and plaque. Maggie didn't know if Olivier had that particular problem. His breath seemed fine to her, but she liked the sound of a green treat and so she'd added it to her basket.

She gave Olivier his treat. He seemed to enjoy it very much and after he'd finished, she picked him up and went to the deck and looked out at the beach. Maggie hated to admit it, but she knew she wasn't just looking at the beach to appreciate its loveliness on this beautiful day. She was hoping she might see Walter walking with Bill Bailey. But the beach was empty and the idea of pacing on her deck, wishing for a glimpse of him as if she were some New England wife on a Widow's Walk, made her feel ridiculous.

Maggie decided that since he hadn't responded to her list of those rejections from famous authors, he must still be in a terrible mood. If she told him about the play idea now, she was certain he'd nix the whole thing. "Maybe I should try one last time to cheer him up, cat," she said to Olivier as she went to her computer. At least for Howie's sake. There must be some nice inspirational things about writing I can find that might help. At least it's worth a try. And then if he chose to stay all gloomy and miserable— so be it. She had better things to do with her time than worry about Walter Hathaway. She wasn't exactly sure what they were right now, but she'd find something. She always had before and she would do it again. It wasn't as if she was going to spend her retirement lying on the couch eating bon-bons; she had plenty of options and in the fall she'd begin to sort it out. She had noticed Mark's Habitat for Humanity shirt when they were on the ferry and that certainly might be something she could look into.

Olivier sat on Maggie's lap as she looked at her computer trying to find quotes and ideas that might inspire a writer. She spent the rest of the afternoon at it, ate an early dinner, then went back to it for several more hours. By seven o'clock she'd compiled quite a list. She printed it out and went out on the deck to sift through it all to choose the best ones. There were a lot of wonderful quotes, but she didn't want to overwhelm him so she decided on three. Maggie went back to the computer, typed them, formatting them so they only took one page, and printed it out. Then she put a handwritten note to him on the top of the page and left for his mailbox.

It was after nine and although the sun had set, it was not yet dark. A full moon was rising and Maggie didn't need a flashlight. It was a quiet night and the only sounds she heard were the gravel on Baker's Beach Road crunching under her feet and a dog barking somewhere in the distance. She got to Walter's mailbox and hesitated, unfolding her note to him and re-reading it in the dusky light. Then she heard something rustling in the bushes on the edge of Walter's lot and although she was sure it was a deer or a raccoon, she suddenly felt nervous and immediately felt like a fool. The whole thing reminded her of passing notes to boys in junior high. Was it Dave Barry who said, "You can only be young once, but you can always be immature"? Well, this would be the last hurrah. If he didn't respond to this, she'd be quite direct, take it head-on like a grown-up. No games, just tell him straight out about the play and hope he'd see what a waste it would be if he just gave up. Maggie opened the mailbox and stuck in the note.

Dear Walter,

I wanted you to see these. You have a gift.

The only time you guarantee failure is when you quit.

(The first one is from the Irish poet Brendan Kennelly. It's about poetry, but I think it goes for other writers, too.)

Love,
Maggie

Poetry is, above all, a singing art of natural and magical connection because, though it is born out of one person's solitude, it has the ability to reach out and touch in a humane and warmly illuminating way the solitude, even the loneliness, of others. That is why, to me, poetry is one of the most vital treasures that humanity possesses; it is a bridge between separated souls.

"All sorrows can be borne, if you put them into a story."
Isak Dinesen

Walter, I don't know the source of this last one.
But I think whoever wrote it is spot on.
M.

A good book can open you to know and experience and love more of the world, when you write you will have preserved a little bit of yourself forever in the world. You will have a true thing.

Maggie heard her phone ringing just as she got back to the house. She ran up the porch steps and as she flung open the door Olivier got under her legs and she tripped over him, tumbling over the arm of the couch.

"Damn! Watch yourself, cat!" Maggie struggled to get up from the couch to go to the phone, but Olivier jumped in her lap just as the phone stopped ringing. "Oh, well," she said, quickly forgiving him, "might as well wait to see if the caller will leave a message, right cat?" She stroked Olivier's back and looked out at the water. The light from the full moon rippled across the cove and she thought it looked as though the man in the moon had flung a path of silver sequins across the sea. It was hard not to feel romantic on a warm summer night like this. Then the red light on the phone blinked and she kissed the top of Olivier's head and went to pick up the message.

"Maggie, so sorry I missed you," Leslie gushed. "I haven't forgotten you, I've just been so terribly busy."

Pity. Maggie twirled the phone cord and looked out at the moonlight on the water.

"It's going to be another week and then I'll be a real Vashon Islander!" Leslie's voice trilled.

Great. My dream come true.

"And Maggie, the surprise is taking shape. The one I told you about, of course I didn't really tell you what it was or it wouldn't be a surprise," Leslie giggled. "And I've found the most darling young man to drive my car up from LA so I can fly up. He's just so cute...young of course..."

"That never stopped you, Mrs. Robinson," Maggie barked into the phone, wishing for a minute that she wasn't just talking to the message.

"...but very mature and he's going to start a few days before I leave so he can get to Seattle and pick me up at the airport. And I can hardly wait to see my darling Olivier, and you too, Maggie. And I'll be staying at your house the first night and then the next day the moving van arrives and I'll be actually living in my new house! See you in a week! Bye for now!"

Oh bluuck. Maggie hung up the phone and scooped up Olivier. *We are fam-i-ly...I got all my sisters with me...Get up ev'ry body and sing...* She sang in a loud voice, holding the phone and bouncing around with Olivier. "Just call me Sister Sledge, cat." Then she stopped and put Olivier down. This is absurd. I was doing so well not hearing from Leslie and now I'm losing my grip.

She carried him to the kitchen and was giving him another Savory Salmon Feline Greenies Cat Treat when the phone rang. Now what? Maggie looked at her watch; it was almost ten, rather late to be calling. Probably Leslie again, she'd never give a thought to the time. Maggie put Olivier down and went to the phone.

"Maggie?" Walter's voice was low and quiet.

"Oh hi, Walter." She tried to sound nonchalant. She bit her lip as her heart quickened.

"I saw you and—"

"You saw me? Sounds like stalker...ha-ha," she blurted, and then laughed, a high-pitched nervous little fart of a laugh. *Oh God. I can't believe I said that...*

Walter laughed. "Believe me, I've thought about stalking you the past couple days, but I've been stuck and haven't been able to get my butt out of my chair. Anyway, tonight I was out at my compost bin and I saw you through the trees at my mailbox and well, I just want to thank you. I wondered if you'd like to come over for dessert? Or uh..." he began to stammer, "uh maybe coffee or uh anything...tea...decaf...uh it's late I know and—"

"I thought I heard something, but I thought it was a deer."

"It was me. Aren't I dear?"

"Walter, that's really a dumb joke."

"I know. Will you come over?"

"Okay."

Maggie got the woven Guatemalan bag she used for a purse and took it to the bathroom. She brushed her hair and threw the hairbrush in the bag. Then she reached for her toothbrush and threw it in. Just in case.

The night sky was covered with a canopy of stars as she headed over to Walter's cabin. The wild sweet pea was still blooming and the scent filled the warm air. She'd taken a flashlight but she didn't need it. Except for a few places where the firs created dark shadows, most of the path between her property and Walter's was clearly visible in the bright light of the moon. There were gentle waves washing up on the beach and in the moonlight they looked like long silver spools rolling on the shore.

Walter was waiting for her on his deck and the minute she emerged from the path he came down the steps and hurried to meet her.

"Maggie—" He put his good arm around her and pulled her to him and held her against him. She could feel his heart through his sweatshirt and lay her head against his chest, careful not to disturb the sling that held his injured arm. Bill Bailey came bounding up and danced around them. Walter kissed the top of her head and then took her hand and they walked through the tall grass to his cabin.

"You know I think my favorite was the genius who told George Orwell it was impossible to sell animal stories in the US," he said, laughing, as they went up the steps. He opened the door for her, then went to the kitchen. "I have a pot of decaf on, want some?"

"Sure." Maggie smiled and sat on the couch.

Walter brought Maggie her coffee and then went back for his and sat across from her next to the fireplace. "But I also loved tonight's mail drop." He reached in his pocket and took out the paper and unfolded it, then picked up his readers from the table next to his chair and put them on. "The part where it said, 'you will have preserved a little bit of yourself forever in the world. You will have a true thing.'" That resonated with me, and it makes me feel better when I think about *Fric* and the other work I did over the years."

Maggie frowned. "You sound like it's all in the past."

"I don't have the stomach for it, Maggie. I don't want to keep sending it out and getting back this crap about tweet and pitch and platform. Screw 'em. I've had enough."

"Well, I haven't." Walter looked puzzled so she continued. "What I mean is that I love *A Goose Called Hope* and the other night I had dinner at Martha Jane's and Howie and Mark were there and I told them about it and—"

"You what?"

"Just hear me out, okay?" She saw him look at Bill Bailey and roll his eyes, but he didn't say anything. "I can't remember whose idea it was, it doesn't matter, maybe it was Martha Jane, but anyway Howie wants to work with you to adapt the book for a play."

"I don't know about this," he muttered.

"Howie thought he could pull a production together by Labor Day weekend and he wants to ask his friend Harv Rubin about reserving the theater for it. I really think you should do this, Walter."

Walter shook his head and continued to pat Bill Bailey.

"There's no agents, no editors, no marketing committees, no acquisition committees, no gatekeepers. No one to stop people on the island from hearing your wonderful story."

Walter took off his glasses, laid his head back against the top of his chair and closed his eyes. "I know you mean well, but—"

"Let me ask you something. Did you write to make money?"

"No. I always liked writing, it's the way I make sense of the world I suppose, or at least try to make sense of how I feel about it. I think I told you before I wanted to write a Vietnam novel but couldn't do it. I just fell into writing for kids. Found I loved it, but I never thought anything would come of it."

"So if money was never the motivation, why does it matter that *A Goose Called Hope* becomes a play for just a small number of people? Does a thing have value only because of numbers? What if just one person loves it, why should that have any less value?" Maggie leaned forward. "I think it's like cooking a big feast, choosing a menu, buying ingredients, cooking and baking for days and then, Walter...then not inviting anyone to eat it. To me writing this book is like that, if you just put it away and let it die." Maggie paused for a minute. "And besides, Mark told me that Howie needs this."

"He did?" Walter perked up a little.

"Yes. He said that he's really missed directing since he retired two years ago and the idea of putting on a show here on the island and working with the author, the playwright, to develop it has really given Howie a lift."

"Can I sleep on it?" Walter smiled.

"Of course."

He stood up and went to her. Walter bent down and lifted her chin. "Can I sleep on it with you?"

Maggie stood up and he put his arm around her and she was startled when they kissed by the strong current of longing and of need. Like a tide coming in that you couldn't halt.

CHAPTER TWENTY-TWO

Maggie yawned, stretched and smiled as Bill Bailey came bounding in, leaped on the bed and snuggled next to her. Walter had let him out and fed him and was in the kitchen getting coffee. She patted Bill's head and thought about when Becky was a toddler, how she'd often climb in bed in the mornings with her and George. It was another life. A chapter that had closed and she was another person. The memory was bittersweet, but elusive. Again evoking the now too familiar question: where did the time go?

Walter came in with her coffee. "Bill didn't waste any time getting back to you, I see." He kissed her forehead and put the mug on the nightstand next to the bed. In a few minutes he came back with his coffee and opened the shades, letting in the early morning light. He climbed in bed and sat next to her. "I love waking up to this view," Walter looked out at the water, then turned to her. "And I love waking up to you. And who'd have thought," he said, wistfully. "This hardly was the plan when I moved to the island. I wanted to focus on my work, I didn't imagine having a lot of people in my life. Or even one person…I'm good at solitude, writers have to be and now, well, things have flipped upside down."

"Disorienting?" Maggie sipped her coffee.

"A little. But in the most delightful way, Maggie." Walter sighed a deep sigh. "And just so you know, I guess I've decided to work with Howie on the play."

Maggie was surprised at the lump in her throat. "I think that's a very good idea."

"I have another good idea." Walter put his coffee down and reached for her.

Walter wasn't the only one who felt his life had turned upside down. This first summer at the dawn of her retirement was one that Maggie had seen as a segue summer: a transition to be filled with quiet reflection. She expected to think about what had given her the deepest satisfaction in the past. Then she would look ahead, contemplating her options, and design her life in a way that would bring the most contentment. She was a frugal person and for the most part lived a simple life. With the pension she had from her years at the school district, if she was careful, she didn't think money would be a huge worry. But part of that equation was counting on social security and Medicare and she refused to think about what might happen if she couldn't rely on that. And so far, she'd been blessed with good health.

Other than the times she spent with her granddaughter, Maggie didn't envision a life filled with joy. But she did believe a deeply satisfying life was attainable. A contented life. The last thing she expected this summer was another wild ride with Walter Hathaway. And part of what felt so wild was the fact that she had been pulled into this adventure without exercising any of the caution with which she'd led her life. Her first encounter with him really had been an aberration. And now what was she getting herself in for? She asked herself how this had happened, but Maggie knew the answer. Even from the first, Walter had been different. She had met a lot of authors through her committee work for the American Library Association and more than a few only wanted to talk about themselves. Walter had shown a true interest in her. In who she was as a person, not just as someone who might help his career. And there was the chemistry between them. It was irrefutable, irrepressible. It felt combustible. She loved his broad shoulders, his deep bass voice, his bushy white eyebrows, his thick white hair, the beautiful smile that lit up his craggy face. She could get lost in his eyes, still so clear and blue that she got silly with poetic images when she thought of them...the depth of the midnight sea...the cloudless, shining cobalt sky...Good Lord...even sapphires! It felt giddy and a little ridiculous; because the intoxicating adolescent excitement was a mixed brew of exhilaration spiked with foolishness and fear.

Walter had been working with Howie on the script for most of the week and was quite simply having a ball. He had opened up, his defenses collapsing like an old fence blown down in a little gust of wind. He was friendly to everyone at Baker's Beach, chatting with people he met walking at low tide, at the post office and the grocery store. Martha Jane overheard him chatting with Jordan's grandmother, Sondra Wiggins. Sondra was on her way back from the mailbox and had bumped into Walter as he was going over to Howie's. He asked her about Jordan and told her what a great help he'd been to him. Martha Jane had heard him when she was on her deck and told Maggie about it when she came in from kayaking.

"Walter's quite a jolly fellow, I'd say," Martha Jane said with a chuckle. "I don't suppose you have anything to do with it, Maggie dear?" Martha Jane winked.

"Maybe." Maggie smiled...oh why be coy? Maybe she should tell her that she loved the way Walter made her feel. He appreciated what she always thought of as her most ordinary, boring qualities, her steadfastness and her reliability. He liked to make her laugh. He loved her matronly, broad-hipped, tall, big-boned, earth mother body and he told her about that. He brought her coffee in bed. He cooked with his one good arm. He cared about what she thought, and not just what she thought about him. He was passionate and wild and incredibly tender. And he needed her. Not the way Leslie had needed her, which always felt exploitive and a one-way street. He needed who she was; she fed his soul and he gave back. He wanted to please her in every way he could.

Their days together were spent doing things people listed on dating websites. Walking on the beach, watching sunsets, listening to music, cooking together and they laughed about how they were living a romantic cliché.

Maggie looked in the direction of Howie and Mark's house where Walter was working with Howie. "Actually, Martha Jane, I think I'm in love with him."

Martha Jane clapped her hands. "Wonderful!"

"It is, but it could be terrible. I have no clue where this is headed and I could be setting myself up for a knife in the heart if Walter changes his mind or—" Maggie bit her lip.

"Or what, dear?"

"Or if something happened to him."

"It will," Martha Jane said with quiet authority.

"It will?"

"Of course. He'll die. We all die. None of us knows when and if you love someone, if you love to be with him...I, for one, don't think it's wise to avoid happiness because death is inevitable."

"Oh, my...I'm sure you're right...but—"

"Of course I am, dear."

"I just don't know what's ahead. We haven't talked about it, and this is such a U turn for me. I mean for years I've thought why would I even want a man in my life?" Maggie laughed. "What for? If I needed to move the furniture I'd just ask Howie and Mark."

"Speaking of them, Howie's having a dandy time working with Walter. This morning after he fed the chickens he came by for coffee and he told me he wants all of us to be in the play."

"You're kidding? Walter hasn't mentioned that."

"I think Howie just got the idea this morning. But he said he thought they'd be ready to cast it and begin rehearsals next week."

"I don't know about my acting ability, but maybe I could help with costumes or something. It would be great fun to all be involved." Maggie sighed. "Frankly, the timing couldn't be better. My sister arrives next week. A project like the play would give me a good excuse to avoid getting caught up in her dramas. Drama is like food to Leslie, she can't live without it."

For days after her conversation with Martha Jane, Maggie thought a lot about what she had said about death, its inevitability not being a reason to shy away from a relationship. But what about health? One morning when she lay next to Walter, with their legs entwined and her head on his chest, she felt the beating of his heart. It sounded strong and steady, but was it really? And how long would it stay that way? How long would his health hold up? Wasn't that another risk of getting involved at this time in her life? That she'd only have a few good years. Or it could even be just months with someone and then she could get stuck as a caregiver for some very sick old man. Or specifically for Walter. If he became a very sick old man? Hadn't she had enough responsibility when she was young after her father died…why set herself up for more at this time in her life? Now that she had retired, she didn't even have her job to tie her down. Why on earth would she take the risk of getting entangled and burdened with some old geezer albatross? And what about her health? Wouldn't Walter be worried about having some sick old crone on his hands? But the only mention of their health came after making love one night. They'd both laughed that it was sure to be improving their circulation, reducing stress and aiding their prospects for longevity. But Maggie knew that love, by its very nature, encompassed responsibility. Anything less wasn't love; it was a fling. And although they had yet to speak the words, Maggie knew that what she and Walter had, for both of them, wasn't a fling.

The afternoon Leslie arrived, Walter had finished work with Howie and was on his way home when Leslie drove up in her silver Lexus. Maggie went out to meet her and Leslie emerged from the car, carefully extending one golden tanned leg, then the other, like a woman in a car commercial. She pranced over to Maggie, hugging her, and gushed in her breathy little-girl voice,

"Oh Maggie, I'm finally here! And I can hardly wait to see Olivier—it's just been so long."

Maggie looked over the top of Leslie's blonde perfectly coiffed hair at Walter crossing the road. Better get it over with. "Walter, come over a second, will you? I'd like you to meet my sister."

Walter stood next to the Lexus and Maggie made the introductions, explaining to Leslie that Walter lived at the north end of Baker's Beach.

"I'm so happy to meet you," Leslie said, shaking his hand, covering it for a minute with both hands in an exceptionally warm greeting. "I'm so looking forward to meeting my neighbors."

"Welcome to Baker's Beach." Walter smiled and withdrew his hand. "Well, I've got to get home to feed Bill. Nice to meet you."

Walter trotted down the path toward his house as Leslie went to the back of the car, opened the trunk and reached in for a small carry-on bag. "Who's Bill?" she whispered to Maggie as she lifted the bag out. "Is he gay?" Leslie pursed her lips, looking regretful.

"His dog."

"His dog. Oh, that's so cute. My dog Bill. Remember that old song? 'My Man Bill,'" she laughed, suddenly quite cheerful. "Oh, I remember now, he's the guy who sang to call his dog. See, I knew there was a song in there somewhere—so, who is he?"

"Walter Hathaway, I just introduced you."

"I know you did. That's not what I meant. I meant, you know—maybe you mentioned it before—is he married? What does he do? That sort of thing. And what happened to his arm?"

"He fell. Don't you want to see Olivier?" Maggie turned and went in the house as Leslie scurried after her. Olivier was asleep in Maggie's reading chair. Leslie dropped her bag and ran to him.

"Oh, my darling boy!" She scooped him up and he opened his eyes and began meowing the eerie wail that Maggie suddenly found quite irritating. Leslie stroked him and rubbed her face against his head. In a few minutes he began to purr and she covered his face with little kisses and then put him down. Olivier went to Maggie and rubbed against her legs.

"He seems to like you," Leslie didn't sound all that pleased.

"We got along."

Leslie went to the door where she had dropped her bag and took it in the guest room. "So what about him, Maggie?" she called.

Maggie went to the kitchen and looked for a bottle of wine. She had hardly been drinking since she'd begun spending so much time with Walter. She didn't even miss it. 'Til now. There was a bottle of chardonnay toward the back of the refrigerator and she pulled it out, took a jelly glass down from the cupboard and poured herself a glass. She supposed she should offer one to Leslie. She looked at the cupboard and thought about getting another glass, but instead, sat down at the kitchen table and drank her wine.

Leslie had changed her clothes and came in the kitchen. "I can't remember if I told you, but I'm having dinner tonight with Betty Sue."

"That's fine."

She glanced at the wine bottle. "You're having wine?"

"Yep." Maggie took a big gulp as Leslie stood by the table, waiting for Maggie to offer her some. Maggie kept drinking.

Finally, Leslie said. "I'll just get a glass, too. Where are the glasses again?"

Maggie waved her hand to her left. "Cupboard next to the fridge."

"So what about him?" Leslie asked again, finding a wine glass. She sat next to Maggie and poured the wine.

"I fed him that Fancy Feast Tuna and kept the doors and windows shut—"

"No I mean, the guy."

"What guy?"

"That Walter guy, the one with the dog named Bill."

Maggie gulped her wine. She was not going to be able to avoid this. She would have to tell her, she'd find out anyway, so she might as well find out from her. She sighed and said, "Walter is single and—"

"Really?" Leslie arched her eyebrows. Maggie could almost see her licking her lips.

"And he's a writer and—"

"Really?" She leaned forward. "Has he written anything I might have heard of?"

"He writes kids' books."

"Oh." Leslie leaned back and sipped her wine.

It really fried Maggie the way children's writers were dismissed as somehow being less than writers who wrote for adults. As if anyone could do it. "Walter Hathaway wrote *The Adventures of Fric the Chick*," Maggie announced, sticking her chin out.

"That's a movie!" Leslie said, excitedly. "I remember that! Did he write the screenplay, too?"

"He did." Maggie nodded. "Look, I might as well tell you that Walter and I, well, we see a lot of each other and we're very close, that's all."

"He's a very sexy old guy. So, are you sleeping with him?" Leslie folded her fingers back against her palm and examined her nails.

"You know I've always wondered why some older men are sexy old guys while others are dirty old men." Maggie poured a little more wine in her glass. "I suppose the dirty old men are the ones that chase women the age of their daughters and granddaughters."

"So you *are* sleeping with him!" Leslie dropped her hand and laughed. Then she leaned forward, put her elbows on the table and rested her chin in her hands. "Is he any good?"

Maggie just smiled. "You're so surprised."

"I just never thought of you in that way."

"No. You thought of me as a mother and most people don't think about sex and their mothers." Leslie didn't say anything. "You're not the only one that lost a mother, Les. She checked out on me, too."

"But you were older," Leslie said, defensively.

"Teenage girls still need mothers. They're like boats practicing to leave their mooring. They go out a little, then come back, then they go out a little farther and they need the mooring to be rock solid. I was out there by myself."

"Remember the time you tried to make chocolate chip cookies for me and you brought home this roll of dough wrapped in plastic that we kept in the refrigerator and finally we just opened

it and ate all the dough." Leslie bent down and picked up Olivier. All the diamonds on her fingers flashed in the afternoon sun
streaming in the window. "It's one of my happy memories. You
and me, eating that cookie dough."

"Oh my God, that is so pathetic. We were so pathetic."
Maggie laughed and shook her head. "Remember when I took
you trick-or-treating and your bag broke on the front steps just
as we got home. And there was some dog in the neighborhood
following us and he ran around gobbling it all up."

"And he threw up." Leslie laughed. "That dog's name was
Wendell, he was a big black lab. Served him right, but then you
felt sorry for him. But I didn't." Leslie put her hand on Maggie's
arm. "I can't wait anymore. I'm going to tell you my surprise.
I just know you're going to be excited for me, Maggie." Leslie
paused dramatically and then stood up. She walked across the
kitchen and looked out the window over the sink for a minute.
Then she turned back and leaned against the kitchen counter.
"When I lived in New York and was doing theater there, I was
the understudy for the lead in a Tennessee Williams play. It was
a fantastic part and I loved it so much I could have done it in my
sleep. I still can," she said in her high breathy voice. "Back then
the girl who had the part never got sick so I could never perform."

"Too bad."

"Yes, it was. Not that I wanted her to get sick—"

"No, of course you didn't." It was all Maggie could do to keep
from choking.

"But I knew if I'd gotten the chance I would have been great.
And now, I have that chance because Betty Sue—" Leslie saw
Maggie scowl. "Betty Sue, you remember. My realtor, well, she's
put me in touch with the theater here and I'm going to produce
that show right here on Vashon Island! I'll be bringing up a director and a cast from LA. I've made a very substantial donation
to the Vashon Island Theater and they are just thrilled with
the whole project!" Leslie patted her hair, and grinned. Maggie
sipped her wine. "This is such a quiet place, it will be perfect for

me to concentrate and put together a really first-rate show. And remember when I said the surprise had to do with your name?"

"Did you say that?" Maggie winced. "I guess I forgot."

"It's Maggie! I'm producing *Cat on a Hot Tin Roof* and I'm Maggie the Cat!"

Maggie stared, speechless, as Leslie stuck out her chest and swung her hips seductively and leaned back against the refrigerator and took a long, slow drag on an imaginary cigarette. Then she put her hands on her hips. "Maggie the cat is ALIVE!" Leslie bellowed in what Maggie thought was supposed to be a Southern drawl. "I'M AH-LIVE!"

Maggie continued staring, still speechless...Maggie the Cat was supposed to be young, ripe, juicy, fertile. Not a post-menopausal, botoxed old babe. This was beyond denial. Leslie had lost contact with reality...she was delusional! *Oh Lord...give me strength*, she could hear their mother's voice.

Maggie realized that Leslie assumed that Maggie's obvious astonishment was because she had been blown away by this sample of what would be her incredible performance as "Maggie the cat." She watched Leslie sit back down at the kitchen table and attempt to project a modest smile.

"I'm stunned," Maggie finally muttered when the silence started to feel awkward. But she just had to say something, at least try to help ward off this disaster. "Leslie, look, I don't want to be unkind, but aren't you a little old to be playing this part? A lot of actresses as they age do character roles, like Betty White. She's fabulous. Why not be like Betty White, she's had a great career and she's still considered a hot property," Maggie said, cheerily.

"I can't believe you said that!" Leslie glared at Maggie and stood up. "Betty White is EIGHTY!" she screeched. She scooped up Olivier and stomped out, yelling over her shoulder. "AND I'M *NOT* EIGHTY!"

CHAPTER TWENTY-THREE

The afternoon that Walter finished the script, he went straight home from Howie and Mark's and called Maggie. He wanted to celebrate and thought they should go out for dinner. "You're probably sick of my cooking anyway," he said, "and we need to get out of our rut, don't you think?"

"I love your cooking, but sure, I think it would be fun to go out. It'll give me a good excuse to dress up, which means wash my jeans."

"Five-thirty okay? We can eat with all the other old people."

"That's most of the island. Seems like everyone looks alike around here, all these aging hippies with white hair. I suppose I'm one of 'em, too." Maggie laughed. "Want me to walk over? Around five-fifteen?"

"No, we're going on a date. I'll pick you up and I'm not some bonehead that pulls up and honks. I'm coming to the door."

"Maybe I should iron my jeans. Although come to think of it, I don't know if I have an iron."

When they arrived at The Hardware Store, the restaurant was packed and Maggie thought it was a good thing Walter had made reservations and asked for a booth. It was cozy and more private. Or as private as you could be on the island, where, like most small towns, everyone seemed to know everyone's business. When their server came, they ordered Virgin Mary's; Maggie didn't miss wine when she was with Walter. He'd told her he didn't mind if she wanted a glass, but she said she'd already had a drink with her sister. "As soon as she appears I seem to want a drink. She's like some kind of trigger for a craving and I don't think it's a good habit. This afternoon she came over to borrow mousetraps. Seems there was quite a collection of mouse turds around the house she just bought and she was quite upset."

"So, she really is planning on living here?" he asked, shaking his head. "I only just met her, but she doesn't seem quite the type for this place."

"I know. The Lexus, the Fendi clothes, the Louis Vuitton luggage—Leslie's whole package isn't really in tune with Vashon's slightly shabby, recycled style." Maggie chewed on the celery stalk from her drink. "Her stuff looks more than ostentatious here, if I'm honest about it, I have to say it strikes me as almost vulgar. And then all the bling."

"Yeah. I know what you mean."

"Really?" Maggie grinned. "Most men think she's dazzling."

"I've never liked topiaries."

The server came and they both ordered the buttermilk fried chicken with mashed potatoes and chicken gravy. Maggie reached for the bread, took a piece and dunked it in the little dish of olive oil. "What about topiaries?"

"Sure. Like your sister. Those perfectly pruned trees in fake shapes. Some people think they're beautiful, but I don't. I think you're beautiful. You're full and lush and not all pruned up and everything." He laughed. "I guess that's not a very poetic compliment."

"I'll take it, buddy." Maggie blew him a kiss.

"Why did she move to Vashon, anyway?" he asked.

"Her marriage just ended and she said she wanted to be near family, which is only me. Although I've hardly seen her since she got here." Maggie proceeded to tell him about Leslie's project, that she was going to produce *Cat on a Hot Tin Roof* so she could play "Maggie the Cat."

"Isn't she pretty old for that?"

"Oh, you noticed?" she laughed. "When she told me she was going to do a Tennessee Williams play I thought for sure it would be *A Streetcar Named Desire* so she could play Blanche DuBois."

"That would make more sense," he said, "be a lot more believable."

"And there's Blanche DuBois' famous line," Maggie reached for another piece of bread, "'I have always depended on the kindness of strangers,' which is perfect for my sister who has depended on their kindness, if the strangers are rich men. Although to be fair, Leslie worked, too. Made a lot of money from doing television commercials. But even so, sadly, there's a lot of Blanche in Leslie." Maggie chomped on the bread, then continued. "When she announced this whole thing, she said ever since she was the understudy, back in the last century, I might add, she says it's been her dream to do *Cat on a Hot Tin Roof.* She'll be bringing up a director from LA and some actors. It should keep her busy for months. She told me the name of the guy who's going to play Big Daddy..." Maggie hesitated a minute, "I think she said his name is Ronald Whitehorn and he played the lead in a Broadway play called *Talking Dirty in the Beauty Shop*, but I never heard of it, or of him. But that doesn't mean he wasn't well known. I remember one time Martha Jane's friend, Annie Duppstadt, said she didn't know who the people in *People* magazine were. And that goes for me, too. I'm pretty out of it."

"I'm mostly ignorant about that sort of thing, too, but it doesn't bother me. Does it bother you?"

"No. When it comes to knowing who's who is this world, I have to say that other than trying to keep up with my friends and the names of their grandchildren, mostly I just want to know the names of birds."

"We're a good match," he said, nodding, as he reached across the table for her hand.

After dinner Walter drove her home and parked his truck in her drive. They held each other and they stayed in the car kissing like teenagers. "I'd like to wrap you in a blanket and dance you around," Walter whispered.

Maggie leaned her head back. "You what?"

"It's a line from one of my favorite songs. 'Qu'Appelle Valley Saskatchewan.' Do you remember Buffy Sainte-Marie?"

"Sure. I love her."

"You would. You're someone who would love her." He stroked her face. "The song says 'wrap me in your blanket...dance me around, take me back to where my heart belongs. You can travel all alone, or you can come along with me'—"

"Qu'Appelle Valley, Sas-katch-e-wan—I remember it now. It used to make me cry."

"Sometimes I wonder what my life would have been like if I'd gone to Canada. Hadn't gone to Vietnam. And if some guys I knew hadn't gone. For sure some would be alive—and maybe I wouldn't have drowned in booze, but maybe I would have. You never know."

Maggie put her head on his chest and her hand was under his shirt, her fingers spread and moving slowly across his warm skin.

"What are we doing in this truck?"

"Beats me." Maggie closed her eyes. "Want to come in?" Maggie whispered.

"Is the Pope Catholic?"

On Wednesday of the next week, the first reading for *A Goose Called Hope* was held at Howie and Mark's house. Howie had asked Martha Jane, Maggie and Jordan to come over to read through the play so he and Walter could listen and make any necessary changes. It had rained the morning of the reading, and by the time everyone got to Howie and Mark's that afternoon, it still hadn't let up. It was a steady, light rain and they gathered in the living room instead of on the deck as Howie had hoped.

"I'm grateful for the rain," Martha Jane said, looking out. "We've had such a lovely stretch of cool, bright air and full sunlight, but everything around my house looks parched. Although your garden is just beautiful," she said to Howie and Mark. "The smell of the oriental lilies between our houses is intoxicating and that fuchsia hanging down from the porch is simply superb."

"That's Mark's work," Howie patted Mark on the shoulder and then began handing out the scripts. "So, let's get started. I'll assign parts and then we'll read it through and Walter and I will take notes. But first, Walter, if you could just summarize the story so everyone has a sense of it before you read it."

"Sure. Although I have to say I never thought I was much good at describing my stuff, but here goes. I'll try to be brief."

Maggie listened while he gave them his condensed version of the story. She loved the sound of his deep voice. She wondered if it showed because Martha Jane gave her what she thought was a knowing look. When he finished everyone clapped and Walter looked a little embarrassed.

"That was great, thanks Walter." Howie sat forward. "Okay, so I thought for this read-through that Martha Jane could be 'Hope,' Mark will be 'Mr. Hedgehopper' and Jordan and Maggie you will be 'Goose #1' and 'Goose #2' and then for the scenes with the townspeople, you'll be 'Town #1' and 'Town #2.'"

"Don't I get a name?" Jordan looked disappointed. "Can't I be something besides 'Goose #1'?"

Howie looked at Walter. "Fine by me. Okay with you Walter?"

Walter nodded. "Did you have a name in mind, Jordan?"

"Um-well, how 'bout G-Gooze. That's way cooler than Goose #1." He leaned back and shoved his hands in his pockets.

"Do you want a name, too, Maggie? We've got to be fair here," Howie said.

"What's good for the goose is good for the gander," Walter grinned, a little sheepishly. Everyone groaned except Martha Jane, who laughed. Walter ran a hand through his hair. "Sorry. Couldn't resist that,"

"Okay, well if I'm going to have a name, I'd like to be "'Maggie the Goose.'"

Walter cracked up and when no one else laughed, Maggie explained, "It's kind of an in-joke."

"Fine, well let's get started. I'll read the stage directions," Howie stood up and went to the window and sat against the windowsill. As the script was read, Walter took a few notes and Howie jotted notes on the margin of his script. It took about an hour to get through the whole thing, and when they got to the end, everyone put down their scripts and clapped.

"Awesome!" Jordan jumped up and pumped the air.

"Great job, everybody," Howie said. "You sound like you've been doing theater all your lives." Howie looked at his script. "I have a few notes and I know you do, too, Walter but before we discuss those, does anybody want to add anything, any reactions?"

Mark stroked his chin. "I was thinking about an underlying political theme, about geese in flight and how they need both the left and the right wings, kind of a subtle healing message about unity and so forth."

"Yeah and I think G-Gooze should have these special powers and he can sneak into the town meeting and he has this special stare when he points at someone and like it freezes people and zaps them and stuff!" Jordan jumped up and held his arm out straight, pointing out the window at Bill Bailey and Tanner, Mark and Howie's dog, who were romping along the beach. He turned to Howie. "Get the idea?"

"I like it the way it is," Martha Jane said. "It seems to be about the triumph of the ordinary."

Howie looked at Walter who nodded in agreement. "Good, I agree with Martha Jane. I think Walter and I can mostly polish what we've got, which shouldn't take too long. And then we'll have to begin blocking it."

"What's that?" Jordan asked.

"Working out the movements, the action. What each character's business is, which means what each one is doing." Howie paused for a minute. "How would each of you like to take these parts for the show?"

"I'm quite flattered," Martha Jane said, quietly. "But you see I could never remember the lines. I wish it weren't the case, but

'Hope' has a big part and I'm so sorry but I'm just not up to it, but I'd love to be in the crowd scenes."

"If you could turn Hope into a guy, I'd do it," Jordan volunteered. "Instead of 'Hope' the goose could be 'Harry' you know, like Harry Potter."

Maggie looked at Walter whose fingers were pressing the bridge of his nose.

"Jordan, did you know that in Shakespeare's time all the women's parts were played by men?" Howie asked.

"Didn't know that."

"It's true. And a great actor can take on a role of a character very different from his or her true self. And I think from what I just heard, as you read the part of G-Gooze that you have the ability to star in this show. To be our 'Hope,'" Howie said, confidently, and made a note on his script.

"Really? Star, huh?...well, yeah, I guess so. I mean even if 'Hope' can't be a dude, I guess I can do it." Jordan grinned.

"Fine, then it's settled," Howie smiled and began collecting the scripts. "Maggie will be 'Maggie the Goose' and Mark will be 'Mr. Hedgehopper' and I'm going to ask some people I know to be the geese and the townspeople for the crowd scenes along with Martha Jane. And someone for the other goose that Jordan was going to play. They only have one or two lines so we can just bring them in for the last couple of rehearsals.

"What about costumes?" Martha Jane asked. "Shouldn't we look like geese?"

"I was thinking about everyone stuffing a pillow under a gray sweatshirt that has a hood, and wrapping wide black ribbon around the neck. Then getting hats and scarves for the townspeople at the thrift shop, at Granny's Attic. Would you and Maggie like to be in charge of that?" Howie asked.

With Maggie's help, Martha Jane slowly pulled herself up out of the chair. "I'd love to do that and I'm sure you'd help me, right Maggie dear?"

"Love to." Maggie nodded and Martha Jane patted her cheek. "This is going to be a splendid play! Everyone will just love it!"

Walter stayed with Howie to work a little more, and after Maggie walked Martha Jane to her house, she practically floated home. The rain had stopped and the air was fresh and clean. Sunlight danced on the water of the cove and everything felt new. Walter was thrilled with the reading. He hadn't said it in so many words, but Maggie could tell. She was learning to read him and she was brimming with gratitude: for this day, for her friends, for Walter. And for having had the chance to help him and make a difference in his life. Martha Jane once told her that without gratitude there can merely be pleasure, which is momentary and fleeting; that only with a grateful heart can true happiness be obtained. And Maggie agreed.

She was in the glow of such happiness that a half-hour later when Leslie stormed over to her house and charged in, red-faced and perspiring, without so much as a "hello," and flung herself on Maggie's couch—it hardly fazed her. Maggie watched, somewhat detached, as her sister, apparently having a mini meltdown, threw her arms in the air and shouted, "I can't believe this place! This is ridiculous! No one told me it was so isolated!"

Maggie sighed. "What happened, Les?" she asked, calmly.

"Ronald had to—"

"Who's Ronald again?"

"*Ronald Whitehorn*! I told you, he's playing Big Daddy and I kept his script by mistake and he left LA for New York for just a couple of days and he asked me to send it to him Express so he'd get it tomorrow and I went to the post office and they won't guarantee that it will get there overnight! I never heard of such a thing! They said it would take two days to get to New York...*two days!* Then they told me to go to the Country Store and try to send it FedEX and I went to the mailroom in the back of the store and they said the FedEX guy had left for the day, and then going back to my car, I had to go back through the shed filled with packages but now there was a chicken sitting in the rafters, a grayish puffy chicken, with a beak and everything—right over my head—I can't believe just to mail stuff you have to worry about getting bombarded with chicken shit!"

"I know that chicken. It's a very nice chicken. And the Country Store is charming and really, Les, you'd never get bombarded with chicken shit." Maggie sat on the arm of the couch. "Look, the thing is, you have to understand that when you live on an island you don't have all the conveniences of the city, the pace is slower. Living on 'island time' means things don't run like clockwork and you need to have patience."

Leslie took a deep breath. She seemed to be trying to collect herself. After a few minutes she said, "It's such a coup my getting Ronald, that it was very upsetting to me not to be able to do as he asked."

"Will another day matter that much?"

"I suppose not." She was quiet for a long time. She examined her nails, then she looked at Maggie. "You know, you always had patience. It came easily to you."

"I'm not so sure about that."

"Remember when Aunt Rose stayed with us?" Leslie began to smile. "You were more patient with her than I was. I think I cried all the time."

"It's not that I had patience, I was just ten years older." Maggie shook her head. "Oh my, I haven't thought about Aunt Rose in years. I think she came after Dad died and Mom was in the hospital for a few days for some tests, she had collapsed or something, so I was sixteen and you were six. And Rose had it in for Dad since she invested money in one of his schemes and lost it all, and she couldn't stand Mom because Mom wasn't Jewish."

"I don't remember that stuff. All I remember is that she made us stay at the table until we finished all her disgusting food. She never let us watch TV and she called us brats. But didn't we do something to her?" Leslie asked. "Some sort of trick or something?"

Maggie grinned. "We did. It was your idea, but I thought it was great. Aunt Rose had an ulcer and drank milk for it and we put green food coloring in it. She went nuts, but we did it right before Mom was coming home so it was our goodbye gift to Thorny Aunt Rose."

"Thorny Rose." Leslie smiled. "That's a good joke, Maggie."

"Thank you, but quite corny. Walter makes jokes like that and I think it's rubbing off on me."

"How are things with you and Walter?"

"Great. He's in such a good place, he's written a play, a children's play and it's wonderful."

"How sweet." Leslie stood up and went toward the door. "Maggie, do you remember that mink neck thing that Mom had? I was thinking about the kind of clothes 'Maggie the Cat' might wear and I remembered Mom's mink thing. I was fascinated by it."

"I was too, but now it seems pretty awful."

"Terrible!" Leslie laughed. "There were like three pelts and they had the heads and tails."

"And the mouth had a hinge and it hooked on the other mink, like it was biting it," Maggie said, shaking her head, "and they had little claws. Good Lord, what was she thinking wearing those dead animals with little glass eyes?"

"It was the style, I guess." Leslie went to the door. "Um, Maggie, I'm going to be going back and forth to LA a lot while we're getting the reading together and I wondered if it would be okay if I left Olivier with you?"

"Sure. He kind of grew on me, you know."

"Thanks so much!"

"My pleasure." Maggie smiled as Leslie gave her a big hug.

CHAPTER TWENTY-FOUR

The dog days of August. Maggie seemed to remember that "dog days" was derived from Roman times, when they thought the hot weather came from the ancient rising of the dog star, Sirius. As she looked at Bill Bailey and Tanner, she thought the common interpretation, people lying around in the heat, dog tired, was more apt. The dogs were lying in the shade, sprawled with their tongues hanging out, near the door of the new theater space in the building that housed the Island Community for the Arts. The dogs came to all the rehearsals and they were good friends, usually romping and chasing about. But today, with the temperature near ninety, they lay unmoving, like furry sacks of cement.

Howie and Walter had polished the script with just a few tweaks and had confidence that Jordan, whose voice hadn't yet changed, would be believable as a female. There was only one exception: the final scene where a young mother goose, a descendant of Hope, is telling the story to her gosling. Both Howie and Walter didn't think Jordan could make a shift to a younger voice without sounding like Minnie Mouse. Jordan seemed to shine in the part when Hope was rallying the geese and came up with the plan to clog Hedgehopper's toilet. But in the last scene where it required a nuanced, more emotional range he didn't execute as well. They decided that the solution would be to have a narrator to both open and close the story, and Howie didn't have to work too hard to convince Walter to do it.

"You're quite wonderful, you know," Maggie told him after they'd run through the script with the new version. They were sitting in the dark at the back of the theater and he reached for her hand. "I'm a bit of ham," he said, looking a little embarrassed. "But you should know, you make a brilliant 'Maggie the Goose.'"

"It's sure new for me, my sister's the actor in our family."

"What does she say about your coming debut?" he asked.

"Oh, I mentioned the play, but she wasn't that interested since it's a play for kids, so I didn't tell her I was in it," Maggie said, "I actually haven't seen much of her. The guy who's playing Big Daddy wants to rehearse in LA and only come up here for a day or two before the show."

"When are they having it?" Walter asked.

"Leslie hasn't said, I think she likes going back and forth between here and LA. It gives her a good excuse to get her hair done, go to her spa, go shopping, that sort of thing. I guess she's hired everyone now. She told me the name of the guy who's going to play Brick and supposedly he was in a TV show that had a good run a few years ago. But of course, I'd never heard of him either." Maggie laughed. "I'm so yesterday."

Walter put his head on her shoulder and whispered, "Yesterday, love was such an easy game to play...Suddenly, I'm not half the man I used to be—"

"Who is half of what they used to be?" Maggie laughed. "But you do all right, Walter." She looked at her watch. "I better get going. I've got to pick up Martha Jane, we're going to Granny's today to get the rest of the costumes." She picked her bag up from the floor. "Have you decided what you're going to wear?"

"I have an old sport coat somewhere and summer slacks, but if it's hot like this, I'll just wear a short-sleeved dress shirt. I think I have one, but if I can't find it, I can pick one up in Seattle. I never thought this day would get here, but I've finally got an appointment to get this off." He tapped his cast. "I should be back in time for the dress rehearsal Friday night. And the timing is great, because now that I'm in the show, I'd like to have both arms."

"Do you need a ride or anything?"

"Thanks, no. One of the advantages of my truck is the automatic transmission," he paused, and then said quietly, "You do too much for me anyway, Maggie. This is all because of you." He pointed to the stage. "I have to tell you, I get a real charge out of hearing my words up there. It's a first-rate space and I'm proud to have the play here. And if I'm honest, it's more than just hearing the play. There are times when I'll get an email from one of those agents not wanting my stuff, and it's still a bit of a blow. But then, I think about the play. And about having it produced in this new theater, it's a real gem. And the blow, well, it rolls off, like water off a goose's back." Maggie laughed at "goose" and Walter grinned. "Then, I just send them a reply and like the Brits say, I tell them to bugger off. It's very satisfying." He stood up and kissed her cheek. "See you tonight."

Over the years, Maggie had learned to allow a lot of time whenever she took Martha Jane anywhere. Martha Jane often had trouble finding her purse, or her keys to lock the house, and then there was just getting from point A to point B, such as walking from the house to Maggie's car and then walking from the car to wherever they were going. In this case Granny's Attic. Martha Jane's gait was slow and halting. She shuffled along, pausing every few minutes to catch her breath. When they finally got to the car, just getting in—slowly bending over to sit on the seat, finally sitting, then slowly pulling her legs in, to say nothing of finding the seatbelt and then getting it buckled—it was all quite an undertaking. The patience it required was the same that Maggie had needed to draw on when she was trying to get Becky ready and out of the house to go to preschool all those years ago. When she was around Martha Jane, it always struck her how the first years and the last years of life could be so similar. And it sometimes made her wonder who would be there for her, if she lived to be Martha Jane's age. But Maggie wasn't dwelling on that thought as often as she once did. She was having too much fun.

She looked at the horses, llamas, and sheep that grazed behind fences along Westside Highway and at Martha Jane sitting quietly in the passenger seat, enjoying the outing. It had cooled off a bit and the summer sky was filled with huge fluffy, white clouds. The sun had disappeared behind one of them and Maggie glanced up to see a silver lining shining behind it, and smiled as she thought about the play and what it meant to Walter.

She turned left onto Cemetery Road and drove east until they got to the intersection at Vashon Highway. At the stop sign, she was about to turn right when a car on the north side of the intersection started honking. It was quite unusual because no one honked on the island, or at least rarely. People just weren't in that much of a hurry, unless they were trying to catch the ferry. There wasn't a single stop light on the whole island to make someone impatient if you sat there not seeing it had turned green. Occasionally someone in the ferry line would fall asleep and when the boat began boarding, the car behind would have to honk, but that was about it. The car, a silver Lexus, kept honking and Leslie waved and smiled as she cruised through the intersection and on down the highway.

"I don't see that well, but wasn't that your sister?" Martha Jane asked.

"It is. I guess she's back from LA."

"How's it working out, Maggie dear? Having her live here? I remember you said you'd been worried about it. Or maybe that wasn't it, maybe I'm thinking of something else—" her voice trailed off.

"No, you're right, I was worried. But I have to say it really hasn't been a problem. The only thing she's wanted from me is to borrow some mousetraps. And vent a bit after she'd had a problem at the post office. But I'm used to that with her, so I think it'll be okay."

"Maria Montessori used to take care of the mice for me. I took her bell off when she was in the house and then put it back on when she went out so she wouldn't get the birds. But unfortunately, it didn't always work and then I would be so upset when she brought one as a gift and presented it at my feet. I believe that I heard somewhere that the number one killer of birds was cats. Pity isn't it?"

"It is a pity. But then it's useful if they get the mice. My sister has a cat, but I don't think Olivier's the mouser type." Maggie turned right on 210th Street and found a space in the parking lot in front of Granny's Attic. She went around to hold the door for Martha Jane. "But like I said, it really has gone well with Leslie, because she's back and forth to LA all the time and she's got a project she's working on, so I hardly see her when she is here. We've had dinner a couple of times and it's really turned out much better than I ever thought."

It would have been easier if Maggie had just gone to Granny's Attic by herself. Not only because of the time it required to get Martha Jane in and out of the car, but once in the thrift shop, Martha Jane seemed to become a little confused as to their mission. Today it was to get fabric pieces to dye blue to make the set for the lakefront of the town. But Martha Jane kept trying on hats and scarves for her role as the townsperson, while Maggie was in the back room getting fabric. "We're just here for the fabric, today," Maggie said, gently. "And I've found plenty of fabric that can work. We're all set for the townspeople costumes. We got those last week."

"Oh, yes of course." Martha Jane said, cheerfully, as Maggie paid for the fabric. Maggie noticed that it didn't seem to bother Martha Jane that she'd forgotten they'd gotten the clothes for the townspeople last week. Maybe that was part of aging with grace. Just not letting it bother you when you forgot stuff. After all, what good would it do to get all riled up about it? Maggie was convinced her friend had the right attitude.

When they got back to Baker's Beach, after Maggie dropped Martha Jane off at her house and walked her to the door, she drove home and was just getting out of the car when Howie came running over. His ponytail bobbed against his neck, his face was red and when he got to Maggie he was out of breath and quite rattled.

"I've got to talk to you," he said, panting. Then he leaned over and put his hands on his knees, trying to catch his breath. "Is this a good time?"

"Sure, come on in. Can I get you anything?" she asked, as he followed her inside.

"Just water would be great."

Maggie took a glass down from the cupboard, let the water run for a few minutes, then filled it and handed it to him. "Thanks." He took a big gulp, then wiped his mouth with the back of his hand and sat at the kitchen table. "Maggie, we can't have the space on Saturday." Howie put the glass down and slumped in the chair. "I got a call a half hour ago from Harv."

"You're kidding." Maggie stared at him.

"I wish I were." Howie reached for the glass and drank another big gulp.

"What happened?"

"He got a better offer. It seems a substantial donation has been made to Island Community for the Arts and the result is that your sister is going to have a staged reading that night of *Cat on a Hot Tin Roof*."

"Oh for God's sake!" Maggie shoved her chair back with a screech and folded her arms across her chest, shaking her head and fuming. "I knew it." She slammed her fist on the table. "I just knew it. Things had been too easy with her. But the same night! As Walter's play! Why the hell couldn't she do it some other night?"

Howie stood up and went to the sink and got more water. "Supposedly, it wasn't intentional. Something about scheduling for one of the actors and this was the only day the guy could come up from LA."

"So why doesn't she do it down there?" Maggie could barely control her rage.

"You'd have to ask her. All I know is that we've been dumped. Harv offered me a bunch of other days, but Jordan has to leave on Sunday. His school starts the day after Labor Day."

"He's going to be crushed. He told me he's been texting all his friends about it and he asked Sophie, Audrey Katovsky's granddaughter, to take a photo on his phone during the performance so he can send it to his friends." Maggie sat forward with her elbows on the table, pressing her fingers against her forehead. And what about Walter? She hated to think what it might do to him. It was one thing to be rejected by a bunch of agents in New York, but to have his wonderful play dumped from the theater on this little island. How humiliating was that? "Does Walter know?"

"I told him." Howie sighed.

"How did he react?" Maggie felt her heart quicken. "Was he okay?"

"Actually, he seemed pretty stoic about it. I suggested we get the cast together. Not the whole cast, but you, Mark, Jordan, and Martha Jane and see what we can come up with. I asked him if we could get together at his place tonight after dinner." Howie paused. "I was afraid if it was my place he might not come. But he seemed okay with it. Sort of."

"Fine, but I don't want to cave without seeing if I can get Leslie to find another date." She gritted her teeth, trying to contain her fury. "At least I have to try!"

CHAPTER TWENTY-FIVE

Maggie knocked on the door, banging it so hard her fist hurt. No answer.

More banging...*bam bam bam*...still no answer. The silver Lexus was in the drive, Leslie had to be there. Maggie banged again and again—still no answer—and she started to imagine grabbing an axe and just breaking down the damn door. But the name Lizzie Borden whooshed into her mind, the suspected axe murderess who was thought to have murdered some family members, and the imaginary axe evaporated...too violent an image—she was not a violent person. But as a figure of speech? Yes, absolutely. She wanted to clobber her sister.

Finally, after what seemed to Maggie to be at least five minutes of steady pounding, Leslie opened the door holding her cell phone. "Just a minute, Ronald," she said, her whispery, gooey voice oozing with apology, "so sorry, there's someone at the door--" She glared at Maggie and motioned for her to come in, then turned and ran to her bedroom, closing the door to finish her call.

Maggie paced back and forth, going from the slate entry, across the pale oak floors and then back to the entry like a caged tiger. It made her think about that tiger in Las Vegas that bit its trainer a while ago. All those years of doing what the trainer wanted and one day it snapped, took a chunk out of the guy and the act was over.

Leslie finally scurried out of the bedroom, smoothing her hair. "What in the world? All that banging—"

"I can't believe you've done this!" Maggie grabbed the back of the couch and leaned forward, digging her nails into the pale blond, buttery leather.

"What are you talking about?" Leslie looked genuinely confused.

"The play. Your God-damned play-—bribing ICA with all that money so you could get what you want!" Maggie shouted. "Didn't you know that Walter's play was on Saturday? Don't tell me you didn't know," she scoffed.

"It was mentioned, but it didn't seem to be a big deal. You people live here, you don't have the scheduling challenges we have. We're professionals, Maggie."

"You're a professional pain in the ass, you know that? All you think about is yourself and what you want and what's good for you!"

"Ronald Whitehorn has a part in a film they're shooting in Toronto and they've changed the schedule and he has to leave on Sunday. He said he'd be willing to stop here on his way. He said he didn't want to disappoint me and we could have a staged reading and then work on the full production after he's done with the film." Leslie's eyes were wide. "I can't pass up this opportunity, Maggie, how can you *not* understand that? Don't you care about me at all?"

"How cleverly you do that. You're a real pro all right."

"Do what?"

"Turn the tables so you're the victim and I'm this hard-ass, uncaring person."

"Your friend's play is just a little kid thing. I'm doing Tennessee Williams, Maggie," she said, her voice dripping with condescension.

"It would have made a hell of a lot more sense if you were playing Blanche DuBois."

"Why would I want to play Blanche DuBois?" Leslie bristled, "She's old and pathetic."

"If the foo shits."

"So you just came over here to insult me, is that it?" Leslie's eyes narrowed.

"No. I'm asking you to re-schedule your staged reading."

"Well, I can't do that, Maggie." She folded her arms across her chest. "Working with Ronald is a real boost for my career and I can't believe you won't support me. I suppose you won't even come to my reading."

"How perceptive of you." Maggie turned and stomped out. "I'll come to your friggin' reading the day hell freezes over, you selfish jerk!" she shouted, slamming the door.

When Maggie got home, still reeling from her dust-up with Leslie, a voice mail message was waiting from Walter, inviting her for dinner before everyone else came over. His voice sounded fine, but she wondered if he was handling things as well as Howie thought. The memory of how he'd turned on her when she told him the bad news about his agent was like a freshly dug grave. Why was it that bad memories always seemed stronger than good ones? Maggie realized it was difficult for her to know how Walter was going to react to things. True, she was learning to read him in some situations, but it was hardly like they were a couple that had been together for years and knew everything about each other, could finish each other's sentences, knew each other's thoughts. And were they really a couple?

Walter was out when she called to say that she'd love to come to dinner, so she left a message. She wondered what he'd say when she told him about her outburst with Leslie. Would he be surprised? How well did Walter think he knew *her*? For a few minutes, it had been positively exhilarating to let Leslie have it. But the elation was quite short lived. It seemed like she had only been back at her house a short time when the reverberating energy of all that anger gave way to something old and sadly familiar. It was as if she'd been harboring a slow, toxic gas leak in her connection to Leslie and when Walter's play got dumped, it was the spark that finally ignited it. But the explosion now left her flattened in a rubble of guilt.

Maggie sat down and rubbed her temples...she'd let her mother down...she'd let her father down...she wasn't taking care of her little sister the way she was supposed to...She put her head back and closed her eyes. *Oh, for God's sake...would that old script ever be rewritten?* Her stomach hurt and she was suddenly exhausted.

Better get some rest. She'd need a nap if she was going to be any kind of company for Walter. At least Howie had been the one to tell him about losing the theater space and she didn't have to break the news. Even though Howie said Walter was taking it okay, Maggie still wondered if he was trying to put on a good front. Either way, the last thing he'd need would be for her to come to dinner all gloomy and depressed.

She kicked off her shoes and fell into bed. Her shoulders were knotted and the muscles in her arms and legs ached as if she'd just run a long race, or had been driving for hours without stopping. She slept soundly, only to wake a few hours later when she thought she heard a small child wailing. Maggie opened her eyes. She was groggy and the wailing seemed so real it took her a minute to realize she'd been dreaming. She was fully awake, but the dream was still vivid. There was a small girl weeping, collapsed in the middle of a road, as a car drove away. The car was driven by a woman, but only her back was visible as she disappeared down the road. Nothing else. That was when she'd woken up.

Maggie kept thinking about it as she showered. At first she was sure that Leslie was the child and she was the woman. That seemed pretty obvious. But then, at the same time, it felt like she was the child, too. It was unsettling, but Maggie didn't want to dwell on it. She needed to get ready to go to Walter's and it was quite enough to be worrying about how he was doing.

Along the path on the way to Walter's house, Maggie noticed that the vine maples were showing a tiny hint of gold. The nights were cool now with a hint of fall in the air and the days were getting shorter. It made her sad to think of this summer ending. And she couldn't help wondering if Walter would see his writing career ending, that the cancellation of his play would be the nail in the coffin. When she got to his house, she braced herself, taking a deep breath before she knocked.

"Maggie—" he greeted her with a hug. A very long hug, followed by a very long kiss.

"Walter, I'm so sorry about—"

"Shh—" he pressed his finger to her lips, then kissed her again. "I'll get us drinks, come on in and just sit down."

"Something sure smells good," Maggie said, trying to sound cheerful.

"It's my old standby. I'm kind of in a rut with the Costco lasagna, but as soon as I get this damn thing off my arm, I'll have a whole new repertoire." Walter brought Maggie her Virgin Mary, then got his and sat on the couch next to her.

Maggie took a sip. "This is good."

"Not too spicy?"

"Perfect." Maggie set her drink down and leaned toward him. "Listen, I have to say this. I can't believe Leslie did this. Although I don't know why I'm surprised because it's exactly the kind of thing she's done her whole life and well, I feel terrible about it. I just want you to know that."

Walter stroked the top of Bill Bailey's head. "It's not your fault."

"I know, it's just—"

"Look, I'm not sure what the point is of everyone coming over later, but Howie seemed to think we needed to meet. Maybe he wants to tell them as a group."

"Are you okay?" Maggie asked. "I mean, you seem okay and I—"

"I'm not a fragile wimp, Maggie." He smiled, but she thought his eyes looked sad.

"I didn't mean that."

"I know." He took a sip of his drink and scratched Bill Bailey behind his ears. Finally he said, "Of course, I wasn't thrilled when Howie told me. And if I'm honest, it seemed like old Walter had gotten dumped again." He paused and took another sip. "Frankly...I felt pretty shitty and I had to get out of here. I took

Bill Bailey for a walk and when we got to Peter Point, that place where you saved his life, I threw a stick for him a couple of times and while I was looking at the water and the mountains, I realized that this has been the best summer of my life. Or at least in years and years, and nothing can take that away."

Maggie felt tearful as Walter suddenly stood up and went to the kitchen to check on the lasagna. "Few more minutes and then we can eat." He took a salad from the refrigerator and put it on the counter, then went back for a bottle of dressing. He lifted it to his mouth and held the cap with his teeth and unscrewed it. "I'm getting good with one hand, don't you think?"

"Very impressive," she said, quietly squeezing her eyes shut. "Can't I help?"

"Nope. I'm all set." He poured the dressing on the salad, then got a big salad fork and tossed it around. "The thing of it is, like I told Bill on our walk…it's probably time I think of a new career anyway." He carried the salad to the table and looked up to see that she was about to object. "I'll always write for myself. It's how I make sense of things—not that I wouldn't like another hit—you always want a home run. But I'm better off if I give up that idea. This isn't the first time I've thought I should find something else. And it's not the finances, I'm okay, and in a lot better shape than a lot of people my age who've retired. But I don't play golf or bridge or anything like that, so when I say career, I guess I mean a new focus. Maybe a different kind of identity because as a published writer, I'm a has-been."

"I don't see it that way. Kids are always discovering your books—they live on whether you're writing new things or not."

"Maybe, but the prevailing sentiment is all that matters is what you're doing now and how much money it makes. For most people in this business, success usually lasts about a nanosecond."

Maggie stirred her drink with the celery stalk. She suddenly felt anxious. She remembered he'd said he'd come to the island to write. If he was thinking of doing something else, it could mean he was thinking about leaving. "Well, what else do you see yourself doing?" she asked, trying to sound casual.

"I thought I might want to be a Food Bank Elf."

Maggie tried to keep a straight face. Was he serious?

"Of course it's seasonal," he said, smiling. "But all you have to do is stand at the main intersection of Vashon Highway and Bank Road and ring the bell. And the outfit is kind of fun. The Santa hat and the red and white striped stockings. It seems like a good thing to be. You just stand there and say 'hello' and hold out the bucket and then the people who put something in feel very good and you thank them, and everyone feels good."

Maggie didn't have the heart to tell him that not everyone loved the Food Bank Elves. She remembered hearing someone at the post office complaining about traffic being tied up and how it made the people who didn't put anything in the bucket feel stingy. But she was relieved he'd thought of something on the island. "Well, I love the Food Bank Elves and I think you'd look great in the outfit," she said. "But they're just out there at the holidays."

"It's also a metaphor for some kind of volunteer job." Walter went back to the kitchen and took the lasagna out of the oven. "I'll figure something out. See, I figured that it's time I thought of being a Pip and not Gladys Knight, if we're speaking metaphorically. 'Midnight Train to Georgia' is one of my favorite songs and I always liked the Pips' part. They call *All Aboard* and then make this train whistle sound…*whoo-whoo*…I always thought I'd like to do that."

"Oh Walter," Maggie went to the kitchen and put her arms around his neck.

Walter closed his eyes and sang. "*L.A. proved too much for the man…*

"*So he's leavin' the life he's come to know …*

"*He said he's goin' back…to a simpler place and time…*"

It was the first time Maggie had ever heard him sing anything other than the Bill Bailey song and she kissed his cheek, holding him tight, careful not to press too hard against his arm.

Howie and Mark arrived just as they were clearing the table, and a few minutes later, Jordan came with Martha Jane. From their long faces it was clear that Howie had told them about what had happened. Walter put the kettle on for tea for Martha Jane and Mark, and Maggie poured coffee for herself, Walter and Howie.

"Is there anything I can get you?" Walter asked Jordan. "I'm afraid I don't have any Coke or anything, but I've got some orange juice."

"I'm okay, thanks." Jordan sat on the floor, patting Bill Bailey. "So what are we going to do, Mr. Hathaway?"

"I'm not sure what the options are. Maybe we're here to commiserate," Walter said, sitting next to the fireplace. Maggie and Martha Jane sat next to each other on the couch, and Mark and Howie pulled up chairs from the kitchen table.

Maggie sat forward. "I've said this to Howie and Walter, but I just want everyone to know for the record. I'm so terribly sorry about my sister." The minute she said it, Maggie felt tears well up and it completely surprised her. She knew how mad she was at Leslie, she just hadn't realized how hurt.

Jordan jumped up and raised his fist. "One monkey don't stop no show!" he shouted, then sat back down as everyone started laughing.

"Where'd that come from?" Martha Jane asked, chuckling.

"My friend Jamil says it whenever we can't get someone to play basketball with us. But I'm serious peeps, uh, I mean Mrs. Lewis, Mr. Hathaway. Why can't we just have the show on the beach?"

Howie went over to the window and looked out, and after a few moments he turned to Jordan. "I like the idea, but it's Labor Day weekend and there are lots of people walking on the beach and lots of dogs and more boats around. Plus, our beach is pretty rocky. I'm not sure how we'd get the sets to stand up."

"More tea anybody?" Mark asked, as he went to the kitchen.

"None for me...thanks, dear." Martha Jane shook her head.

Mark poured himself a cup, took a sip and leaned against the kitchen counter. "As soon as Howie told me what happened, I checked around all the usual places, and Café Luna, the Red Bicycle, the Blue Heron, and the O Space all have stuff going on,"

Howie turned the kitchen chair around and straddled it, folding his arms across the top of the back. "So I guess the alternatives are to scale back the production and have it in someone's house or schedule it for next summer when Jordan comes back. Can anyone think of anything I haven't mentioned?"

"I have an idea!" Martha Jane sat forward. "What if I call Fred Weiss and see if we could use his meadow?" He has plenty of space to park, it's surrounded by big firs so there's not a lot of wind and it truly is just the most beautiful spot."

"But what if it rains?" Maggie asked.

"I know where I can get a tent." Howie whipped out his cell phone and handed it to Martha Jane. "Do you know Fred's number?"

"I have it at home."

Walter got the Vashon phone book, which was about the size of a comic book. Then he put on his readers and it only took him a second to find Fred Weiss. "Here it is, ready?"

"Ready." Martha Jane adjusted her glasses and held her fingers over the key pad as Walter slowly read off the number.

CHAPTER TWENTY-SIX

The morning of the first run-through at Fred Weiss's meadow, the sun spread hazily through wisps of clouds and the air again had the tinge of autumn. There was hardly any wind and Maggie saw a few sailboats near Sunset Beach floating with their sails flapping, barely moving. Bill Bailey sat in the truck between Maggie and Walter, his head almost even with theirs. When Walter turned off SW Cove Road onto Margot Road, all three of them jiggled along, bouncing into each other on the rutted country lane. A mile down, on the waterside, overlooking Colvos Passage, Maggie saw the bright yellow farmhouse Martha Jane had described. She'd said to look for the green mailbox and Maggie spotted it at the end of the drive. Next to it, hanging from a piece of driftwood, was the sign, "Foster" and "Weiss."

"Martha Jane told us to park in front of the studio, it's supposed to be about a half-mile beyond his daughter's place," Maggie said, putting her arm around Bill Bailey to steady him.

Walter passed the house and drove up a hill where a small, cedar shake building was situated on the edge of a meadow, a broad expanse surrounded by tall alder and fir. A green tractor mower was parked near the studio and the meadow looked as though it had been freshly cut.

Walter pulled next to Howie and Mark's truck behind Martha Jane's ancient red Mercedes. There were several other cars Maggie didn't recognize and she thought they probably belonged to the folks Howie had recruited to play the parts of the geese and the townspeople.

"Guess we're the last ones," Walter said, as he turned off the ignition and put the truck into park.

"We have a good excuse," she whispered, thinking about how they'd ended up making love in the morning, and then both fell back to sleep.

"The best." Walter grinned. "But I don't think we need to explain."

"Not at all," she laughed. "Besides, most people are on island time anyway."

In front of the studio, Martha Jane was chatting with Fred Weiss and motioned for them to come over. Maggie was surprised when she saw Fred. She'd heard Martha Jane talk about him with such admiration that somehow she'd had the picture of someone much larger. She'd imagined someone with a sensitive face, but more force-ful looking. Sort of a tall, Charlie Rose type with white hair. Fred was quite short, not that much taller than Martha Jane, and stocky with a medium build and a craggy face. She knew he was eighty-one because Martha Jane had invited him to dinner for his birthday last March, but there didn't appear to be that much difference in their ages. That seemed so much the case as people got older, Maggie thought. It was so different from babies, toddlers and prepubescent kids, where you had a pretty good idea of their age by what they could do developmentally. Adults had hair dye, face lifts and you could be off by decades trying to guess someone's age. And then all those women who spent their lives in the gym; sometimes they looked like someone stuck a granny head on a Barbie doll. That was one of Maggie's favorite things about Martha Jane—the acceptance she had of her age and her gratitude for every day. She seemed espe-cially vibrant that morning as she introduced them to Fred.

"We certainly appreciate this," Maggie said.

"This is a beautiful piece of property." Walter shook his hand after Maggie did and looked around admiringly. "It's very kind of you,"

"We were delighted to be asked. This belongs to my daugh-ter and son-in-law—there's about five acres, most of it's wooded surrounding the meadow, which, I have to say, seems like it's made for putting on a play." Then Tanner came up with Fred's dog Pablo, an old black and tan lab mix with a gray muzzle. He moved slowly and waddled as if he had some arthritis in his hips, but the minute he saw Bill Bailey, he perked up and the dogs took off, chasing each other around the meadow.

Maggie and Walter waved to Howie, Mark, and Jordan, who were starting to unload a tent from the back of Howie's truck.

"I don't think you'll need the tent," Fred looked at the clear sky.

"Probably not, but we'll all feel more secure." Martha Jane reached over and patted his shoulder. "You're a dear to let us do this."

"Well, my daughter and son-in-law got a vote, too. They love theater and are very excited about it. One of Melissa's favorite movies was *The Adventures of Fric the Chick*."

"Glad to hear it," Walter said and Maggie could see he was quite pleased. She squelched her impulse to shout, "I told you so! Your work has a life you don't even know about!" Maggie was a believer in "I-told-you-so's" and gloating whenever a good opportunity presented itself. But because Fred and Martha Jane were there, she felt limited to just giving Walter a very smug smile.

Fred pointed to a yurt at the back of the property. "The only thing we don't have is bathrooms for a large crowd. There's just the one in my yurt. That's where I live, over there, and my daughter's house has two. I've been hoping to get a permit from the King County Health Department to put a bathroom in the studio, but it's starting to feel like waiting for Godot."

"Fred dear, I think we're going to be okay," Martha Jane patted his shoulder again. "It's not a long play, and word's gotten out about the television person who will be doing the *Hot Cat on the Roof*," she paused, "…is that right?…doesn't sound right—"

"Close enough," Maggie muttered, thinking, Yeah, right… Leslie, The Hot Cat…*In her dreams*.

Martha Jane continued, "Well, anyway…that cat performance will be very well attended…so, I think we'll just get a few families with kids, mostly relatives and friends of the cast in Walter's fine play. And they'll be young, Fred dear," she said, laughing, "with young bladders."

"There's always the bushes," Walter added.

Howie came over with the rest of the cast and introduced everyone, but Maggie already knew Henry Freed, Rosetta Taylor, Mike and Marcia Olson, and Elaine Yamashita. The other two, Eva Jean Wilke and Terry Pfeiffer, looked familiar the way so many people on the island did, although she hadn't met them before. Howie had found it easy to recruit people for the play. Especially since the geese parts only required honking and the townspeople just had a few lines like, "Kill the geese!"

It took most of the morning to put up the set, rehearse a few times, and then break down the set so it could be kept in Fred's studio for the night. The set had been made from three large plywood panels painted to look like the front of Mr. Hedgehopper's bicycle shop, the weeds near the lake, and the lake itself. Vashon was teeming with artists, and it hadn't been hard for Howie to find some who wanted to help. Several of the artists, Eva Jean Wilke and Henry Freed, had also wanted to be actors for the crowd scenes. Henry painted primitive folk art and had done wonderful work on the set. He had also developed an impressive honk, which he belted out with great enthusiasm.

"Whew," Walter wiped his brow as they walked to his truck. "That was a hell of a workout, getting that set up and down. And I didn't do half of what the rest of you did." He tapped the cast on his arm as he opened the passenger door and Bill Bailey hopped in the front seat. "I won't be shedding any tears when I say goodbye to this thing tomorrow morning." Maggie got in next to Bill Bailey and shut the door. "It sure would have been easier in the theater," she grumbled, as she fastened the seatbelt. "I can't figure out why my sister didn't just have her play in LA. She's been back and forth the whole time. The cast and the director are there—I just don't get it."

"It's best to forget it. Everyone's excited about being in the meadow under the tent." Walter put the key in the ignition and started the truck. "Besides, I get why she doesn't want to do it in LA."

"You do?"

He nodded as he looked over his shoulder and backed around. "It'd be like me trying to produce *A Goose Called Hope* as a street theater piece in front of Simon and Schuster on Avenue of the Americas in New York. If she does her play in LA in some storefront theater or church basement, the contrast between her days on that TV show, when she was up and coming...what was the name of it again?"

"*Bottoms Up*—it was sort of a *Cheers* spin-off."

"Yeah, well the contrast is too hard to digest that way. Up here on this little island where nobody knows her, she's protected from the truth."

"What truth?"

"That she's a has-been. It's not easy to be a has-been, Maggie. And even if it wasn't just one long glory road, there just aren't that many miles left."

"Didn't you hear Fred say this morning that *Fric* was of his daughter's favorites? Your work has a life you don't even know about. In libraries and schools, and people's minds and hearts. You're *not* a has-been," she said, emphatically.

"In the eyes of the money people who decide what to publish, I am. But the difference between me and your sister is that I don't care anymore." Walter laughed. "Frankly, Scarlett, I don't give a damn."

Walter dropped Maggie off and she hadn't been home ten minutes before he called. "I just found my old sport coat and it has a couple of holes it," he said. "Moths had some dinner, I guess. Do you think I should try to get a new one after I'm through at the clinic tomorrow, or just wear a shirt?"

"I don't think you need to worry about getting a new one just for the play." Maggie wondered if he was getting stage fright. "You'll be great in whatever you wear."

"Should I wear a light blue shirt or a white one?" he asked, then he paused. "...I can't believe I'm asking you about my wardrobe. I don't even have what you'd call a wardrobe, I must be losing my grip here."

"Walter, trust me. People will love the play and you will be wonderful as the narrator."

"You really think so?"

"Absolutely."

"Okay. I'll wear my blue shirt."

CHAPTER TWENTY-SEVEN

The morning of the dress rehearsal, Maggie pulled a gray sweatshirt over her head and when she got the arms through the sleeves, they hung down over her hands, almost covering her finger tips. She'd gotten a man's extra large at Granny's and had to roll up the sleeves, but she thought the big size would work well once she got the pillows. In the guest bedroom she took both pillows from the bed and stuffed them under the sweatshirt then looked down at her plump front. Mother Goose. More like granny goose…a fat old goose, that's for sure. The old grey goose, she ain't what she used to be…or was that the old grey mare? She went to her bedroom to get the black ribbon. Maggie took it to the bathroom, wrapped it around her neck and looked at herself in the mirror. Ridiculous. She looked ridiculous. Oh well, Howie had said the goose costumes were just to give a suggestion of geese, just to give an impression. Like a few strokes of a pen in a drawing can create the idea of an object. Maggie hoped he was right, because in the mirror all she saw was a fatter version of herself wearing a black ribbon around her neck and she looked absurd. What we won't do for art…Walter better appreciate this. She went back to the bedroom and was unwrapping the ribbon from around her neck when the phone rang. At the desk, she looked at the caller ID on the phone. Walter's cell number. More stage fright? she wondered. At least being the narrator he didn't have to wear a costume.

"Hi Walter." She pulled the pillows out from under the sweatshirt.

"Maggie..." Walter's voice was tired. "It seems they want to keep me here."

"Keep you where?" Maggie sat down at the desk and kicked the pillow to the side. "Where are you right now?"

"I've just been admitted to Swedish Hospital. I'm fine...it's ridiculous."

"Is it your arm? Was something wrong when they took the cast off?" Maggie asked, trying to sound calm. She picked up the pillow and held it to her chest.

"No, it's fine. I guess I blacked out or something and they were concerned I'd had another one of those little strokes, and also my heart went into jackhammer mode. They want to keep me overnight."

Maggie stood up, heart pounding, still clutching the pillow. "I'll get the next boat."

"Don't come, Maggie. Just take care of Bill." He coughed and his voice was so weak she could hardly hear him. Finally he said, "Haven't we done this before?"

"Déjà vu all over again. Look, you do sound really tired—I'm sure it's best to be cautious, they must have a good reason to keep you." Maggie activated her Ms. Lewis–the–Librarian persona, her voice steady with confident authority, while she squeezed her eyes shut and pressed the pillow against her chest.

"At my funeral I'd like them to play 'Pop Goes the Weasel' and 'The Old Rugged Cross.'"

"For God's sake Walter—" Maggie started laughing. Then she was crying.

"I'm sorry about this."

"If you didn't want to be in the play you should have just told us," she said, trying to laugh, but still crying.

"It wasn't a panic attack or anything...my heart got out of whack. Atrial fibrillation. Maybe Howie can take my part...like Jordan said 'one monkey don't stop no show.'"

Maggie put the pillow on her lap and brushed away her tears, then took a tissue out of her jeans pocket and wiped her nose. "Look, don't worry about anything here. I'll call Howie and I'll go over and take care of Bill. Just get some rest and do what they tell you."

"They said if everything settles down I can probably go home tomorrow, but they want me to take it easy. So if I can get out of here tomorrow, I probably need to lay low tomorrow night."

"Well, you can still see the show. Howie's friend Gary Ratner, the guy that loaned us the tent, is going to be there and make a video. You can see it right after the play's over or Sunday."

"Okay."

"I better get ready for the dress rehearsal. Do you want me to call you when I get back?"

Walter coughed several times. "Maggie?"

"Yes?"

"I love you."

Maggie's voice caught in her throat.

"Just thought I'd mention it, in case I don't get a chance to tell you." Then he hung up.

Maggie tried to put Walter out of her mind at the dress rehearsal, but it was impossible. They were saying his words, from his heart, from his mind. Instead of her line "Kill the Geese!" she kept thinking of Elizabeth Barrett Browning, *I love you not only for what you are, but for what I am when I am with you*, which meant happier, full of hope, more alive...and what about that...being alive ... what was happening to him? She held it together, but by the time she got home she was drained. Totally exhausted.

The rehearsal had gone well. The set looked wonderful, the costumes were funny, Howie did a fine job as the narrator and only a few people dropped their lines. The night had been clear and beautiful, the velvet sky was covered with glittering stars, but everyone was worried about Walter and their concern for him hung over the tent in the meadow like a huge, black cloud. She fell into bed before ten, not even bothering to brush her teeth. Went to bed...but not to sleep.

Maggie lay awake, her emotions swinging back and forth like the pendulum of an old clock...I don't know how many years I have left...I don't want to be without him...I don't know how many years I have left...I don't want to be the caregiver for some sick old man...I don't know how many years I have left...I don't want to be without him...on and on through a good part of the night. She saw the two of them on the beach with Bill Bailey, cooking together, eating dinner, going to the grocery store. Ordinary, sweet things. The everyday fabric of life and she saw herself in his arms, and in his bed. Their bed. And then the bed was a hospital bed and she saw a respirator, an IV drip, bedpans, a bedside table covered with little plastic pill bottles and her life swamped with clinic appointments, trips to the pharmacy, hospital vigils. The last time she looked at the clock it was after three a.m.

CHAPTER TWENTY-EIGHT

Maggie peeked around the edge of the set and couldn't believe how many people were sitting in the meadow. If each of the twelve cast members invited a few friends, Howie had said they might get around fifty people. But it looked to Maggie like there were at least three times that. What a relief! She'd been worried that they'd only get a handful of people since Leslie's staged reading was turning out to be a big deal. The *Beachcomber* had run a front-page story about Ronald Whitehorn next to a huge black and white headshot of the guy. He looked ancient. Very beefy and jowly and Maggie could see why he'd make a good "Big Daddy." Evidently, there were a lot of people on the island who knew him from television, and several people had seen him on Broadway when he was in *Talking Dirty in the Beauty Shop*.

Maggie hadn't spoken to her sister since their little dust-up. She'd heard the reading was sold out and knew Leslie would eventually call to gloat. (When Leslie gloated, Maggie thought it was childish and obnoxious, unlike the occasions when *she* gloated, which were entirely appropriate.)

As she saw more families arriving, Maggie had to admit she was surprised by such a great turnout. It must have been Sondra Wiggins' media blitz. Sondra was quite invested in her grandson being in the play and over Jordan's objections had made posters that featured his name in gigantic Day-Glo letters. She'd put them on the door of the Burton post office, at the Burton coffee stand, in the bathrooms at Café Luna and on the golf club bulletin board. It probably took her mind off what the goats had done to her garden and Maggie thought that was certainly a good thing. But she did feel bad that Sondra's enthusiasm for Jordan's theater debut embarrassed him.

"Maggie dear," Martha Jane whispered. "When do we begin honking?" Martha Jane stood behind the set with the rest of the cast. For the first scene they were dressed as the townspeople, but would be making honking noises off stage. Maggie could see that going back and forth between the two parts was a little confusing for Martha Jane. Maggie looked at her watch and peeked around the set again. "We're supposed to start in a few minutes, but the audience is still arriving. Take a look."

Martha Jane poked her head out. "Oh, my! Well, look at that. It's a full house, or should I say full meadow!"

She began to laugh and Howie put his finger to his lips. "Shhh. Just a few more minutes and then we'll start."

"And I don't wear the feathers at first, do I?" Martha Jane asked Maggie. All the geese wore black ribbons around their necks, but Terry Pfeiffer had found a black feather boa and everyone thought since Martha Jane was the elder goose, she should be the one to wear it.

Maggie bent down and whispered in her ear. "No, that's in the next scene."

Howie looked around the edge of the set and then stepped back behind it. "Okay, folks. We can get started. I'll go out and introduce the play and mention about Walter and—"

Maggie bit her lip. She was trying to get in the spirit of that great show business tradition: the show must go on. But she was worried sick about Walter. He'd called right before she'd left to say that they weren't going to discharge him until tomorrow. When Howie mentioned him, it was all she could do not to cry.

"Break a leg everybody," Howie whispered, and then, with long strides, he emerged from behind the set to take his place on the grass on what they'd marked as center stage. "Welcome everyone! We're so glad you all found your way here. We have a great play for you tonight. But before we begin, there are a number of generous people we want to thank for their support. We're grateful to Fred Weiss and the Fosters for the use of this beautiful meadow, and Gary Ratner for the tent, although it looks like we're in luck tonight and we aren't going to need it." Everyone clapped and then Howie took a list from his pocket and continued thanking all the artists who had helped with the set and Orcas Building Supply for donating the plywood.

"Tonight," he continued, "is a very special night. It's the world premiere of a play that I'm sure you'll love as much as we do, *A Goose Called Hope*, by our fellow islander, the acclaimed children's author, Walter Hathaway!" Maggie listened to the huge applause, wishing more than anything Walter could hear it.

"Unfortunately, due to a last-minute conflict, Walter wasn't able to be with us tonight, but we know he's here in spirit and this will be the first of many performances of *A Goose Called Hope* and we'll have many more chances to recognize this outstanding author..."

"I hope—" Maggie whispered to Martha Jane, putting her hand against her heart, relieved that Howie hadn't given any details about why Walter wasn't there. "And now..." Howie paused and lifted his arms wide, "Let the show begin!"

That was the cue for the geese to honk off stage. Henry Freed began the honking and the cast followed his lead as Mark entered, dressed as Mr. Hedgehopper in a hat, bow tie and tweed jacket. He stood in front of the Hedgehopper Bicycle Shop set, and when he gave his opening line, the geese offstage stopped honking. Except for Martha Jane, who didn't quite understand Mark's line was the cue to stop and Howie had to motion for her to be quiet.

"Look at this goose poop in front of my store! It's a disgrace!" At the word "poop," the audience, the majority of whom were kids, exploded with laughter. Mark paced back and forth with his arms behind his back. "We've got to do something about this. I'm sick and tired of this poop all over the place. I say, get rid of the geese! Round them up and send them back to Canada! I'm mad as hell and I'm not going to take it anymore!"

Jordan, as the goose "Hope," entered stage left in the middle of Mr. Hedgehopper's speech and crouched next to the set painted with weeds. Hope listened while the townspeople entered and assembled for the town meeting. They wore the hats, scarves and jewelry that Maggie and Martha Jane had gotten for their costumes from Granny's Attic and Maggie couldn't help wondering if anyone in the audience might notice an item that once belonged to them. Terry Pfeiffer wore a ratty, maroon cowboy hat with a frayed gold band that would have been easy to identify.

After Mr. Hedgehopper and the townspeople made their exit, Hope had a soliloquy about how she must save the flock. Behind the set, during Hope's speech, the actors took off the hats, scarves and jewelry. Then they put the pillows under their gray sweatshirts, pulled up the hoods, wrapped the black ribbons around their necks and entered honking. Maggie found herself caught up in the performance and was able to stay focused and keep it together through both acts. Her character "Maggie the Goose" had several lines that came in the scene where the geese decided to retaliate and clog the town toilets. She delivered them in a loud, strong voice, projecting well out over the meadow and each of her lines got big laughs. But when the play was over, when the cast all held hands and bowed to a standing ovation, tears spilled down her cheeks. She knew she was exhausted, she'd had so little sleep the night before, but all she could think about was Walter.

Maggie saw, without a doubt, that *A Goose Called Hope* was a hit. There had been a few glitches: a bicycle that had been a prop in front of Mr. Hedgehopper's shop fell over and Mark had to ad-lib quite a bit, the panel for the set that was the lake toppled when Jordan lost his balance and backed into it, and Martha Jane did get confused about when to wear the townsperson costume and when to change to be a goose. At one point she was honking in a hat and jewelry. And Jordan and Mark both dropped a few lines. But the audience loved it and Maggie couldn't wait 'til she got home to tell Walter about it. She stayed at the meadow to help break down the set and load the tent in Howie's truck, but it all took a lot longer than she expected. By the time she got home, she knew it was too late to call the hospital. But she'd call him first thing tomorrow.

It was seven-thirty and Maggie was still asleep when the phone rang the next morning. Even Bill Bailey had been asleep. Groggily, she reached for the phone.

"Mornin' Maggie. I hope I'm not calling too early."

"Oh, no. I was just getting up," she lied, slowly sitting up. Bill Bailey woke up and whined by the bedroom door. "Hang on just a second, Walter, I've just got to let Bill out." Maggie went to the living room, let the dog out and then picked up the phone on the desk. "Sorry about that. Can you come home? How are you?"

"Well, I just want to tell you, they're saying I might be out of here around noon." Walter sounded a little subdued, maybe even nervous, although she couldn't tell for sure. "So, how did it go?" he asked. "Did anybody come to see it?"

"Walter, I can't wait for you to see the video. The play was just a smash hit! I was going to call you last night but I got home too late. Everyone absolutely loved it, and I just hope they got some of the audience in the video so you can see the kids react. We must have had a hundred and fifty people in that meadow. Mostly kids."

"Really?" He sounded surprised. "Really, that many?"

"Yeah, really."

"Sure wish I'd been there." There was a long pause, then he asked, "How's Bill?"

"Bill's fine. I'll take him back to your house when I go to the store. But how are *you*?"

"I'm fine. The cardiologist wants to me to quit coffee for a while, and I have to get a prescription filled for something called metoprolol and then he wants to see me in a month. But everything checked out."

"What a relief," she said, quietly. Maggie closed her eyes for a moment. "You're really doing okay?"

"Maggie, I knew there wasn't anything to worry about. Look, they could only give me a ballpark time, so I'm not sure exactly when they'll let me go or what ferry I'll be on. I think it may depend on when the doctor makes rounds."

"Just get here when you can and come over. We can have an early dinner."

After she got off the phone, Maggie made a list of things to get at Thriftway and put down herbal tea, since Walter was supposed to quit coffee. Then she took Bill Bailey to Walter's cabin. As she put him inside, Maggie realized how comfortable he'd been spending the night at her house. What a contrast to his howling misery the first time Walter went to the hospital. It was hard for her to believe that had been less than two months ago.

It was around four-thirty that afternoon when Maggie was in the kitchen getting dinner ready that she heard Walter's footsteps on the porch. Her heart quickened as she went to let him in. She didn't know what she'd been expecting, but when she opened the door, she stared at him, then blurted, "You...you look...*great.*"

"Don't sound so surprised." He came in and kissed her on the cheek.

"No, I mean...well—I was worried—"

"I told you it was nothing, the whole thing was silly." He held out his arm. "Look Ma, two arms." He wrapped his arms around her and pulled her close to him.

"We probably won't have to be so careful now when we...you know—" Maggie held tight to him.

"Funny, I've had the same thought," Walter said, before he kissed her.

After a minute, she took his hand. "Come on in the kitchen. The computer's on the table and I've got the DVD in it, Howie brought it over this morning."

"So it really went okay?" Walter sat at the table.

"Absolutely. Jordan did a great job, everyone did." Maggie went to the refrigerator and got ice cubes and filled glasses for their Virgin Mary's. "There were only a few little things that went wrong."

"Like what?"

"You'll probably see on the video, but no big deal. Part of the set fell over, but the audience just laughed." She took two celery stalks from the refrigerator and stuck them in their drinks, then brought them to the table and sat next to him.

"Can I help with anything?" he asked.

"Thanks, I'm all set. I made salmon niçoise this morning, all I have to do is take it out of the refrigerator. I got everything at the farmer's market yesterday before the play...green beans, tomatoes, onion, and potatoes. All local except the olives and capers. I got those at Thriftway. Well, and the salmon, too. But the eggs are from Howie and Mark's chickens. Howie did a great job as the narrator, by the way."

"Good."

"But you would have been better," she said, leaning her head on his shoulder.

"I doubt that. But glad to hear it went well."

Maggie turned on the DVD and while Walter watched the play, Maggie watched Walter. He didn't say much, but he was nodding and smiling and she could see he was enjoying it.

"Guess you were right about the toilet humor," he said. "Some of those kids look like they became hysterical every time Mark said 'poop.'"

"I told you so!" Maggie said, not wanting to waste an opportunity to gloat. When the play was almost over, she got up to set the table.

"Well, well," Walter said, as the video ended. He shut off the computer. "Where do you want this?"

"Just on the desk in the living room, thanks." Maggie took the platter with the salad out of the refrigerator and brought it to the table.

"I love that," Walter said from the living room.

"The play? Wasn't it great?" Maggie set a pitcher of ice water on the table.

"I mean that salad," he said, as he came back in the kitchen. "Are we ready?"

"Come and sit down." Maggie sat across from him and put her napkin on her lap. "So, what did you think of it? Martha Jane can't wait to perform it again, by the way, and you should know, the video doesn't do it justice. The cast, the audience, everyone really loved it, Walter."

"It didn't seem to matter when Jordan dropped a few lines."

"I don't know if you noticed in the video, but Martha Jane got the costume changes confused and still had the feathers when she was supposed to be the townsperson. She got a little rattled, but then she started hamming it up like it was a stole, bless her heart."

Walter rubbed his arm before he picked up his fork. "It's sure good to have that thing off." He took a bite of salmon. "This is delicious by the way. And yes, I liked the play. I liked it very much." Then he learned forward. "Maggie, remember when I said I thought I knew what I'd like to do next?"

"Be a Food Bank Elf?"

He nodded. "When they kept me in the hospital, I got to thinking—"

The phone rang and Maggie started to get up, then changed her mind. "Sorry. I won't get that. Go ahead, what were you saying?"

Then she saw the message light blinking. She put down her fork and took her napkin off her lap. "Maybe I better listen to this, just in case it's life or death or something." She went to the phone, then suddenly felt rude and embarrassed about jumping up and leaving him.

She held the phone, and turned away from Walter as she listened to the message.

"Maggie," Leslie's little-girl voice was breathy with excitement. "I just wanted you to know that Ronald has asked me to go to Toronto with him and I'm leaving tomorrow. Betty Sue is going to rent my Vashon place, she says she doesn't think she'll have any trouble finding someone. *Oh, and our reading was a-MAZing!* Everyone said so and they were just thrilled to have real pros, you know, right here on this little island. Just thrilled. Well, I'll keep in touch. Take care of yourself, Maggie. Bye for now."

Maggie put the phone down. Predictable. Totally predictable. Wasn't that just typical? She makes a mess, then leaves abruptly and acts like nothing happened. The big surprise would have been if she'd showed any remorse, any empathy. That would be the shock all right, but this? This was just vintage Leslie.

Maggie went back to the kitchen and sat across from Walter. "That was my sister. She says she's leaving for Toronto with this Ronald guy. I knew she'd never last here, the whole thing is so predictable, it's almost boring. Leslie makes a mess—there's always some drama—and then she's on to the next thing and it's like none of it ever happened. And she just assumes I'll be there the next time she wants something." Maggie took a sip of her water.

"Will you?" he asked.

"Probably," Maggie sighed. "Maybe I'll get better at setting some limits, but I know that the dance won't end. We'll be in each other's lives until one of us dies." Maggie was quiet for a minute. "The truth is, I'm her only family and she's the only person I know who knew my parents, who lived in that same house." Maggie sounded sad, but still she had to laugh. "She's the only one who knows about the dead animals my mother used to wear around her neck."

"Dead animals?" Walter raised his eyebrows.

"Minks, it was a neckpiece sort of thing."

"Mordecai Siegal said, 'Acquiring a dog may be the only opportunity a human ever has to choose a relative.'" Walter smiled.

"Who was he?"

"A writer. Wrote a lot of good books about pets." He took a bite of salmon.

"Well, to be honest, I wouldn't choose Leslie for a relative, but she is my sister and I guess our shared history means something. She drives me nuts, but when I think about if I even love her, I suppose I do in that we both come from a place of the earliest love, the kind of love that's based on the earliest history. The kind of bond you have if you grow up in the same family. Whatever it is, I know it will last as long as we do." Maggie shook her head. "Walter, I'm sorry, before I got the phone…you were going to tell me something."

Walter looked away. "Maybe it's not the best time…I'm going to leave in a minute anyway, I've got to go home and feed Bill and I think I'll turn in early tonight."

"No, please, you were talking about when you were in the hospital."

Walter leaned back in his chair and folded his arms. "Well, okay. For what it's worth. I was thinking that maybe you and I could work with kids, on writing. I mean, I know I could do it myself, I don't need anyone else to be with me to volunteer. But I think it would be more fun to do it together. I know there aren't any do-overs. But I like to finish what I start, and I never finished that visit to your school." Walter stood up. "You don't have to say anything now. Maybe just think about it."

"I don't have to think about it." Maggie walked him to the door and put her arms around him. "Remember what you said about being a Pip?"

"Yeah."

"It's plural. There's more than one Pip. It's not Gladys Knight and the *Pip*. It's *Pips*. Gladys Knight and the Pip-*s*. And I'd like to be one, too, Walter. Metaphorically speaking." Maggie looked up at him. "And that song, about the midnight train...the song says 'I'd rather live in his world, than live without him in mine.' So, maybe just think about that."

Walter kissed her, closing his eyes. Then he said, "I'd want to stay if I weren't so tired."

"Go home to Bill Bailey. Tomorrow's another day."

Maggie stood at the window and watched him walk down the steps and head for the path between their houses, her heart filled with tenderness. The dark sky was lavish with stars and the August moon shone on the water of Baker's Cove. She had been relieved when it turned out that all he wanted was to ask her to make school visits with him. She didn't know if she wanted to get married again. Or even live with someone. Would his health be okay? Would hers? But she smiled, watching him disappear down the path between the towering firs. All she knew for sure was that she wanted to be with Walter. And she'd take it one day at a time.

ABOUT THE AUTHOR

JEAN DAVIES OKIMOTO is an author and playwright whose books and short stories have been translated into Japanese, Italian, Chinese, German and Hebrew. She is the recipient of numerous awards including *Smithsonian* Notable Book, the American Library Association Best Book for Young Adults, the Washington Governor's Award and the International Reading Association Readers Choice Award. Jeanie began writing for adults when she and her husband Joe retired to Vashon Island in 2004 where they are visited by deer, a raccoon named George who is missing a tail, and their six grandchildren.

CPSIA information can be obtained at www.ICGtesting.com
Printed in the USA
BVOW021748260312

286098BV00001B/1/P

9 780983 711513